**W9-CCT-356**

# CRITICS ARE CHARMED BY ALISSA JOHNSON'S *AS LUCK WOULD HAVE IT*!

"Quite enjoyable…lively and fun."
—The Good, the Bad, and the Unread

"*As Luck Would Have It* is a tale written with a wicked web of intrigue. The author has created a delicious combination of luscious ingredients, a pleasure for all, leaving the reader fervently looking forward to Ms. Johnson's next romance."
—*Affaire de Coeur*

"A seductive debut filled with rapier-sharp repartee, passion and espionage."
—RITA Award-winning author Sophia Nash

"Brimming with humor and tenderness, Johnson's debut is a joyous book from a bright new star."
—Kathe Robin, *Romantic Times BOOKreviews*

# KISMET

"My eyes are the color they've always been," Mirabelle said. "Maybe they're a slightly different hue when I'm angry."

"And I've only ever seen them angry," Whit noted with a nod. "Why is that, imp? Why have we never gotten on at all before now?"

"You said once it was fate," she reminded him.

"Ah, yes, the divine ordinance argument. Clever of me."

"Quite."

He stopped the horses suddenly and turned in his seat to look at her. "I don't believe in fate, actually."

"You don't?"

"No. Aside from the inescapable realities of birth and death, we're responsible for the paths our lives take. We each make our own choices." He bent his head and whispered against her lips. "And I choose to do this."

It was Mirabelle's very first kiss.

It was everything she imagined a kiss would be—and absolutely nothing like she would have expected a kiss from Whit to be—not that she ever allowed herself to imagine kissing Whit. But if she had it would have been forceful and—

Whit pulled back until he could see her eyes. "Stop thinking, imp."

She reached out, took hold of his cravat, and brought him closer. "Stop talking, cretin."

Other *Leisure* books by Alissa Johnson:

**AS LUCK WOULD HAVE IT**

# Tempting Fate

## Alissa Johnson

LEISURE BOOKS  NEW YORK CITY

*For Ty Johnson and Brandon Hudson, because you cooked nearly every meal I ate for a year. Chumps.*
*Love you.*

A LEISURE BOOK®

February 2009

Published by

Dorchester Publishing Co., Inc.
200 Madison Avenue
New York, NY 10016

ISBN 10: 0-8439-6156-2
ISBN 13: 978-0-8439-6156-0
E-ISBN: 1-4285-0599-7

The name "Leisure Books" and the stylized "L" with design are trademarks of Dorchester Publishing Co., Inc.

Printed in the United States of America.

10 9 8 7 6 5 4 3 2 1

Visit us on the web at www.dorchesterpub.com.

# ACKNOWLEDGMENTS

My sincere thanks to Emmanuelle Alspaugh and Leah Hultenschmidt, without whom Whit and Mirabelle would never have discovered their fate.

# Tempting Fate

# ❋ Prologue ❋

1796

There is no messenger quite so unwelcome as the one who comes bearing the news of death.

William Fletcher rather felt he ought to know.

To date, he had been present at more than a dozen such deliveries.

But he hadn't been made to feel unwelcome at Haldon Hall. On the contrary, upon his arrival William had been told by the countess that the earl was out—as he almost inevitably was—then she had sat him down, poured him tea with a generous splash of whiskey, and politely turned her head when his young voice cracked with grief.

It was no mere colleague's death he heralded today. It was a friend's.

"Will you speak to the boy, or shall I?" the countess asked from where she'd taken up a position by the window.

He knew what, or rather who, she was watching—her son, Whittaker Cole, heir to the Earl of Thurston. Whit was lining up tin soldiers on the lawn with Alex Durmant—the newly orphaned Duke of Rockeforte.

"I would prefer . . ." He cleared his throat. "That is, I would very much like to speak to Alex myself, if you could see your way to allowing it."

She shot an annoyed look over her shoulder. "You are as much his family as I, William."

"I . . . I should have been quicker. I could have—"

"Posh and nonsense. The duke knew the risks of working for the War Department, just as every Rockeforte has"—she returned her attention to the children outside—"and will. Do you mean to honor his final wishes?"

"I do. I gave my word."

"It's ridiculous you know, a grown man playing match-maker." She crossed the room to sit beside him.

"I'm aware of it," he grumbled. "As was he, I assure you."

Her lips curved into a fond smile. "He was a consummate jokester. It seems fitting that he should have died with a laugh. He neglected one small detail, however."

"What detail would that be?" And if his voice betrayed some hope at the possibility of being released from a very troublesome vow, it couldn't be helped.

"Two of those children have a mother . . . with definite plans of her own."

William was spared from a response when the front door swung open and an argument poured inside.

"You crushed them to pieces, imp!"

"Well you shouldn't have left them scattered about willy-nilly in the grass, cretin!"

"They were not scattered willy-nilly. They were *positioned!*"

"Positioned for what?"

"For the advanced raid, you—!"

"Whittaker Vincent!"

At the countess's surprisingly robust shout, the voices quieted and moved off down the hall.

She cleared her throat delicately and picked up her cup of tea for a sip.

"As I said, I have plans of my own."

# ❋ One ❋

1813

There was some disagreement regarding the origins of the long-standing and bitter feud between Miss Mirabelle Browning and Whittaker Cole, the Earl of Thurston.

The lady in question was of the opinion that the discord had begun the first time the gentleman—and she used the term most loosely—deigned to open his mouth and thereby proved himself to be an ass.

The gentleman—loathe to be outdone—argued that the dislike had appeared directly upon sight, which was an obvious indication of fate. And as providence was the domain of the Heavenly Father himself, any and all unseemly behavior toward Miss Browning on his part was clearly an indication of the Almighty's disfavor with the lady, and he but an instrument of God's wrath.

The lady felt this opinion argued strongly in favor of the gentleman being an ass.

Some said it all began when a young Mirabelle caused the slightly older Whit to fall headfirst out of a rowboat in front of the lovely Miss Wilheim, who promptly slipped and fell overboard herself, putting an end to their brief but dramatic romance. Others maintained that the whole business had started when a mischievous Whit had put a large bug down the back of Mirabelle's dress during a musicale, causing the girl to jump, scream, swat madly, and otherwise endanger the people around her.

Still others insisted they really had no care for when or how it had all begun, merely that they wished it to end. Immediately, if not sooner. Everyone, however, was in accord over the fact that the two, quite simply, did not get on.

So infamous was their rivalry, that had anyone been watching as the two of them scowled at each other over a dandy horse on the back lawn of Haldon Hall, the Thurston estate, he or she would have sighed in resignation even while beating a sensible, and hasty, retreat to safety.

Fortunately for the group of people currently attending the house party, Whit and Mirabelle stood alone, each with a hand on the new wheeled contraption and, much like two children fighting over a toy, each equally determined to gain sole purchase.

As a sensible and—under most conditions—respectably reserved young woman, Mirabelle was perfectly aware of the ridiculousness and pettiness of the situation. As an honest young woman, she could admit that very little else would suit her current mood quite so well as the ridiculous and petty.

A rousing good argument was just what she needed. As always, Whit was more than willing to oblige.

"Let go, imp."

As was his habit when truly annoyed, Whit clenched his jaw when he spoke. Mirabelle was fond of pointing out that the resulting muffled effect took something away from the impact. Just now, however, she was feeling a bit more mulish than witty.

"I see no reason I should," she retorted, tipping her chin up.

"Likely because you couldn't see reason if it were perched on the end of your nose." He gave the horse a tug, which only succeeded in making her dig her heels into the soft ground. "You don't even know how to use it."

"I certainly do. One sits there between the two wheels,

holds on to the bars, and pushes with the feet. I'll show you—"

"No. You're not riding it."

A mere ten minutes ago, she hadn't given a single thought to riding the blasted thing. She'd merely been curious about it. But while she'd been standing there in the warm sun, amusing herself by turning the machine this way and that to discover how it was all put together, Whit had come round the house and ordered her, *ordered* her, not to get on it.

She'd taken a good look at him, with his light brown hair tousled by the breeze, his cool blue eyes sparking, and his aristocratic features set in grim lines. Every inch of his tall, lanky frame spoke of power that took root in wealth, title, lands, and the sheer luck of having been born a man. The very same sort of power her uncle used to keep her under his thumb.

And she decided she wanted to ride the damn thing after all.

"You said it was for guests, cretin," she pointed out.

"You're not a guest at Haldon."

She let go and stepped back, completely stunned by six words that meant more to her than he could possibly know. "I . . . that is the *kindest*—"

"You're an affliction," he clarified, hefting the horse up. "Like dry rot."

She lunged and grabbed hold of the seat with both hands.

A brief tugging match ensued. Whit was stronger, of course, but he couldn't very well pull the horse from her tight grasp without possibly doing her an injury. And while Mirabelle considered him a flawed man—a very, very flawed man—she knew he wouldn't go so far as to risk causing a woman bodily harm. She took some satisfaction in knowing, at the moment, he was likely chafing at that particular code of honor.

Resigned to the fact that she wasn't going to be able to pull the horse away from him, she briefly considered simply tugging as hard as possible before letting go abruptly, with the hope he'd fall hard on his backside. But when a door behind Whit opened, and she caught a glimpse of bronze silk and gray hair, she decided on a different plan.

A mean, childish, and terribly unfair plan.

A perfect plan.

She let go, took a step back and put her hands up, palms out. "I couldn't *possibly*, Whit. Please, I don't think it's safe."

"What the devil are you——?"

"Whittaker Vincent! Are you encouraging Mira to ride that ghastly machine?"

At the sound of his mother's voice employing that time-honored and dreaded phrase—the first and middle name—Whit paled, then flushed, then narrowed steely eyes at Mirabelle.

"You'll pay dearly for this," he hissed.

Probably so, she conceded. But it would be well worth it.

Whit turned and smiled at his mother. She was a small woman, with the blue eyes of her children and the rounded features she inherited from her father. Demurely dressed, rosy cheeked, and soft of voice, she often reminded people of a kindly aunt or younger version of their dear grandmama. It was a misleading impression Lady Thurston had long ago learned to use to her full advantage.

Whit swallowed hard. "Of course not. I was——"

"Are you insinuating I am old?" Lady Thurston inquired.

"I . . ." Confused, wary, Whit fell back on charm. "You are the picture of youth, Mother."

"Very prettily put. But are you certain? Nothing wrong with my hearing, then? My eyesight?"

There was a pause as he recognized the trap, and then another as he realized there was nothing he could do but walk into it. Mirabelle was hard-pressed not to laugh out loud.

"Not a thing, I'm sure," he finally managed.

"What a relief to hear it. For a moment, I thought perhaps you were going to tell me I had misread the situation. That can happen, you know, as one ages and the senses begin to dull. Very confusing, I imagine."

"I imagine," Whit muttered.

"Well, now that we've cleared up that misunderstanding, give your apologies to Mira, Whit, and put that thing away. I'll not have one of my guests breaking open his head."

Mirabelle, feeling immensely pleased with Lady Thurston just then, poked her head around Whit's shoulder.

"What if Miss Willory should care for a ride?" she inquired with an innocent expression.

Lady Thurston appeared to ponder that for a moment. "No, head wounds bleed profusely. And I'm quite fond of my carpets."

Mirabelle laughed and watched Lady Thurston leave in a whirl of bronze skirts. "I'm waiting, Whittaker Vincent."

Whit spun around to face her. "For what?" he snapped.

"My apology, of course."

"Good. Keep waiting."

She laughed and turned to leave, satisfied with the idea that he'd be glowering at her back until she was out of sight.

She jolted when his hand caught her arm and spun her back around again.

"Oh, we're not quite finished here, imp."

Walk away. Let it alone.

Whit knew he ought to, but even as the small voice of reason urged him to do what he knew was best, the louder, and infinitely more appealing, voice of pride insisted he seek revenge. As a soft and seductive afterthought, it suggested he might as well enjoy it.

Mirabelle wasn't the only person at Haldon Hall laboring under a dark mood that afternoon.

Whit had spent the last three days at one of his smaller holdings, settling a dispute involving two tenant farmers, a patch of broken fence, a milk cow, an incompetent overseer and—unless he was much mistaken—a certain attractive barmaid who likely had more to do with the dispute than the fence, cow, or overseer.

He'd held his temper in check through the entire process, and again when he returned home very late last night to find his sister still up and moving about in her room, without an acceptable explanation for her nocturnal activities—again.

And he'd been remarkably restrained when he'd been awoken early by the sound of two upstairs maids arguing heatedly over a spilled tray. And when he'd gone to the stables to discover his favorite horse had come up lame. *And* when his second choice threw a shoe an hour into his ride, necessitating a very long walk back from the fields to the stables.

He'd been returning from that very spot, grumbling, swearing, disgusted with the knowledge that he'd missed the noon meal, and otherwise relinquishing any lingering pretense at finding the day a pleasant one, when he'd seen her in the distance.

His first reaction had been a familiar one—a pleasant quickening of the blood, the instinctive tensing of muscles, a slow and involuntary smile. A rousing argument was just what he needed.

Mirabelle was delightfully easy to bait—never able to let a comment pass and typically loathe to back down from any challenge. It was the chit's best feature, really, and there was little he enjoyed quite so much as harassing her until her temper flared.

True, the consequences for him were sometimes unpleasant, occasionally even disastrous—witness the humiliating episode with his mother—but there was something exceedingly satisfying in watching her eyes narrow, her color heighten and then . . . and then the most astonishing things came out of the girl's mouth. She never failed to amuse him, even if he was too angry—or even injured—at the time to appreciate it.

It was a bit like playing with fire, he supposed—distinctly unwise, but wholly irresistible.

He set down the dandy horse slowly. In part to give himself adequate time to consider his plan of attack, in part to settle his temper, and in part for the simple pleasure of seeing her squirm. And squirm she did, twisting her arm this way and that in a fruitless attempt to free herself from his grasp.

"Are we going to stand here all day, then?" she asked on a huff, finally giving up her struggles.

"It's a possibility," he informed her. "I haven't decided."

"You'll be as bored as I in a moment."

"Oh, I doubt it. I've all manner of interesting things to ponder."

"Ah, he's endeavoring to think." She nodded in exaggerated understanding. "That would explain the delay."

"Revenge is a weighty matter. It requires a certain deliberation."

"It requires intelligence and a modicum of creativity." She tapped her foot with impatience. "Perhaps you'd like to sit down."

He smiled slowly and released her arm. "No need. I believe I've hit on just the thing."

She rolled her eyes dramatically, but made no move to leave. "What's it to be then? Will you pull my hair? Insult me in public? Put a reptile in my dress?"

"Your dress might well appreciate the improvement, but no, I've something else in mind."

"Well, out with it. I'm all aflutter to hear your cunning scheme."

"I don't think so." He gave her a menacing smile. "You'll just have to wait."

She furrowed her brow. "What do you mean, I'll have to wait?"

"Just that. You'll have to wait."

"Is this your revenge, then?" she asked, fisting her hands on her hips. "You think to keep me wondering, worrying, what nasty trick you might pull."

"A welcome side benefit."

She pursed her lips thoughtfully. "A decent strategy, really, or would be, if you were capable of keeping more than two thoughts in your head at a time. You'll forget by dinner."

"How can you be sure my cunning scheme won't play out before dinner."

"I . . ." She opened her mouth, closed it again.

"Cat got your tongue?" he inquired. "Or are you struck mute by worry?"

She snorted derisively and spun on her heel to leave. The sun broke from behind a cloud and, for the briefest moment, highlighted her in soft amber. She seemed, he thought, brighter all of a sudden—different. He blinked, taken aback. Why the devil should she look different?

"Just a minute." He reached out and caught her arm a second time.

She groaned but let herself be turned around. "What's the matter, cretin, a third thought push the first two out so soon? I'll own myself surprised that you had that many in so short a time. Perhaps, if you had someone to write it all down for you . . ."

He stopped listening in favor of looking her over. It was the imp, certainly: average height and build, same brown hair and brown eyes, thin nose, oval face. Looking fairly nondescript, as was her wont, but something was off—changed or missing. He just couldn't seem to put his finger on what that something was.

Was it her skin? Was she paler, tanner, yellower? He didn't think so, but he couldn't say for certain, having never really paid any attention to her skin in the past.

"There's something different about you," he muttered, more to himself than to her, but he noted that she blinked once before opening her eyes wide in an expression that displayed both surprise and skepticism.

So there *was* something different. What the devil was it? Same widow's peak on her forehead. Same high cheekbones. Had she always had that little mole just above her lip? He couldn't recall, but rather doubted it had appeared overnight. Certainly her color was a little higher than it was a minute ago, but that wasn't what was stumping him now.

"It's the damndest thing, imp. I can't seem to . . ."

He cocked his head the other way and ignored her exasperated expression. He just couldn't puzzle out what was altered about the chit. He knew something had changed and he knew that, for some inexplicable reason, he didn't like it. The alteration made him uncomfortable, uneasy somehow. And so it seemed a perfectly natural thing to straighten up and ask,

"Have you been ill?"

# ❊ Two ❊

*M*irabelle's trip around the side of the house was not so much a walk, as it was an extended fit of huffing.

*Have you been ill,* indeed.

It might have made more sense for her to simply use the back door, but in order to do that, she would have had to walk past Whit. And an exit was never quite so dramatic as when one could spin on one's heel and storm off in the opposite direction, which was exactly what she'd done after Whit had voiced his supremely asinine question.

*Have you been ill?*

She kicked at a small rock and watched it tumble through the grass. Maybe . . . possibly . . . she shouldn't have been quite so contrary with him. But she'd been in a foul mood all day. Ever since that blasted note from her uncle had been delivered to her at breakfast.

Twice a year, every bloody year, she was forced to make the two-mile trip to her uncle's home for one of his hunting parties. And every year, he sent a missive in advance of those occasions to remind her she was to come. And every single year, no matter how hard she tried to make it otherwise, the note left her with a sick dread that lingered for the whole of the week.

She despised her uncle, loathed his parties, and abhorred nearly every dissipated, dissolute, and debauched sot who attended them.

She'd much rather stay here, at Haldon. She stopped for a moment to stare at the great stone house. She'd been a child the first time she'd seen it. A small girl who'd lost her parents to an outbreak of influenza and come to live with her uncle only a month before. Reeling from the change in her circumstances, and finding herself unwelcome in her new home, she soon came to look at Haldon as both a haven and an enchanted fortress. It was an enormous combination of the old, the new, and everything in between. There were cavernous rooms, narrow halls, sweeping stairs, and secret passages. There were gilded ceilings in one room, lowered beams in another—an oddly endearing collection of the past eight earls' tastes and lifestyles. A person could, and occasionally did, get lost in the maze of it all. If only, she thought, she could get lost and never find her way out again.

Well, she couldn't, she reminded herself, and resumed her walk.

She was to play hostess for her uncle, and there was nothing to be done about it. Except, of course, to prepare for what she knew was coming. She'd tried very hard this time not to let it ruin her stay at Haldon, even having gone so far as to have a new gown made up.

She hadn't put on a new dress in . . . oh, forever it seemed. The pittance her uncle gave her for pin money didn't allow for extravagant purchases. It barely allowed enough for basic necessities.

In retrospect, perhaps she shouldn't have dipped into her savings, but after the note arrived, she'd gone straight to her room and put on her new dress. It was silly, really, how much better it made her feel . . . almost pretty. She'd rather expected someone might comment upon it.

*Have you been ill?*

She found the rock again and kicked it hard enough to feel the bite against her toe.

Really, Whit was about as perceptive as a . . . well she didn't know exactly. Something blind and deaf. Pity he wasn't mute in the bargain.

Mirabelle stopped to take a deep calming breath. It was

pointless for her to become so worked up over one little comment. In particular when said comment had come from Whit. It wasn't anywhere near the most offensive insult he'd ever handed her, and the fact that she was so angry over such a small slight only served to make her . . . well, angrier.

She turned and pushed through a side door into the house, turned her steps toward her room, and tried to sort through her muddled feelings. It wasn't all anger, she realized. There was hurt, too, and disappointment. He had just stood there, with that famous lopsided devil-may-care grin that had half the *ton* in love with him, and for an instant it seemed as if he might actually say something pleasant. For reasons she chose not to examine too closely, she had very much wanted him to say something pleasant to her. Something along the lines of: "Why, Mirabelle . . ."

"Why, Mirabelle, what a lovely dress."

Mirabelle whirled to find Evie Cole exiting a room behind her. A curvaceous young woman with light brown hair and dark eyes, Evie's appearance would have been described as lovely were it not for a slight limp and the long thin scar that ran from her temple to her jaw, both remnants of a carriage accident during childhood.

Though it was not known outside the family, it was that very accident that had brought Evie to Haldon Hall. Her father—Whit's uncle—had been taken that night, and her mother—not an attentive parent to begin with by all accounts—had chosen to dwell in grief rather than see to the care of her child. According to Evie, Mrs. Cole had been all too happy to accept Lady Thurston's offer to raise Evie at Haldon.

After years of neglect, it was no great surprise that Evie arrived a painfully shy child. It had taken months to coax her out of her shell. When she finally emerged, Mirabelle had been astounded to find not a proper and demure little girl, but an opinionated bluestocking. Evie had an incredible gift for mathematics and a personal, albeit currently secret, goal to free the world's—or at the very least England's—female population from the oppressive rule of the subspecies she referred to as the male gender. In short, she was a radical.

She was also unerringly loyal, wickedly clever, and rather incongruently fashion conscious. There was little chance of Evie failing to notice a friend's pretty new dress.

Mirabelle felt herself smiling broadly.

"Does this mean your uncle has finally loosened his death grip on the purse strings, then?" Evie inquired, plucking at the lavender sleeve of the dress.

"Hardly," Mirabelle scoffed. "It would take a good deal more than the grim reaper to pry that man's fingers from his money."

At Evie's questioning expression, Mirabelle took her hand and led her to a small sitting room at the end of the hall. "Come, I'll explain when Kate returns from her ride. In the meantime, ring for tea and some of those delicious biscuits Cook makes. I know it's early, but I'm starved. And now that I have you cornered, I insist you finally tell me all about your trip to Bath last month."

"You're always hungry," Evie mumbled after pulling the bell cord and sending the answering servant for refreshments. "And I've told you, Bath was Bath. A goodly number of ugly people in pretty clothing, drinking filthy water. I wrote you quite faithfully," she finished, taking a seat.

"You turned out one letter, and its entire contents were centered on a dreadful musicale you were forced to attend at the Watlingtons'. I want the high points."

"That *was* the high point," Evie insisted. "Miss Mary Willory tripped on the hem of her skirt and upended the cellist before her head connected soundly with the back of his chair, and by way of clarification, one letter *is* faithful correspondence where I'm concerned."

"I know," Mirabelle chuckled. "It's fortunate others are fond of writing letters or I should never know what happens on your adventures."

"Nothing happens on my adventures, that's why I write so little. It takes up half a week of my time composing enough material to fill one page, and to be honest, a good deal of it is exaggerated—for dramatic purposes, you understand."

"Naturally. The Miss Willory incident?"

Evie grinned wickedly. "Oh no, my recounting of that event was true down to the last blessed detail. God knows I made every effort to memorize the scene. I shall live off the memory for years."

Mirabelle tried and failed not to smile. "I suppose we hardly do ourselves credit by sinking to her level of spitefulness. Besides, she could have been injured."

"Oh, she was," Evie replied, unrepentantly cheerful. "She had a lump on her forehead the size of a hen's egg." She smiled wistfully at the memory. "It was glorious—all black and blue and red around the edges."

"God, that sounds painful."

"One can only hope. And it turned the most spectacular shade of green after several days. I've never seen the like. I was tempted to invite her to the modiste so I might have a gown made in the same shade in honor of the occasion, but I didn't think I could stand her company for quite so long a time."

A rattling at the door and the appearance of a bedraggled young woman stopped Mirabelle's reply.

"Kate!" Both girls cried, half in pleased greeting and half in dismay over her state.

Lady Kate Cole, under better circumstances, was a beauty—tall enough to wear the current high-waisted fashions with

ease, but still petite enough to appear respectably delicate—
and endowed with enough curves to keep men's eyes and
thoughts off either one of those concerns. She'd had the
good fortune to be born with the pale blonde hair and soft
blue eyes the *ton* was currently raving over, as well as a
straight blade of nose, an adorable little chin, and a perfect
rosebud mouth. Normally, she was a vision. At the moment,
however, her hair was half undone from its pins, hanging in
damp lanks down her neck. Her dress was torn, and the
front of it splattered liberally in mud.

"Oh, Kate," Evie sighed, standing up to take her cousin's
hand. "Whatever happened?"

Kate blew an errant lock out of her eyes. "I fell off my
horse."

Both Mirabelle and Evie gasped. Kate's mishaps were
common, but rarely were they dangerous.

"You what!"

"Are you hurt? Should we call for a physician?"

"Does your mother know?"

"You should sit. Immediately."

Kate let herself be led to one of the chairs where she sat
down with a disgruntled sigh. "I fell off my horse, and I'm
perfectly well, I assure you. I don't need a doctor, *or* my
mother. Has anyone rung for tea, I'm in desperate need—".

"Yes, yes," Mirabelle cried impatiently, "but are you sure
you're uninjured? Being thrown from a horse is no small
matter, Kate. Maybe we should—"

Mirabelle stopped at Kate's sheepish grimace.

"Daisy didn't throw me," Kate supplied reluctantly. "I fell
off."

There was a moment of silence before Evie raised her
eyebrows and said, "Well, I'll concede there is a difference."

Kate nodded and waved at her friends to resume their
seats. "I was in the east pasture, and I stopped to look at a little flower just starting to bloom quite in the middle of

nowhere, and so early as well. I thought if I could find out what it was, I could plant some of them along that far side of the walled garden that gets so little sun. You know the spot, where nothing ever seems to grow but spiny weeds and—"

"Kate," Mirabelle admonished gently.

"Right, well . . . I leaned down for a closer peek and my dress, or maybe it was my heel . . ." She paused to look down questioningly at her feet. "Something, at any rate, caught on something else, and the next thing I knew, I was face down in the mud. Daisy was standing perfectly still."

Evie and Mirabelle winced sympathetically. Mirabelle couldn't help but ask one more time if she was all right.

"I'm fine. Truly," Kate replied. "Nothing was injured besides my riding habit, which can be replaced, and my pride—which, fortunately, has developed a healthy callus over the years and shall no doubt heal completely before the day is out. Oh, and the flower. I landed on it."

"That's a shame," Evie remarked.

"Rather. Now I'll never know what it was."

"I'm sure there are others," Mirabelle assured her. "I think you should go change your dress before you catch a chill."

"Oh no, it isn't necessary. I'm dry as a bone underneath all the mud. Speaking of dresses, you look quite lovely today, Mira. Is that a new gown?"

"It is." She plucked at the skirts. "My uncle sent his note this morning. I rather thought the dress might cheer me up."

Kate leaned forward and grasped her hand. "You don't have to go, you know. If you'd just tell Mother you want to stay, she'd see it done."

Mirabelle turned her hand over and gave her friend's a squeeze. Lady Thurston would no doubt try. Unfortunately, according to the terms set out in her parents' will, Mirabelle's guardian received a yearly stipend of three hundred pounds, until she reached the age of seven-and-twenty, provided she spent a minimum of six weeks every year under his roof. Mirabelle assumed it was a precaution taken to ensure she wasn't simply shipped off to the poorhouse. Good intentions that had done more harm than good.

"I know, but my uncle would make it so difficult, and I won't bring that sort of battle into your home."

"How much longer until the will runs out and you're ours for good?" Evie inquired.

"Not long, less than two years."

That knowledge had played a key factor in her decision to purchase a new gown. She would no longer need her paltry savings of eighty pounds after her twenty-seventh birthday. Her parents had evidently decided that if she hadn't managed to land a husband by that age, it was likely she never would, and then her inheritance of five thousand pounds—currently a dowry—would be hers to do with as she pleased.

It would please her very much, she thought, to have a house of her own—where people would come to visit *her* for a change.

Her musings were interrupted when Thompson, the butler, entered the room.

"The Duke and Duchess of Rockeforte have arrived," he informed them before wisely stepping aside as the three women made a dash for the door.

# ❋ Three ❋

The duke and duchess—better known to their close friends as Alex and Sophie—were, in Mirabelle's opinion, the most delightful couple in all of England. She could see the pair now through the open front doors as they descended from the carriage—a markedly handsome man handing down a beautiful and obviously pregnant young woman.

Mirabelle had known Alex since childhood. His mother and Lady Thurston had been lifelong friends, and when a young Alex had been left orphaned, Lady Thurston had opened her doors and her heart to him and had become, in essence, a second mother. He was as tall as Whit, but a bit broader in the arms and chest. His hair was a rich coffee color, and his eyes a misty green that once had a wariness about them, but were now filled with laughter.

Mirabelle had made Sophie's acquaintance less than two years previously, but they had become the fastest of friends in a matter of days. She was a fascinating woman, having traveled the world for years before she married Alex, and been involved in any number of outrageous adventures along the way. Her hair was a dark mahogany and her eyes a crisp blue, which, like Alex's, usually shone bright and happy. Just now, however, they were snapping with irritation.

"While I'm sure numbness about the hands is a widely held complaint amongst women in my condition," she was saying in a tone simply dripping with sarcasm, "I find that I am miraculously unaffected. Please hand me my reticule."

"No."

Mirabelle may not have recognized the language Sophie responded in, but she could fathom the content well enough. Curses had a sort of ring about them.

Sophie broke off when she caught sight of the group from the house. What followed was not the *ton*'s usual round of stilted greetings. There was no formality here as the women laughed and embraced, speaking over each other in their excitement. It was, Mirabelle thought, the way of family—of sisters and brothers.

The newcomers were ushered into the house with a great deal of noise and movement. Boxes and trunks were hauled from the carriage and into the hall, a maid was called to take coats and hats, and refreshments were offered in the parlor.

"I'm sure Alex would prefer to take his tea with Whit," Sophie interjected before Alex could speak.

"I would, in fact, but only if you'll promise to sit down while you take yours." Alex grinned at his wife and planted a brief and gentle kiss on her cheek. It was an easy affection Mirabelle supposed he probably indulged in several times a day, but there was a sweetness to it that had her wondering, as she had a time or two in the past, what it might be like to know that sort of love. It was a thought she quickly pushed aside. Love was reserved for the beautiful, the lucky, and the incurably romantic. She wasn't even remotely qualified.

Sophie pursed her lips at her husband. "Sitting *is* the usual way of taking tea."

"So it is, but as the usual way and *your* way so rarely coincide—"

"I'll sit," Sophie ground out.

"Excellent. Is Whit in the study?" Alex asked Thompson.

"He is, Your Grace."

Sophie rolled her eyes at Alex's retreating back before walking into the parlor and—true to her word—taking a seat in an overstuffed chair.

"Would you like something to eat?" Evie asked as Kate poured tea.

Sophie groaned and pressed a hand to her belly. "I can't. I just can't."

Mirabelle felt a sliver of alarm at her friend's pained expression. "Are you unwell? Is something wrong?"

"I'm in perfect health," Sophie assured her. "It's only that I've eaten more in the last six months than I have in the whole of my lifetime. It's Alex. The man won't stop feeding me. It's some sort of horrible illness with him. 'Have some stew, Sophie. A few more carrots, Sophie. Just one more bite of fish, Sophie, one more piece of toast, one more slice of . . .'" She straightened in her chair. "Are those lemon tarts?"

"Er . . . yes."

"Thank God." Sophie snagged one, bit in, and spoke around the food. "If he'd foist this sort of food on me, I'd be less inclined to complain, but it isn't desserts with him. It's pounds and pounds—tons, really—of breads and meat and vegetables. Mother of God, the vegetables. The man's so bloody careful. Do you have any idea how long it took us to reach here?"

Three heads shook in unison.

"Four days," Sophie informed them, taking another bite. "Four endless days, and we not forty miles from Haldon. He made our driver stop every two hours so I could rest. Have you ever heard anything so ridiculous? And he was a dreadful traveling companion, let me tell you. I couldn't so much as shift in the seat without him fussing over me, or calling out to our man to have a care with the ruts in the road. Not that there were any ruts, mind you, or that we'd enough speed to have felt them if there were, the man's simply come unhinged."

"I'm surprised he agreed to let you come at all," Evie ventured.

"Oh, he didn't initially. There was a . . . discussion." Sophie's expression went from exasperated to grim as she set down the remainder of the tart. "Good Lord, listen to me. He's driven me to ranting. It won't do. I have to get away from him, for a few hours at the very least. I beg of you, help me."

"Why don't we go into Benton for a bit of shopping," Evie suggested. "Mirabelle needs a bonnet and gloves to go with her new dress—matching reticule as well if one can be found."

"I certainly do not," Mirabelle objected on a laugh. She held up a hand before Evie could argue. "But I'm not averse to purchasing something small. Something small, pretty, and pointless." She reached for a tart and bit in. "I rather feel like pampering myself."

"For once," Evie commented.

"Alex will want to join us." Sophie pointed out.

"Well, we'll simply have to find an excuse to become separated," Evie said. "Take him aside at some point and tell him you need to purchase some clothing items of an embarrassingly feminine nature."

"Oh, he'll *insist* on joining me for that."

"Well then, tell him *I* need to purchase some clothing items of an embarrassingly feminine nature."

"That, I think, should do it," Sophie agreed with a grin as Kate and Mirabelle laughed. "*Do* you need them?"

Evie merely shrugged. "One can never have too many undergarments, so it needn't be a lie."

They were still laughing when Whit poked his head in the door. "Ladies . . . imp . . . Alex and I are for—"

"Benton," Kate piped in and shot a covert glance at Sophie. "Sophie has expressed an interest in Mrs. Gage's pastries. You don't mind do you, Whit?"

Whit frowned at the food the servants had brought into the room. He opened his mouth, but Sophie—devious and clever girl that she was—cut off any argument by lifting her hand to run gentle circles across her extended belly.

"I don't wish to be a bother," she said with a soft voice and angelic smile. "But I'm simply ravenous for something . . ." Her eyes scanned the plates in the room. "Chocolate. There doesn't seem to be any here."

"You're not a bother," Whit replied. In the manner of men who have limited experience with expectant mothers, he was exceedingly careful to keep his gaze on her face, or over her shoulder, or anywhere other than the obvious mound under her dress. "If you want Mrs. Gage's pastries, you'll have them. Alex and I will ride into town—"

"Oh, but I don't know which kind I might prefer, exactly, and I'd very much like to spend some time shopping with my friends before all the . . ." She waved a weak hand in the air. "Fuss and noise of the party. But if it's too much trouble for you, we can walk."

*"Walk?"*

"Yes, of course." She began to lever herself out of the chair with all the strength and grace of a woman on her deathbed. "It's not more than three miles, and I'm not an invalid, you know."

Whit was inside the room and gently pushing her back into the chair in under a second. Mirabelle managed, only barely, to keep from laughing. Oh, but Sophie was a wily creature, she thought. Outright weakness might make a man like Whit inclined to pamper a bit, but quiet bravery would destroy him.

"Sit down, Sophie, please. There's no need for you to walk, for pity's sake. Alex and I will take you into town."

"Well, if you're sure—"

"Of course. Of course, I'm sure. You'll have all the pastries you like."

"Looks as if the carriage is nearly ready, ladies," Whit commented later as their transport, along with his and Alex's mounts, were brought to the front of the house. "We need only hitch the imp to the front of the team."

Mirabelle sent him a sneer and climbed in behind a freshly attired Kate. "Rest assured, cretin, if I were to suddenly find myself a horse, the first thing I'd do would be to kick you in—"

"We're ready to go now!" Sophie inserted enthusiastically as she clambered in and sat beside Mirabelle, making room also for Kate and Evie.

"—the head," Mirabelle shouted after him before turning to Sophie with a furrowed brow. "What did you think I was going to say?"

"Er . . . something else. Something . . ." Kate waved her hand to indicate the lower half of her body.

Realization dawned on Mirabelle's face, and with it, a delighted grin. "Oh. Oh, that's very good." She poked her head back out the window to amend her earlier threat, but found Whit gone. "Blast."

There was only one dress shop in all of Benton, but as the dress shop was run by Madame Duvalle, one was all that was needed. A London modiste of some import in the previous decade, Madame Duvalle had fallen out of fashion in part because of the capriciousness of the *ton,* and in part because of her unwillingness to compromise her work to the demands of silly young girls—but according to Lady Thurston, that could only be counted as a mark in her favor.

She'd made the short move to Benton at Lady Thurston's urging, and kept up a lively business catering to the Coles, their frequent guests, and the surrounding gentry.

Madame Duvalle also held the unusual distinction of being an actual native of France, having been born, raised, and trained in her art in Paris. And just so there would be no misunderstanding on the girls' part, what Madame Duvalle created was art.

The shop was located with the other shops of quality in the heart of the town. A young woman with a friendly smile greeted them at the door, then disappeared into a back room to discreetly inform Madame that her most prestigious patrons had arrived. Before Mirabelle had had a chance to glance at the new materials, a very tall and somewhat plump woman sailed out of the door the young woman had recently exited. She stopped abruptly, let out an enormous sigh, and clasped her hands to her heart.

*"Mes chéries!"*

It was an entrance the young women had long grown accustomed to, but as it was no less sincere than it was dramatic, they returned the greeting with smiles.

*"Mes belles,* look at you," Madame Duvalle crooned. "Why I should bother to put such effort into your gowns, I do not know. You would make a draped sheet appear a masterpiece of thread and needle. But I am most delighted to see all of you . . . except for you," she informed Mirabelle with a sniff and a twinkling eye. "You are too stubborn."

Mirabelle laughed and, unable to resist, leaned up to kiss a cheek. "You were able to convince me to choose the lavender gown over the brown," she reminded her.

"Yes, but it was the ivory I wanted you to have."

And it was the ivory that *she* had wanted to have, Mirabelle recalled, but it had been too dear, and far less practical than the deep lavender, which would hide stains more easily.

"I'm here twice in as many weeks with the intention of making a purchase, surely that must count for something."

*"Oui,* it counts for much." She gave Mirabelle a hopeful smile. "The ivory this time?"

"Nothing quite so grand, I'm afraid. We're in need of undergarments."

"Ah." Madame Duvalle looked over as newcomers arrived. "You know the way, of course. I will give you time to look while I see to these ladies, yes?"

Unlike the bolts of cloth and the ready-made gowns, items of a more intimate nature were displayed in a separate, windowless room.

"Have you any idea what you might want?" Kate asked Evie as the women took in the contents of the room.

"No, but I'll own myself intrigued by this."

Mirabelle looked up from where she'd been studying a fashion plate to see Evie point out a . . . a something, displayed on a seamstress's form. Light blue satin cut much too simply to be a gown, hugged rather than draped over the model.

"Well, for heaven's sake," Mirabelle laughed. "What is the point of such a garment?"

"I've no idea," was both Kate's and Evie's reply.

"To feel delicious," was Sophie's. Three heads immediately spun in her direction. She shrugged, a slight bloom of red showing on her cheeks. "Perhaps one needs to be married to appreciate the prettiness of it."

"Or be in the market for something pretty and pointless," Evie added with a pointed look at Mirabelle.

"That's absurd, Evie," Mirabelle chuckled. "We don't even know what it is."

"Sophie appears to."

"Not really," Sophie admitted. "I just think it's lovely. Perhaps it's a chemise."

"It's too long." Mirabelle argued. "It would reach near the ankles. And the material isn't right."

Chemises were made of sturdy material that could withstand the abuse of repeated washings. The fabric before her looked as if it might melt in a hard rain. She reached out to run a finger down the material. And fell instantly in love.

"Oh my," she breathed. "Have you ever felt anything so soft?"

"Ah, you have found my little experiment, I see."

At the sound of Madame Duvalle's voice, Mirabelle

snatched her hand back with a guilty start. "I beg your pardon, I shouldn't have—"

"Pfft. If I did not want it admired, I would not have left it out. What do you make of it?"

"It's divine," Mirabelle whispered and had four pairs of eyes blinking at her. "Well, it is," she defended. "It feels like . . . like water. What's it for?"

"It is a chemise."

"But . . ."

"But it is most impractical, yes. And so every woman of means has informed me." She gave an annoyed huff. "It is odd, is it not, that even the most frivolous of women would not be eager to indulge themselves thus?"

"Because they can't display it where others could see and envy," Evie murmured.

"Exactly so, my clever girl."

"A woman with a husband could," Sophie said, considering.

"This is true," Madame Duvalle laughed. "But this piece is not for you, *juene mère*. It is for Miss Browning."

Mirabelle wouldn't have been more stunned if she'd been offered the deed to the shop. Which is likely why she failed to see the look of understanding pass between Madame Duvalle and Kate.

"For me? But I couldn't. I couldn't possibly. I . . ." She trailed off. "Couldn't," she felt, summed up her position quite well. She couldn't afford it. Couldn't find a use for it. Couldn't all sorts of things.

Her objections feel on deaf ears. "I insist. I would have my creation appreciated, not sitting in this room collecting dust." Madame Duvalle began to pull the chemise off the model. "I ask three shillings and will do the alterations for free, yes?"

Three shillings? It was a ridiculously low price.

"Three shillings? That's absurd. The material alone—"

"Three shillings, stubborn girl, and also the currency of gossip. I would hear of the guests." She held the material up against Mirabelle and squinted. "No alterations needed, I think. We are fortunate."

"A very hard bargain," Evie cut in before Mirabelle could continue her argument. "But she'll take it. Which gossip would you care to hear first?"

Outnumbered, outmaneuvered, and not all that interested in having her way, if truth be known, Mirabelle dug into her reticule for the three shillings. "I'll take good care of it," she promised. "Thank you."

"Of course you will." Madame Duvalle moved into the front of the store, which was—to Mirabelle's vast relief—once again empty. "Now, tell me what you make of the Mr. Hunter who has come to visit."

Kate shrugged. "He has business with Whit. We haven't met him as yet."

"I've met him in London," Sophie told them. "He seems pleasant enough."

"Yes, a very pleasant man," Madame Duvalle responded as she set the chemise on a table and began to wrap it in tissue. "That is how, I am told, the London actresses and opera singers speak of him, a most pleasant gentleman."

"Oh, dear." Mirabelle and Kate didn't bother to hide their frowns. Sophie and Evie didn't bother to hide their grins. And Madame Duvalle didn't bother to consider that either reaction might be anything other than encouragement.

"His conquests are quite legendary, but it is said he does not dally with the innocent or the married, as many young men seem to feel they must, and that is something, no?"

Evie gave a scoffing laugh. "It's quite all right, then, for him to seduce legions of women so long as they're actresses and courtesans?"

Madame Duvalle gave a very Gallic shrug and put the chemise in a box. "One cannot expect him to exist as a monk, after all."

"Why not?" Evie demanded. "Women are expected to live as nuns. It's most unfair."

"*C'est vrai, ma petite,* but so it has always been for women, no? If life were fair, I would be forever young and beautiful, I would have a delectable young man to dance attendance upon me, and all my customers would be as much fun as the four of you."

"I think, Madame Duvalle," said Sophie, "that if you were forever young and beautiful, it would be distinctly unfair to the rest of us."

Madame Duvalle smiled slyly. "Don't be silly, I would share my dancing man."

# ❈ *Four* ❈

To Mirabelle's mind, it was just a touch unsettling to traipse about Benton carrying a box that held an unconventional undergarment. As such, she thought it might be best if she dropped her purchase off at the carriage while the others went ahead to the bookseller's.

But if she had known she would run into Whit on the sidewalk, she would have carried the box from one end of town to the other without complaint. There were, after all, varying degrees of unsettling.

"Whit. Hello. It's a very nice day, isn't it? The others have gone to the bookseller's. Where's Alex?"

She was chattering. She knew she was chattering, she just couldn't seem to stop herself. It was amazing she was able to get out anything at all, considering she had an entirely different—and entirely involuntary—sort of conversation running through her head.

*Whit. Hello. I'm carrying a blue chemise in this box. I think it might be some sort of satin. Isn't that lovely?*

She peeked over his shoulder at the carriage and wondered if she could sneak by him without being too obvious about it. She rather thought not. Certainly not with him suddenly looking at her so intently.

She felt the heat creep up from her chest to spread across her neck and face. She was blushing. Five-and-twenty years of age and she was blushing. It was ridiculous. And dangerous. Whit was watching her with amused curiosity, his blue eyes narrowing with an interest that alarmed her.

"Alex is at Maver's Tavern. What are you hiding, imp?"

"What?" The word came out too loud, but good Lord, how could he possibly know? Had he seen her? Mirabelle glanced back at the modiste's shop. No, the windows reflected the afternoon sunlight, no one could see inside without standing mere inches away, and she was fairly certain someone would have mentioned if the Earl of Thurston were pressing his nose against the glass.

She cleared her throat nervously. "I haven't the faintest idea what you're talking about, Whit."

Her voice came out too soft this time. Damn it, she was only making things harder for herself.

"You're only making things harder for yourself," he said, and smiled at her scowl. "You're so nervous, I half expect you to bolt."

The idea had merit. Her whole body was tensed for flight. She forced her muscles to relax. But not too much. She liked to keep all her options open.

"I'm hot," she offered lamely. It didn't come within a mile of explaining her tension, but it was the best she could manage under the circumstances.

Apparently, her best was none too good for Whit because he ignored her last statement entirely. "Are you making excuses for the rest of the ladies?"

She blinked at the non sequitur. "Er . . . no," she stuttered, honestly confused. "I told you, they're at the bookseller's. Kate wished to see if a particular Wollenscroft book was available."

Whit groaned and leaned around her to peer down the street. She heard him mumble something about "trash" and "putting my foot down," and she jumped at the chance to change the subject.

"They're quite horrid, it's true, but I can't see any harm in her reading them."

"They'll rot her brain."

"Oh, I doubt that. Even if it were a possibility, which I don't believe for a minute, we would have seen the effects by now. She's been reading books like those for years."

"Maybe we just haven't recognized the damage they've done."

"Such as . . ."

Whit shrugged. "She's one-and-twenty," he replied distractedly. "She should have been married by now." He moved to step around her.

Well, *that,* she decided, was a bit much. She stepped in his path.

"You can't really be so obtuse as to hold those books responsible for your sister's unmarried state."

He stared at her for a moment, his eyes boring into her own. "Actually, I have an entirely different theory on what, or who, is responsible."

That rather hurt. It shouldn't after so many years of traded insults, but it did. Briefly, she was taken aback by the force of her feelings, by the realization that all of his unkind comments over the course of the day had affected her more strongly than ever before. She felt a lump form in her throat, but then, to her vast relief, the thought that this coldhearted man had so completely upset her composure spurred her to anger. That he should suspect her of standing in the way of his sister's happiness was unimaginable, insupportable, and just . . . very, very stupid.

"If you honestly believe that I ever have anything but the greatest of care for your sister's happiness, then you are a greater fool than even I imagined. Furthermore, if you honestly believe that your sister hasn't the backbone to tell me and my great care to go straight to the devil, should it please her, then you're a disloyal brother *and* a fool. Furthermore . . ."

In a blink of an eye, he had the box from her hands.

One moment she had been heartily enjoying her tirade, which she had punctuated with sharp little jabs of her finger to his chest, and the next he was standing several feet away, holding her box, absently rubbing his chest, and grinning like the fool she had just accused him of being.

"God, you're fun to rile," he laughed. "And so delightfully easy. You'll believe near to anything, won't you?"

Mirabelle felt a brief flash of relief that he hadn't meant his earlier accusation, but it was almost immediately replaced by indignation at the insinuation that she was gullible, and *that* was very promptly pushed aside by dread at the thought of her blue chemise. Whit's fingers moved to idly play with the strings keeping the box closed, and her emotions shifted yet again, to something dangerously close to panic. She took several deep breaths to calm herself. The effects were negligible.

"What is it in this box that has you so jumpy?" Whit asked, toying with the knot.

She was mortified, but she'd submit to every torture known to man before she let Whit know it. "Good Lord, cretin, how did you ever convince your nanny to let you out of your gowns?"

Whit shrugged nonchalantly and she fought the urge to slap him, and blue satin be damned. "One of the benefits of being so charming. You get to wear whatever you like."

"This is beneath even you."

Whit raised the box to his ear and shook it. "Actually, I can't imagine anyone it *wouldn't* be beneath, but I find my curiosity has gotten the better of me. I've never seen you look so guilty." He frowned thoughtfully and gave the box another shake. "So what is it, imp? It's soft . . . rather light . . ."

"I'm humbled by your brilliance, your lordship," Mirabelle drawled. "It's soft, it's light, and I've just come from the modiste's."

Whit shook the box again.

"The modiste's, Whit. It's cloth, it's light, and I was . . . uncomfortable. Must I spell it out for you?"

By the glint in his eye, there was clearly no need.

"On the contrary, I just wanted to see if you could bring yourself to say the word."

She glared at him.

"You can't, can you? Very well, I shall do the dirty for you." He wiggled his eyebrows ridiculously and, in his best rake's voice, whispered, "Unmentionables." Ignoring her eye roll, he continued on in his normal tone. "Silly name for a garment, or a set of garments as the case may be. Why go through the bother of naming them, then deciding they can't be mentioned, then mentioning them as unmentionables, as if that somehow negates the fact they were just mentioned?"

"Yes, it's a fascinating puzzle. May I have my box back now?"

"Of course not, this is far too great a prize to relinquish without payment."

"I've already paid for what's in it."

"You haven't paid me."

"It doesn't belong to you," she managed to spit out through gritted teeth.

"Nonetheless, I have the box now, and for its return I require recompense."

"I cannot begin to imagine . . ."

"No? How sadly uncreative of you. I can think of at least a dozen varieties of payment, some of them quite interesting."

"What is it you want, Whit?"

He settled the box securely under his arm. "A favor," he replied clearly. Mirabelle couldn't help but notice his tone and expression had suddenly become rather serious.

"What is the nature of this favor?" she asked suspiciously.

"Its nature is pleasant enough, just not honorable." He shot her a grin. "That's why I'm asking you."

"*Are* you asking me?"

"Not really. I want you to tell me what Kate has been doing at night."

Her face must have shown her shock because he continued on. "Don't look at me like that. I'm not suggesting the sort of behavior you're clearly thinking of. She's been writing, and I want to know what, and to whom."

She folded her arms across her chest. "Go on."

He shrugged. "Not much else to tell. I sometimes see a light coming from under her door in the small hours of the morning. I want to know what she's doing."

Mirabelle wanted to know what *he* was doing up in the small hours of the morning, but thought it best not to ask. Despite Whit's earlier assertion, she was creative enough to think of a few reasons he might be sneaking in at dawn, and they were nothing she cared to dwell on.

"Why don't you simply ask her?" she inquired instead.

"I have. She claims she can't sleep some nights and keeps busy writing letters." He scowled absently. "I don't believe it."

Neither do I, she thought. "Kate really isn't one for lying." Mostly. "And she is a faithful correspondent."

Whit shook his head. "I need to know for certain."

"You're asking me to spy on my friend, your sister."

"Yes."

"Only you aren't really asking."

"No."

"And if I refuse?"

Keeping his eyes pinned on hers, Whit reached over and untied the knot at the top of the box.

"You wouldn't dare," Mirabelle gasped.

"Of course I would. You know I don't bluff."

"I know nothing of the sort. And it doesn't signify. Even an earl can't pull out a lady's unmentionables in the middle of the street and get away with it."

"You'd be surprised what an earl can get away with."

"Probably," she grumbled.

"Besides, I've no intention of just pulling out your undergarments in the middle of a sidewalk." He gave her a wicked smile. "I plan on tripping over that curb and spilling the contents in the street. We Coles are notoriously clumsy, you know."

"No one who knows you would believe such a pathetic excuse—"

"I'm an earl," he reminded her with a shrug. "My excuses don't have to be believable, just available."

"You'd do this?" she asked quietly. "You'd humiliate me like this?"

Whit looked at her hard. "My sister is very important to me."

*And you are not.* It was amazing how loud unspoken words could sound. And infuriating. The man was an arrogant, selfish, spoiled ass, and it was on the tip of her tongue to tell him to go to hell and take the box with him, and she would have, if the box had contained just the usual sturdy, practical variety of undergarments. But that damn blue satin chemise was inside. Unmarried, gently reared young women were not supposed to have unusual undergarments. At best she'd be a laughingstock, at worse she'd be utterly ruined.

Seething with resentment, she clenched her fists, ground her teeth, and glared at the man in front of her. "Fine, you coldhearted ass. I'll do it."

An emotion passed over Whit's face, but it was gone before she could interpret it. She decided she was too angry to care.

"On your honor, imp."

She snorted. "Would that be the honor in succumbing to blackmail, the honor in betraying a friend's confidence, or the honor you accused me of not having?"

"I want your word you'll do as I've asked."

"Demanded."

"Your word."

"My word, then. Are you quite satisfied?"

She knew he would be. In Whit's world, there was no conceivable excuse for breaking one's word of honor—everyone could afford rigid principles. Whit never, *ever* broke his word. He was famous for it, and if she were a little less angry with him, she would admit that she respected him for that. But Mirabelle's experiences had taught her a somewhat different lesson. Sometimes, those principles were a luxury only the rich and powerful could afford. The richer and more powerful, the more honorable they could afford to be. The rest of the world did the best they could with what fate handed them.

In Mirabelle's case, self-preservation demanded that her sense of morality be occasionally flexible. She didn't condone lying. In fact, she was fundamentally opposed to dishonesty, but like Whit's willingness to use blackmail, some evils were unavoidable.

She wasn't about to betray Kate's trust, but she wasn't going to have her undergarments tossed into the street either.

Whit, clearly sensing something amiss, stared at her a moment longer, but apparently deciding he wasn't about to receive further reassurances, nodded once and handed her the box.

Looking back, Mirabelle would be forced to admit that what happened next was not Whit's fault. Not directly anyway.

She was in full possession of the box, but her hands had grown clammy and the sweat had seeped through the cheap material of her gloves. She'd been too eager to get the knot retied, and it was so awkward trying to hold the box and manipulate the string at the same time. In retrospect, she should have set the box down first, because the next thing she knew, it was making a slow descent to the ground.

And it truly was slow. Mirabelle knew it took forever because she had time to mentally recite every invective she had ever heard, some she didn't even remember hearing until just that moment. Strangely, while her mind rushed, her body seemed frozen in place. She managed only one feeble grasp with her fingers and a soft cry before the bottom of the box hit the pavement with a soft thud. The lid lifted up briefly from the force of the impact, betraying a flash of bright blue, before settling neatly back in place.

*Sweet merciful heaven. Thank you.*

Her heart beating loudly in her ears, she shot a panicked look toward Whit. He was looking at something across the street. He hadn't seen.

*Thank you, thank you, thank you.*

She glanced around furtively to see if anyone had witnessed the accident. Assured of her still untarnished reputation, she quickly made a mental apology for every foul word that had crossed her mind. Then she tied the lid back on with a very secure triple knot, picked up the box with both hands, and headed for the carriage. Where she would wait for the others. She was quite done with shopping.

Whit couldn't recall the return trip from Benton to Haldon ever taking quite so long. It wasn't that the horses were moving slower than usual, or that they'd lost a wheel, or met with some other misfortune.

It was just that he was so damnably uncomfortable.

He turned his eyes to the carriage for what he estimated was the dozenth time in the last quarter hour. He couldn't seem to stop himself. He couldn't seem to do anything but recall the way the lid of Mirabelle's box had lifted to reveal a glimpse of something blue, glossy, and quite obviously flimsy.

He'd been appalled.

He'd been fascinated.

He'd pretended not to have seen. In retrospect, that might not have been the best choice of reactions—how could he ask, let alone tease, her about something he hadn't seen? But for the first few seconds after the lid had opened, he'd been stunned into speechlessness. And since then, he'd been repeatedly stunned by persistent, and entirely unwelcome, images of the imp wearing flimsy blue undergarments.

Undergarments that looked to be satin, now that he thought on it.

Not that he was going to continue thinking on it. Absolutely not. He certainly wasn't going to dwell on how it would feel . . . like the skin it would so scarcely cover, he imagined—soft, and cool to the touch, until it warmed under his palms. He'd bunch it up slowly, inch by tantalizing inch, to discover the smooth flesh underneath. He'd use just his hands at first, teasing them both as his mouth found that delightful beauty mark just above her lip. When she was near to begging, when she was writhing beneath him, he'd . . . he'd . . .

*Holy hell.*

He shifted in his saddle, now uncomfortable on several levels.

It had to stop. He *would* stop. He wasn't a boy of fifteen, to be panting at the mere glimpse of a woman's unmentionables. Even if they were blue, and soft, and flimsy.

*Blast.*

He eyed the carriage again, wondering what Mirabelle was after, purchasing something like that.

And he wondered why he couldn't stop wondering.

# ❊ *Five* ❊

$\mathcal{D}$inners at Haldon Hall might have carried the reputation of being unusually informal, with lively conversation and children as young as eight allowed to attend, but there was no mistaking the gathering for a simple meal with friends and family. Dinner was an *event*—a six-course feast that often stretched for hours and offered everything from the delicacies of lobsters and calf brains to the comforting favorites of roasted fowl and bread pudding. The food was prepared by an efficient kitchen, cooked and seasoned to perfection by the inestimable Mrs. Lowell, and swiftly transferred upstairs to be presented and served by a veritable fleet of footmen.

In her customary seat at the foot of the table, Lady Thurston surveyed her staff with approval, her guests with amusement, and her children with love and—in the cases of Whit and Mirabelle—no small amount of annoyance.

Whatever had she been thinking, she wondered, to have

seated them within shouting distance of each other? Not that they were actually shouting, mind you—they knew better than to engage in a yelling match at her table. But even from the other end of the table, she could see that Whit's face was tight as he spoke, and Mirabelle, she couldn't help but notice, was grasping a salad fork in a manner that made the countess just a little bit anxious.

Something, she decided, must be done.

"I had hoped it wouldn't come to this," she murmured.

"Beg pardon?" William Fletcher, noticeably aged (particularly about the hairline) since his days as the bearer of sad tidings regarding the late Duke of Rockeforte, reluctantly turned his attention from the truly superb trout on his plate to follow his hostess's gaze. "Ah. At it again, are they?"

"Ever and always." She watched the pair for a moment more. "I have decided, William, to take advantage of your gracious offer. If it is still available?"

"Yes. Yes, of course it is," he replied carefully. He scratched at his bulbous nose. "But if you're not comfortable with the idea, we could give them a bit more time—"

"They've been given time enough. I should have agreed to something like this years ago, when you first suggested the idea." She sighed deeply. "Only, I had rather thought they would have progressed beyond this by now. I had envisioned things coming to their natural conclusion . . . well, naturally."

"And so they would, eventually."

"Eventually," she decreed, "is taking entirely too long. I'll speak with Whittaker tonight."

After seeing her guests retire for the evening, Lady Thurston made her way to Whit's study. It was nearing midnight, but she knew he wouldn't be in his bedchamber. Not for hours yet. Her late husband, she mused, had spent less time in that study over the entire course of his life than her son did in the course of a sennight. There were times she wasn't sure which of them had the better way of it.

As she had long ago learned the benefits of taking her children by surprise, she didn't bother knocking on the door.

"Am I interrupting?" she asked as she crossed the room and took a seat in front of the desk. "Oh, never mind, I don't really care. I wish to speak with you, Whittaker."

Whit started slightly in his chair before groaning and setting down his quill. "Mother, I love you. I adore you. I'll admit freely and openly to anyone who cares to listen that it is an honor and a privilege to be your son. I would lay down my life for you, but so help me God, if you're here to lecture me on my duty to beget an heir, I will pack you off to the continent. Tonight. This minute."

"That was quite the loveliest thing you have ever said to me," she replied with a sniff, clearly unfazed by his threat. "The first part, I mean, and so I forgive you for the latter, which I know to be an empty threat as you could never handle the girls on your own."

"I am most certainly capable—"

"And I love you too," she continued as if he hadn't been speaking at all. "You do know that, don't you? I sometimes worry I don't say it enough, or too often as if it's a trifle."

Whit came out from behind the desk and placed an affectionate kiss on her cheek. "You needn't worry on either score."

She sighed happily. "Excellent. Now go sit down. I have something important to discuss with you."

"Mother—"

"Would it further my cause if I brought up the subject of an heir on a daily basis?"

"No."

"I didn't think so. Oh, well. As it happens that's not why I'm here."

"Why are you here? Not that you aren't welcome."

"Delighted to hear it. Now sit." She withdrew her hand and used it to make a little shooing motion.

Ever the obedient, if somewhat harassed, son, Whit returned to his seat and gave her a pointed look. She wasted no time.

"It is time you set aside your differences with Mirabelle."

Whit was on guard immediately. "Has she said something to you?"

That wasn't like the imp, he thought. She had never before complained to his mother about their arguments. She threatened to on a regular basis, but she'd never actually gone through with it.

"No," Lady Thurston replied, her eyes narrowing. "Should she have?"

Whit thought it best not to answer that. "I'm surprised by the request, that's all."

She gave him a long look before replying. "It is not a request, Whittaker," she stated coolly. "In my presence, the two of you may play nice for my benefit, but I am not a fool. All the *ton* knows of your adversarial relationship."

Whit scowled. "I should think people would have more interesting matters to discuss." At least by now, he silently amended. The animosity between Mirabelle and him was old hat.

"Aside from poverty, oppression, and injustice, there is no matter too insignificant for the *ton* not to notice," Lady Thurston replied wryly, "and an earl's obvious animosity toward a young unmarried woman is always good gossip. I have left you two to your little squabbles because it does you good to lose your head from time to time, and because Mirabelle doesn't appear to suffer unduly from it, but—"

"What do you mean by 'unduly'?" Whit cut in. "I have never—"

"Raised a hand to her? Publicly humiliated her since becoming an adult? Yes, I know."

"The same can hardly be said for her," he replied, recalling several injuries he'd incurred at her hand.

She gave a small nod. "I'm aware of it. It's another reason I've been reluctant to intervene. In your passion to become the antithesis of your father, you occasionally become a trifle self-righteous. I do admire you, Whit, but it's not healthy to have the fawning respect and admiration of every human being that crosses your path. Mirabelle is good for you."

"She broke my nose," he informed her with a grumble.

"Did she?" She sat up straighter in her chair with unabashed interest. "Did she really?"

"Twice."

Lady Thurston thought about that for a moment. "Care to tell me why?"

Whit barely stopped himself from grimacing. The first time had been with a billiards ball more than ten years ago—in retaliation for an extremely lewd comment he made when Mirabelle had interrupted a round of serious imbibing with his friend Alex. The second time had been for attempting to lock her in the library during a house party.

Whit shifted uncomfortably in his seat. "I will admit, there were some extenuating circumstances."

"I thought there might be. You lose your head with her from time to time. It's good for you."

Whit frowned at her assessment. He didn't want to lose control around the imp. He didn't want to lose control at all. He'd worked to remedy the scandals his father had caused, and also the financial straits in which the man had left the family. Whit had worked too hard to ruin things with a rash temper.

The Thurston earldom was one of the oldest and least respected titles in the country. No one could even remember why the Cole family had gained an earldom, but anyone caring to do the least bit of research would find that not a single generation had done a thing to further the family name. The Thurston earls had been an assorted lot of cheats, rakes, and wastrels, with the family fortune ebbing and flowing dramatically while their reputation remained unerringly low. His late father had carried on the tradition with great fervor—drinking, sporting, throwing lavish parties, and finally dying in a duel over a woman who was not the Lady Thurston.

To the *ton,* however, the newest Earl of Thurston was everything a peer of the realm should be: honorable, charming, handsome, loyal, levelheaded and, thanks to a great deal of hard work and a little good luck, respectably wealthy. Whit cultivated that image diligently, encouraging his sister and cousin to do the same. He was determined that future generations would be proud of their name.

His resolve to be the perfect gentleman, however, was occasionally forgotten when he was in the company of Mirabelle Browning. He'd always known it to be the case, but he hadn't realized people still paid any attention to their little disagreements. They'd been at it for years, and he'd never tossed her out of the house or ruined her good name (despite his threats), and she'd never cast aspersions on his honor or his status as a gentlemen (in public, at any rate.) The worst of their disagreements occurred in private, and the smaller public insults were no more dramatic than the usual barbs traded amongst the *ton.*

But if people were talking, then it needed to stop.

"Come to a decision, have you?"

Whit blinked as he came out of his musings. "My apologies, I was lost in thought."

"No apology necessary, I am pleased you are giving serious consideration to what I have said."

Whit nodded absently. "I'll speak with the . . . with Miss Browning. I'm sure we can come to some understanding."

"Excellent," Lady Thurston replied. She stood to take her leave but was stopped short of the door by Whit's question.

"Why bring this up now?"

She turned to give him her full attention. Never one to sit in the presence of a standing lady, Whit was on his feet behind the desk, his brow furrowed thoughtfully as he fiddled with a quill. "Why have you kept quiet all these years, only to speak up today?"

"She was wearing a new gown today. That small but significant change, along with several others, leads me to believe she may finally be looking to acquire a husband."

Whit set the quill down and stared at her. "A husband? The imp?" he managed to choke out.

"Yes, a husband," Lady Thurston replied. "She is a woman after all, not wealthy, and in case you have not noticed, there are very few options open to us when it comes to securing our means of support."

"I always thought she'd choose to be a governess, or someone's companion."

That wasn't really true. He hadn't thought much on it at all, to be honest. He had always just assumed Mirabelle would remain unmarried, that she would forever be about the London town house and Haldon Hall. During one of his more fanciful moments he had imagined the two of them, old and grey, seated before the fire in the front parlor and taking swings at each other with their canes.

"Well, she won't," he heard his mother say, and it took him a minute to work out that she was speaking of Mirabelle's possible career as a governess and not her aim with a walking stick.

Because he could think of nothing else to say, he settled for a simple, "Are you certain of this?"

"Not at all. It is merely a guess, but in the event that it is true, I will not have her chances ruined by hostility between the two of you. It is time she had a family and home of her own."

*She has a home and family here.*

The thought was no less vehement for having come unbidden, and the force of it rendered him momentarily stunned. Uncomfortable, he set it aside. "I'll not stand in her way."

"Of course you won't, dear."

Whit nodded and watched his mother leave. A new dress. That was the difference he'd been unable to identify that morning. As a general rule, Mirabelle wore rather drab colors of indeterminate material and unremarkable cut. This morning she'd been wearing something light and flowing. Had it been purple? He couldn't remember. Whatever it had been, it had been unlike her.

As was the blue satin he'd seen in her box. Then again, perhaps such undergarments were the new rage in ladies' trousseaus. How the devil should he know?

He turned the quill over with his fingers, unaware that he was scowling.

Was she really looking for a husband?

Probably not, he decided. Mirabelle had been on the marriage mart for years now and had never shown the least interest in catching a husband. Her new wardrobe must be a result of something else.

Whit mulled over the possibilities in his head for awhile before giving it up and deciding simply to ask her when he informed her of their new truce. And as he had some idea of where she could be found at present, he decided now was as good a time as any to do just that.

Mirabelle made the short walk from her room to Kate's, blissfully unaware she was the topic of conversation in another part of the house.

She had decided after dinner that it was time to address the ridiculous issue of spying with Kate. With that purpose in mind, she checked to make certain there was light coming from under the door before knocking softly. She was answered with a moderate-sized crash of what sounded like a chair hitting the wooden floor, followed by a great deal of indecipherable noise and movement. As it was Kate's room, Mirabelle wasn't the least surprised by the sound of furniture being knocked over, but the rest was a mystery.

"Kate?" she called quietly against the wood. "Kate, are you all right?"

There was a moment of complete stillness from inside and then the sound of footsteps and the clack of the bolt being thrown back. Kate's face, when it finally appeared, was flushed, distracted, and just a little bit annoyed.

"Why didn't you say it was only you?"

Mirabelle's brows rose. "Who else were you expecting?"

"I don't know," Kate answered, peeking her head out to look down the hall. "Whit, I suppose. He came nosing about last night. And there's that new friend of his, Mr. Hunter. I didn't care for the way he was staring at me over dinner."

Unable to stop herself, Mirabelle looked over her shoulders. "Do you really think a guest would be so bold as to show up at your door?"

"I suppose not. I . . . did you get a clear look at him?" Kate asked, pulling back. "Did he seem at all . . . familiar to you?"

Mirabelle pictured the handsome, dark-haired man who'd sat farther down the table from her. "Yes, I saw him, and no, he didn't seem familiar." She grinned wickedly. "Although, he seemed rather interested in becoming familiar with you."

Kate merely snorted and peeked around the corner again. "The interest isn't returned."

"Are you going to let me in, Kate, or shall we drag a pair of chairs out and enjoy the fine hall air while we eat the biscuits I know you secreted from the kitchen? It'd be almost alfresco."

"Hmm. What? Oh!" Kate smiled sheepishly and stepped back, closing and locking the door after Mirabelle. "I'm sorry, Mira. I'm a bit distracted."

"Yes, I gathered as much."

Mirabelle took in the familiar room with a glance. It was something of a mess, as was usual. Gowns, gloves, and bonnets had been neatly tucked away, but there were papers littering the desk, piled in toppling stacks and sticking out from drawers. The bed was unmade—the pale blue counterpane twisted and pulled back as if Kate had crawled in, tossed and turned for awhile, and then crawled back out again. Books had been piled haphazardly next to the bed and on the window seat. The desk chair was overturned, a hairbrush had been knocked off the vanity, and for some inexplicable reason, there was a teacup on the floor.

"Where's Lizzy?" Mirabelle asked, looking into the empty adjoining room where Kate and Evie's abigail usually slept.

Kate stepped across the room and righted the chair. "She wasn't feeling quite the thing and asked to sleep in Evie's room where the light wouldn't bother her."

"Is she all right?" Mirabelle inquired. She was rather fond of the girl, though the maid was always after fussing with her hair and clothes.

"Just a touch of the headache," Kate assured her. "I brought her a powder earlier in the evening and she went straight to sleep. I expect she'll be fully recovered by morning."

Mirabelle nodded and wandered over to poke at the papers on the desk. "What is all this?"

"Music," Kate answered. "I'm composing."

That certainly made sense, she thought. Although . . .

"There's quite a lot of it. Are you working on several pieces at once?"

"No, strictly speaking, it's the same piece."

"Is it?" She looked over the piles of paper again. "Are you having difficulty? Is that why you've been up so late?"

"No I . . ." Kate's hands tugged on her dressing gown—a telling gesture of nerves. "It's a symphony."

Mirabelle's mouth dropped open. "A symphony? Truly? You've mentioned the possibility before, but . . ." She gazed at the papers. She was always just a bit in awe of Kate's musical talent, a bit amazed at the magic and beauty her friend could create with such incredible skill. And now a symphony. Pleasure and pride bloomed, and quick to follow were excitement and delight. She laughed and threw her arms around her friend. "Oh, but this is wonderful, Kate!"

"Do you think so? It's not proper, not really, for a lady to—"

"Nonsense," Mirabelle snapped, pulling back. "That's complete and utter nonsense, and well you know it. You've been given an amazing gift, Kate, and it's only right that you should use it to the best of your ability. The notion that a woman of your skill, your talent, should deny her abilities in the interest of making a few small-minded individuals more comfortable is preposterous, I'd go so far as to say blasphemous. Why would God have given you such a gift, if He hadn't wished for you to use it? If Evie hears you speaking this way—"

"Well, good Lord, Mira."

"I . . . I'm ranting a bit aren't I?" She let her hands drop from where they'd been gripping Kate's shoulders.

"A bit," Kate agreed.

"Sorry." Mirabelle dragged herself over to sit on the edge of the bed. "It's been something of a long day."

Kate crossed the room to sit beside her. "As your ranting was in defense of my work, I won't hold it against you.

How did you know I'd been up late? I don't recall mentioning it."

"You didn't," Mirabelle admitted without hesitation. "Whit mentioned it and—and this is part of my very long day—I agreed to spy on you."

"Did you?" Kate asked, looking more intrigued than offended. "Did you really? How did he manage to acquire your cooperation?"

"He blackmailed me."

"Oh, he did not," Kate laughed with a playful poke to Mirabelle's shoulders.

"He did, and quite effectively too. He cornered me—metaphorically speaking—in Benton and threatened to upend the contents of my box—the one I'd only just brought from Madame Duvalle's—in the middle of the street."

Kate's eyes grew round with a kind of excited horror. "Did he know what was in it?"

"Only in a general sense."

An odd and very suspicious sound emerged from Kate's throat. "He blackmailed you into spying on me by threatening to expose your unmentionables?"

"It's not funny, Kate."

"No." The sound came again, louder this time, and accompanied by a loud puff of air. "No. I'm sorry, you're right." A slightly less than delicate snort escaped. "Absolutely right." Her lips twitched violently. "Not in the least funny." After a snort, a hiccup, and a noise that put Mirabelle to mind of sheep, Kate erupted into fits of laughter.

Mirabelle crossed her arms and waited for the storm to pass.

It took some time.

"Oh, I'm sorry," Kate choked out eventually. "I'm terribly sorry."

Mirabelle felt a corner of her mouth quirk up involuntarily. "No, you're not."

"You're right, I'm not. At least—not *very*. It's just so ridiculous"

"He could have ruined me," Mirabelle pointed out.

"He wouldn't have done it. Surely you know he wouldn't have done it. It's just the sort of harmless bullying brothers do."

Thoughtful, Mirabelle picked at the counterpane. "But he's not my brother, is he?"

# ❋ *Six* ❋

*M*irabelle left Kate's room feeling quite a bit better than she had all evening. Nothing could lift the spirits quite so quickly as a middle-of-the-night laugh with a dear friend.

And nothing could send them plummeting with the same speed as the sight of Whit's lanky frame lounging against the wall in the darkened hallway.

"Just the imp I wanted to see," he said softly, and straightened.

"Have you been waiting for me?"

"Of course not," he answered, just fast enough to tell her he'd been doing exactly that. "But since you're here . . ."

As quick as you please, he had his hand under her elbow and was leading her away.

"What do you think you're doing?" she whispered with a frightened glance down both ends of the hallway.

"Escorting you to my study."

She stopped walking. "We most certainly will not be going—"

"Would you prefer my room?"

"Are you mad?" she gasped, struggling to pull her arm from his grasp. "You'll ruin me."

"The study it is," he decided and led her forward at a leisurely rate. "It occurs to me that you are forever bemoaning the possibility of ruin, and yet your good name remains intact."

"No thanks to you," she bit out.

"Nor you," he retorted without heat. "Wandering the halls at night as you are."

"I most certainly was not wandering. I was visiting Kate—whose door, I'll remind you, is only three down from my own."

"A lot can happen to a young woman in the space of three doors."

"Like being dragged off by a fiend disguised as a gentleman?" she asked pointedly.

"Why yes, that was the very thing I was thinking. How funny you should mention it."

"Hilarious." She gave up trying to free herself. "If you must be an overbearing ass, Whit, couldn't you at least do it more expediently?"

When he failed to move any faster, she leaned up to hiss in his ear. "If we're discovered, your mother will insist you do the honorable thing and offer for me."

His pace increased exponentially, until they were very nearly trotting. The relief she felt was instantaneous, as was her annoyance at the obvious insult.

"Not that I'd have you," she huffed.

"Here we are." He pulled her into his study where several candles were already—or possibly still—glowing. He shut and locked the door behind them.

"We're safe enough now, I think," he said, no longer whispering.

"Hush, what if someone should hear you?"

"There's no one close enough to hear anything," he assured her.

"You can't possibly know that. People are always skulking about at house parties." She tossed her arms up. "Look at us."

Unconcerned, he walked over to lean a hip against the enormous oak desk. "Yes, and as it's my house, I'm perfectly aware of *where* each and every one of them is skulking about."

"That's absurd, you can't possibly—"

"Mr. Dooley is passed out drunk in the orangery," he began, folding his arms across his chest. "The lonely Mrs. Dooley is consoling herself in the arms of Mr. Jaffrey. Mrs. Jaffrey, well aware of her husband's roving ways, has taken her revenge upon him by slipping into Lord Habbot's room. Lady Habbot isn't in residence, of course, but her nephew Mr. West is busy entertaining the willing Mary—Mrs. Renwald's lady's maid—while Mrs. Renwald herself, is occupied in the stable with Mr. Bolerhack's grooms. Mr. Renwald, blissfully unaware of his wife's proclivities, is fast asleep—"

"I beg your pardon." She just had to ask. "Did you . . . did you say *grooms?*"

"I did." He grinned at her wickedly. "I did indeed."

"But what . . . how . . . I . . ."

"Would you care for an explanation, imp? A description, perhaps?"

"No." Good Lord. "Thank you. I'd rather you explain why you dragged me in here."

"In a moment. Did you speak with Kate?"

Deciding she might as well make herself comfortable while she was being annoyed, she took a seat at a small settee in front of the fireplace. It might have made more sense to have chosen the chair in front of the desk, but she rather felt as if that position would have put her in the role of subordinate, and the man's arrogance was intolerable as it was.

"I did speak with Kate," she informed him stiffly. "And as it happens, you've made a fuss over nothing. She's composing."

"Composing," he echoed.

"Yes, I assume you've heard of the phenomenon? Little dots on paper representing musical notes?"

"I've some grasp of the concept." A line formed across his brow. "Why did she lie to me? And why did she act as a child sneaking treats when I asked her what she was about? For God's sake, I've seen feral cats less skittish."

"The fact that you're frightening to children and small animals is hardly cause—"

"You gave your word, Mirabelle," he reminded her in a cool tone.

"Oh, very well." She leaned back against the cushions for a clearer view of his face. "She's working on a symphony."

"And . . ." he prompted when she said nothing more.

"And, what?" she asked. "She's working on a symphony and has been for some time now. She's excited and nervous, and she's worried. It isn't entirely acceptable for a young lady to pursue music as anything more substantial than a hobby. She's concerned you won't approve."

"That's absurd," he snapped. "I can't hum two notes without sending the dogs to barking. What business would I have instructing my sister on how to use her talent? What business has anyone, come to that? If someone's said something to her—"

"You needn't shout at me, Whit. I'm not arguing with you."

He blinked. "You're not, are you?"

"No. Unlike you, I've a lovely singing voice," she informed him. "But my musical aptitude is nothing, less than nothing really, in comparison to Kate's. I'm in full support of her endeavor. It won't be easy for her, I suspect. The goal itself is a lofty one, and she'll be subject to some criticism and censure once she obtains it."

He settled his gaze on her, considering. "And you're certain she'll obtain it?"

"Of course," she responded, returning the challenging stare. "Aren't you?"

"Absolutely," he said without hesitation. He rubbed the back of his hand against his chin. "Well, this is interesting."

"I suppose, though not exactly shocking, is it? When one thinks about it, it was only a matter of time before Kate delved into—"

"I wasn't referring to Kate—I'll sort this out with her tomorrow—I was referring to us. We're in agreement on something."

"I . . . so we are." And it felt, she suddenly realized, a bit odd. Uncomfortable, she rose and ran her hand down her skirts. "Well, stranger things have happened, I imagine."

"Not much stranger."

She dropped her hands and rolled her eyes. "I'm sure you've lived in constant dread of this dark day, but perhaps now that it's finally here, you can find the strength to move past it and get on with your life."

"I'll put some thought into that. Why don't you sit back down, imp. We're not quite finished here."

"I'd rather stand, thank you." It was a lie, but she felt foolish sitting again when she'd only just risen. "What else is it you wanted?"

"It isn't a matter of what I want, but of what my mother has . . . requested."

"Your mother?" A tickle of unease formed in her throat.

"She's asked that we set aside our differences for a time—call a truce of sorts." He twisted his lips in thought. "Perhaps she was more put out this morning than I realized."

"I . . ." She paled. She knew she paled because she could feel every drop of blood drain from her head to pool in her stomach where it sloshed about, making her queasy.

It wasn't possible to have been at Haldon so often as a

child and not earned Lady Thurston's disapproval from time to time. Poor judgment and poor behavior are inescapable facts of childhood. But Mirabelle had put an enormous amount of energy into avoiding Lady Thurston's censure— certainly, a great deal more than most children would have—and *oh,* how she hated when she failed. She owed so much to the countess, and to repay her kindness with worry or vexation was unforgivably selfish.

"Is she very angry with me?" she asked in a strangled whisper.

"She's not—" Whit broke off with a curse and stepped forward to take her arm. "Sit down. You look half ready to faint."

"I don't faint," she argued unconvincingly, but let herself be guided back to the settee. "What did she say to you, Whit?"

"Nothing that warrants this sort of reaction," he replied, but his words were gentled by a soothing pat on her arm, and by the good-sized glass of brandy he poured and pushed into her hand. "Drink it down."

She made a face at the amber liquid. She didn't think spirits would settle well in her stomach at present. "I don't want it. I want to know what your mother—"

"And I'll tell you, after you have a drink." He tapped the bottom of the glass to nudge it closer. "Go ahead."

She scowled at him, but drank the contents of the glass in one quick swallow. She coughed, wheezed, and spluttered her way back. "Oh, ack!"

Chuckling softly, Whit took the glass from her and set it aside. "Brandy's generally sipped."

"Well, I'm not drinking a second," she informed him after a hard breath. "So my way will have to do."

"Fair enough." He searched her face. "Feeling better?"

"No." Which she really wasn't. "There was nothing wrong with me to begin with." Which there really was.

"Huh," was his inarticulate and—she was forced to

admit—diplomatic reply. He straightened and looked down at her. "I forget sometimes how much you care for her."

"Lady Thurston? I love her, with all my heart."

"I know you do. But I forget." He patted her arm again. "She's not angry with you in the least. Nor with me. She . . . Are you looking for a husband?"

"Am I . . . ?" She gaped at him, wondering if the inquiry had really come from nowhere, or if the brandy had begun working much faster than anticipated. "I beg your pardon?"

"It's a simple enough question. Are you considering marriage?"

Because it was Whit asking, she stared at him long and hard without answering.

"Imp?"

She held up a finger. "A moment—I'm trying to ascertain if there's an insult in the question."

He straightened his shoulders. "I assure you, when I insult you, you'll know it."

"You do lack subtlety," she agreed and ignored his sneer in favor of thinking aloud. "The question then, was a preamble to the insult. Are you going to offer up an unsuitable candidate for the position? Someone like . . ." She pursed her lips, thinking. "Jim, for example? That's cruel, you know. He has troubles enough without people poking fun at him."

"I've no intention of . . . Who the devil is Jim?"

"Jim Bunt," she supplied. "Short man with a missing leg? Spends his days outside of Maver's Tavern, always with a bottle about him? Surely you've seen him."

He blew out an aggrieved breath. "Yes, I've seen him, though I can't begin to imagine how it is you've come to use his given name—"

"Oh, Kate and Evie and I often bring him food and—"

He cut her off with a curt wave of his hand. "Never mind. If you would just see your way to answering the question. Are you looking for a husband?"

"No," she said clearly. "I most certainly am not. Does this have something to do with your mother's request?"

He leaned forward a bit and searched her face, much as he'd done almost moments ago, but it wasn't concern in his blue eyes now, it was the inexplicable heat of temper. Why ever would he still be irritated, she wondered. She'd answered the question, hadn't she? Of course, Whit was irritated with her as a rule—her presence alone was sufficient to spark his ire. But there was something different this time. Unable to put her finger on just what, she watched him in return, fascinated as the fire was banked, if not entirely extinguished.

He straightened once more with a quick nod, as if coming to some decision. "Mother is under the impression that you're seeking marriage, and that our disagreements could hamper your attempts to find an eligible gentleman."

"That's absurd," she scoffed. "She knows very well I've no interest in chaining myself to a husband."

"Chaining yourself?" He pulled a chair over to sit across from her, close enough that their knees almost brushed as he sat. "That's a rather grim view of marriage, don't you think?"

"No," she replied with all sincerity. "And I doubt you do as well, given that you're past thirty and still unwed."

"Taking a wife is an entirely different matter. It's a responsibility that requires a great deal of forethought, planning, and—"

"I had no idea you were such a romantic," she drawled.

He shot her a hard look. "My wife, when I take one, will want for nothing—including romance."

She sighed, suddenly tired and a little fuzzy from the brandy. "I know," she reached over and patted his knee congenially. "You'll make some fortunate girl an excellent husband one day, Whit."

Whit shifted slightly in his seat. He wasn't about to let her see how her brief touch, her nearness, was suddenly, surprisingly, interfering with his train of thought.

She laughed at his wary stare. "No insult. I'm in earnest. You're a catch and not just because of your wealth and title, though I can't imagine that's a detriment."

"Will you admit to having said this tomorrow, in front of witnesses?"

"Oh, I'll suffer the tortures of the damned first."

"Thought so. You're just a bit foxed, aren't you?"

She thought about it, but having never before been foxed, she decided she couldn't quite say for certain. She'd had a glass or two more champagne than was wise in the past, however, and rather thought she felt now as she had on those occasions.

"I believe I'm a bit tipsy," she admitted. "It's your own fault, pushing that brandy on me."

"I hadn't expected you to down it in one gulp," he pointed out.

She shrugged. "Quickest way to get rid of the vile stuff."

"A man once offered fifty pounds for a bottle of that vile stuff," he informed her.

"Really?" She puffed out a breath and shrugged. "Well, there's no accounting for taste, is there?"

"Apparently, not."

"I prefer champagne myself," she said a bit dreamily, leaning back against the cushions.

"Do you?" he asked on a chuckle.

"Hmm. The bubbles are very agreeable."

"They are that . . . Perhaps we should resume this conversation in the morning."

It occurred to her that she should probably be offended by the laughter in his voice. And she would be, she decided— later. When it would be easier to concentrate on the matter. For now, she needed to turn her mind to Lady Thurston's request.

"I don't think it's necessary to postpone this," she said, attempting to instill a touch of sobriety in her words. "I'm a bit worse for wear, I'll admit, but I can follow the conversation well enough. Your mother has asked us to call a truce, correct?"

"Yes," he replied, and she decided to ignore the twitch of his lips.

"Very well. For how long?"

"Until . . ." He frowned thoughtfully. "I've no idea. If my mother had been right, I'd have suggested we'd keep at it until you were comfortably settled with a husband."

"Ah, so it would be a permanent sort of arrangement. That might be asking a bit much for the two of us."

"I agree. I suggest we do the thing in stages." He leaned back in his chair and steepled his fingers in front of his chest. "We'll start by agreeing to remain civil for the duration of this house party and any events hereafter in which my mother—or someone likely to report to my mother—is present. Should we find the task to be accomplishable without any great hardship, we can reevaluate and decide at that time if we wish to make it a permanent arrangement."

"That sounds immensely sensible." She bobbed her head good-naturedly before tilting it to study him. "You've great gobs of sense in that head of yours, don't you, Whit? You must, to have turned your family's fortunes around in so short a time."

"It's true," he agreed with another twitch of his lips. "I am all that is good and wise. And my astounding intellect tells me now that it is past time for you to crawl into bed and sleep off the brandy—not that I don't like you this way," he added.

"And what way might that be?"

"Inebriated," he supplied with a grin. "And pleasant."

She made a face at him. She wasn't sure what sort of face it was, exactly, as she was experiencing some numbness about the nose and lips, but she was relatively certain it was some form of scowl—possibly even a haughty glower. "I'm not pleasant . . . that is . . . I'm not inebriated. I'm only—"

"Tipsy, I know." He stood and took her hand. "Up you go, then."

She allowed herself to be pulled to her feet.

"Do you really think we can—" She broke off when she realized he wasn't listening to her. He wasn't even looking at her.

Well, he *was* actually, and quite intently. But his gaze was clearly focused below her face. A breathlessness stole over her, and her skin seemed to prickle and warm as he did a slow sweep of her figure, his expression one of . . .

What did one call that? Irritated bemusement? Reluctant interest?

She found the irritated and reluctant aspects a touch insulting. She dropped his hand.

"Is something the matter?" she asked in what she hoped was a cool tone.

"The matter?" he echoed without raising his eyes.

"Yes, the matter," she repeated. Tucking her chin for a better view of her gown, she trailed her fingers along the neckline.

"Have I a spot?" Oh dear, what if she'd dribbled brandy down the front of herself without realizing? "You might have mentioned earlier, you know," she grumbled.

She looked up when he didn't respond and found his gaze focused on where her hand rested against her chest. He looked just as intent as he had a moment ago—standing absolutely still, with his brow furrowed and his jaw clenched. But he didn't look half as reluctant. And she suddenly felt twice as breathless.

"Whit," she snapped, a little amazed she'd found the necessary air.

His eyes snapped up to hers. "What? Yes. No. I beg your pardon?"

"Whatever is the matter with you?"

"Not a thing," he offered, then blinked, waited a beat and added, "I'm checking for swaying."

"For . . . oh." The logical explanation made her feel silly. What else would he have been doing? "Right, well, I'm not. Swaying that is." She quietly slid her right foot out a little.

"So I can see," he said with enough lingering amusement that she was reminded of the question she'd meant to ask.

"Do you *really* think we can manage to behave civilly to each other for the whole of the week?"

"Of course. Nothing to it—for me, at any rate. You'll need to employ your skills as an actress." He gave that some thought. "Or perhaps we should just keep you in brandy."

She merely lifted an eyebrow, which had him swearing, which, in turn, had both her eyebrows lifting.

"From insulting a lady, to swearing at her." She tsked at him. "You're beginning very badly, you know."

"We'll start tomorrow."

She turned her head pointedly—if a little wobbly—toward a clock on the mantel. Its hands indicated that it was well past midnight.

"We'll start," he ground out, "at sunrise."

"You see? Gobs and gobs of sense."

Whit saw Mirabelle back to her room before heading toward his own. She'd probably been capable of finding her way on her own, he mused as he pushed open his door, but he had just as soon not have her stumbling about in the dark. He'd never seen her quite so tipsy before—or perhaps "fuddled" suited better, he thought with a private laugh.

Certainly, he'd never seen her smile at him for such an extended length of time. She had a rather nice smile, he decided, as he pulled off his cravat and tossed it over a chair. It made her nose wrinkle just a little, and the humor in her expression reached all the way up to her chocolate eyes.

He stopped in the act of unbuttoning his shirt. She didn't have chocolate eyes, did she? Surely not. The imp's eyes were brown. Just your everyday sort of brown. Where had he gotten the idea they were something else? And what the devil had he been thinking, looking the chit over as if she were a bit of muslin?

Damn blue satin, he mentally groused. That's what he'd been thinking.

"Been working too hard," he decided and resumed undressing.

"If I may be so bold, my lord—yes you have."

Whit tossed a smile over his shoulder at his valet. Even half asleep the man looked a fashion plate in his dressing gown and quickly, but effectively, arranged hair. "Go back to bed, Stidham."

"Of course, my lord. Let me help you with that—"

"If I needed help undressing, you may be sure I would have had the foresight to find a pretty young thing to see to the job."

It felt odd enough, having another man pick out his clothes as if he were a child or an incompetent fool. Under no circumstances, outside of complete physical incapacitation, was he going to let said man undress him as well. In truth, he'd just as soon take care of the whole business on his own, but a gentleman of his station was expected to retain the services of a valet. Besides, he was quite fond of Stidham.

"I'm sure there are a host of pretty young things in the house who would be all too eager to oblige you," Stidham said with a straight face. "Shall I fetch one for you?"

"Generous of you, but I'll pass for tonight."

"Very good. If you have no need of me then, I'll wish you a good night."

"Good ni . . . Stidham?"

"My lord?"

"You've been here with me at Haldon for some years now."

"I have."

"What . . ." He hesitated, wondered if there might be a way to form the question without making a complete ass of himself. And came to the conclusion that there really wasn't. "What color are the imp's eyes?"

"Miss Browning?" If Stidham was surprised, or amused, by the inquiry, he was too dignified to show it. "I believe they're a very dark brown, my lord."

"Very dark brown," he repeated. "Would that be another way of saying chocolate?"

"I suppose it would."

In the small hours of the morning, while the rest of the house slept, a man and a woman stood in the darkest corner of the library and spoke in hurried whispers.

"Is this it, then?" the man asked, reaching for the small box wrapped in brown paper that the woman held.

"It is." She drew her hand back, out of his reach. "I'll have your word this won't come back to haunt my family."

"I'd like to give it," he said gently. "I'd like nothing more, but it'll be for Whit to decide what's done."

She nodded once and pressed the package into his hand.

"You've great faith in the boy," he murmured.

"When one has trust and respect, faith becomes irrelevant."

"Then it is to be hoped our trust is not misplaced."

# ❊ *Seven* ❊

*M*irabelle hadn't enough personal experience with over-imbibing to fully appreciate her good fortune in waking the next morning feeling whole and hale, but she could appreciate fine health on a warm spring day in a general sort of way. She was a trifle muzzy perhaps, but that was easily countered with a cup of hot chocolate and some fresh air.

She avoided the guests in the breakfast room, preferring to take her cup from the kitchen to a small bench in the garden. There wasn't anyone presently up and about she cared to speak with, at any rate. Kate, Evie, and Sophie were all still in bed. The first two by choice, and the last, no doubt, by virtue of having an overprotective husband. It would be an hour yet, maybe two, before any of them emerged from their rooms.

As she had tiptoed past the breakfast room, she had heard Lady Thurston's soft voice mingling with the guests', along with Whit's deeper one, but she wasn't ready yet to face either of them.

To make pleasant conversation with a man she'd spent more than half her life dreading the very sight of . . .

No . . . no, that wasn't quite right.

She sipped at her hot chocolate, contemplative. She'd never dreaded the sight of Whit. Not once, that she could recall, had she been unhappy to see him. It seems she had always been unhappy *with* him—annoyed, irritated, angry, furious and . . . and *pleased,* she realized with a start.

She'd always been at least a little bit pleased to be annoyed, irritated, angry, or furious.

She set her cup down on her knee with a small thump, failing even to notice when some of the liquid splashed over the rim onto her dress.

Good Lord, what was the *matter* with her? What sort of person enjoyed being aggravated—and aggrava*ting?*

She gave that a great deal of thought and decided that it was the very same sort of person as Whit.

She wasn't solely to blame for their continuing rivalry, after all, and she certainly wasn't the only one to gain pleasure from it. He had initiated their disagreements as often as she, and she could recall, quite vividly, more than one occasion in which he'd clearly been having a grand time of it while they went at each other with slights and barbs.

She blew out a short breath and rubbed a hand on her thigh.

They were both deranged. It was as simple as that. She suspected seeing their way to *not* being deranged would be a much more complicated matter, but Lady Thurston wanted it done. In Mirabelle's opinion, standing in opposition to the countess was not only the act of the deranged, but of the plainly stupid. She'd just as soon not be both in one day.

She heard the distant approach of footfalls on the gravel path leading to her bench. Her muscles tightened instinctively, so that she had to force herself to relax them again. Was it strange that she should know the sound of his walk, she wondered? Perhaps not—she knew Sophie's quick and light steps, and Evie's steady and uneven ones. Kate's were slow and meandering. Lady Thurston's were brisk and . . .

And this was silly, concentrating on the way her friends walked in an attempt to still her sudden nerves. She wasn't a green girl to be ruffled by the idea of speaking with a man—a man upon whose head she'd once dumped an entire plate of eggs. Remembering that fine occasion, she relaxed, smiled, and waited.

She was still smiling when Whit stopped to stand in front of her.

"Good morning, Miss Browning," he offered.

He looked almost adorable, she thought, with his hands clasped behind his back and his blue eyes brimming with such determined sincerity.

"Good morning," she returned.

"How are you feeling this morning?"

"Er . . . very well, thank you. And yourself?"

"Fine, fine."

Determination or not, what followed after that painfully stilted conversation was a long and awkward silence.

She scraped her toes against the gravel path.

He rocked on his heels.

"Lovely weather we're having," he tried again.

"Yes. Yes, very."

Whit waited a moment more. Then lifted a brow and tilted his head forward and to the side. Unable to decipher what that could possibly mean, Mirabelle just stared at him until he gave up and blew out an exasperated breath.

"You have to say something I can respond to, imp. 'Yes, very' is hardly sufficient to keep a conversation going."

"Oh, right! Right . . . Er . . ." She bit her lip and struggled to come up with something suitably benign to say. "Oh! Have you any plans for today?"

He nodded once, though whether it was in response to, or in approval of, her question, she couldn't say. "I do, in fact. Several of the young ladies expressed an interest this morning in a tour of the grounds, and I've agreed to act as a guide."

"That was kind of you, Whit. I wonder, which of the . . . Why are you glowering at me now?"

"I don't think it's appropriate for you to call me Whit," he told her.

"Whittaker then?" she asked with a sugary smile. "Or would you prefer Whittaker Vincent?"

"You're edging perilously close to being insulting. You'll address me as 'my lord.' "

Mirabelle snorted, twice, at the mere thought. "I will not."

"It's only proper. I addressed you as Miss Browning, so—"

"Then don't," she suggested. "It doesn't sound right coming from you, at any rate. Why don't we refer to each other by our given names? Your mother has asked us to behave as friends, not new acquaintances. And I can't very well start—"

"You're arguing, imp."

"No I'm not, I'm—" She heard the beginnings of temper in her voice and cut herself off. She took a very deep breath, held it, then let it out. When she spoke again, it was in careful, measured tones. "You're absolutely right, I am. But in the interest of doing this thing well, I must tell you—in a calm and objective manner, of course—"

"Of course."

"—that I am uncomfortable with, and therefore unlikely to, refer to you as 'my lord.' As we have known each other from earliest childhood, I believe it would seem odd and forced."

"Very well, I'm willing to—"

"Also, it is improbable that I shall remember."

"You're making this exceedingly difficult—"

"*Also,* I think it best you refrain from calling me 'imp.'"

"I swear to—" He started and broke off as her words filtered through frustration. "Have I called you 'imp'? This morning, I mean?"

"More than once."

"I . . . really?" He squinted as if trying to remember. "I hadn't realized."

Mirabelle shrugged. "I don't mind, but your mother might take offense."

"You don't mind?"

"Not in the least. Does it bother you when I call you 'cretin'?"

He slanted her a look. "Yes."

"Very well. I'll not call you 'my lord,' but I'll refrain from referring to you as 'cretin.'"

"Among other insulting names."

"Among other insulting names," she agreed. "I'll address you as 'Whit' or 'Whittaker.' You may address me as 'Mira,' 'Mirabelle,' or even 'imp' if you think your mother won't mind."

"I don't think it will bother her overmuch."

"Are we in agreement, then?" she asked, and wondered if two intelligent people had ever had a more ridiculous conversation.

"I'll agree, but for the record, 'Whittaker Vincent' is out of the question."

"So noted."

On the other side of the lawn, Lady Thurston stood in the cool shade of a willow tree and watched the young couple with mounting frustration. Even from a distance, she could see their discomfort in the way they held themselves so rigidly. Whit with his polite tilt of the head and Mirabelle with her ramrod-straight back. She could just imagine the infuriatingly formal tone of their conversation.

*Lovely weather we're having. So unusual for this time of year.*
*Yes, very.*

She scowled in their direction. Then scowled at the man standing next to her. "Well for heaven's sake, this isn't working at all. The next thing we know they'll be addressing each other as Lord Thurston and Miss Browning."

William studied the couple a moment longer before answering. "It does seem to be headed in that direction."

"I thought you'd done this sort of thing before."

He shifted at the quiet hint of accusation. "I have, and with some success, I'll remind you."

She nodded toward the pair. "And was this the way your earlier success proceeded?"

"The two cases are entirely different." When she only stared at him, one eyebrow raised, he coughed nervously into his fist. "There were, I'll admit, one or two . . . er, complications."

"Complications," she repeated with narrowed eyes.

"Well, they do happen," he said in a defensive tone. "I've taken a lesson from them and tried to go a bit more simple this time 'round, but I'm not a fortune-teller, am I?"

She blew out a quick breath and reached to give his arm a gentle squeeze. "No, of course not. Please accept my apologies. I'm a bit concerned is all. Her uncle's hunting

party is at the end of the week and I had rather hoped she
wouldn't have to go."

"If all goes well, it'll be the last she need ever attend. Did
the invitation arrive?"

"Same time every year," she affirmed. "The man's an idiot. A vile, drunken idiot."

"I'll not argue it," he said softly. "But Mirabelle's safe
enough, my lady. As safe as any of us can make her at present."

"I know." She turned to give him a smile filled with gratitude. "I'll never be able to repay you adequately for that
kindness. It's a priceless gift you've given me."

"Well now." He coughed into his hand a second time and
shuffled his feet. "It's nothing. Nothing at all. Just a favor
for an old friend."

"You give it too little credit. I'm in your debt."

"No, no—"

"But as for the other matter we discussed." She turned to
face him. "Whit may be a man fully grown, but he is still
and always will be my son. If he comes to harm while under your command, I'll use every resource at my disposal to
see you suffer. And you may be sure my methods will be a
good deal more . . . thorough than anything your clever but
unimaginative men ever thought to devise."

His only response was an audible swallow.

Satisfied she'd made herself perfectly clear, she smiled and
gave him a soft pat on the arm before leaving. "Wipe your
boots when you come inside, dear."

Mirabelle scooted over to make room for Whit on the small
bench. Having successfully concluded the monumental task
of agreeing on names, they were now once again at a loss
for what to discuss.

"Well," he said pointlessly and looked about him, searching for inspiration.

"Well," she returned, feeling several degrees beyond foolish.

She was generally rather good at making friendly chatter. She was a popular dance partner during the London Season for that very reason. Yet here she was, quite unable to think of a single topic of conversation. Or perhaps more to the point, quite unable to think of a topic of conversation that wouldn't have one or the both of them up in arms within minutes.

Truth be known, the one thought that kept popping into her mind just now, was that she couldn't recall a time before in which she'd ever sat so close to Whit.

Physical avoidance had been included in their feud. Probably less out of a conscious distaste for the contact than out of a concern for safety—Whit's primarily. But their knees and shoulders were brushing this morning, and she could feel the heat of his form through her gown. There seemed to be an awful lot of it, she noted. An awful lot of him.

Why that should make her uncomfortable now, when they were sitting together in peaceful—if awkward— silence, was a question she'd just as soon not answer. She might recognize the little jolt her heart gave at the contact, but it didn't stand that she had to acknowledge it.

She reached for something to say, something to take her mind off their closeness.

"Whit, I—"

"Would you care to join the tour this morning?" he asked suddenly.

She snapped her mouth shut, whatever she was about to say instantly forgotten. Until that moment, Mirabelle would have been unable—even upon pain of death—to recall a single instance before in which Whit had extended her an invitation without his mother's immediate prompting. Unless, of course, she'd been allowed to count the times he'd invited her to go to the devil, in which case she'd have had ample examples—

"Mirabelle?"

"Oh, sorry. I was woolgathering."

"I guessed as much. Merino or just your everyday sort of wool?"

"Merino," she decided with a smile. "And I think I'd like to go for that walk this morning. Where will we be going?"

"The lake path, if it suits the ladies."

"Really?" Mirabelle asked, genuinely pleased. "That's my favorite."

"Is it?" He studied her face. "Honestly, or are we still being polite?"

"Both, I suppose. We're behaving remarkably well, in my opinion. And it truly is my favorite walk. I particularly enjoy the curve on the far eastern side, where that enormous old oak stands and the reeds grow high as my waist. Did you know, last spring, there was a nest of ducklings right on the other side of that tree?"

"I did, though I hadn't realized anyone else knew it was there." His face lit up with a knowing smile. "Fattest chicks I've ever seen."

Mirabelle found herself smiling in return. "They were enormous . . . I fed them regularly."

"Yes, me too."

Delighted with the picture of a grown man sneaking behind an old tree to feed baby ducks, Mirabelle laughed out loud.

Feeling comfortable, Whit stretched his legs out before him. She had a nice laugh, he thought. Soft and low, like a warm wind over water. He'd heard it before, countless times. But never had he heard it directed at him. No, that wasn't right. She'd laughed *at* him more times than he cared to remember. Never before had she laughed *for* him. It was a completely different experience, and one he was finding surprisingly pleasant.

A whole world more pleasant than the experience of hearing the tittering giggles of Miss Willory and her followers, which, unfortunately, was the very sound currently emerging from the back door. He felt Mirabelle tense as the group spotted them and began to head in their direction. He could hardly fault her for the reaction.

Miss Willory may not have been the most pretentious and mean-spirited young woman of his acquaintance, but she was a contender. And it didn't help matters that she was so often surrounded by Miss Fanny Stills and Miss Charlotte Sullivan, her greatest admirers and mimics. And Miss Rebecca Heins . . . well, Miss Heins seemed a sweet creature, actually, but the group as a whole was a disquieting sight to behold.

"These are the ladies you spoke of?" Mirabelle asked, still watching the group.

"They are."

"I see," she said slowly. "You didn't think of this outing, did you?"

"Oh, I've had a great many thoughts regarding this outing," he assured her. "None of which I should voice in mixed company."

There was a pause before she said, "Your mother made you do this."

"Yes." He made himself smile as the giggling group drew closer. "Yes, she did."

Mirabelle rose from the bench and cast a longing glance at the house. "Do you know, I think I may have forgotten to—"

"If you leave now," Whit whispered quickly as he stood beside her, "they'll think they ran you off, and crow over the accomplishment for days."

"I . . . Damn." She straightened her shoulders, lifted her chin, and managed a strained expression he assumed was meant to be a kind of smile.

It took considerable restraint for Whit to hold in his sigh of relief. Mirabelle would be staying. He'd rather thought she would . . . at least, he'd certainly hoped. Very well, he had prayed to every god known to man that she wouldn't leave him alone to face this group on his own.

Unmarried women of the *ton* made him distinctly uneasy. Title-hungry and blatantly conniving young women with ambitious mamas flatly terrified him. And if Miss Willory didn't qualify as such as creature, he rather thought no one would.

She ought to be beautiful, he thought as Miss Willory and her band stopped before them. She had all the hallmarks of beauty—the pale hair and eyes, the ivory skin, the delicate features. Her hair was perfectly coiffed, her fashionable figure perfectly turned out.

But he didn't find her beautiful. He didn't even find her pretty. He just found her irritating.

"Here we are, Lord Thurston," she chirped gaily. "I do hope we didn't keep you waiting, but poor Miss Heins, we just couldn't seem to set her bonnet straight. We quite gave up on the matter."

Miss Heins reached a startled hand up to her bonnet, which looked perfectly adequate as far as Whit could tell. He thought to mention as much, but Mirabelle beat him to it.

"It's a lovely bonnet, Miss Heins," she said with a bright smile for the blushing girl. "Did you do the work yourself?"

"I . . . I did, yes."

Miss Willory started and blinked at Mirabelle as if only just realizing she were there.

"Oh, Miss Browning, will you be joining us? How . . . unexpected." She sent Whit an overly sympathetic smile and reached out as if to pat his arm.

In a move too smooth to insult, he avoided the contact by stepping over to Mirabelle and offering his arm. There were, it seemed, unexpected benefits to this truce with her. Not the least of which was dodging Miss Willory's advances.

"Mirabelle agreed to join our group at my insistence."

"Oh." Miss Willory floundered for a moment before pasting on a doting expression. "How very, very sweet of you, my lord. You must be terribly excited, Miss Browning."

If he hadn't been holding her arm, Whit likely wouldn't have noticed the way Mirabelle tensed. Her face remained impassive, and she gave a small shrug of indifference.

"I've always enjoyed this particular trail," she said. "It's best viewed in the fall, mind you, but there's plenty to appreciate in the spring, as well. Perhaps next year, if you're about, you might have the opportunity to view the western shore—as we'll only be making a half trip of it today. The flora on that side are not to be missed . . . if one can help it."

Neatly reminded that Mirabelle had regular access to both Haldon Hall and its master, Miss Willory could do little more than hold her false smile and speak through her teeth.

"I'm sure it's lovely."

"Oh," Mirabelle breathed sweetly and took a good hold of his arm. "You have no idea."

"Shall we begin?" Whit suggested quickly.

Conversation between Whit and Mirabelle along the trail was stiff and awkward. It was still so new, this not arguing, and there were long stretches of silence between them. Mirabelle wished dearly for long stretches of silence from the others, but while there was a notable dearth of intelligent discourse, there seemed to her no lack of pointless jabbering.

"How pretty everything is!" Miss Willory crooned. "I vow I could live on this path!"

"But what of the gypsies?" Miss Stills gasped, as if there

was a real risk of Miss Willory forsaking all her worldly
goods to live in the Haldon Woods.

"Or the hermit McAlistair," Miss Sullivan added. "Oh,
do look at these big round things!"

"Oh! They're prickly."

"Oh! Whatever could they be? Lord—"

"Chestnuts," Mirabelle informed them, though she'd
have wagered they knew quite well.

"Don't be silly, Miss Browning," Miss Willory snapped,
clearly put out by having her question answered by someone other than his lordship. "I know what a chestnut shell
looks like. My uncle's quite fond of them. Lord Thur—"

"It's the outer casing," Mirabelle snuck in. It was no
doubt small of her to gain such satisfaction at thwarting
Miss Willory, but she just couldn't bring herself to care.

Miss Heins nudged one with the toe of her boot. "Looks
to be a chestnut."

"Lord Thurston?" Miss Willory asked, ignoring her.

"It's a chestnut," he confirmed.

"How clever you are," she simpered. "You simply must
give us a lesson on—"

"Miss Browning would be a better choice of tutor. She's
made quite a study of the local flora and fauna."

"It's only a hobby," Mirabelle said with a startled glance
at Whit. She hadn't realized he knew of her interests.

"Are you a bluestocking then, Miss Browning," Miss
Willory asked in a patronizing tone. "A great scholar of
plants?"

"Hardly, but I've some passing knowledge. For example,
the tree you're standing next to is a sessile oak, and the vine
wrapped around it is *Toxicodendron radicans,* a species introduced from the Americas—better known as poison ivy."

"Oh!"

The vine was actually a harmless everyday variety of ivy,

but Mirabelle didn't think it would mind the lie. "Shall we continue?"

The lake path followed the curve of the shore for the most part. But there was a small section that required the group walk up a steep hill and through the trees. It was tougher going, but well worth it in Mirabelle's opinion. The advantage of height and the distance from the lake allowed for the most spectacular views of the water. She didn't even mind stopping when some of the others needed a rest from the climb.

"It's beautiful," Miss Heins said softly when they'd reached the top of the hill.

"What it is," Miss Willory complained, "is muddy."

It was almost always a bit damp at the top of the hill. The steep side received more sunlight and allowed for draining, but the combination of a thicker canopy and a flat expanse meant the top often had several small puddles of mud, and one larger stretch of it that disappeared around a curve.

"We simply must turn back."

"It's not so terrible," Mirabelle assured her. "The worst of it can be gotten around."

"Well, I'm certain you don't mind, Miss Browning, not in that old thing. How wonderfully clever of you to wear a . . ." She waved her hand about as if searching for the right word. ". . . dress one wouldn't mind having splattered hem to neck in mud."

"That old thing" had been her best day gown until she'd purchased the lavender dress. She opened her mouth to deliver a scathing reply.

But Miss Willory continued babbling. "Mine was made by Madame Rousseau, you know. I don't suppose you've heard of her. She's terribly select in her clientele. I dare say she'd be quite displeased to see the hem of one of her creations covered in mire. And my little half boots—"

Whit stepped forward and cut her off. "You're absolutely right, Miss Willory. Such a charming ensemble shouldn't suffer the indignities of mud. Do you see that path we just passed there on the right?" He turned her about to point down the hill. "Not more than ten yards down? It leads back around to the house. I'm certain you, and your very fine gown, will be more comfortable there. Miss Browning and I—and anyone else who cares to join us—will continue on this way."

Miss Willory spluttered for a moment. "You're very kind I'm sure, my lord, but—"

"Not at all. Can't have that pretty white muslin ruined, can we?"

"I'm sure my maid—"

"Now, now, there's no need to be brave about it." He gave her a slightly less than gentle nudge. "Off you go, then."

"Lord Thurston—"

"Miss Willory," Whit said with just enough coolness to have Miss Willory blinking, "I insist."

After that, there was nothing Miss Willory could do—short of begging—to retain her position in the group. But because there is nothing misery likes quite so much as company—particularly when felt by the likes of Miss Willory—she made a concerted effort to ruin everyone else's fun as well.

"Come along then, Charlotte and Fanny," she snapped. "Your mothers will have your heads if they hear you've been traipsing through the woods like common gypsies. And those worn boots of yours, Miss Heins, are likely seeping already, you'll catch the ague." She spun on her heel and began marching down the path, her reluctant followers trailing behind.

"Hurry along, Rebecca," Miss Sullivan called out. "We'll not wait for you."

"I—" Miss Heins gave Mirabelle and Whit an embarrassed smile. "It was kind of you to let me join you this morning. I wish . . . well . . . it was kind of you."

"Why don't you stay," Mirabelle suggested gently. "After the curve, this trail's actually quite a bit nicer than the other. Not that they need to know."

"It's very kind of you to offer, but I—"

"I'd only be kind," Whit pointed out, "if your company wasn't genuinely desired, and I assure you, it is."

"Oh . . . oh." She turned a charming shade of pink and ducked her head.

"Do say you'll come along," Mirabelle pleaded.

Miss Heins looked toward the trail where the others, having kept their word and not waited for her, had disappeared. "I suppose, perhaps. They might wonder what happened to me."

Mirabelle sincerely doubted they'd give it a single thought, but didn't have the heart to voice the opinion. "Why don't you run ahead and let them know where you'll be? Whit and I will wait."

"Well . . . all right." A smile bloomed on her face. "Yes, all right. I'll only be a moment."

Mirabelle watched her scamper down the path.

"She's like a lost kitten," she murmured, and grimaced at her own words. "I didn't mean that to sound insulting. There's just something so endearing and helpless about her."

"There is, isn't there?" Whit agreed. "And that makes it all the more unforgivable for someone to kick at her."

"I wonder why she keeps company with Miss Willory and her group?" Mirabelle asked as she wandered to the edge to look out over the water.

"I couldn't say. I make a point not to involve myself in the social peculiarities of females. Perhaps there's some sort of family friendship."

"Well, her family could do better," she grumbled, pacing a bit in her agitation. "Butter wouldn't melt in Miss Willory's mouth."

"No," he agreed. "But it might sour."

That drew a laugh from her and had the knots in her belly easing. "*Can* butter sour?"

"I've no idea," he admitted. "Shall we test it and see? You fetch the butter. I'll hold her down."

"Oh, Lord," she gasped on another laugh. "Can you imagine? I wonder if we'd be lauded as heroes or villains."

"Lunatics, would be my guess."

"It might be worth it, just to—"

Her words cut off as she felt her heel sink, then slip in mud. If she hadn't been so distracted, she might have noticed how close she'd been walking to the edge. She certainly would have taken care in how she righted her stumble, and where she put her next step.

Because where it landed, was in the air.


# ❋ *Eight* ❋


To a bystander, the act of falling off a hill might seem to be a very sudden thing. One moment a person is standing there, and the next moment she's not, ergo—sudden.

But for the unfortunate individual actually engaged in the act of falling, it is an event that takes an inordinate amount of time—at least initially.

Mirabelle had the opportunity to remember the box she'd watched drop slowly to the sidewalk the day before, and she had the time to think she really—really and truly—ought to be able to grab hold of a branch or a bush before it was too late. But even as her fingers reached out, the long hill rushed up before her.

After that, things moved along at a very brisk pace, indeed.

She hit, she rolled, she bumped and slid. Sky and ground raced past in a dizzying circle. She slid to a stop a good fifty yards from the top, and still a distance from the water. For one terrible second she couldn't feel her limbs and feared she might have lost them sometime during the tumble.

Then the pain came—stings and burns mostly, that niggled more than truly hurt. Her ankle, on the other hand, positively screamed, and had her bolting up to grab hold of her leg.

"Oooh, *ow!* Ow . . . ow . . . ow!" Between each exclamation of pain, Mirabelle mentally injected the list of invectives she'd apologized for only the day before.

With an oath of his own, Whit came crashing through the brambles to crouch at her feet.

"Look at me, imp. Look at me. Do you know where you are?"

Hurting, and irritated with what she considered a tremendously stupid question—had the man been struck blind in the last five minutes?—she shook her head at him and concentrated on breathing hard through her teeth.

His hands cupped her face, forcing her to look from her throbbing ankle to his worried gaze. "Tell me where you are."

She glared at him. "Bottom of a hill."

"Good." He pulled one hand away to hold in front of her. "How many fingers am I holding up?"

Understanding began to seep in, and she made herself count the slightly blurry fingers. "Two."

He flicked his eyes along her forehead before turning his attention to her leg.

"Move your hands. Let me see what you've done to yourself."

"No! Don't touch it!" She swatted at him. It was an instinctual response brought on by fear and pain, and Whit didn't react to it other than to reach up and run a soothing hand down her arm.

"No more than a sprain, I imagine. The worst of the pain will pass in a moment. But just to be safe, be a brave little girl and let me have a look."

Mirabelle stopped rocking—a motion she hadn't even been aware of making—and narrowed her eyes at him. "Little girl?"

"There now, feeling better already, aren't you?"

She was, actually, and because distracting her from the pain had apparently been his sole reason for delivering the insult, she couldn't very well be angry with him for it. Besides, he actually looked a bit pale, and there was a line of worry across his brow.

Lord, was he lying about the sprain? Could she have seriously injured herself?

She swallowed hard and released her grip on her ankle. "Don't move it or . . . just don't move it, Whit. Please."

"I'll have to, I'm afraid. Just a little," he assured her when her hands came back up and tried to push his away. "Just to make certain it isn't broken."

He unlaced her boot and pulled the leather away with exquisite care. Using only the tips of his fingers, he prodded gently at her ankle. It hardly hurt at all, she realized. In fact, it felt rather nice, rather comforting. She felt herself begin to relax under the soothing ministrations. Then the flat of his hand pressed against the bottom of her foot and he pushed her toes up and her heel down.

"Ahh!"

He winced and immediately stopped. "I'm sorry, sweetheart. It had to be done."

She couldn't manage anything more than a stifled moan and a nod.

Whit tucked behind her ear a lock of hair that had fallen loose. "It's all right, now. It's done. Take a deep breath. There you are. Better?"

She nodded again, and found her voice as well. "Is it broken? My ankle?"

"No, only a sprain. You'll be up and about in a few days—a week at most."

Just in time for her uncle's party, she thought miserably. There were times life seemed distinctly unfair. She may have grumbled about it a bit, but Whit distracted her by slipping out of his coat and carefully draping it over her shoulders.

Confused, she blinked at him. "I'm not cold."

"You're shaking."

That was true, she could feel the trembles well enough. "I'm a bit agitated, but you don't have to—"

"And your dress is half gone." He gently pulled the coat closed.

*"What?"* Horrified, she pulled the material away from her chest and took a peek.

Half gone, she decided, was something of an exaggeration. The left shoulder of her gown and chemise were torn from neck to upper arm, and the material had gaped open to reveal skin that was generally left covered. But she wasn't exactly indecent—or at least, not *fully* indecent. The bodice of her gown was still intact, after all.

While she felt some small measure of relief at the relative decency of her gown, the state of her shoulder and collarbone had her gasping in stunned dismay. She was a mess—her skin a raw mass of cuts and abrasions. Blood was beginning to ooze in small drops from several of the deeper scrapes. Instictively, she touched a fingertip to the red and swollen flesh, and hissed at the resulting sting.

Whit pulled her hand away. "Stop touching it."

She looked at him, bewildered. "I'm bleeding."

"Yes, I noticed." He pulled a handkerchief out and carefully inserted it between her skin and the rough coat. "Nothing too deep. You'll be all right."

"Am I bleeding anywhere else?"

He reached up and feathered his fingers along the edge of her widow's peak, where his eyes had tracked before. "Here a bit."

"Oh."

Whit caught her hand before she could reach the injury. "Stop poking."

"I can't help it." She really couldn't. There was something about a fresh injury that insisted a person prod. "Is it very bad?"

"No." He ran a comforting hand down her hair, discreetly pulled away a leaf. "No, it's shallow. Hardly bleeding at all, really."

She barely noticed when he smoothed her hair again, and was far too distracted by her own discomfort to notice his hand was less than steady.

"You're certain?" Though her mind was rapidly clearing—enough for her to realize there wasn't a river of blood seeping from her forehead—she wanted the reassurance.

"I am." He rubbed her uninjured shoulder. "You'll be fine. Let's get you—"

He broke off at the soft voice calling for them.

"Lord Thurston? Miss Browning?"

"Down here!" Whit shouted, and waited until Miss Heins saw them. "Miss Browning took something of a tumble and turned her ankle."

"Oh, dear." Miss Heins used a tree to balance herself as she peered down the hill. "Oh, dear. Miss Browning, how dreadful for you. Is there anything I can do to help? The others have gone on ahead, I'm afraid, but I could try catching them again and—"

"I'm very glad it's you who came back," Mirabelle called

out, and immediately wished she hadn't. Her battered body strongly protested the exertion.

"Keep still," Whit ordered before turning back to Miss Heinz. "Would you be so good as to return to the house and have one of the grooms bring a mount for Miss Browning?"

"Yes, of course."

"And ask my mother to send for the physician—"

"I don't need a physician." Mirabelle objected.

Whit merely slanted her an annoyed look at the interruption. "To send for the physician," he repeated pointedly, "and to the kitchen for some hot tea and a cold—"

"For heaven's sake, Whit."

"I'll make certain everything is ready for her," Miss Heins assured them. "I'll be as fast as I can."

"Nothing needs to be made ready." Mirabelle tried arguing, but Miss Heins had already taken off down the path. Exasperated, she turned to Whit instead. "The whole house will be in an uproar now. It would have started off as merely 'Miss Browning took a tumble down a hill and turned her ankle' and have grown to 'Miss Browning is lying broken and bleeding at the bottom of a two-hundred-foot cliff' in the course of a quarter hour."

"Every respectable house party should contain at least one high drama."

"Every respectable high drama should be based on something a bit more . . ." She waved her hand around.

"Dramatic?" he offered helpfully.

"Interesting," she replied, mostly because she felt she ought to be able to complete her own sentences. "Perhaps you should go with Miss Heins to keep the hysterics down—"

"Not a chance."

He brushed her skirts aside and carefully slid an arm under her knees and the other around her back. In one smooth move, he had her in his arms and against his chest.

Something, somewhere inside of Mirabelle thrilled at the

action, but the feeling was tangled inextricably with the far more recognizable emotions of shock and embarrassment.

"What in the world do you think you're doing?" she gasped.

"I'm taking you to the top of the hill," he replied, hauling her up with an ease that surprised her. "There's too much bramble here for a horse to make it safely down."

Instinct made her put her arms around his neck as he began to climb. Lord, the man was strong. She'd had no idea there was so much strength in his lean form. The chest she was pressed against was hard and warm, and the arms that held her were banded with muscle. He carried her up the side of the hill without so much as a hitch in his step—or his breath.

There was such power in him, she thought—beyond the wealth and title. How had she not appreciated it?

He adjusted his grip, lifting her higher against his chest, his large hand settling comfortably on the side of her knee. And something inside her thrilled again, louder this time. It was all too similar to the jolt she'd felt in his study, and sitting next to him on the bench, and because of that, she pushed it aside and fought to concentrate on something else all together. Something along the lines of how best to extract herself from her current situation.

She shifted a little in an effort to create a meager amount of space between their bodies. It was a pointless effort, really, but she couldn't stop herself from at least trying.

"This is entirely unnecessary," she said. "If you'd just put me down, I could hobble along well enough."

"No doubt you could, but why should you?"

It was an annoyingly reasonable question, and the fact that she hadn't a reasonable answer made it all the more irritating. "Because . . . I . . . it's unseemly."

"Stop squirming before you do us both an injury," he warned, obviously unimpressed with her logic. "Under the circumstances, it's an insult to describe my behavior as 'unseemly.' It's been nothing short of chivalrous—heroic even."

The vision of her and Whit both rolling down the hill put a quick end to her struggles, and his ridiculous statement had her snorting out a laugh. "Perhaps you'll get a medal."

"I'd settle for the fawning admiration of the ladies."

"Oh, I'm sure Miss Willory will be in raptures," she said sweetly. "No doubt, she'll follow you about doggedly, insisting you relate the tale of your gallant deed over, and over, and over, and—"

"That's just cruel," he interrupted with a wince. "You're an appallingly bad damsel in distress, you know."

She sniffed. "I'm being admirably stoic, in my opinion."

He sidestepped a series of large roots. "And in my opinion, if you have to mention you're being stoic, you no longer are by definition."

She thought about that. "You have a point. I've been commendably reserved in my reaction, then. I think that's a fair assessment, given how very much I wished to swear"— he jostled her slightly and had her gritting her teeth—"and still do."

"Sorry, imp. It's tough going here, but don't hold back on my account. I've heard you curse the air blue before today."

Intent on taking him up on his offer, she opened her mouth . . . then shut it again. "It's just not the same when one's *expected* to do it."

Whit laughed and maneuvered around a sapling. "Oh, I don't know. It's expected for men to swear in the company of other men. I do so regularly and enjoy it immensely."

They reached the path, but rather than put her on her feet, he continued toward the house.

"Perhaps it's an acquired skill." She craned her neck to look down the path. "Aren't you going to set me down?"

"No point in it. We'll meet the horse and groom on the way."

"But you must be tired," she insisted. "I'm no longer a child, Whit."

"No, you are not," he replied softly, and for a brief second, his eyes changed from laughter and concern to something else, something she couldn't read.

"I . . ." She wanted to ask him what that something was, but it was gone before she could work up the courage to form the words. "I think I hear hoofbeats," she finished lamely.

"And the cavalry arrives. I could carry you back, if you like. It's bound to be more comfortable than having your injury jostled about on the horse."

"It's a quarter-mile walk, Whit. You can't carry me all that way."

"I certainly could."

Before answering, Mirabelle was careful to take into consideration what Evie referred to as "the innate fragility of male vanity."

"You'd know your limitations better than I, I'm sure," she said prudently. "But it would be unkind not to use the horse after Miss Heins went through the trouble of fetching it for us."

After a few minutes on that horse, Mirabelle was willing to reconsider Whit's offer. She *was* uncomfortable riding. No matter how slowly and carefully Whit led the mare, her sore ankle bounced painfully. And though she may have liked the distraction of conversation, she was forced to give up all attempts at it in favor of gritting her teeth.

By the time they reached the house, she was too exhausted to object when Whit scooped her off the mare's back and carried her inside. One of the dozen or so servants who—along with Lady Thurston—had been waiting for them could have managed the job, but it seemed a waste of energy to point it out.

"Which of the guest rooms are empty?" Whit asked the group at large.

"This way." Lady Thurston led them down the hall, calmly giving instructions as she went. "We'll need some of your special tea, Mrs. Hanson, and some extra wood for the fire, Lizzy. If you'd be so kind to see if my niece and daughter have returned from their ride, Hilcox? And I believe the Duke and Duchess of Rockeforte can be roused. The man can't make her sleep forever."

Mirabelle managed a half smile for Whit. "Aren't you going to take me to my room?"

Her room, they both knew, was located in the family wing at the other end of the house—on the second floor.

"I'll take you after the physician—"

"I really don't need a doctor, Whit," she cut in. "And I don't need to be brought to my room. I was only jesting."

"Needed or not, jesting or not, you'll have both," he informed her as they crossed the threshold into the guest room.

She didn't argue with him. She wasn't given the opportunity. No sooner had he laid her gently on the bed than he was being forcefully pushed out the door again by his mother, Mrs. Hanson, and several hovering maids.

"Thank you, my lord. I believe we can handle things quite well from here. "

"I'm certain you can, Mrs. Hanson, but—"

"Tisn't proper for you to be about while we look at her injuries, your lordship."

"I've already seen them, Lizzy. I want a physician—"

"It's only a sprained ankle."

"Nonetheless—"

"Out!" This last came from Lady Thurston, and she

punctuated the command with a quick nudge that propelled him the last inch out the door.

Thusly banished, and none too happy about it, Whit stood in the hallway and scowled at the door for a moment before turning away.

He wasn't going to pace outside the room, waiting for some scrap of news like a lovesick pup. He was going to his study, where he could pour himself a very large brandy.

Possibly two very large brandies.

Perhaps he'd omit the pouring altogether and drink straight from the bottle. Whatever it took to erase the memory of Mirabelle bleeding at the bottom of a steep hill.

Remembering now, his heart contracted painfully in his chest, an echo of the panic he'd felt when he'd seen her disappear from the path. The relief upon finding her conscious and relatively whole at the bottom had been near staggering. As had the desire to gather her in and rock and pet and stroke until the lines of pain in her face were soothed away.

It was, he decided now, a completely natural reaction to the sight of a woman in danger and discomfort. And since he'd pushed the panic away and handled the situation satisfactorily, he saw no reason to dwell on the matter.

It wasn't that he was embarrassed, *exactly*, he was simply a good deal *more* embarrassed by what had come after—when the intial fear for her well-being had passed and he'd picked her up. She'd been soft and warm and rumpled against his chest, and she'd had her arms twined around his neck. She'd smelled of earth and roses.

And for the third time in two days, he had found himself reacting to Mirabelle as a man reacts to a woman. Not a little girl, not an aggravating houseguest, and not an opponent, but a woman.

Suddenly, he'd wanted to touch for reasons other than to comfort, to hear her moan and whimper in something other than distress. Or, perhaps more honestly, in a very different sort of distress.

He'd seen himself laying her back down on the soft earth, stripping away her torn gown, and letting his hands take over. He'd imagined tasting that intriguing beauty mark above her lip, then working his way over to her ear, down her neck and lower. Then lower still.

He'd wondered if he might find that blue satin somewhere.

When she'd twisted in his arms, his eyes had dropped to where his coat covered her, and the sight of it aroused a sense of possession in him . . . and a considerable amount of self-recrimination.

She was injured, for God's sake. And he was having erotic fantasies of taking her in the dirt. He had more control than that.

He certainly had more finesse.

Suffering now from the unfortunate combination of worry and lust, he pushed through the study and headed directly to the sideboard.

"A bit early in the day for that, isn't it?"

Whit didn't bother to turn at the sound of Alex's voice. His oldest friend didn't need an invitation to come in and make himself comfortable in his favorite seat by the fire, would have laughed at the formality, in fact. Whit concentrated on pouring a full glass instead.

"The length of some days can be measured by how much time one *feels* has passed, rather than what the clock reads. And by my calculations, it is now"—Whit blew out a long breath—"tomorrow."

He picked up the drink, but before he could take a sip, an image of his father, smelling of spirits before noon, sprang to mind. He put the glass back down. "Hell."

"Why don't you ring for something else?" Alex asked, taking a seat.

"Because I don't want anything else." He shot his friend an annoyed glance. "Aren't you interested in Mirabelle's condition?"

"I am, which is why I spoke to one of the maids. A sprained ankle, isn't it?" Alex sent him a patronizing smile. "Overreacting a bit, don't you think?"

Whit raised a brow at the mocking tone. "And how is Sophie this morning?"

A corner of Alex's mouth's twitched. "Touché. But Sophie is my wife. Mirabelle's been little more to you than a nuisance."

"And it follows I should enjoy the sight of her in pain?"

"Nothing of the sort," Alex assured him easily. "But I'd have expected you to see a touch of humor in the situation."

"You find her injury amusing?" Whit asked coolly.

"No, but I find the image of you carrying the imp up the side of a hill and halfway back to the house *immensely* entertaining. I can't imagine a more reluctant knight in shining armor."

Whit remembered just how unreluctant he'd been, and to his everlasting horror, he felt the heat of embarrassment spread in his chest and crawl up his neck.

Alex leaned forward in his chair. "Holy hell, are you . . . blushing, Whit?"

"I bloody well am not." Please, God, make it true.

"You bloody well are," Alex countered and threw his head back to roar with laughter. "I haven't seen you redden like that since we were children."

"I am not blushing," Whit ground out. Men, by God, did not blush.

"I beg your pardon," Alex offered with an exaggerated—and unconvincing as he was still chuckling—courtesy. "I haven't seen you flushed, then, since childhood. Or would you prefer, 'I haven't seen your color up since—'?"

"I haven't planted you a facer since childhood either. Would you care for a reminder of what that was like?"

Alex held a hand up in peace. "Tempting as it may be, your mother would have both our heads if we indulged in fisticuffs."

"She'd have mine. There wouldn't be enough left of yours to be of use to her."

Competitive as only a brother could be, Alex sneered gamely. "A round at Jack's, next time we're in London," he challenged. "A hundred pounds."

"One-fifty."

"Done."

They shook on it, both of them grinning, as pleased with themselves as they were sure of their victory.

Feeling considerably better, Whit took a seat across from Alex and watched in some amusement as his friend made a guilty glance at the door. "I'd appreciate it if you'd not mention this little wager to Sophie."

"Any particular reason?"

"You know how women can be about these sorts of things," Alex replied, turning back. "And she has enough to occupy her mind at present. Which reminds me—she's asked that Kate, Evie, and Mirabelle be present at the . . . er . . . event."

"Present?" he asked, taken aback. "In the room, do you mean?"

"I don't," Alex assured him, "but it's entirely possible that she does. She acquired some very strange ideas on her travels. Will you bring the girls?"

"Me? I—" He was going to offer to have his mother bring them, but stopped himself just in time. A man didn't abandon a friend in need, and Alex, for all his jesting, was clearly anxious. And rightly so—birthing was a dangerous, and terrifyingly female, event. He had some clear memories of his sister's birth—memories he contrived very hard not to dwell on.

"We'll all be there. How long until . . ." He waved his hand about.

"A little under three months."

"So soon?" It seemed as if it ought to be further away. Years and years away. "Only three months and then . . ."

"Yes, and then," Alex responded grimly.

"I see." Whit tapped a nervous finger on the chair.

Without being aware of it, Alex mimicked the movement. "Yes. Exactly."

"Hmm."

Alex shot a considering glance at the brandy.

"It's not *that* early, really."

"It certainly isn't," Whit agreed, and made a hasty trip to the sideboard.

# ❈ *Nine* ❈

*W*hile Whit and Alex consoled themselves in the study, Mirabelle was poked, prodded, and then—when it was ultimately decided she would survive—fussed over extensively. A footman came to carry her to her own room, which she only demurred against a little. She *was* more comfortable in her own space than in the guest quarters, and she was *much* more comfortable with the idea of someone other than Whit carrying her there.

Loyal friends that they were, Kate, Sophie, and Evie joined her to make all the requisite sympathetic noises. They also made quite a few nonrequisite ones in the form of teasing jokes, but Mirabelle had expected no less.

"You'll not live to hear the end of it, you know," Evie said. "Not if you live to be a hundred. It's much too entertaining to the rest of us—Whit, forced to carry the imp up a jagged cliff—"

"It was a hill," Mirabelle corrected.

"Not in a hundred years, it won't be," Evie assured her. "It'll have grown to biblical proportions."

"Someone will write an opera based on the tale," Kate predicted. "A comedy."

"Composed by Lady Kate, like as not."

"I think it's romantic," Sophie interjected. When that statement was greeted with stunned silence, she merely shrugged. "Well, he didn't have to haul you up, did he?"

"Of course he did," Mirabelle countered. "It was too steep for a horse—"

"You see? Jagged cliff."

"—and he was the only one there," Mirabelle finished, poking Evie in the ribs for the interruption.

"All right now, ladies," Mrs. Hanson broke in. "It's past time Miss Browning got the rest she needs. Off with you."

"But I don't want to rest," Mirabelle argued as the housekeeper made shooing noises at the girls. "It's the middle of the day."

"Didn't ask what you wanted, did I? Said it was what you needed. Off you go, girls. You too, Your Grace. Lady Kate, you should be seeing to your guests, and you, Miss Cole, I believe you promised a tea party with young Isabelle Waters."

Sophie grinned at Mrs. Hanson as she was pushed to the door. "You really must conquer this unfortunate propensity to cower in the presence of rank, Mrs. Hanson."

Mrs. Hanson gave a good-humored snort and another push. "I may not have changed your nappies, Your Grace, but I had occasion to change the duke's a time or two."

Sophie laughed as she left, then stuck her head back in before Mrs. Hanson could close the door.

"Whit could have waited for help, you know," she told Mirabelle. "No one would have faulted him for it."

That final comment left Mirabelle gaping. First at the door Mrs. Hanson promptly shut after Sophie's head had disappeared, and then at Mrs. Hanson as she and Lizzy put the room to rights. When it finally occurred to Mirabelle that she really didn't have a reason to be gaping at the housekeeper, she closed her mouth and picked up her tea.

Sophie was right. Whit needn't have carried her up the hill. It hadn't been required of him. It hadn't even been expected of him. He must have known he'd be teased for it later, and while he might have a greater appreciation of the absurd than most peers of the realm, no man she knew actively enjoyed being poked fun at.

So, why hadn't he waited?

He'd been worried at first—that much had been clear—but not once he'd seen she wasn't seriously injured. Had he? He had seemed perfectly calm. He could have hidden it, she supposed, but that explanation only opened up a whole other set of questions. Why would he have continued to worry? Why would he bother hiding it? Why carry a person up a hill when one can worry just as well with their arms unencumbered?

"Are you after seeing your future, Miss Browning?"

"I . . ." She blinked herself out of her musings to find Mrs. Hanson smiling at her. "I beg your pardon?"

"I asked if you were after reading the tea leaves. But as I can see you haven't gotten around to drinking the tea, I'll assume you're not."

"Oh," Mirabelle frowned into her cup. "I don't mean to be rude, Mrs. Hanson, but it tastes a trifle off. I think whoever prepared it was overenthusiastic with the sugar."

"That's just my special brew, dear. Now you drink it down."

"But—"

"Or I'll fetch Lady Thurston, and you may be sure she'll see it done."

"I'll drink it," Mirabelle promised on a grumble.

"That's a dear. I need to see to the dinner preparations, but Lizzy here will wait for the cup so it won't be left sitting about when you're through."

"And so you'll know I drank it," Mirabelle added.

"That as well," Mrs. Hanson admitted without even a hint of shame. "Get some rest."

Mirabelle waited for the sound of the housekeeper's footsteps to disappear down the hall before turning to Lizzy. "I'll give you two pounds if you'll toss this out the window and tell her I drank it."

Lizzy laughed but shook her head. "Not worth my position, miss."

"Two pounds, half."

"Nor my head, which is what I'd lose if Mrs. Hanson caught wind."

"You're a very selfish girl, Lizzy," Mirabelle admonished. "Kate has a novel in which the heroine's abigail sacrifices her very life for her mistress. It was most touching."

"I believe I read it, miss." Lizzy casually folded a blanket at the end of the bed. "I recall thinking at the time that it was very kind of the lady to employ the infirm and that it was probably best the poor girl went at the end. Can't have that sort of thing being passed down, can we?"

Mirabelle laughed until Lizzy pointed a finger at the cup. "Hold your nose and gulp it down quick. It's the only way to take that sort of medicine."

"You're right," Mirabelle agreed on a sigh, and followed the instructions. "Ugh, that's dreadful."

A light knocking and the appearance of Whit's head at the door kept Lizzy from responding.

"Am I interrupting?" he asked before his eyes fell on

the head of the bed and Mirabelle. "Ah. And how are you feeling?"

"Sore, but otherwise well." She watched him enter the room fully, his hands hidden behind his back.

"I'll just see to the cup," Lizzy began.

"If you'd be so kind as to stay," Whit said. "I'd like a few words with Miss Browning."

"Certainly, my lord."

"Take a book," Mirabelle suggested, knowing the girl wouldn't do so without invitation while Whit was in the room. "I believe you'll find several of Kate's recommendations on the vanity."

"Thank you, miss." Lizzy selected one before settling herself in a chair at the far corner of the room.

"Won't you sit down, Whit?" Mirabelle asked, while wondering how she might go about asking him why he'd chosen to carry her up the hill.

"In a moment. I've brought something for you."

She sat up straighter in the bed. She adored presents. Not charity, which smarted the pride, but presents for an occasion—and she rather thought being injured was an occasion—were always welcome. "Have you? Are you holding it behind your back? What is it?"

He grinned and pulled his hands out to show her.

"A cane," she laughed.

"It's something of a relic, I'm afraid," he said, handing it to her. "The last member of the house to require assistance walking was my great-great-grandmother. It seems the Cole women are a sturdy lot."

"Very sturdy," she commented, hefting the cane experimentally. It felt stout enough to hold up a lame horse.

"If you'd prefer something more fashionable, I'm sure I could find something in Benton for you."

"This will do beautifully," she said, still inspecting the cane. "Thank you."

"My pleasure." Whit moved to sit in a chair by the bed. "Mirabelle?"

"Hmm?"

"Were you aware that Evie doesn't own one of those?"

"Yes." She looked up and took in his thoughtful frown. "I take it you were not."

"No." He picked idly at the arm of the chair. "I stopped by her room, thinking to borrow one for you, and she informed me she's had no need of them."

"Evie's leg is strong, Whit, and it rarely bothers her except in extreme cold."

"I hadn't realized it bothered her at all," he said more to himself than her. "Why would she keep that from me?"

"She hasn't," Mirabelle responded instantly, uncomfortable with the brief glimpse of hurt she saw cloud his eyes. "Certainly, not intentionally. It simply isn't something she speaks of. It just *is*—much like your blue eyes or my drab hair. And since there's nothing she can do other than take a hot soak on cold days—"

"There are physicians who specialize in these sorts of things."

"You take too much on yourself, Whit."

He visibly started at the comment. "I do nothing of the sort. Evie is an unmarried woman under my care. It's my responsibility to see to her well-being, her protection—"

"She'd buy a cane fast enough if she heard you speaking of her like that," Mirabelle scoffed. "If only to beat you about the head with it."

"I've every right to—" He cut himself off and blew out a frustrated breath. "She would, wouldn't she?"

"With great fervor. And without mercy."

"She's a bloodythirsty wench. And you may tell your mistress I said so," he added in a louder voice for Lizzy.

"Very good, my lord."

"I would have told her in any case," Mirabelle informed

him. And then, quite out of nowhere, she asked, "Why did you carry me up the hill?"

If Whit was surprised by the abrupt question—and she couldn't imagine anyone *not* being surprised by such an abrupt question—it was nothing compared to her own shock. Where the devil had that come from? Had she hit her head?

She must have hit her head.

Hit it so tremendously hard during her fall that the impact removed all memory—along with all common sense—of . . . of having hit it at all. It was the only explanation, even if it didn't seem to make sense to her at the moment.

"I told you why," Whit answered with a concerned tilt of his head. "It was too steep and full of bramble for a horse to traverse."

"Yes, but . . ." She trailed off when his face blurred before her eyes.

"I've tired you," she heard Whit murmur.

"No, I'm not tired." Oh, but she was. Suddenly, she was very, very tired.

"Your head is drooping."

"Isn't," she countered, and was still lucid enough to recognize how childish that sounded. She willed her head to clear. "Mrs. Hanson put something suspicious in my tea."

Whit took the cup and sniffed at it. "Sweet," he commented. "Laudanum, I'd wager."

"Laudanum?" She jerked herself awake—relatively, at least. "She put—?"

"No more than a drop."

"But I don't want—"

"It's too late to do much about it now." He reached over to pull the blankets up to her shoulders. "Go to sleep, imp."

"Later," she muttered.

"All right, later."

She was vaguely aware of movement in the room, of hushed voices and the door opening with a creak.

"Mirabelle?"

"Mm-hmm?"

"Your hair's not drab."

"All ri—" Her eyes snapped open again. "What's that?"

"It's the color of the chestnut tree we saw today. I find it to be rather nice."

Before she could even begin to respond to the comment—and really, how *did* one respond to having one's hair compared to a tree—he was gone, and she was asleep.

Those persons who spend an above average portion of their time attending secret meetings in the dead of night—for reasons other than a pleasant tryst—often prefer to hold said meetings in varying and out-of-the-way places, so as to keep their secrets, secret. As such, the two gentlemen whispering to each other now were not doing so in the library, but rather the currently vacant nanny's quarters, where even the nosiest guests were unlikely to visit.

"Is this it?" the younger gentleman asked as an older man held out a brown package.

"It is."

"And where do you want it?"

"In the study if you can manage it. Anywhere it can be found, but not stumbled upon."

"Easy enough." The younger man turned the package over in his hands. "Are you certain you want the both of them involved in this?"

"Of course. There's no reason for her not to be. It would defeat half the purpose, really."

"If something happens to her—"

"You'll break my nose," the older man interrupted with a much put-upon sigh. "I know."

"Whit will break your nose," the younger corrected. "I'll break your legs. And the women will take turns breaking everything else."

# ❊ Ten ❊

*W*as there anything more lovely, Mirabelle wondered, than spending a lazy day in Haldon's library, curled up in a window seat with a good book, while the warm sun played against one's skin?

She pondered that for several minutes before being forced to admit that, yes—yes, there certainly was. In fact, there were any number of more appealing things to do on a warm and sunny day.

One could go for a picnic, for example. The picnic most of the guests were even now gathering in preparation for, outside. At least, one could if one wasn't surrounded by overprotective worrywarts.

She gave up trying to make the best of her situation, snapped her book shut, and tossed it aside. She absolutely refused to acknowledge the shot of pain that movement caused her ankle. She considered it her own small penance for telling the worst of the worrywarts her injury might look a bit ghastly, but hardly hurt at all. She hadn't cared for the lie, but there'd been nothing else for it. She'd simply *had* to get out of bed, or go stark raving mad.

At the insistence of Lady Thurston, Mrs. Hanson, and Kate—the traitor—she'd spent the whole of yesterday in that bed, resting. She hadn't done it willingly, or even particularly gracefully, but she'd done it. And now she wanted to do something, *anything,* besides rest.

She wanted to go on that damnable picnic.

It was only a sprained ankle, for heaven's sake, and she'd found she could get about well enough with the cane Whit had brought her. There wasn't a single reason she could see for keeping her confined to the house.

"Ready to go, imp?"

Her head snapped around at the sound of Whit's voice. A voice that sounded tremendously jovial at the moment, which, given her current circumstances and mood, she found tremendously irritating.

"Ready to go where? I . . ." She trailed off and narrowed her eyes at him. "If you think I'm spending one more second of daylight in that bed, you are utterly, *utterly* mistaken." To emphasize the point, she reached for the cane and grasped it as one might a weapon.

"This is quite a reversal from the last time I saw you." He studied her with concerned eyes. "Is your ankle paining you? Let me see—"

She lifted the cane and sent him a scowl she very much hoped came off as menacing. "My ankle has never felt better," she bit out. "But my patience has suffered irreparable damage."

"Don't be a brat," he chided. "Lift your skirts."

She raised her makeshift club another inch. "Stay away from me. I thought we'd agreed not to insult each other."

"So we have."

"You just called me a brat."

"No, I advised you against behaving like one. That's entirely different," he informed her.

"In that case, I advise you to stick your head in—"

"If you choose not to take my advice," he continued in a casual tone. "I'll simply assume your foul mood is a result of your injury and leave you to heal."

If her arm wasn't already tiring, she would have lifted the cane a bit higher. "I'm not—"

"If you do behave, however, I'll take it as a sign you're feeling better. Possibly even well enough to join us on our little picnic."

She dropped the cane with a clatter. "Do you mean it?"

"Are you going to let me inspect your ankle?"

Without so much as a hint of hesitation or embarrassment, she pulled up the hem of her skirts and stuck out her leg. "Inspect away."

Whit stood where he was and frowned. "I'm uncertain as to whether I'm pleased or unnerved by how quickly you just did that."

She rolled her eyes, but didn't take offense. "It's not as if I'd let just any man see my ankles, Whit."

"That's reassuring." He stepped forward to kneel at her feet and press his fingers against the tender skin. It hurt, just as it had when she moved so quickly to extend it to him, but she was determined not to let on.

"But as we very nearly grew up together," she continued after forcing her teeth to unclench, "and you've seen them a dozen times or more in the past—including only yesterday, I'd like to point out—I think it's only sensible to let *you* take a look if need be."

"I see."

"And the physician, of course."

"Naturally."

"And Alex, if it were absolutely necessary."

His gaze shot up to hers. "Alex doesn't need to be looking at your bare ankles."

"Not at the moment, of course not, but if the situation arose in which—"

"Ever," Whit qualified and pulled down her skirts.

"Have I passed your inspection? May I go?"

"Grab your cane," was his somewhat gruff reply.

He had a curricle ready. The spot chosen for the picnic wasn't far, just on the other side of the lake, and the others would be making the short trip on foot. With her ankle injured, however, it would have been an arduous journey for Mirabelle. She'd have managed it, she was certain, but the curricle made everything so much simpler.

"It'll take some time," Whit informed her as he helped her up. "As the road veers away from the water before it cuts back again."

"It's perfect weather for a drive," Mirabelle replied.

It was perfect weather to be doing anything outside.

The fresh air and sunshine did more for her than all the other medicine and rest combined. Once they were both settled and the curricle moving, she let out a long heartfelt sigh. "This is lovely. Absolutely lovely. Thank you, Whit."

He tossed a quick smile at her and adjusted his grip on the reins. "My pleasure."

She very much doubted it, as her behavior so far had been decidedly less than pleasant. She didn't mind a show of temper as a rule—hers or others—but an explanation and an apology were in order if one didn't have a good reason for the outburst. Two days ago, she wouldn't have troubled to offer them to Whit—she'd always felt he was reason enough for a good show of temper—but things, she was all too aware, had changed.

Still, she waited until they were a considerable distance from the house before working up the courage to turn her face in his general direction and speak.

"I should like . . ." She cleared her throat and fixed her gaze over his shoulder. "I should like to . . . to . . ." She cleared her throat again and had Whit frowning at her.

"Are you coming down with a cold, imp?"

"Am I . . . ?" She blinked at him. "Oh. Oh, no. I just . . ." She managed, barely, to keep from clearing her throat again. "It's only that I . . ."

"Because you sound as if you are."

"No, no—"

"Have Cook fix you a pot of her special tea—the one for head colds—when we return. It does wonders with a sore throat."

"I'm perfectly well, Whit, honestly."

But she wouldn't be, she knew, if the family and staff developed the impression that she was both injured *and* ill. And because Whit was looking at her as if seriously considering the possibility of consumption, she took a deep breath and—God help her, she just couldn't stop herself—cleared her throat for the fourth time.

"I want to apologize for my behavior in the library," she began in a rush. "You were—*have been*—very kind to me, and rather than thank you as I should have, I"—threatened to do you bodily harm with your great-great-grandmother's cane, she thought with a wince—"I was inexcusably antagonistic. Being uncomfortable makes me testy, and I'll admit my ankle does give me some pain. I don't mean to use that as a justification, I—"

"It's all right, imp. Apology accepted."

She waited a beat before asking, "That's it?"

"What more were you expecting?"

"Well, I rather thought you might milk it a bit," she replied, a trifle surprised.

"I might have, a few days ago," he admitted. "But we made an agreement, if you recall. Any particular reason you waited to tell me this?"

She wanted, badly, to shift in her seat. "I didn't want to give you an excuse to leave me behind."

"I'm not in the habit of reacting to an apology with spite," he said a little indignantly.

"Of course not," she was quick to agree. "But I wasn't certain you'd react to my admission of pain by letting me come along either."

"And made the decision to postpone your conscience until we were safely away from Haldon?"

This time she did shift in her seat. "Essentially."

He nodded. "I thought as much."

She risked a glance at him. "You're not angry, then?"

"No, I'm not. In fact, I'm delighted you behaved in such a way as to require an apology."

"I beg your pardon?"

"I've one of my own to make," he began by way of explanation. "And after having your own so generously, so selflessly, so—"

"I believe I grasp the general idea, Whit."

"—charitably accepted," he finished. "You really have no other choice but to do the same in return, or else run the risk of appearing petty and vindictive by comparison."

"That's a twisted bit of logic."

"But sound if one takes the time to follow it."

"And equally irrefutable if one doesn't care to be bothered—which, I confess, I don't." She twisted further in her seat to look at him. Now that she'd finished with her apology, it didn't seem so hard a thing to catch his eye. "What could you possibly have to apologize for?"

"For maneuvering you into spying on Kate," he said, suddenly serious. "It was ill done of me."

"Yes," she agreed without the heat of anger. "It certainly was."

"I'm sorry for it."

A corner of her mouth quirked up. "Are you only sorry now that it's become apparent that spying was unnecessary?"

"I don't recall asking you to qualify *your* apology," he evaded, suddenly paying much closer attention to his driving.

"You asked why I waited to offer it," she pointed out.

"Only after accepting it to start."

"You're right," she laughed and sat back against the cushions. "And it hardly matters now anyway. Apology accepted, Whit. Although, I don't think it will do for us to start expressing regret for *every* past misdeed. We'd never speak of anything else."

"You have a point." He gave the matter some thought.

"Perhaps we should agree not to extend any more apologies for crimes committed against each other before the house party."

"Will I have to apologize for getting you into trouble with your mother, then?" She grinned at him. "Because I'm not sorry I did it."

"You would have been," he promised her, looking quite smug. "Once I enacted my revenge."

"Well if you're *certain* of it, there's really no reason for me to tell you I'm sorry. It would be redundant." She tapped a gloved hand against her leg. "What was your revenge going to be?"

Whit shook his head. "I don't think you should know. There's no guessing how long our truce will last, and I'd just as soon keep it in reserve."

Mirabelle had always found it aggravating to be kept out of a secret—which was only natural to her mind—and as this particular secret pertained directly to her, she found its continuing secrecy twice as aggravating. This would require, she decided, twice the usual tenacity in finding it out.

"How's this," she tried, "I'll say I'm sorry—"

"Only you're not."

"True, but you're certain I *would* have been, and that amounts to the same thing, really," she explained reasonably. "But you first have to agree to tell me what you had planned."

"I've done more agreeing in the last two days than I typically do in a year," Whit chuckled.

"Can't be helped," she said dismissively. "What do you say to my offer?"

He thought about it—which she found perfectly reasonable—and thought about it—which she could forgive him for—and thought about it some more—which was a little annoying—and then finally decided.

"No. No, I don't think I will."

Which was entirely unacceptable.

"Why ever not?" she demanded.

"I don't wish to," he answered with a roll of his shoulders.

"You're being stubborn, Whit. I don't think that's allowed under the terms of our agreement."

"Of course it is. You're just not allowed to criticize me for it."

"That"—is probably true, she conceded, but only to herself—"is ridiculous," was what she said to him.

"That might also be the case, but again, you're not allowed to mention it." He transferred the reins to one hand and rubbed his chin thoughtfully, his blue eyes dancing. "In fact, now that I think of it, I can say or do near to anything now—as long as it's not insulting to you—and you can't disparage me in any way."

"There's always later."

"Yes, but I'm a man who lives for the present."

"You're a braggart is what you are—and I mean that in the nicest way possible," she was quick to assure him.

"I don't think it is possible to call someone a 'braggart' without being insulting," he scoffed.

"Of course it is. I've my own—and entirely uninsulting—definition for the word."

He blinked at her. "That's . . ."

"Yes? Go on, Whit," she prompted with a silly grin. "Is it ridiculous? Absurd? Is it—"

"I'm at a loss for words," he admitted with a laugh. "And it's for the best, as it seems we've arrived."

And so they had. Mirabelle craned her neck to see through the small line of trees that separated the road from the field beyond. The lake path they'd taken the day before may have been her favorite place to walk, but there wasn't a spot on the Haldon grounds more ideally suited for a picnic. It had a wonderful feeling of seclusion about it, with the road hidden from view and the forest closing in on three other sides.

The occasional oak and maple had been allowed to thrive in the midst of the green and even now servants were spreading out blankets and depositing baskets of food under the shading branches.

The first guests were beginning to arrive, mostly the very young who had no doubt grown impatient with the adults' leisurely pace and scampered ahead, but a few others were there as well—Kate and Evie among them.

"We abandoned poor Sophie to the wolves," Evie informed them as Mirabelle and Whit made their way into the field. "But Alex wouldn't let her walk any faster, and I couldn't stand another second of Miss Willory's tittering."

"Do you know," Kate said as they chose a blanket and sat, "that before I met her, I hadn't known a person outside of a book *could* titter?"

"It's a rare skill," Mirabelle replied. "With any luck, we'll never meet another who's acquired it."

Luck, as it happened, was on their side that morning. By the time Miss Willory arrived, the spaces on their two blankets had been filled. Perhaps not with their favorite guests, as the pompous Mrs. Jarles and silly Miss Sullivan numbered among them—the latter of whom received a very nasty look from the isolated Miss Willory—but it was a more pleasant group than might have been expected. Alex and Sophie failed to arrive in time to claim a space, but Miss Heins had.

The topic on everyone's mind, of course, was Mirabelle's unfortunate—and, in her opinion, embarrassing—tumble down the hill and subsequent—and even more embarrassing—rescue.

"It's not like you to pay so little attention," Kate commented. "It's really more something I would do."

"Perhaps the hermit McAlistair was hiding behind a tree and snuck up behind to give you a push," Miss Sullivan breathed. "I shall be terrified to go into the woods alone again."

Mirabelle couldn't imagine the pampered Miss Sullivan ever having had the urge, or the occasion, to go into the woods alone, but knew better than to voice that opinion out loud.

"McAlistair is no threat to you," Whit assured the group. "And as he hasn't seen fit to show himself to guests for the past eight years, I can't imagine why he would suddenly choose to do so now."

"McAlistair isn't even real," Kate said with an eye roll. "Whit made him up years ago with the express purpose of frightening three poor unsuspecting little girls."

Whit snorted at the image. "The two of you were already out of the nursery," he pointed out to Mirabelle and Evie. "And you—" he continued, looking at Kate, "—may have been a little girl, but you were neither poor nor unsuspecting. You've refused to believe it from the start."

"I *was* rather clever for my age," Kate conceded.

"If Whit had wanted to f . . . frighten us," Evie said softly, her discomfort with being the center of attention manifesting in a stammer, "it seems to me he'd have made McAlistair more . . . well, frightening."

"Never say you believe in such rubbish, Miss Cole," Mrs. Jarles admonished.

Evie ducked her head and made a small movement of her shoulders. "I don't c . . . care to discount things before they've been proven one way or the other."

"Which goes to prove one needn't always grow out of their childhood cleverness," Whit commented with a smile and a gentle tug on Kate's bonnet ribbon.

"The woods are safe enough," he continued. "But I'll have to ask you ladies to stay away from the far north pasture for the remainder of the party."

"That pasture is more than three miles away," Kate murmured. "Why . . . Oh! Have the Rom returned, then?"

"Just this morning, I was informed."

"Gypsies! Here?" Mrs. Jarles spun her head about as if expecting one to pop out from behind the nearest tree.

"Not here," Whit assured her. "Not at the moment."

"But on your land! You've allowed them on your land?"

"I have, as I do every spring and fall when this particular clan passes through. As they keep to themselves, I see no harm in it."

"No harm in it?" Mrs. Jarles very nearly screeched. "We could all be murdered! Murdered in our own beds!"

"Would you prefer the parlor?" Whit inquired with a politely interested tone.

Mirabelle covered a surprised laugh with a cough, but even over the distraction she could clearly hear Mrs. Jarles wheeze out a loud breath.

"I beg your pardon?"

Whit shrugged and reached for another piece of cake. "You seemed so set against the deed being performed in your bed, I thought you must have someplace else in mind."

"I . . . I . . ." Mrs. Jarles stammered and blinked rapidly.

"Personally, I'd just as soon be asleep," Whit said nonchalantly. "If one *must* be cut open by a drove of murderous gypsies, one would probably be better off being unaware of the whole nasty business."

Evie and Kate turned bright red with suppressed laughter, while Mirabelle debated whether she could contain her own mirth long enough to see how the conversation—such as it was—played out.

Mrs. Jarles drew herself up as far as her position on the blanket, and sadly inconsequential height, allowed. "The indignity—" she began, and in such a way that Mirabelle was uncertain whether she was referring to Whit's comments or her possible death at the hands of the gypsies.

"Would hardly signify," Whit assured her easily. "As you and everyone you know would be dead."

"Scattered about the house in their literal and figurative

deathbeds of choice," Evie spluttered out in one quick breath before turning a brighter shade of red and gaining her feet. "Excuse me, I need to . . . I need . . ."

The remainder of her sentence was drowned out with a coughing fit and the sound of her quickly retreating steps.

"I'll just go see if she's all right," Kate mumbled and followed her friend's retreat with a coughing fit of her own.

"How odd," Whit commented, biting into his cake. "I wonder if perhaps the cook used a heavier hand than usual with the spice. Between the marauding locals and poor food, I shan't take offense, Mrs. Jarles, if you choose to cut your visit short."

He sent a wicked glance at Mirabelle. "You look a little peckish yourself, Mirabelle. Do you need to follow Kate and Evie?"

Mirabelle bit her lip, hard, and shook her head. Then nodded, grabbed her cane, and made a stumbling escape.

Mrs. Jarles would not have been surprised to discover that there *was* a man hiding in the cover of the trees. A man who was no stranger to murder. A man who knew all too well what it felt like to steal life from a sleeping form.

But he hadn't come today to kill.

He'd come to watch, as he always watched.

And to yearn, as he always yearned.

No, Mrs. Jarles would not have been surprised to see the dark form crouching in the woods. She would have been *very* surprised, however, to learn that someone else knew the man was there.

# ❈ Eleven ❈

The picnic ran later than expected—as all successful outings do—and the sun was making its golden descent by the time Whit again helped Mirabelle into the curricle.

"What are you looking for, Whit?"

"Hmm?" Whit turned his attention from the trees and started the horses forward with a soft flick of the reins. "Nothing. Thought I saw a deer, a buck."

"Why didn't you say something? The children would have loved to have seen a buck."

"I only just noticed—"

"You've been peering into the woods for the last twenty minutes."

"My mind's been wandering a bit. Have your eyes always been chocolate?"

"I . . ." She was too startled by the question to consider that its purpose was to change the subject. Confused, she reached a hand up to touch her cheek. "They're brown."

"No, they're richer than brown. Perhaps it's only noticeable in candlelight or when the sun turns gold."

Was he being poetic? she wondered, and wished she had a way of knowing. She'd never inspired poetry in a man before—confidence perhaps, and friendship certainly, but never the pretty words that were invariably reserved for beautiful women. The fact that she wasn't a beautiful woman answered the question well enough, she concluded.

"First you tell me I have hair the color of bark, and now I've chocolate eyes." Her lips twitched with humor. "I'm a cacao tree."

"Do cacao beans grow on trees? I rather thought it was bushes."

"Trees," she assured him. "At any rate, my eyes are the color they've always been. Maybe they're a slightly different hue when I'm angry."

"And I've only ever seen them angry," he said with a nod. "Why is that, imp? Why have we never gotten on at all before now?"

"You said once it was fate," she reminded him.

"Ah, yes, the divine ordinance argument. Clever of me."

"Quite."

He stopped the horses suddenly, and turned in his seat to look at her. "I don't believe in fate, actually."

"You don't?"

"No. Aside from the inescapable realities of birth and death, we're responsible for the paths our lives take. We each make our own choices." He bent his head and whispered against her lips. "And I choose to do this."

It was Mirabelle's very first kiss. She was the eldest of her friends, but until this moment, she was the only one of them to have gone unkissed. Even Kate had stolen a kiss with Lord Martin—her heart's greatest desire at one time— during her first Season. Kate had decided shortly thereafter, for reasons she kept to herself, that her heart had been sadly misinformed.

Mirabelle wondered if hers was as well . . . until Whit's lips met her own. Nothing, she decided then, absolutely nothing could possibly be wrong about kissing Whit.

It was everything she imagined a kiss would be—and absolutely nothing like she would have expected a kiss from Whit to be—not that she ever allowed herself to imagine kissing Whit. But if she had it would have been forceful and—

Whit pulled back until he could see her eyes. "Stop thinking, imp."

She reached out, took hold of his cravat, and brought him closer.

"Stop talking, cretin."

He grinned against her mouth for a moment, and then he was kissing her again. Despite her eagerness, he kept things soft and gentle, a tender brushing of lips and breath. Her hand relaxed against his chest, and his own came up to lightly cup her face.

He kissed her as if she were an unfamiliar treat, in small careful tastes that had a pleasant warmth spreading in her chest.

He nibbled softly on the corner of her mouth, and the warm sensation bloomed and spread until her limbs felt heavy and her head felt light. His tongue swept her bottom lip and that pleasant warmth turned to an aching heat. She squirmed on the cushions, wanting closer, wanting more, wanting something she wasn't certain how to ask for.

Whit's thumb brushed down her cheek to press gently on her chin.

"Open for me, sweetheart."

When she did, and his tongue darted inside, the ache became a demand.

Her hand fisted again and she heard herself whimper into his mouth. He stilled for just a second. Then in one quick move, he wrapped an arm around her waist, another in her hair, dragged her hard against him . . .

And took.

Later, much later, she would think that this was what she expected a kiss from Whit to be like. It was demanding, frantic, a battle of tongues and lips and teeth. But for now, thought was lost to her. She could do nothing more than grab handfuls of his coat, hold him close, and take in return.

His mouth slanted over hers again and again, until she was lost in the taste and feel of him. She struggled closer, her hands moving to his shoulders, his hair. Her mouth moved under his in desperate need. She wanted more. She wanted closer. She wanted something she hadn't the name for.

But to her frustration, his own hands and mouth gentled and slowed to the easy tastes he'd started with.

And then he pulled away, leaving her breathless and thrilled and confused.

"I'll not apologize for that," he whispered.

"All right."

"I'm not sorry I did it."

"Neither am I." But she was more than a little sorry he had stopped. "Why did you? Kiss me, I mean?"

He tilted her chin up with his finger. "Why did you?"

"I . . ." It was a fair question, she'd been kissing as much as she'd been kissed, but she wasn't at all sure how to give it a fair answer. Not when her heart and mind were still racing.

"I kissed you for the same reason," he said, straightening fully. He smiled just a bit and took the reins again to start them forward. "That gives us something to think about, doesn't it?"

"I suppose it does."

It was, Mirabelle thought, a very good thing the curricle pulled into the drive just then because for the life of her, she couldn't think of another thing to say to Whit. She was rather surprised she was capable of thought at all.

At least nothing beyond—

She had kissed Whit. Whit had kissed her. They had kissed each other.

She managed, somehow, to greet the group waiting on the front steps with a smile. She responded to questions, asked one or two of her own and otherwise made a very fine job of pretending she hadn't just had her world turned upside down. But when someone suggested a game of whist in the front parlor, she demurred, using the excuse of her sore ankle to retreat to her room.

She slipped—or hobbled to be more precise—away before Whit could offer his assistance, and after a laborious climb up the stairs, made it to her room where she collapsed in a dazed heap on the soft chair by the window. She looked through the glass without seeing what lay beyond. Her mind remained steeped in the kiss. That lovely and terrifying kiss.

Why had it happened, when only days ago they would both have sneered at the idea of Whit so much as kissing her hand?

*Would* she have sneered at it? She shifted in her seat as if gaining physical comfort could somehow compensate for the discomfort of the truth. And the truth was, she would have let him kiss her hand. If she had known he did so with sincerity, that it wasn't a joke or the beginnings of an insult, she would have taken that compliment and cherished it.

And if her recent reactions to touching him were any indication, she would have wished for more. She had felt the jolt of awareness when he'd sat next to her on the bench that morning, and the shock of excitement when he'd picked her up in his arms and carried her up the hill.

With the certainty that nothing could come of it, she'd done her best to ignore her physical response to him. Now something *had* come of it. There could be no more pretending not to notice the way her heart leapt, and her skin felt hot and sensitive whenever he was close enough to touch.

Wondering what that meant, and if it meant anything at all to Whit, she snuggled deeper into her chair. There was so much to sort through—too much, she decided, to attempt to make sense of all at once. Particularly while her ankle throbbed, her mind whirled, and her heart skipped uncomfortably in her chest. Giving into exhaustion, she closed her eyes and slept.

She woke several hours later stiff and cramped, her neck twisted at an awkward angle against the back of the chair. She groaned softly as she fought off the dregs of sleep, sitting upright to look at the clock on her mantel. It was dark out, but not yet eight. She had time to straighten her appearance and perhaps stretch out the worst of her kinks with a short walk before dinner.

With her ankle injured and exhaustion still lingering, she found it difficult to undress and dress. But if she rang the bell for assistance now, it would likely be Lizzy who came, which increased the probability of Evie or Kate appearing as well. As much as she loved her friends, Mirabelle wanted some quiet time before dinner to clear her head and settle her thoughts.

She took one of the secondary staircases down in the hopes of avoiding everyone, but as she reached the bottom, raised voices in the hall told her solitude was not to be had.

"Stop it! You give her back!"

Mirabelle stepped around the corner to find little Isabelle Waters, no more than six years of age, confronting a thirteen-year-old Victor Jarles.

"Give her back!" Isabelle stomped her foot in temper even as the first tears fell. "You give her back!"

"What's all this?" Mirabelle asked, stepping between the two.

"Victor's taken my Caro!"

Mirabelle turned to the boy and noticed he was holding a small doll. "Is that true, Victor?"

The boy shrugged and tossed the doll at Isabelle's feet. She snatched it up and ran to the corner where she cradled her toy and sniffled.

"I was only playing," Victor said carelessly.

"It didn't look as if she wanted to play your sort of game."

"What does she know? She's only a baby."

"I am not!" the little girl wailed. "I'm six! Nearly."

"Aren't you a bit old to be teasing a six-year-old?" Mirabelle inquired, fisting her hands on her hips.

Victor sniffed and tugged regally at his cuffs. "Can't see how it's any of your concern. Mirabelle."

Her eyes narrowed at the insult. The boy was every inch his father, she thought, a man whose drunken attentions she'd twice had to fend off in the past. The second, and final time, had required Sophie's unique skill with knives.

"It is Miss Browning," she corrected sternly. "You'll apologize to Isabelle and to me."

"I won't. She's a brat. And you're not but one step removed from a servant," Victor returned derisively. "Servants are referred to by their Christian names."

Patience, she told herself, even as she felt that particular virtue dwindling away at an astounding rate. "I am but one step removed from a baron—"

"A baron no one knows," he interrupted snidely. "My father says you're poor as paupers."

It was difficult to argue with the truth, so she made an attempt to argue around it. "I am also your elder and a guest—"

"An ape leader, is what you are," Victor returned with a tight smile and a jeering voice. "My mother says you're too plain and poor to ever catch a husband."

And with that, her patience was gone. She leaned down until they were nose to nose and gifted him with her most intimidating glare—an expression she had usually reserved for the occasions when she met with pompous adults, and for Whit in general.

"I need neither beauty nor coin to turn you over my knee. Some pleasures can be had for free."

His face turned a shade of red that, had she cared one wit for his health at the moment, might have been alarming. "You wouldn't."

"Care to place a wager? I could use the funds, you know."

"I'm thirteen! You can't—"

"Can and will." She sized him up. "Or I'll fetch someone else to see to the job. That would be a trifle embarrassing for you, wouldn't it?"

He pressed his lips together and said nothing.

She straightened. "Right. Shall I send the Duke of Rockeforte here, then?" she asked calmly, and watched his eyes widen at the reminder that she wasn't wholly unconnected.

"Or shall I send him to your mother's room?"

"I'm sorry," he snapped at Isabelle.

"And?" Mirabelle prompted.

"I'm sorry," he ground out in her general direction.

"Apology accepted. Now—"

"But not nearly as sorry as *you'll* be," he hissed, and bolted down the hall.

Mirabelle watched him disappear around a corner. "Atrocious little monster," she grumbled. "Spendthrift father should pay for a few manners."

"What's this?" a new voice asked. "And whose father is a spendthrift?"

She turned to find Whit striding toward her from the opposite end of the hall. Her heart made an extra beat, just at the sight of him.

"To hear the young men tell it, whose father isn't?" she laughed when he reached her, hoping to cover her sudden nerves with humor.

"He called her names," a soft voice said. "He's very naughty."

Mirabelle turned her head to discover Isabelle still standing in the corner. She'd forgotten the child was there.

"Who called her—?" Whit began.

"Isabelle," Mirabelle interrupted. "Why don't you take Caro to the nursery for a nap?"

The girl's face turned mulish in an instant. "I don't need a nap."

"Certainly not," Mirabelle was quick to agree. "But your Caro looks to be a very young infant, and they tire easily, particularly after a great deal of fuss."

"They do?"

"Absolutely."

"Oh, all right then."

Mirabelle watched the little girl scamper down the hall cradling and murmuring to her doll. "If only they were all like her," she sighed.

"Well behaved?" Whit asked.

"Female."

"Ah." He cocked his head at her. "Are you going to answer my questions?"

"It was nothing," she assured him. "Just a minor disagreement with a young tyrant—a child," she hastened to add when his face darkened.

"I could ask Isabelle."

"I know," she replied with a nod. "But I'm asking you to let me deal with this as I see fit."

"I'll allow it," he decided after a moment. "For now. But you'll inform me if it becomes anything more substantial than a minor disagreement."

It was a testament to how tired she was and how far they'd come in their truce that she didn't take offense at his high-handedness. At least, not so much that she couldn't see past it to the underlying concern, and what it cost him to make the concession.

"I'll inform you," she agreed.

"Good. Do you need help getting to . . . where were you headed?"

"To dinner, but . . ." She blew out a breath and swallowed her pride. "Would it be a bother to have something brought to my room, instead? I'll admit, I feel a trifle worn."

He reached over to tuck a lock of hair behind her ear, the light brush of fingertips leaving a trail of warmth against her cheek. "I'll see to it."

She watched him as he turned and left the way he'd come.

Wherever was this truce with Whit headed, she wondered, and turning her own steps back toward her room, decided she would figure it out tomorrow.

For most young women, the sight of a large man crawling through one's bedroom window in the dead of night might constitute a serious cause for alarm. For the occupant of this particular bedroom, however, the intrusion was not only expected, but welcome.

"What happened?" she demanded as the man slipped agilely from the sill. "You were gone for ages."

"Slight change of plans. I had to hide the package in the bedroom rather than the study."

"Whatever for?" she asked, rising from a chair.

"The baron fell asleep at his desk." He stepped across the room to plant a quick kiss on her forehead. "The man has the most tremendous snore I've ever encountered. I half feared he'd bring the roof down on our heads. The place is falling to ruins."

"I rather wondered." She sighed deeply. "She speaks so little of it."

"Well, she needn't speak of it at all much longer."

"You're certain this will work?"

"Of course. How can you doubt it?"

"How can you not?" she asked on a snort. "It was a very near thing the last time."

"Nonsense. It was fated."

"It was luck."

"That would be fitting, wouldn't it? Do you know, of all the missions I've had a part in, I think this one may prove to be my favorite?" He took in her narrow-eyed glare. "Er, second favorite."

## ❋ Twelve ❋

Whit had always been proud of Haldon Hall—even when its master had been a keen embarrassment. Its elaborate design, the extensive grounds, and—and he wasn't ashamed to admit it—the sheer size of the manor, had always been a source of pride for him.

On occasion, however, he was forced to concede that certain tasks would be a trifle easier if his home wasn't *quite* so grand. Tasks like hunting down Evie for his mother. His cousin had promised to assist with decorating the ballroom that morning, but had yet to arrive. Whit could empathize with her reluctance, but a promise made was a promise kept at Haldon.

It took quite a bit of time to track her down, but eventually he heard her voice float through a window from the western side of the lawn. He made his way to a door leading outside, opened it . . . and froze.

Whit had never considered himself a coward. There were, however, a whole list of terrifying things a man could— and should, really—be able to go his entire life without witnessing. And the women of his family throwing daggers was most decidedly one of those things. In fact, he rather thought it should be somewhere near the top of the list.

But there they were—Evie and Mirabelle standing before a makeshift target while Sophie instructed them on the fine art of knife throwing.

"Pay attention to your lead foot and take care to aim it in the direction where you'd like the knife to go." She stepped forward and with one swift and—he might admit in the very distant future—graceful move, had the knife slicing through the air to stick dead center in the target with a solid *thunk.*

"Mother of God."

"Oh, hello, Whit."

His sister's voice jarred him out of his wide-eyed stupor. He whipped his head around to find her sitting next to Alex, a small traveling chess board spread out between them.

"Sophie's giving lessons on knife throwing," Kate informed him as she angled her bishop forward two spaces. "Isn't it exciting?"

As a rule, Whit preferred to react to unsettling situations in a manner that befitted a man of his stature. And, as a rule, men of his stature did not pale and stammer.

*But sweet hell, Kate throwing knives?*

"Are you . . . is she . . . for pity's sake, Kate."

She turned cool blue eyes on him. "Have you always thought me an idiot?"

He blinked, remembering the conversation he'd had with their mother on the back lawn not long ago, and how swiftly he'd been maneuvered into that trap. He took what he hoped would prove a settling breath.

"No." He made the mistake of glancing again at the knives. "The possibility has only just occurred to me."

"Does it look as if I'm participating in the lesson, or does it appear, *perhaps,* as if I'm enjoying a game of chess with Alex while we watch?"

He didn't bother to hide a wince. "Point taken, Kate—"

Kate sniffed and turned back to the game. "Clumsiness isn't synonymous with idiocy, you know."

"I know, and I apologize." He stepped over to plant a soft kiss on her cheek. "It was ill done of me."

"As for the rest of you . . ." Whit turned to Alex, steadfastly ignoring the amused glint in his eyes. "I can't believe you're allowing this."

"I can't believe you expect me to argue with a group of armed women," Alex countered.

"I don't expect you to argue. I expect you to disarm them."

"Ah, don't know why I didn't think of that. Well, you're here now." Alex waved his hand at him. "Have at it."

He turned, intending to do just that, but when he opened his mouth, he met three pairs of annoyed eyes, and decided instead to hold out his hand in silent demand.

No one moved.

"The knives please, ladies," he prompted.

"You've known him longer," Sophie said to the others. "Is he being brave, or merely stupid?"

"That would depend, wouldn't it?" Mirabelle replied.

"On what?"

"On whether or not we skewer him."

"I vote you make him stupid," Kate piped in. "He called me an idiot."

Whit shot a sharp look at his sister. "Stay out of this, Kate. No one here will be skewered, because, in a moment, I'll be holding all the knives."

"Just not in his hand," Evie added.

"You," he shot at Evie, "are supposed to be helping Mother with preparations for the ball."

"Oh, oh no, I'd forgotten." Evie actually paled, which made him feel a touch guilty.

"She's not upset with you, Evie, she was only wondering where you were."

She wasn't listening to him. She passed her knife to Sophie and ran for the house.

"I should go with her," Kate murmured and followed Evie into the house.

"She'll feel terrible about that for days," Mirabelle said with an accusing glance at Whit.

"I'll speak with her, after you give me the knives." He pointed a finger at her. "You made a promise not to fight with me."

"I'm not fighting with you. I'm quietly disobeying," she countered. "It's entirely different."

"Mirabelle."

"Oh, all right." She gave up her knife, but like Evie, she handed it to Sophie. "I should see if Lady Thurston requires more help, anyway."

Whit watched her go, mostly because he just couldn't seem to stop himself from looking at her. The slight limp did the most interesting things to her backside, and he had a brief image of following her inside and . . .

*Damn it.*

He spun away before he embarrassed himself and concentrated on his remaining opponent. It felt a bit off, giving orders to Sophie when Alex was right there, and she was such a stubborn creature to boot, almost as bad as the imp. But surely she could be made to see reason.

"For God's sake Sophie, you . . . you're . . . ." He waved his hand in the general vicinity of her belly. "You know."

She didn't, apparently, because her only response was a blank stare. Feeling a little desperate—and not a little foolish—he tried the other hand, then both, then added in a jerk of his chin.

"I believe he means you're with child," Alex prompted with a grin.

"Oh, yes," Sophie assured him without changing her expression. "I managed to translate that. Somehow. But I'm trying to fathom what one thing could possibly have to do with the other."

"It's just . . ." Wrong, he thought. So very, very wrong, on so very many levels. "Unsafe."

Again, the blank look.

"You could be injured," he added.

"For heaven's sake," she finally said on a laugh. *"How?"*

He honestly didn't know, but he wasn't about to admit to that. "I'd prefer not to dwell on it. Give me the knives, Sophie."

"They're daggers, actually, and I won't give them to you because they belong to me." She sighed and stepped over to pick a leather satchel off the ground. "But since you ran off my students, I might as well put them away for now."

It was on the tip of his tongue to say "for good" but he decided to swallow the argument and take the victory he'd been handed. Mostly.

"It would be appreciated if you were to keep them put away for the remainder of the house party."

"Appreciated by whom? Certainly not Evie and Mirabelle. They've a right to learn how to best defend themselves."

"They know how to best defend themselves—they come to me."

"Or me," Alex added, though from the amused look on his face, the comment wasn't an indication he wished to join the argument, just add to it here and there.

"The two of you are not always available," Sophie countered.

"Careful where you tread, Sophie," Whit advised.

"I mean no offense. I know you to be the most faithful and reliable of brothers, Whit, and I can certainly attest that you're the most protective of husbands, Alex, but you can't be with every one of your women at every moment, can you?"

"If anyone ever attempted to harm one of you—"

"Then they might very well succeed if they caught Evie or Mirabelle alone, and there'd be nothing you could do but demand satisfaction after the fact. That would be gratifying, no doubt, but would hardly undo what had been done."

"It's my responsibility to see that they're never in a position—"

"I know, and you do an admirable job of it. I don't mean to argue with you—well, yes," she amended after reconsidering, "I do, but I don't wish to anymore. Consider what I've said, Whit." She swept past him towards the house. "Even the most sheltered of women have had to face danger alone, and even the most trusted of men aren't privy to every secret."

"What the devil does that mean?" he called out to her retreating back. When she slipped inside without answering, he whirled on Alex. "What did she mean by that?"

"Why are you asking me?"

"She's your wife."

"Doesn't mean I understand her half the time." He gazed at the door Sophie had just passed through. "Amazing, isn't she?"

"Delightful," he ground out. "Has something happened to one of them?"

"Do you think I wouldn't have told you, if I knew of such a thing?" Alex shot him a reprimanding look. "I'm not one of the women to be keeping secrets."

Whit swore and dragged a hand through his hair.

Alex took pity on him. "I'm sure she was speaking theoretically, Whit. Passionately, I'll grant, but you did interrupt one of her great pleasures."

"Knife throwing," Whit muttered. "I can't fathom why you've allowed it."

"It was a compromise. One of a great many made to keep her safely distanced from my work with William."

"She knows of that?"

"She does, and a bloody load of trouble it's been too," Alex grumbled.

"Then why did you tell her?"

"I didn't, though I suspect I would have eventually. I wouldn't care to keep something like that from her."

"How did she come to know of your work, then?"

"It's a long story. I'll relate it some other time." Alex turned to leave. "I need to check on Sophie. Like as not, she's halfway up a ladder by now, hanging garlands."

By nine o'clock that evening, Mirabelle was starving, exhausted, and immensely grateful that Lady Thurston hosted only one ball during her pre-Season house party rather than her famous three as she did during her larger end-of-Season gathering.

She had worked through the noon meal, as well as tea, assisting Lady Thurston in everything from decorations to seating choices for the meal. Mirabelle didn't mind in the least, but she was now more than ready for the chance to sit down and eat.

She stopped by her room for a quick wash and change. Most of the guests would be in the parlor by now, waiting for the announcement that dinner was served. She was finishing her hair, repinning the parts that had fallen during the day, when she saw it—the slightest movement on the bed.

It was nothing more than a twitch of her pillow, but it had her arms falling to her sides and her mouth opening in surprise.

Someone had put something in her bed, and she'd bet her last pence she knew who that someone was. More amused than annoyed, she stalked over to pull the bed linens away.

She very nearly laughed at the small frightened lizard cowering under her pillow.

"Oh, for goodness sake."

If Victor Jarles had been a mischievous young man rather than a cruel one, she might have brought the small reptile back into his room to lay under his blankets. It would have been a grand laugh for the both of them in the morning. But the little monster would likely kill the thing as not, so she fetched a basin and towel instead.

"Poor little thing," she murmured, scooping up the lizard and gently placing him in the deep bowl. "Scared half to death, I wager. Not to worry, I'll set you free."

"Who the devil are you talking to?"

Mirabelle started at the sound of the masculine voice and glanced over to see a very confused looking Whit standing in the open doorway.

"You startled me. I didn't hear you knock," she said as she draped the towel over the basin.

"Likely because I didn't. Your door was open." Whit made a quick search for witnesses in the hallway before entering the room and closing the door behind him. "What have you got there?"

"A very frightened lizard I found hiding in my bed. A gift from young Victor Jarles, I suspect."

Whit crouched to peek under the towel.

"Huh." he murmured, obviously unimpressed. "That's a bit disappointing, isn't it? I'd have expected more from the likes of him."

"I'm terribly sorry he failed to live up to your expectations," Mirabelle drawled. "Perhaps you could take him aside and give him a few pointers."

"The idea has merit," he said, returning to a stand. "If one is going to be a troublesome little boy, after all, one ought to make the effort to do it properly."

"He's not little," she grumbled. "And he'd not troublesome. He's just trouble."

He narrowed his eyes. "Trouble enough to call a lady names?"

"Would that elevate him to the status of a properly troublesome little boy in your estimation?"

"Mirabelle."

She brushed an errant lock of hair out of her eyes and stood. "Let it alone, Whit. And for heaven's sake, get out of my room before someone comes along and makes a fuss."

"Door's closed. Who's to know?"

"My eight o'clock assignation. He's the jealous sort, and generally quite prompt."

"He'd be generally quite dead if he were real," Whit only half jested. He ignored her dramatic eye roll in favor of holding out his arm. "May I escort you to dinner?"

It would be nice, she thought, to be seen on Whit's arm. But it wasn't appropriate. "You can't, I'm not the highest ranking woman in the house."

"I can do what I like, but if it makes you uneasy—may I at least escort you to the parlor?"

"I'd like that," she replied with a broad smile. "But check the hallway first, won't you? And if anyone should ask, we ran into each other on the back stairs."

As it happened, no one asked outright how Whit came to escort Mirabelle into the parlor. There was quite a bit of conspicuous whispering among the most gossip-minded partygoers, but none of them were interested in the truth of the matter so much as discussing the possibilities.

The what-ifs and do-you-thinks lasted through dinner, but Mirabelle and Whit barely noticed. They were seated too far apart to have a discussion of their own, but from time to time (with rarely more than ten seconds between each time) they caught each other's eyes across the table, and shared a smile.

# ❊ Thirteen ❊

$M$irabelle woke the next morning to the discovery that her ankle had healed well enough to put away the cane. It was still swollen and tender, and protested loudly if she twisted it the wrong way, but with a little care, she was able to move about without so much as a discernible limp.

She celebrated the improvement with a morning walk in the gardens before going in for breakfast.

She loved the gardens best in the spring. They weren't at their peak yet. Lady Thurston preferred the rich colors of fall blooms over the soft, bright shades of spring. But for Mirabelle, there was nothing so beautiful as the first signs of life. She could, and sometimes did, spend hours walking the paths, finding and delighting in those first green shoots and buds struggling through the soil or the remains of last year's growth.

It was comforting in a way, to know the plants had been there all along, waiting out the cold, dark winter until the sun warmed the ground again, giving them the opportunity to grow and bloom.

She thought of her five-thousand-pound inheritance. Less than two years, and winter would be over for her, as well. A woman could do a great deal of growing and blooming with five thousand pounds at her disposal.

"Staring at the larkspur won't make it grow any faster," Whit said from behind her.

She turned to find him not five feet away. "I hadn't realized you were standing there."

"I'm not surprised, you seemed lost in your thoughts."

"I was," she admitted before gesturing at the plant she'd been staring at without realizing it. "You know their names, then?"

"Only so far as my mother used to chastise Alex and I for playing in them. The roses, mostly, as there's something about thorny bushes that draws small boys like moths to flame. Nearly as irresistible as mud."

"I wonder why that is?" She laughed.

"One of the great mysteries of life." He tilted his head at her. "You look a picture, you know, standing in the garden with the sunlight in your hair."

"Oh." She felt her cheeks growing hot. Would he kiss her again, she wondered, and immediately wished she hadn't, since it only served to make her cheeks grow hotter. "Um . . . thank you."

Straightening, clearly enjoying himself, he gripped his hands behind his back and rocked on his heels. "Not accustomed to compliments in general, or just not from me?"

Not accustomed to wondering if I'll be kissed, she thought, but what she said was, "Both, I suppose."

He took a step closer to her. "An unforgivable oversight."

Perhaps he *would* kiss her, and because she found it impossible to make room for any thought beyond that, she once again said, "Oh. Er . . . thank you?"

He chuckled softly and took another step. "You're welcome. Won't you take a step forward, imp? I wouldn't mind kissing you, but I'd rather we kiss each other again."

"Oh . . . er—"

"Don't thank me."

"What? No, of course not. Um . . ." She dragged her foot one miniscule inch forward, then brought the other up to match.

Whit glanced down at her feet and smiled. "It's a start, I suppose. But I've taken two, you'll recall."

"Two. Right." She begin to scoot her foot forward again, then stopped. "This is absurd."

"I'll say. If your sole doesn't leave the ground this time, I'm not counting it."

She choked back a laugh. "That's not what I meant."

"I know."

"I don't know why you're doing this," she said suddenly.

His expression remained somewhere between bland and faintly amused. "Don't you? I'd have thought it obvious. Didn't I just mention kissing?"

"No. I mean, yes, you did." She blew out an exasperated breath. "But why do you want to kiss me?"

"We're going to kiss each other."

"Yes, and I know why *I* want to—"

"Do tell."

She ignored that. "But why do you? Up until a few days ago, you hated me."

He recoiled a bit at the accusation. "That's something of an overstatement, don't you think?"

"I'm not sure," she answered honestly. "You sometimes looked physically ill when your mother made you dance with me."

"That wasn't hate," he argued. "That was fear."

"I'm in earnest."

"So am I. You can be quite fierce, you know."

She bit her lip, uncertain of what to say.

Whit studied her face. "I've never hated you, Mirabelle. There were times I've badly wanted to muzzle you, but I've never hated you." He swallowed hard. "Did you hate me?"

She opened her mouth, not to speak, but in surprise, then turned her head and nodded thoughtfully.

"Dear God," he whispered, appalled, "you did."

"What?" She started and blinked. "Oh! Oh, no . . . I was thinking of something else."

"One would think this conversation was significant enough to warrant a person's full attention," he grumbled.

"It does. It has. I was considering my own behavior, and how it could have led you to believe I didn't care for you . . . that is . . ."

Oh, how mortifying.

Whit didn't seem to notice her discomfiture. He simply nodded in understanding and closed the distance between them.

His head slowly bent down to hers until she could smell the faintest hint of coffee on his breath. She liked that, she decided, closing her eyes. She liked it very much.

"Mira! Mira, are you out here?" Kate's voice, not far down the path, had her jerking back.

"We'll finish this another time," Whit whispered against her lips before stepping away. No sooner had he retreated, than Kate came into view. "There you are. Evie thought you'd be in the library, but I knew you'd be here this time of year. Good morning, Whit."

Because his sister's bright smile and distracted eyes never failed to both touch and amuse, Whit bent to kiss the top of her head in greeting.

"Good morning," he returned. "It's early for you and Evie to be up, isn't it?"

"Mother wants help with some last-minute arrangements for the ball. Will you come, Mira?"

"Er . . . Yes, of course."

Kate took her hand and began tugging her down the path. "I'd make myself scarce if I were you, Whit. She's looking for someone to take the ladies into town for a spot of shopping."

Last-minute arrangements turned out to be everything from greeting and settling the musicians to overseeing candle replacement in the half-dozen ballroom chandeliers.

Morning gave way to midday, and it was past time for tea when Mirabelle finally made it back to her room.

She'd barely started to wash up a bit when Kate knocked on her door and, carrying a gown of pale blue, let herself in.

"Would you like this? I bought it because mother insisted the color matched my eyes, but it doesn't in the least, and I'm a hair too tall for the cut as well." She frowned thoughtfully at the dress. "It's not like Madame Duvalle to make mistakes. I wonder if she has a new girl working for her."

"Why don't you bring it back and have her fix it?"

Kate looked appalled. "I'll not be responsible for having some poor girl sacked."

"Give it to Lizzy, then."

"I tried," she replied. "But she has more gowns from me and Evie than she knows what to do with. She says she has a pile of dresses to sell already, and if Evie and I give her one more, she'll quit our employ and open a shop. Won't you at least try it on, Mira? I hate to think of it going to waste or—"

"All right!" Mirabelle laughed and took the gown. "Lord, I've never met a more convincing babbler in my life."

"I've many gifts, babbling is but one of them." Kate made a shooing movement. "Go and try it on."

Mirabelle stepped behind a screen and replaced her old gown with the new one. It took a bit of work. "It's too tight," she decided yanking on the material. "My stays show, and my chemise bunches terribly."

"It's not a dress one wears with stays," Kate called.

"Oh." She shimmied out of the half-corset and tried again. "My chemise is still bunching, and it's too light a material to go without one. I'm afraid it just won't work. Pity too—it's lovely."

"What a shame . . . Oh! Why don't you try it with your new chemise underneath?"

"Will that work, do you think?" she asked stepping out from behind the screen.

"It can't hurt to try."

"I suppose you're right." Mirabelle rummaged through an armoire and pulled out the box from Madame Duvalle's. It took her a moment to untie the triple knot, but eventually she succeeded in freeing the blue cloth. "It looks to be near the same color. A bit darker perhaps, but the same hue."

She stepped behind the screen and changed yet again, slipping the new chemise on with a sigh of pleasure as the soft material brushed her skin.

"It's the most heavenly thing," she murmured.

"What's that?"

"The chemise, it's wonderful. I may start sleeping in it."

"What if there's a fire?"

"A very good point." She pulled the dress on next. "It fits," she said, a bit stunned. "It fits perfectly. It even covers the scratches on my shoulder."

"Let me see," Kate needled.

Mirabelle stepped out from the screen, still gazing down at the gown. It was simply cut with puff sleeves and only a wide band of ribbon along the hem for decoration, but it was far more fashionable than anything she could normally afford. The blue material appeared even paler than when Kate had first handed it to her, and there was a sheerness to it that allowed the darker chemise to show from underneath, giving the overall effect of layered colors.

"Oh, Mira. It's lovely. Absolutely lovely."

"It is, isn't it?"

"Yes. You'll wear it tonight, won't you? And you'll let Lizzy fix your hair."

"I don't know . . ." She caught sight of herself in the mirror and grinned. The gown nearly glowed. "All right . . . Yes, all right."

"Excellent. Why don't we have tea here, then? It'll save us time. I'll just go tell the others."

★　★　★

When Kate left Mirabelle's room, it was to discover an eager Lizzy standing in the hall. "She take it, miss?" the maid asked in a rushed whisper.

Kate hooked her arm through Lizzy's and headed to their rooms. "Were you eavesdropping, Lizzy?"

"Of course I was," the maid said, completely unrepentant. "But I couldn't make out but every third word."

"I expected better from you," Kate chided. "You should have brought a glass to press against the door."

"There wasn't one handy, and Cook would have my head if I took one out of the kitchen. Did she take it?"

"Did Cook take what?"

"No, Miss Browning, and the dress."

"Oh. She did." Kate patted her friend's arm. "It was a clever scheme you concocted."

"Not so difficult, seeing as how she and I are of a size and Madame Dupree likes nothing better than a challenge and a secret."

"And a sizable fee from my mother."

"That as well." Lizzy agreed. "I wager that dress fit her like a dream."

"It did, indeed."

They walked together in companionable silence for a time before Lizzy spoke again. "Lady Kate?"

"Hmm?"

"Do you still have that novel where the lady's maid dies for her mistress?"

"Lord, no," Kate laughed. "One read-through of *Lady Charlotte the Cowardly and Her Prodigiously Stupid Maid* was enough for me. Why?" Kate stopped and gawked at her. "Never say you *liked* that book?"

"No." Lizzy smiled and started them forward again. "No, I didn't."

# ❈ Fourteen ❈

She wasn't beautiful.

Mirabelle knew she was not a beautiful woman, and no amount of blue silk or hair pins would change that fact. But for the first time in her life, she realized that she wasn't quite as plain as she had always imagined either. In fact, tonight she looked decidedly—pretty. Certainly there was a world of difference between being beautiful and being pretty. Mirabelle ran her fingers down the silk at her waist and hips without attempting to hide her grin. After all, there was an equally large difference between being pretty and being plain, and she had certainly leapt to the winning side of that gap tonight.

"It's the smile, you know."

Mirabelle turned around at the sound of Kate's voice to find her friends watching her reaction.

"Your smile," Kate repeated. "It's one of your best features."

"It's true," Sophie agreed. "It completes the picture."

"Like the finale of a good symphony."

Mirabelle beamed at Kate's comment but shook her head in denial. "I'm no symphony," she replied before returning her attention to the mirror. Catching sight of her friends' disgruntled reflections she added, "but I'll not argue against a sonata."

The girls laughed before Kate cocked her head thoughtfully to one side and said, "Do you know, I think that's the very reason I've never thought of Miss Willory as truly beautiful? She never smiles with her eyes. Her expressions are always so practiced, so calculated."

"Like a tavern ditty without the invectives," Evie offered.

"A pointless endeavor," Sophie agreed laughing. "Rather sad."

Kate rolled her eyes but appeared amused nonetheless. "Come on, Sophie, Evie, we need to get ready. I'd hug you, Mira, but I'm afraid to muss you."

"I had planned on being a dramatic opera," Evie remarked casually. "But I think I'll aim for a wicked sailor's tune instead. Curses included. That should put Miss Willory's nose out of joint."

Mirabelle laughed and waved her friends out the door with one final reassurance that she would do nothing to endanger all their hard work.

Because she hadn't the startling looks or the inherent talent for drama that some of the other young women possessed, Mirabelle's entrance into the ballroom that night went largely unnoticed. Except, of course, by her friends—and Whit.

"That can't be . . . is that . . . *Mirabelle?*"

"You look a little surprised, Whit," Kate commented casually, her eyes sparkling.

Whit brought his drink up for a long swallow. "What the devil happened to her?"

"Nothing too remarkable," remarked Sophie. "Just a new dress, and Kate insisted on Lizzy doing Mira's hair tonight. Excellent job she did of it too."

"Didn't she?" Kate agreed.

Whit finished his drink. Just a dress? *Just* a dress! The garment in question was a concoction of pale blue silk that flattered Mirabelle to perfection. The cut hugged her subtle curves faultlessly—and the color made her skin look like fresh cream and her dark eyes shine brighter than he had ever seen them.

And when a man begins thinking a woman's dark eyes could shine brightly, he was well and truly sunk.

Bloody hell.

He glanced down at his empty glass, wondered if he could have another drink so early in the evening without thinking less of himself, then glanced up again to see a young man leaning over Mirabelle's hand.

He handed the glass to Kate without looking, who took it with a smug smile he was too preoccupied to see. He'd made several strides across the floor before a hand reached out to grip his arm.

"Do you intend to dance alone?" Alex inquired.

Whit stopped and reluctantly turned his gaze from Mirabelle. "What are you talking about?"

Alex dropped his arm and jerked his head at the dance floor. "The dancers are lining up. It'd look a bit strange for you to be up there by yourself. What were you planning to do?"

Temper had him answering before reason could get a thought in edgewise. "She doesn't need to be dancing with the likes of him."

"Who?" Alex asked. "And who?"

"Mirabelle and . . ." He actually had to look to remind himself who he'd seen kissing her hand. "Mr. Kittlesby."

"Why not? Kittlesby's a good sort."

He was, actually, but that wasn't the point. The point was . . . the point was . . . "She shouldn't be up there . . . wearing that sort of gown."

Alex glanced over. "Seems a perfectly normal sort of gown to me. I think she looks rather nice."

"Well stop thinking on it. You're a married man."

"Didn't say I was thinking of taking the dress off her. But now that you mention it—" When Whit turned on him, blood in his eyes, Alex laughed and held up a hand in peace. "I'm only having a bit of fun with you. I *am* a married man and very much in love with my wife. Besides that, I see no great difference in her tonight other than a pretty dress."

"Then you're a blind man."

"Or perhaps I've seen all along what you have not."

Because he was beginning to suspect there was some truth to that, and didn't care in the least for admitting to it, Whit offered only a grunt in response.

"It's not as if every man in the room is suddenly vying for her attention, Whit," Alex pointed out, and then added in a mutter, "and believe me, that can happen."

"One is enough."

"I suppose it is," Alex agreed and gave him a bolstering pat on the back. "I've left my wife alone long enough. Try not to do anything rash while I'm away."

Whit barely noticed his friend's departure. While the dance continued, he worked on clearing his head. What *had* he planned on doing, whisking Mirabelle away in front of everyone? That was the action of an impulsive man, and by God, he was not an impulsive man. He was a reasonable, sensible, respected peer of the realm. He would not make a spectacle of himself.

She'd danced with others before, he reminded himself. She was smart and witty and friendly, and during the London Season, when men were pressed by their mothers into dancing with one of the less fashionable girls, she was often their first choice. It had never bothered him in the past.

But then, she hadn't been *his* in the past.

And she bloody well was now.

He wasn't certain what that meant yet, but he was damn certain he wasn't going to let someone else fawn over her while he sorted it out.

He clenched and unclenched his fists, and waited for the dance to end. The moment it did, he was at Mirabelle's side. "Won't you take a stroll about the room with me, Miss Browning?"

She looked at him, baffled, which was no wonder as he hadn't waited for Mr. Kittlesby to return her to her chair.

"Oh, ah." Her eyes darted to Mr. Kittlesby and back again. "Er . . . yes. That is, it'd be my pleasure. You'll excuse us, won't you, Mr. Kittlesby?"

"Of course," the young man answered in a tight voice.

He needn't have bothered, as Whit had already pulled Mirabelle off into the crowd. Keeping a firm grip on her elbow, he maneuvered her through the press of people and out onto the terrace. It wasn't nearly as packed as the ballroom, but it was a near thing.

"Blast."

"Is something wrong, Whit?"

"I want a moment of your time," he responded, sweeping his gaze from one end of the terrace to the other.

"Well, you've taken it. Rudely, I might add."

He ignored her censure and led her to the far end where the light was dimmer.

"You've made a habit recently of grabbing my arm," she commented.

"Perhaps I simply like touching you."

"I . . . There's no way for me to respond to that without embarrassing myself."

"No response required." He pulled her into a recessed portion of the terrace. "Here we are."

"I don't know that this is proper."

"Answer a question for me, and I'll let you go."

She scowled at him. "I hadn't realized I was being held captive."

Likely better that she didn't, he decided, and opted out of replying. "Where did you get that dress?"

She blinked at him and glanced down at her gown. "Why, is something the matter with it?"

He very nearly told her *exactly* what was the matter with it—it was beautiful. She was beautiful in it. Every man in the house could see she was a beautiful woman in a beautiful gown. He had just enough common sense left, however, to know those words, spoken as an accusation, would accomplish nothing—nothing good, anyway. And now that he'd removed her from the ballroom, the worst of his temper was settling to a manageable burn. He took a deep breath. "There is nothing at all the matter with it." And because he worried his behavior may have caused her to think otherwise, he added, "You look lovely."

And to that he added a silent, and heartfelt *Damn it*.

"Oh. Thank you. I'm glad you like it. I . . ." She dropped her gaze, and fiddled with the material at her waist. "I should probably tell you . . . the cost of it will come to you. I didn't do that on purpose. Kate bought the dress, but it didn't fit her properly, and she gave it to me. If you like I can—"

"Why should I care where the bill was sent?" he asked, honestly baffled. "Have I ever complained before?"

"Before?" She shook her head. "I don't understand."

"Your other gowns," he clarified. "The other bills—" He cut himself off when she continued to shake her head. "The bills haven't been sent to me?"

"Of course not."

He scowled in thought. He never paid attention to the details of the bills from the modiste, he simply paid them. "Your uncle, then?"

"No," she replied and tilted her chin up a fraction. "I pay for my own gowns . . . usually, anyway. And if it bothers you—"

"It bloody well doesn't bother me," he snapped.

"It rather sounds like it bothers you," she pointed out.

He drew a frustrated hand down his face. "Why would you pay for your own gowns when you knew perfectly well I'd see to the expense for you?"

"Well, I didn't know perfectly well, did I?"

He sent her a dubious look. "Do you mean to tell me that my mother never offered?"

"Of course she did, but—"

"But you refused," he finished for her. "Why?"

"A woman has a right to her pride as much as any man," she answered. "I take enough from your mother—from your family."

"You've taken nothing that wasn't freely offered."

"All the same—"

"It's only a gown, for God's sake," he continued with an impatient wave of his hand.

"Exactly. I fail to see why you're so upset." She shook her head when he opened his mouth to argue. "This isn't the place to discuss this."

"You're right." He stepped back to a window and slid it open. "Climb through."

She stared at him, then the window, then him again. *"What?"*

"Climb through," he repeated gesturing with his hand. "It's the study."

"Of course it's your study," she replied sarcastically. "Where else would you play fast and loose with my reputation?"

"I'm not playing with anything. No one can see, Mirabelle, and I want a private conversation with you. Climb through."

"No."

"Climb through," he ground out, "or I'll toss you through."

Mirabelle glowered at him, caught somewhere between dumbfounded and furious. It was on the tip of her tongue to say something along the lines of *you wouldn't dare*. But by the set look on his face, he *would* dare.

She stepped up to the window.

"You're not following the rules of our agreement," she grumbled as she sat down and swung her legs over the sill and into the adjoining room.

"You can take me to court for breach of contract tomorrow. Now hop down."

She did, and turned to watch as he climbed through the window, closing it and the drapes behind him.

"This is entirely unnecessary," she announced as he lit two candles on the desk. "I'm not going to apologize for paying for my own clothing."

"I don't want your apology," he informed her. "I want you to listen to mine."

Baffled, she watched him finish with the candles and cross the room. "I . . . you haven't anything to apologize for."

"You've been uncomfortable at Haldon," he replied. "Uncomfortable with asking for or taking what you needed. That's my fault."

"There is no fault," she retorted. "I haven't been uncomfortable—"

"Don't lie to me, imp."

"Very well, I haven't been any more uncomfortable taking your charity than I would be taking anyone else's."

He swore softly. "It's not charity."

"Of course it is. Freely given as you said, but charity all the same. How would you feel in my position?"

"It isn't the same thing."

"Oh? Why not?"

"Because I'm a man."

"And you're allowed a pride I am not?" she asked hotly.

"No. I am allowed to work," he corrected. "It is my responsibility to see to the care of those who are not."

"I could be a governess, or a paid companion—"

His expression turned hard. "You bloody well won't."

"I'll bloody well do whatever—" She cut herself off, held up a hand when he opened his mouth to fill the silence. "We aren't going to agree on this, Whit. Couldn't we agree to disagree?"

"No."

"If we're to keep the peace between us—as we promised your mother," she reminded him, "we'll have to find a compromise."

It was a moment before he spoke. "What sort of compromise?"

"I'll admit that my pride has made me, perhaps, a little stubborn." She ignored his snort of derision and continued. "And I shall endeavor to be more receptive to your mother's offers of assistance in the future. But you must agree not to push at the matter. My pride is part of who I am. I won't trade it for a pretty wardrobe."

"You're such a reasonable sort," he said after a moment. "How did we manage to never get along in the past?"

"I wasn't at all reasonable when it came to you. Does the compromise suit you?"

He crossed his arms over his chest. "No, but I'll agree to it, for now."

He looked so handsome when he was annoyed, she thought, with his dark gold hair tousled from the outside breeze, his strong jaw clenched, and his blue eyes dark and brooding. The muscles in his arms and across his chest tensed and moved under his shirt and coat. She wondered again how she had never before noticed the strength in him, or how it made her skin heat, and her breath catch . . .

"A penny for your thoughts, imp."

She started at his voice and lifted her gaze to find his eyes no longer brooding, but laughing.

"Oh, they're worth ten pounds at least. I certainly couldn't let them go for anything less than five, and at that a bargain." Her voice came out a little breathy, but she was so flustered, she was grateful it came out at all. Really, how embarrassing.

"Done. Five pounds."

Mirabelle blinked rapidly. "I beg your pardon?"

"Five pounds for your thoughts just now. The ones that

made you blush. I can pay up front if you doubt my sincerity." He reached behind him and pulled a five-pound bank note from his desk.

"I . . . er . . ."

"Come now, you made the bargain. Surely you don't mean to renege."

"You can't be serious."

"Perfectly, I assure you." To prove his point, he held the money out to her. Mirabelle just stared at it in bewilderment.

Five pounds would be a welcome addition to her emergency funds, particularly as she had recently dipped into them twice.

She had as much pride as the next person, but there was a time and place for everything, she decided. And now was the time and place for a little pragmatism. Beyond that, she was just a little bit curious as to how he might react.

"Very well," she said, snatching the note out of his hand. "I was thinking that your . . . ah . . ." She motioned in the general direction of his chest. "Your shoulders . . ." She swept her hand back and forth. "They're . . . ah . . . they're a bit broader than I remembered," she blurted. Good Lord, that had been awkward.

Whit's smile went from merely mischievous to decidedly wicked. His eyes, amused a moment ago, darkened with something she felt she might be better off not attempting to name. She was blushing quite enough, already.

"Well, good-bye, Whit."

He caught her arm on a soft laugh. "Not quite yet, imp. You can't go about making statements like that to a man and expect—"

"I don't. I've never said anything like that before . . . to anyone but you."

He pulled her toward him slowly. "Nor statements like that one."

She tugged lightly on his arm. "We've been gone too long. People will talk."

"We've time yet." He brought her that last foot forward to stand before him, and then brought his lips to hers.

Whit intended the kiss to be in tune with the moment—sweet and light. A simple matter of a few stolen moments at a ball. Keeping a loose hold, he ran a hand up her back to coax her closer, brushed his mouth across hers to tempt and tease, nipped gently with his teeth in an invitation to play.

The taste and feel of her seeped into him, adding another layer to the need that had been steadily growing for days.

He allowed himself the dangerous luxury of letting it build.

He could enjoy the feel of her small fingers gripping his shoulders and feathering across the back of his neck. He could savor the way she fit against him, her face turned up to his, her breasts pressed against his chest. He could relish the lines of her, and mold his hands along the subtle hips and long waist. He could take his fill of her warm mouth, her fragile skin, her soft sighs.

He had control.

He did.

Until his fingers skimmed along the low back of her dress and, dipping between her gown and shoulder blade, discovered satin.

Smooth, and warmed by the heat of her flesh, the feel of it was unmistakable.

"Whit?"

Mirabelle's breathless voice, sounding uncertain, made him realize he'd gone absolutely still.

"You're wearing it," he whispered.

She blinked at him blurriedly. "Wearing . . . wearing what?"

By way of answer, he trailed his finger along the neckline of her gown, over her uninjured shoulder and down her collarbone to rest on the swell of her breast. Slowly, as if un-wrapping a rare present, he peeled the gown away to expose the soft blue beneath.

"The blue satin."

Had he been watching her face, he'd have noticed her eyes clear.

"You saw," she breathed, and took a step back.

Oh, he'd seen. But not enough. He took a step forward.

"Not nearly enough."

Her eyes went from clear to wide, and she retreated an-other two steps.

He advanced. Then advanced again, beginning a leisurely stalk of her across the room.

She stumbled back against a chair. Gentleman that he was, he simply leaned around her to pull it out of the way.

"I believe you were running?"

"I'm not running," she retorted. And made a quick dart to the left.

Grinning wolfishly, he snagged her around the waist and dragged her against him, then marched her backwards until he had her trapped against the wall. He leaned in, pinning her with his weight.

"What is it, Mirabelle? A chemise?" He traced the mate-rial at her breast with the pad of his thumb. The hand he'd braced against the wall fisted when she shivered. "It is, isn't it?"

"Yes, I—" She broke off with a ragged breath as he drew his hand down, brushing the side of her breast, outlining her waist.

An entire garment of flowing blue satin, he thought. And underneath it all was the imp. His hand tightened reflex-ively on her hip.

*His* imp.

He caught her eyes now. He made certain of it.

"Mine."

Mirabelle had only a chance to wonder at that statement before Whit's mouth was once again on hers. But this time, the kiss wasn't light and sweet. It was dark, and heady, and dangerous.

And she reveled in it—in the rough caress of his hands, the possessive sweep of his tongue.

She ought to push him away, she thought dimly. Or at least stop pulling him closer. She certainly shouldn't be letting him unbutton her gown. But as quickly as those thoughts would occur to her, they would be lost again, washed away in the heat.

It felt so wonderful, so wonderfully right, to have his hands against her skin, his mouth trailing hot kisses down her neck. Sliding a palm up her calf, he caught the back of her knee and hiked her higher against the wall. The hard muscle of his thigh pressed forcefully at the juncture of her legs, and suddenly it no longer felt merely right to touch and be touched, it felt absolutely necessary.

She lost herself in the frantic desire of the moment. As if from a distance, she heard her own gasps and moans.

And Whit's own ragged cursing.

"Enough," he rasped, easing back and letting her slowly slide to the floor. "Enough. I have control."

Control? What the devil was he talking about? She struggled to get closer, to bring him back. She wanted . . . she wanted . . . she wasn't entirely sure what she wanted. But she was damn well certain it wasn't his control.

"Easy." He pressed his lips to her temple. "I'm sorry, I shouldn't have let things go so far."

He held her close, petting and stroking in a manner that soothed rather than aroused.

"Better?" he asked after a time.

No, she thought, a little sourly. "Yes. Yes, I'm fine."

No need to add desperation to the list of her sins.

He nodded once, brushed the back of his fingers across

her cheek, and stepped away. "We've been in here too long. Go to the ballroom. I'll follow after—" He broke off and took a thorough study of her appearance. "On second thought, go to your room first. You're a bit . . . mussed."

She raised an unsteady hand to her hair, found it almost completely undone

"Here, turn around," he suggested.

"What?"

"Your buttons," he explained, and took her shoulders to turn her about. He did up the back of her gown with the rapid efficiency of a man determined not to think too hard on where his hands were.

"There." He turned her about again. "I can't do much about the rest, I'm afraid."

"Oh. That's all right." She stared at him blankly for a moment.

"You should go, Mirabelle."

"Hmm? Oh, right. Right." It took her a moment to regain the use of her legs to the extent that she could walk towards the door without stumbling.

"Mirabelle?"

She spun around with an eagerness that would embarrass her later. "Yes?"

"Dance with me?"

"What . . . *now?*"

He grinned suddenly, the self-satisfied smile of a man who'd befuddled a woman. "I wouldn't say no, if you've a mind to. But we might find it an easier prospect in the ballroom, with music."

"Oh," she said, finally understanding. And then said, "Oh," again in pleasure. Whit had danced with her before, but only out of a sense of obligation . . . and because his mother nagged. Now he was asking for himself. Her feet, already light from the kiss, nearly floated off the floor.

She smiled at him. "I could probably see my way to clearing a space on my dance card for a reel."

"A waltz," he countered. "I want a waltz."

She gave a brief thought to saying something sophisticated and witty, something to offset the delight she was certain her face betrayed. But she had neither the skill nor the inclination to play the flirt.

"A waltz, then."

Although Mirabelle saw Whit the next day, it was only from afar or in passing. The gentlemen engaged in separate activities, preferring cards and a trip to Maver's Tavern over the more staid pursuits of charades in the parlor and walks about the grounds.

Mirabelle made a sincere attempt to not be distracted by thoughts of Whit, but every time she began to attain some success in that endeavor—and by success she meant a solid five to ten minutes of time in which she thought of him only once or twice—she would catch sight of him across the lawn, or hear his voice from the far end of the dinner table, and her heart would beat wildly and her thoughts would scatter, rearrange themselves, and return focused solely on him.

She thought of the way he'd held her close as they'd waltzed a slow circle about the room the night before— how the music drifted over them, his hand solid and warm on the small of her back. From that memory, it was a very small leap to recalling where his hand had been earlier in the study.

It was maddening. It left her feeling tense and anxious. It left her feeling aggravatingly needy. And the fact that he'd appeared perfectly composed the few times she had seen him, only succeeded in making her more agitated.

Shouldn't he be as worked up as she? she wondered as she

let herself into her room after dinner. It didn't seem at all fair that she should be the only one feeling excited and miserable at the same time.

Of course, if she was the only one feeling that way, it had very little to do with what was fair, and with what simply *was*. A few secret kisses likely weren't so very large a thing to someone like Whit. They weren't, after all, *his* first kisses.

Swearing under her breath, she yanked off her gloves and tossed them on the foot of the bed.

The counterpane shifted.

It was only the slightest of movements, but she'd caught it, and sighed.

"Again? Honestly, couldn't the boy come up with something—?"

She broke off, speechless, as she pulled back the covers.

Spiders. Everywhere. A mass of legs and fangs spread out over her bed like a gruesome blanket. A blanket she watched undulate, then tear as the exposed spiders scurried to find refuge.

She didn't scream, not even when one of the little monsters crawled over her hand, and though her pride would be grateful for that later, it wasn't pride that kept her from screeching at the top of her lungs at present. It was the fact she hadn't the breath to manage more than a strangled, "Nyah."

She tossed the counterpane down again and took two steps back.

"Nnn," or something very close to it, emerged around clenched teeth as she shook her hands wildly. She slapped at her skirts, patted at her hair and took another step back, just to be safe.

"Something the matter, imp?"

She whirled to find Whit standing in the doorway, a quizzical smile on his face.

"Are they on me?" she whispered in a strangled voice. "Are they? Get them off. Get them—"

"Is what on you?"

"Spiders!"

"Hold still then, let me have a look." He made what appeared to her to be a cursory glance of her hair and clothes. "Not a thing on you. I wouldn't have thought you'd make such a fuss over one little spider."

"Spiders." She swatted at a tickle on the back of her neck before jabbing a finger at the bed. "Plural. There."

"In your bed, you mean?"

The amusement in his voice had her temper rising, conveniently pushing aside the worst of her jitters. "No, in the imaginary jar sitting atop the bed," she snapped. "Don't you see it? Of course in my bed."

"No need to get testy," he muttered and walked over to grab the counterpane.

He dropped it with a jolt before he'd pulled back more than a corner.

"Well . . . ahem." He reached his hand out again, hesitated, then gripped the material and lifted it a second time. "Well."

"Well?" That was the best the man could do? *Well?*

"Well, it certainly is impressive." He let the material fall and took a step back. "How did someone acquire so many of them, do you suppose?"

His bland tone might have annoyed her if she hadn't seen him shaking his hand off as he turned around again.

"Hellborn babes rarely suffer from a lack of minions," she grumbled. "I suspect he just told them to hop in."

"Victor, again?" he guessed.

"I can't imagine why anyone else would want to do such a thing."

He nodded grimly. "It's time I had a talk with the boy."

She shook her head. "He'll deny any part in this, and his mother will make an ugly fuss over the accusation."

"Mrs. Jarles's ugly fussing doesn't concern me."

"It concerns me, Whit. It would be unpleasant for your mother. I don't want that."

"Nor do I, but there doesn't seem to be a way around it." He glanced again at the counterpane "The boy needs to be punished."

"There's nothing a bully likes less than being ignored." Or having one of his victims get back a little of their own, she decided, but thought it better not to mention as much to Whit. "Let's let it alone for now."

"If that's what you want," he replied, reluctance evident in every syllable.

"It is." She winced at the bed. "What am I suppose to do with this?"

"If you're determined not to have Victor see to his own messes, I'll have the staff take care of it."

"That's hardly fair to them."

"Do *you* want to take care of it?"

She watched one of the spiders crawl off the bed and make a dash across the wall. "Oh, Lord," she gulped. "We can board the room up. Never speak of it again. I won't be able to sleep in here again, at any rate."

And, oh but that made her furious. She adored that room. It had been hers and hers alone since her first visit to Haldon. It was her sanctuary.

Victor Jarles had gone too far this time. In truth, he had gone too far when he'd addressed her as Mirabelle, but while that insult had stung, this prank cut deeper.

She bit her lip when two more spiders made their way out from under the blanket. "Blast."

Whit stepped to her and took her hand. "Go to Kate or Evie's room for tonight. I'll take care of this."

"But—"

He cut her off with a gentle squeeze of her hand and a soft kiss on her forehead. "Go on. We can't clean up in here together, and I won't leave you alone to do it."

"I could—"

"Go on," he repeated and nudged her toward the door.

"Knight-errant again."

"It is becoming something of a habit. Good night, imp."

She was standing alone in the hall before she could answer.

"Well," she said to herself. "Good night."

# ❈ *Fifteen* ❈

$O$ne of the great benefits of centering a social gathering around a meal is that one can always use the excuse of a full mouth to avoid conversation. Whit had been taking advantage of this boon for the last hour. He chewed each bite of dinner slowly and extensively, and he made certain to have the next forkful ready before swallowing.

It was probably rude, no doubt childish, and his jaw was beginning to cramp from the exercise, but it was well worth it to be able to point at his mouth and shake his head apologetically every time Mrs. Jarles leaned over to speak to him. At least his mother had shown him the mercy of balancing the nuisance of Mrs. Jarles sitting to his left, by seating William Fletcher on his right.

Whit would have preferred to have had Mirabelle seated next to him, or at least within shouting distance. He'd barely seen her today and hadn't spoken to her once. When he'd searched her out this morning, the staff had reported that the women had gone "for a stroll."

When they were *still* strolling after midday, Whit quietly sent a pair of footmen out to check on them. They were safe and sound at the edge of the lake, he'd been informed, and a trifle annoyed for having their ladies' outing interrupted.

Whit had been a trifle annoyed in return. It was the last day of the party. Hadn't they spent the whole of yesterday separated into ladies' this and gentlemen's that? Was she seeking ways to avoid him? Perhaps he'd pushed things too far or too quickly. It was damnably hard to say, as he hadn't figured out for himself how far he cared to take things, nor how quickly he wanted to get there.

"I'd like a chance to speak with you."

William's voice pulled Whit away from his musings. He shot a quick look at Mrs. Jarles. Finding her sufficiently occupied with a conversation farther down the table, he relaxed.

"Certainly," he replied to William. "What about?"

"I'd prefer to speak in private."

"Ah," he gave a wry smile. "About that sort of thing."

"Indeed. Will midnight in your study be convenient?"

"It will, provided dinner goes no later than eleven."

"Oh, Lord Thurston," Lady Jarles chimed at the back of his head. "I've been meaning to ask if you intend to visit Almacks when next in London?"

Whit crammed a forkful of food in his mouth before turning his head. He'd have to make the bite last, as the footmen were even now replacing his plate of pork loin with a covered bowl he could only assume contained some sort of soup. There was no chewing of soup.

He needn't have bothered with the ruse, nor worried over how he was to continue it, because even as he was shaking his head to indicate to Mrs. Jarles that he did not intend to visit Almacks, but was unfortunately unable to elaborate at this time, the footmen were uncovering the bowls.

And all hell was breaking loose.

Toads and lizards of varying sizes were bounding, leaping, and scurrying out of what appeared to have been otherwise perfectly good cold soup.

"What the devil?"

"Oh my! Oh my!"

"Catch it!"

"Aiiiieeee!"

"Put the lid back on! Put the lid back on!"

Amidst the screams and shouts of the adults, the wild laughter of the youngest children, and the clattering of chairs and the frantic attempts of the staff to either replace the lids on the bowls that still contained their extra ingredient or catch those that had made good their chance to escape, Whit noticed two things. One—Victor Jarles looked tremendously pleased with the melee, and two—Mirabelle looked respectably shocked and horrified, but she was watching Victor with an evil glint in her eye.

He knew that glint well.

"Enough!" Lady Thurston's voice cut through the riot of noise. "Victor Jarles, you will explain yourself."

"Me?" The boy's expression went from delighted to mutinous in a heartbeat. "Why me? I haven't done anything."

"It is coincidence, then," Lady Thurston inquired coolly, taking her seat once more at the foot of the table, "that your bowl is the only one not to have contained a reptile?"

"That's not my fault." He looked to his mother for help. "It's not my fault."

"I'm certain there's a reasonable explanation for this," Mrs. Jarles insisted. "Perhaps the staff—"

"My staff put these creatures in the soup?"

"Well—I'm certain they didn't," Mrs. Jarles backtracked at Lady Thurston's cold stare. "But I'm sure there's a reason for Victor not to have one in his. And not everyone has taken their lids off—"

"Miss Browning hasn't," Victor cried.

"It seemed imprudent under the circumstances," Mirabelle replied. "I've no great fondness for reptiles . . . particularly lizards."

"Lizar—" Victor's eyes grew round and he squirmed excitably in his seat, pointing at Mirabelle. "She did this! She did! There won't be a thing in her bowl! You! Footman. Take off the lid."

The nearest footman turned to Mirabelle with a questioning look.

"I'd prefer you didn't," Mirabelle said calmly. "We've only just caught the others."

"But he has to do what I say!" Victor snapped.

"Brindle," Lady Thurston addressed the footman, "did you accept an offer of employment from young Mr. Jarles and neglect to inform me?"

The corner of Brindle's mouth gave the slightest twitch. "No, ma'am, not to my recollection."

"Ah, well," Lady Thurston replied turning back to the boy. "It seems you are mistaken, Victor. Now, if you insist on dragging this nonsense out, you may do so, but you'll be quite alone in the matter."

"Fine." He sniffed and stormed around the table toward Mirabelle. "I'll do it myself."

Mirabelle edged away from the table, which should have given the boy something to worry over, but he was determined in his mission to prove her a liar. Mirabelle stepped back when he reached her bowl and stepped back again when he lifted the lid.

A fat toad hopped lazily from the bowl to the table. In a somewhat anticlimactic ending to the whole dramatic affair, Brindle leaned forward and scooped it easily into his hands and back into the bowl.

"Shall I take it away with the others?"

"Please," Lady Thurston replied. "And you, Victor, may take yourself to the nursery, unless your mother would prefer differently. Until you learn to behave as a gentleman, and a gentleman does not attempt to frighten my guests with reptiles, I'll not have you at my table."

"The nursery? But—"

"Come along, dear." Mrs. Jarles bustled her son out of the room.

After several reassurances that the next courses would be up to Haldon's usual standards, the guests returned to their seats and the remainder of the meal. It wasn't overlong before conversation returned to normal—Victor Jarles wasn't the first naughty thirteen-year-old to play a joke during dinner, after all—but Whit kept his eyes on Mirabelle and wondered if Victor had truly been naughty at all.

He had his first chance to ask after dinner when the gentlemen joined the ladies in the parlor. He found her standing in the corner with Kate and Sophie, the three of them conversing in rapid whispers that ceased abruptly as he approached.

Might as well have put guilty signs around their necks, he thought grimly.

"I'd like a word in private with the imp, please."

Mirabelle didn't resist when he tucked her hand around his elbow and escorted her across the room. Of course, she had very little to worry about, as privacy was relative in a crowded parlor, but he managed to secure them a spot by the windows where they wouldn't be overheard.

"Was tonight's debacle your doing?" he asked, letting go of her arm.

She gave him a bland look. "I thought we'd settled this at the table."

"I haven't settled anything as of yet. And until I know for certain who is responsible for embarrassing my mother, I'll not—"

"Whatever else you may think of me, Whit," she interrupted. "You should know I'd rather cut off my own arm than cause Lady Thurston one moment's pain or embarrassment."

He nodded in acknowledgement. "It's only that . . . these

parties mean a great deal to her, and for a guest to take advantage of her hospitality by enacting a joke at her own table—"

"Is that what's bothering you so? That's tremendously sweet, Whit." She smiled at him and then,—to his utter shock and horror—gently patted his cheek. "But she was in on it from the very start."

He shot a quick glance about the room to be certain no one else had seen her little pat. It probably shouldn't have been his first priority given what she'd just said, but a man had a reputation to consider. Reassured no one else had been witness to his embarrassment, he turned to her.

"I beg your pardon?"

She smiled sweetly and leaned against the window sill. "How else could two dozen toads and lizards make their way into dishes straight from the kitchen? Your mother has a wicked sense of humor, you know. And a keen sense of justice."

"Justice? In accusing a boy of a crime he didn't commit?"

"It's not a crime to put reptiles in soup," she pointed out. "And it is justice for his earlier antics."

"You're—"

"Also, I was told just this morning that little Isabelle's doll had all its hair shorn off sometime during the night. I'll not feel bad for him, Whit."

"What if his mother punishes him unfairly?"

She pursed her lips thoughtfully. "Define unfairly."

He sent her a scathing look. "You know very well what it means."

"Yes, I do, and if I thought for even a second that Victor would suffer anything more than a little forced humility—"

"Also known as humiliation."

"Very well, humiliation," she conceded, "then I never would have done the thing. Your mother assured me that Mr.

and Mrs. Jarles dote on the boy and won't lay a hand on him under any circumstances. Really, what do you take us for?"

"Clever women with a vengeful streak a mile wide," he responded dryly.

She shrugged at the backhanded compliment. "Something had to be done. If his mother would discipline him appropriately, one of us would have approached her. But your mother dismissed the idea. The Jarleses won't hear a word against Victor. They'll likely believe his denial of involvement in this as well." She furrowed her brow, contemplating the notion. "Is that irony?"

"Close enough," he murmured. A corner of his mouth twitched. "Dare I ask how you obtained two dozen toads and lizards?"

"The usual way. We caught them."

"My mother—"

"Of course not," she laughed. "Evie, Kate, Sophie, Lizzy, and I made a trip to the lake. Took us near to four hours. It was only to be lizards at first, but it was easier to grab what was available." She grimaced suddenly. "I feel rather bad."

"For framing a thirteen-year-old boy?"

"Heavens, no. I feel childish and immensely gratified for having done that. But I feel sorry for the toads and lizards." She winced. "They must have been scared half to death."

"Insomuch as it's possible for a small reptile to feel afraid, yes. I imagine they were."

"Well, they're back at the lake by now," she said. "I was going to return them myself, but Evie wanted one of her strolls anyway."

"Yes, I know."

She tilted her head at him, curious. "I'm surprised you let her wander about alone after dark."

"She's safe enough if she stays on Haldon grounds and away from the road."

"Yes, but still, it's an unusual freedom—"

"I have my reasons."

Whit's reason was even now nearing the edge of the woods.

Branches and old leaves crunched underfoot. Normally, the man creeping through the trees took better care how he moved. Silence was always best. But to move without sound in a forest required a bit of attention, and his was occupied elsewhere just now.

They'd called him back. Walked straight into his camp and told him it was time—that he was needed.

Bloody, buggering hell.

He might have said no, might have packed his meager belongings and walked away if not for three reasons. He was grateful. He wasn't being asked to resume his former role, and he was in . . .

"Oh!"

He'd unsheathed his hunting knife and bent his knees into a fighting stance before the cry of surprise died away. He recognized the voice as female, but knew full well that a pretty face could hide a blackened heart.

A bright light blinded him momentarily, and he took a quick side step to avoid the glare. When she lowered the lantern, he saw her face.

And everything inside him stilled.

Evie.

"You're M . . . McAlistair," she breathed as he straightened.

He nodded once, slowly and without taking his eyes off hers. He couldn't look away, couldn't so much as blink, afraid and unwilling to lose sight of her even for that short heartbeat of time.

"I . . . I'm Evie . . . Evie Cole."

"I know who you are."

He wasn't surprised to find his voice scratchy and rough from disuse. Nor did he care. He didn't want to speak any more than he wanted to blink. He yearned to hear her voice, not his. It was soft and low, like the echo of her laughter the wind sometimes swept up from the lawn to soothe and torment him in his solitude.

"I . . . The others say you're n–not real."

He hadn't known she stuttered when she was nervous, and stowed that small bit of knowledge away with the precious few he'd gleaned over the years. "I'm real."

She licked her lips, an action he was sure would haunt him for the rest of his nights. "I know," she answered with a small nod. "I saw you once. Th–There." She pointed to a rocky outcrop thirty yards away. "It was almost n–night, and you were skinning a rabbit, I think. You left so quickly. You didn't see me, I suppose, b–but—"

"I saw you."

With the exception of tonight, when he'd been so distracted, he'd always known when she was walking his hills, and always made certain she never walked alone.

"Oh," she whispered softly. "You didn't want me there. Do you want me to leave now?"

He shook his head, a slow motion he was only vaguely aware of making. He was thinking she smelled of lemons and mint, and wondering if she might taste the same.

He had to know. He wasn't capable now of doing what was best for her. Not when she was so near he could hear the hammer of her heart, the quiet pant of her breath. He wasn't strong enough to turn away.

So he bent his head and sampled. Lemons and mint, he thought again as he brushed his lips across hers, warm and soft and comforting as a cup of tea. He only needed a sip, just one small sip to ease the ache inside him. But he kept his hands fisted at his side, knowing if he touched her he might not be able to stop from taking and devouring in big greedy swallows.

He moved his lips over hers slowly, languidly, a careful

dance of advance and retreat. He nipped gently at her bottom lip, and dipped the tip of his tongue inside when she gasped. He withdrew it again to press kisses at the corners of her mouth. She was so lovely, so perfect, his sweet Evie.

And he had no business touching her with his stained hands.

He pulled away. "Don't walk alone for a while. I won't be here to keep you safe."

She blinked at him and brought her fingers up to touch her lips.

He nearly smiled at the movement. It was reassuring to know he hadn't lost the ability to properly kiss a woman.

"Keep me . . ." She dropped her hand. "You've followed me before, haven't you?"

He nodded, and watched her eyes narrow in suspicion and annoyance.

"Whit's idea?" she asked.

"Perhaps." He reached up, unable to resist brushing at a lock of hair. "Will you think of me?"

"Perhaps," she mimicked.

Perhaps would have to be enough, he told himself and turned to lope into the trees.

## ❊ Sixteen ❊

*M*irabelle opened her bedroom door slowly and swept the candlestick back and forth in front of her to illuminate the room. She knew Whit had disposed of the spiders, but it was difficult not to be a touch jumpy. Finding everything in appropriate order, she stepped inside and closed the door.

That was when she noticed the folded paper tacked to

the inside of the door. Frowning, she pulled it down and opened it.

> Miss Browning,
>
> The earl's study. Midnight, tonight. There will be a discussion it is in your best interest to accidentally overhear. The adjoining sitting room will be unoccupied at that time.
>
> Yours most faithfully,
> A concerned friend.

A concerned friend? She flipped the note over, but finding the other side blank, flipped it back and read again. What sort of concerned friend couldn't be bothered to speak to her in person?

She didn't recognize the choppy handwriting, but it was clearly that of an adult, which ruled out the possibility of another of Victor's pranks. Perhaps it came from Miss Heins—she seemed the sort to leave notes. But she would have had to sneak into this room to do so, and Miss Heins didn't seem to be that sort at all.

Baffled, curious, Mirabelle tapped the paper against her hand and debated. Crawl into bed and ignore it, or assuage her curiosity and go back downstairs? She stood there for a moment more before setting the paper on her desk and slipping quietly from the room.

What harm could there be in a little eavesdropping?

Unaware that their conversation was no longer private, Whit sat at his desk and waited while William fished something out of his pocket.

"Thought you might have an interest in this, after your help breaking up that counterfeiting operation last year." William leaned forward in his chair to push a ten-pound bank note across the desk.

Whit took it and frowned. He didn't need to examine it at all to see the forgery. "Not very good, is it? The print is smeared, and this sort of paper could be bought at any stationery shop in London. Sloppy work."

William nodded. "The bank spotted it as a forgery before the poor blighter who'd brought it could even ask to cash it."

"Not his doing, I take it?"

William shook his head. "Got it off Lord Osborn as payment for varied and sundry cooking supplies."

"Lord Osborn? What the devil was *he* doing with a counterfeit bill?"

"Buying sugar and lard, apparently. More importantly, he remembers how he acquired it. He recently sold one of his older carriages to a tavern owner by the name of Mr. Maver."

"A common enough name," Whit countered even as a sense of foreboding washed over him.

"In Benton," William added.

"Bloody hell." He studied the bill. "And he was certain this was the bill used to pay for the purchase?"

"Dead certain. Said he remembered being a bit surprised the man had a ten-pound bank note at the ready."

"One would think he'd give the note a better look, then."

"Yes, well, Lord Osborn isn't the sharpest blade, and I've heard his eyesight's quite poor."

Whit gave a noncommittal grunt in response to the statement. "You need me to speak with Lord Osborn, I take it?"

"No, I need you to become acquainted with the source. That bill was used to pay for a very large, very old debt of Baron Eppersly's." William leaned forward to tap his finger twice on the desk. *"That's"* where the trail ends, and where I believe it begins."

Whit brought to mind what little he knew about his neighbor, Mirabelle's uncle. Lord Eppersly had been a friend of sorts to his father. The closeness of their estates and their mutual love of the hunt had thrown the two together by chance, and their love of drink had made irrelevant the fact that they had very little else in common.

Dashing, charming, and selfish to the core, Whit's father had been a man to relish the attention of the beau monde and demimonde alike. He'd lived for the next ball, the next house party, the next scandal.

Lord Eppersly, on the other hand, was too noticeably unattractive, too slow of mind and tongue, and too low in title and wealth to be of interest to the *ton*. The indifference, as far as Whit could tell, was reciprocal. The man's sole attempt at social interaction these days was centered on a select group of friends who joined him at his estate once or twice a year. If one was to believe the gossip, the men did little but eat, drink, and lie badly about their prowess in the hunt.

Whit knew the staff whispered that Lord Eppersly had become so remarkably fat and lazy in recent years that he no longer truly hunted, preferring instead to sit in a sturdy overstuffed chair on the back lawn and shoot haphazardly at any unfortunate beasts that wandered within range.

He set the note down. "You can't possibly be serious."

William frowned at him. "I assure you, I am. I'm told the man's a living testament to overindulgence."

"In food and drink," Whit scoffed. "Not crime."

"You've an explanation for why he should have a counterfeit note, I take it?"

"I suspect he obtained it the same way as Mr. Maver and Lord Osborn."

"Find the proof. I want you to attend his hunting party—" William held up a hand to forestall an argument. "The baron isn't a man who puts store in being helpful. Innocent or not, any information we acquire from him will have to be obtained with subtlety."

"Subterfuge."

William shrugged. "As you like. Have you developed a sudden aversion for it?"

"No, but I wonder about its necessity in this case. He may not care to be asked the questions, but if it means clearing him of a crime, I can't imagine he'd refuse to answer."

"He didn't. Says he got the note from someone else—"

"Well, there you go." Whit waved his hand. "Just what I—"

"He claims that someone was the Duke of Rockeforte."

He dropped his hand. "Ah."

"He's either an idiot—which leaves the question as to how he could run a counterfeiting operation—or he's simply confused. I want you to find out which. The hunting party starts at the end of the week."

"I've not been invited. I can't very well just pop over . . ." He trailed off at the sight of an envelope bearing the seal of Baron Eppersly. "How the devil did you come by that?"

"I pilfered it from your mail," William admitted without a hint of shame. "It would appear the good baron is a creature of habit, or his secretary is. Either way, he's sent the same invitations to the same people for the last decade."

"It's an invitation for my father."

"It's an invitation," William said slowly, "For the Earl of Thurston."

"Eppersly is likely to argue the point."

"I doubt it. Too much bother for him. But send an acceptance, and we'll see."

Whit nodded. "What of Mirabelle?"

"What of her?"

"She's expected at her uncle's tomorrow," he explained, though he was certain William was aware of it.

"So she is."

"She can't go. She can't—"

"Of course she can," William argued. "And she will. If you arrive, and she doesn't, it will cause undo suspicion."

"The baron will already be suspicious."

"But not unduly so."

"William—"

"I'm not taking chances with this mission. If you can't investigate and keep an eye on the girl at the same time, I'll find someone who can."

The insult stung. "I can bloody well keep her safe."

"Excellent. Now, if you don't mind, I'm for bed. I'm leaving early for London tomorrow. Be back in a day or two."

"Safe journey," Whit grumbled, though at the moment, the vision of William taking a header off his horse wasn't an entirely unwelcome one. In fact, it was pleasant enough to indulge in a moment longer before getting up to blow out the candles and leave.

He'd have to find a way to explain his acceptance of the baron's invitation to his family, and to Mirabelle, but tomorrow morning would be early enough for that, he decided as he closed and locked the study door behind him. He didn't expect any of them to be up at this time of night.

"Good evening, Whittaker."

He straightened, slowly, and he turned, very slowly—hoping, with every heartbeat that passed, that he had imagined Mirabelle's cool voice in his right ear. Praying that his overtired brain was merely playing tricks on him and by the time he finished turning around, it would have righted itself, and the hallway would be empty. He wasn't all that tired, actually, but a man could hope.

Fruitlessly, it seemed, because there she was—standing half in and half out of the doorway one room over with her arms crossed against her chest and her dark eyes glowering.

He swore ripely and reached for her elbow, but she

dodged his grasp and stepped back into the room of her own accord.

"How long have you been sitting in here?" he demanded after following her in and shutting and locking the door behind him. "And not a word about the shut door. I'll slip out the window if need be."

"Give me the key to the door first," she insisted.

Impatient, he dug the key out from where he'd shoved it in his pocket, and held it out to her. "There, now answer my question. How long have—?"

"Long enough," she interrupted as she snatched the key, "to come to the realization that both you and William Fletcher are cracked."

Though he hated repeating himself, he swore again. "You're to forget what you heard. Do you understand? You're to forget every word—"

"Stark, raving mad."

He leaned down until they were nearly nose to nose. "Every. Last. Word."

"No." She said it quietly, but with a determination that made his stomach clutch even as his temper rose.

"You'll be reasonable about this, imp—"

*"Reasonable?"* She laughed derisively. "You've accused my uncle of engaging in counterfeiting and then you have the audacity to begin a lecture on being reasonable? For God's sake, Whit, you know very well he's had nothing to do with this. He has neither the skill nor the connections, nor the intelligence to acquire either."

"If that is the case, you may rest assured I shall find the proof of his innocence."

She twisted her lips. "And yet, somehow, your words leave me feeling neither rested nor assured."

"Mirabelle—"

"I'll deal with this myself."

He reared back. "I beg your pardon?"

"I'll not have you sticking your nose in my family's affairs. Stay here at Haldon. This is my problem, and I'll handle it."

He folded his arms across his chest. "And just how do you propose to go about handling it?"

"Same as you, I imagine," she replied as if the answer was obvious. "I'll find the proof of his innocence, or the lack of proof of his guilt, as is more likely to be the case."

"You wouldn't know what to look for or even where to look for it."

"And you would, I suppose? Are you such an expert, then?"

"I've some experience with these matters, yes."

"And why is that?" she asked softly. She tilted her head to the side and looked at him through suspicious chocolate eyes. "How is it Mr. William Fletcher has private knowledge of my uncle's affairs, and why has he asked you to investigate the matter?"

He reached out to grip her chin in his hand. He tilted it straight again. "*That* is none of your concern."

"You can't command away my memory of tonight's conversation, Whit."

"No, but I can influence your response." His hand drifted to brush the lightest of touches along her cheek. "And I could replace it with other, more interesting, memories."

She knocked his hand away, but not before he saw the flash of heat in her eyes. "That's insulting to both of us."

"It wasn't intended to be," he said honestly. He wasn't interested in insulting, he was interested in extracting her from this mess. "I can't let you have your way in this, Mirabelle."

"You needn't let me have anything. My presence at my uncle's party is required regardless of your feelings, and there's no point in the both of us sneaking about. There's no reason for any of this. My uncle a counterfeiter? It's absurd. Your mother would agree with me, like as not. She'd . . ." She stopped in her rant to glare at him. "What are you going to tell her? She'd never believe you've a sudden itch to better know your neighbor."

"I'll tell her that you've invited me along."

"And not her?" she asked with a derisive laugh. "Or Kate or Evie—?"

"To a hunting party?"

"It's no more ridiculous than my inviting you. It's not *my* party, is it?"

"I know how to concoct a believable story when need be," he informed her.

"You know how to lie, you mean," she corrected. "Are you in the habit of deceiving your mother about these sorts of things?"

"I am in the habit of keeping her separate from business that need not concern her."

"As you would me."

He inclined his head in acknowledgement. "Yes."

"One could argue that as your mother, anything you do concerns her, and I can certainly argue that a plan to spy on a member of my family concerns me."

"It does concern you," he said gently. "I'm not attempting to dismiss what a charge of counterfeiting would mean for you. The damage it could cause the family name."

She blanched, but when he stepped forward with the intent to comfort, she shook her head and changed the subject. "It will never work. Your mother isn't going to believe for a second I invited you to my uncle's hunting party, and my uncle isn't going to believe you've taken it into your head to suddenly become neighborly."

"As I said, I'll handle it."

"It makes more sense for you to stay here and let me—"

"To you perhaps." He cocked his head at her. "Do you know what I think?"

"No," she ground out, "but I know how rarely and how poorly. It's something of a biannual event for you, isn't it?"

"In a good year," he responded, unwilling to let the argument slip into the old pattern of traded insults. "I think you're hiding something."

"Are you accusing *me* of being a counterfeiter now?" she scoffed.

"You know better than that. Why don't you want me to go, imp?"

"Because it's none of your affair," she snapped quickly.

"It's more than that," he said softly. "You haven't mentioned a single word on your uncle's behalf except to say he's incapable of being a criminal. Not a word about his honor."

"I'm not fond of my uncle, it's no secret. He is my family, however, and it's my place, not yours, to clear his name." She spoke assertively, but her eyes darted away from his, and that telltale sign had his own eyes narrowing in suspicion.

"It's his place," he corrected, watching her carefully. "Your hands are shaking."

"I'm angry."

"Your hands fist when you're angry," he countered. "I should know." He brought his gaze up to study her face. "You're more than a little pale, as well."

"I had too much pudding at dinner."

He chose to ignore that preposterous excuse entirely. He looked at her instead, long and hard, and what he saw made his chest hurt. "There's fear in your eyes," he whispered. Without thought, he reached out to grip her shoulders. "What's scared you, imp?"

"Nothing," she answered with a lift of her chin. "I'm not afraid."

"Tell me what's the matter. I'll—"

She knocked his hands away for the second time. "You'll what?" she snapped. "Agree to leave my uncle alone?"

"I can't do that."

"And there's nothing I can say to change your mind?"

He shook his head. "I'm sorry."

She jerked her head once in a nod and handed him back the key. "Then we are at an impasse. I'd like you to go now, please."

"Mirabelle—"

"Go."

He wanted to continue the argument, but reluctantly took the key and let himself out instead. Mirabelle was right—neither of them was willing to give in, and neither was in a position to stop the other from doing what the other pleased.

He stopped in the middle of the hall.

Not in a position to stop her, when what she pleased was to engage in an act of espionage against her own family? What if one of her uncle's guests turned out to be an accomplice and caught Mirabelle poking about where she shouldn't?

*To hell with that.*

He spun around and headed back to the room. She would see reason, damn it—or not—but either way, she would do as she was told. She would do whatever he thought was necessary to keep her safe. He was an earl, for God's sake—that bloody well ought to count for something.

When he entered the room, she was standing at the window with her back to the door. He marched up to her and spoke to the back of her head.

"As this matter involves your safety, I've decided this conversation is not over. It will end when I am satisfied you understand what is at stake here. I have also decided . . ." He trailed off, uneasy suddenly that she hadn't turned around. "Are you listening?"

"No."

He opened his mouth, shut it again at the sound of a sniffle. He took one full step back. "Are you . . . are you *crying?*"

"No." Her response was delivered on a hiccup.

"Dear God, you are." Bewildered, horrified, he stood rooted to the spot, and said the first thing that came to mind. "I sincerely wish you wouldn't."

Even under duress he recognized it was a foolish thing to say, but bloody hell, the imp didn't cry. In all the years he'd known her, he'd never seen her cry. "Mirabelle—"

"Go away."

He was tempted, sorely tempted, to do just that. And it wouldn't be terribly difficult to justify his retreat. A gentleman never pressed his presence on a lady who desired to be left alone. He'd only be acquiescing to her demands if he left. It would be best if he gave her the time to compose herself, then they could work this business out.

But even while his mind whirled with all the reasons he could walk away, he stepped forward and wrapped his arms around her. "Don't . . . imp, don't."

She pulled away from him. He pulled her back. He couldn't stand it.

"I'm sorry, imp. I'm sorry. Please, don't cry."

She stilled against him, but the tears still came. He could hear it in the ragged catches of her breath. He held her, rocking gently, until her breathing smoothed into a steady rhythm.

"Won't you tell me what this is about?" he asked softly, turning her in his arms.

She pulled back to look up at him. "I don't want you to go."

"I know, but I haven't any choice." He wiped a lingering tear from her cheek. "Can't you see—"

"You do have the choice," she cried, pulling out of his arms. "You could stay here. You could let me go alone."

"No," he replied resolutely. "I cannot."

"You won't trust me to see to this myself."

"This has nothing to do with trust." He frowned at her. "Or perhaps a great deal to do with it. Why won't you tell me the reason you're crying?"

"I just did."

"No, not all of it."

She closed her eyes and sighed. "We're right back to where we started."

"We wouldn't have to be, if you'd talk to me."

"And will you talk to me?" she asked with a hint of accusation. "Will you tell me how William knew of this, or why you've experience with counterfeiting, or why—"

"No." He dragged a hand through his hair. "Damn it, I don't want you involved in it. In any of this."

"As I don't want you involved."

"It's entirely different," he snapped.

"No, it's not." She shook her head and moved past him to the door. She paused with her hand on the handle.

"I don't want you to come," she repeatedly quietly. "You won't be welcomed."

The words wounded, deeper than he would have expected or cared to admit, and in a force of habit, he lashed out in return.

"Lack of welcome never discouraged you. Consider it my revenge."

Even as regret had him forming the words of an apology, she nodded once and left.

## ❈ *Seventeen* ❈

*T*here are all kinds of embarrassment—humiliation, mortification, shame—and it occurred to Mirabelle as she made the trip to her uncle's house that she was destined to experience each and every one in the course of a single month. First the fall down the hill, then being tormented by a thirteen-year-old, crying in front of Whit, and now the worst, his visit to her uncle's home.

She'd rather fall off a dozen hills and be set upon by an entire tribe of infantile monsters when she reached the bottom than have any member of the Cole family witness how her uncle lived—and how she lived when forced to be under his roof.

There had always been rumors of her uncle's behavior—whispers of the reclusive baron's fractious nature and fondness for drink—but eccentricity from the titled was tolerated, and his secluded lifestyle kept the full extent of his sins from becoming public knowledge. His reputation—and hers by association—remained essentially intact.

What would Whit do once he learned the truth—that her only living relation was a dissolute scoundrel? Not a counterfeiter, mind you. That absurd piece of business could be cleared up. The remainder of her uncle's offenses, however, could not be denied.

She remembered the time he'd paid for several prostitutes to visit from London. And the memorable dinner at which Mr. Latimer had jokingly offered the baron twenty pounds to take her off his hands. Mr. Hartsinger, overseer of the nearby asylum, St. Brigit's, had then not so jokingly upped the bid to thirty.

In the eyes of many, both occurrences would be enough to ruin her.

If Whit found out . . . Her heart stammered painfully at the thought.

Whit had worked so hard to rebuild his family's good standing in society, and an association with a man like her uncle, or a ruined woman, could undo much of the progress he'd made. Would he distance himself and the rest of the Cole family from her?

It might not be fair that a person be judged by the actions of their relatives, but it was the way of the *ton*. Whit knew that well enough. It had been the actions of his own relatives, after all, that had so damaged the Cole name initially.

And now he would see. He would know. He would *judge*.

And there wasn't a single blasted thing she could do about it.

She had spent the whole of the night frantically trying to find a way out of the situation, but nothing short of running off with the gypsies—or bribing the gypsies to run off with Whit—had occurred to her. The best she could do was to arrive early and attempt to elevate at least some small portion of the house to habitable. With any luck, Whit would be too preoccupied to care overmuch about the condition of the old manor. With an enormous amount of luck, Whit's presence might induce her uncle and his guests to restrict their revelry to the merely embarrassing, rather than the unforgivable.

The idea that they might behave well was nearly laughable. Nearly.

Her pride, she knew, was going to suffer tremendously. She could accept that or, at the very least, learn to accept it.

So long as she wasn't banned from Haldon.

She pressed the back of a shaking hand across trembling lips and wished, as she had wished for years, that her mother and father had cared enough to will her into the care of someone like the Coles.

She'd been seven years old when her parents had died in an outbreak of influenza. In life, they had been indifferent toward their only daughter, choosing to have her raised the *ton* way, by a series of servants.

In death, that indifference proved cruel. They'd warded her to an uncle they barely knew. But the man was a baron, and apparently her mother and father had felt that the title was all the character reference required.

Upon arrival at her uncle's, she had been swiftly relegated to an out-of-the-way room in the back of the house, assigned a disinterested governess, and otherwise ignored by the baron and his staff alike.

After two months of such treatment, Mirabelle had taken it upon herself to seek out her uncle and demand a room with a properly functioning fireplace, regular meals, and, if it wasn't too much to ask, a mattress with its insides on the inside. She was, after all, the daughter of a gentleman and a member of the baron's family.

Her uncle had responded with the back of his hand, an action that had so shocked Mirabelle she had been rendered mute and unable to move. For a moment her head had felt curiously detached from her body and she numbly wondered if she would be forced to spend the remainder of her life on the floor of her uncle's study. But he had quickly dispelled that notion by coming around the desk, grabbing her arm and dragging her forcibly out the study's door. Only when it appeared as if he might follow her, did Mirabelle regain her senses and bolt—down the hall, out the front door, and into the woods on the eastern side of the estate's property.

She had run until she could no longer feel her legs. Until she thought her lungs and heart might burst inside her chest. Until she had turned a corner, lost her footing and tumbled straight down a hill, and into the arms of lovely lady in a crisp white dress that smelled of starch and mint.

The woman had held Mirabelle until the tears stopped. She had checked her over for any serious injuries and admonished her gently for running about the countryside and rolling down hills like a wild animal. Now she would have a bruised eye to show for it, silly child.

Then she had introduced herself as Mrs. Brinkly, governess to young Lady Kate—a small, blonde-haired sprite of a girl who had stepped forward and shyly offered Mirabelle the remains of a sticky bun—more sticky than bun at this point—encased in her little fingers. Mirabelle had accepted the treat gratefully and the silent invitation for friendship that came with it.

Such was her introduction to the Cole family. A kind twist of fate that had made all the difference.

Their estate of Haldon sat not two miles from her uncle's home. Upon hearing that their neighbor had been made guardian to an orphaned child, Lady Thurston had groaned in disgust at the absurdity of the inebriated baron raising a young girl. She immediately saw to it that Mirabelle received an open invitation to Haldon Hall. While visiting, Mirabelle was properly fed, clothed, and educated. The countess had even insisted that Mirabelle accompany the family to London for a come out, and subsequent Seasons.

She'd spent the majority of her childhood in the company of the Coles, and to Mirabelle, Haldon and its inhabitants were straight out of a fairy tale.

But if Haldon had been a shining castle filled with knights and fair maidens, her uncle's home had been a dungeon complete with ogre.

It still was, she thought with a grimace as the stone building came into view around a curve in the road. And it was every bit as glum and unwelcoming as Haldon was bright and gracious. With its pillared front entrance, two rows of windows and multiple chimneys, the old stone building may have carried the hallmarks of respectable—if limited—affluence from a distance, but one needed only to draw a little closer to discover the truth. It was dark, dank, and in disrepair. The pillars were buckling, the windows were cracked, and the chimneys were crumbling.

There were no gardens to speak of, just the moldering ruins of an old half wall and gardener's cottage out back. Nary so much as an herb patch was to be found on the grounds. Her uncle didn't care for vegetables, and she suspected he had lost his sense of taste to spirits some time ago. It would explain why he complained routinely to the kitchen of the lack of food, but never of the food's near inedible nature. Quantity surpassed quality in importance as far as he was concerned.

With her valise in hand, she hopped down from the carriage. She'd brought only two gowns with her from Haldon, and those only because Whit was coming. She'd have made do with the very old dresses she kept at her uncle's home otherwise.

"Shall I carry that for you, miss?"

She smiled and shook her head at the waiting footman. She'd never let any of the staff enter her uncle's home. "Thank you, but no. You should return. I'm certain Lady Thurston could use your help with all the guests packing and leaving today."

"Very good, miss."

She watched the footmen swing lightly back onto the carriage before it rolled away. Then, straightening her shoulders she turned and headed toward the house.

An enormous dog—the sort that looked as if it might fit a person's entire arm in its mouth—was chained at the side of the front steps. A massive beast of questionable lineage, it was fond of snapping at women's skirts and men's ankles as they hurried past, (though whether its purpose was to discourage unwelcome guests or *all* guests was something Mirabelle had never been able to work out.) It had always put her to mind of Cerberus guarding the gates to hell.

Christian, the stable hand and her only friend at the house, had always found this immensely funny. He got along famously with the beast and often took it on long walks in the fields.

Mirabelle had attempted to befriend it as well, bringing it scraps and choice bones from the kitchen. But nothing seemed to work.

As she climbed the steps, the dog lunged and snapped, missing her by a good two feet, but making her jump all the same.

"Ungrateful wretch," she muttered as she pushed open the front doors and made a mental note to have Christian put the animal elsewhere while she was in residence.

She wasn't surprised to find no one available in the foyer or any of the immediate surrounding rooms to help her with her luggage. Her uncle's staff was every bit as disinterested in their work as the Haldon staff was proud of theirs.

She'd heard one or two of Benton's more democratic residents refer to Baron Eppersly as "a great champion of the downtrodden." In truth, her uncle's propensity for employing the old, the infirm and—primarily—the disreputable, had nothing to do with generosity and everything to do with cold calculation. A body in dire need of food and shelter was unlikely to voice complaint over the trifling matters of irregular pay and a few careless swats of a beefy hand.

Fear, however, was a long way from gratitude, and desperation hardly qualified as a skill. As a result, most of the skeletal staff at the house spent the majority of their time either begrudgingly seeing to the baron's demands or doing nothing at all.

"There she is!"

Mirabelle jumped at the deep bellow that echoed from the top of the stairs, but as it was one of the few voices she didn't fear at her uncle's home, she turned to greet its source with a smile.

On any other occasion, Mirabelle might have made a concerted effort to avoid the likes of Mr. Cunningham. The man was loud, coarse, and outrageously crude. He also, for reasons that eluded her, invariably smelled overwhelmingly of vinegar and bad cabbage.

And wasn't it a sad statement of her predicament, she thought, that she should be relieved to see him now? But then, in comparison to the rest of the guests, Mr. Cunningham was very nearly good company. For all his repulsive habits, he was a good-natured sort. She might have even gone so far as to call him jolly. He'd never been one to care-lessly toss cruel insults in her direction, and he'd always had the manners to at least keep his hands to himself.

"Mirabelle, my girl," he bellowed, and as always, ignored the fact that she had long ago reached an age where it was no longer appropriate for him to use her given name. "Good to see you! Good to see you!"

As the sound and smell of him drew closer, she took an instinctive step back, and wondered, not for the first time, why anyone who spoke with enough volume to wake the dead would find it necessary to always repeat himself.

"It's good to see you as well, Mr. Cunningham. Are you headed out?"

"No, no. Not feeling quite the thing, you know. Not quite the thing."

"I'm sorry to hear of it," she said with at least some level of sincerity. "Nothing too serious, I hope?"

"Not at all. Not at all. Touch of the ague, I think. Deuced time to come down with it."

"It is," she replied, because she felt as if she ought to say something. "Can I do anything for you?"

"Well, since you asked, my girl—would you send some-one up with a bit of broth? I rang the bell, but no one came. Not a soul!"

She'd have been surprised to learn someone had. The odds of a functioning bell pull outside her uncle's bedcham-ber and study were slim. The odds of a servant troubling themselves to answer a bell that had originated outside her uncle's bedchamber or study were slim to none. And the odds of both events occurring at once were nonexistent.

"I'll see to it, but just the broth? Isn't there anything else you'd like?"

"Well, I wouldn't object to the broth being carried up by the blonde maid with the generous bosom." He brought his hands up to cup in front of his own appreciative chest.

"Wouldn't object a bit. Sight like that would perk any man up, eh?"

His face lit up, and in a way that had Mirabelle taking another step in retreat. She knew that expression.

"Perk a man up! Right up!" He laughed boisterously at his own joke, sending a cabbage-soaked breath in her direction. "Don't you get it, girl?"

"I do," she gasped.

"Not that I'd be able to do much more than stand to attention, mind you," he admitted over a lingering chuckle. "Or that she'd pay one jot of notice if I did, not with the likes of Lord Thurston in residence. I did hear right, didn't I, girl? Thurston will be joining us?"

"Yes. Unless he falls off his horse and breaks his neck on the way over," she added, and with just enough hopefulness to have him chortling.

"I've caught sight of his lordship once or twice at Tattersall's. Deuced good-looking man—the rotter—don't tell me you wouldn't care for a bit of what he could offer."

"Only if the bit is his head, and it's offered on a platter."

"Oh-ho, I don't believe it. Don't believe a word of it. You may be able to fool others, girl, but not me. Known you since you were knee-high, haven't I? Practically an uncle!"

"If only," she murmured. If she had to have an embarrassing uncle, she'd have preferred this one. "I'd wager the baron would trade me for that roan mare you're always bragging about."

"My Gertie? Trade my only child for a mere niece?" He shook his head. "Wouldn't make any sense. Any sense at all. And she throws fillies besides—doubt you'd be as accommodating."

"Sadly, I do lack that particular skill."

"Well, you've the look of a woman who'll bear strong sons, and that's nothing to thumb your nose at. Nothing at all." He leaned forward, squinting his eyes. "Why aren't you married yet? Must be nearing twenty by now."

She was stunned into silence for a moment before breaking into laughter.

"Bless you, Uncle Cunningham."

She left him to discover if a certain blonde maid wouldn't mind a bit of harmless ogling.

As it happened, the maid in question was only too delighted at the chance to be ogled, and Mirabelle wondered if the pert young woman would be ending the evening a bauble or a few coins wealthier. Not her concern, she told herself, and hardly the most scandalous thing to have happened at a house party—particularly when said party was hosted by her uncle. She put it aside and focused on digging up a few maids and footmen to clean and air out a room for their last-minute guest, Lord Thurston.

They finished just in time. She was coming down the steps, her arms full of the old linens, and a grumbling maid trailing behind her, when a knock sounded at the front door. Since the maid didn't offer to answer the summons, Mirabelle handed over her burden and instructions to see the linens laundered—which she rather doubted would happen—and saw to the door herself.

Though she'd spent the whole of the morning preparing for his arrival, seeing Whit standing on the steps of her uncle's home made her heart jump painfully. Feeling near to panic, she envisioned slamming the door and locking it behind her. If she'd thought for a moment that such an act might induce him to leave, she would have done it without compunction. But he'd only find another way in. Pity Christian had already removed the dog. That might have at least slowed him down.

Steeling herself for what was to come, she lifted her chin and squared her shoulders. "Whittaker."

He frowned at her. "Why are you opening the door?"

"Because I was here. Of course, if I'd known it was you, I wouldn't have bothered."

She wanted to be angry. She *was* angry, but over and beyond that she was terribly, terribly afraid. Because nothing covers fear quite so well as anger, she focused on that.

She held the door open and stepped aside. "Are you coming in or not?"

He stayed where he was, his blue eyes searching. "Is that the way it's to be, then?"

"If you insist of going through with your ridiculous mission."

*Say no. Please, please, please say you've changed your mind.*

"Very well." He stepped around her. "Then play the proper hostess, won't you, darling, and have someone see to my bags?"

She closed the door behind him. "It'd be my pleasure. I know just the hole—very deep, very muddy."

"Who is it, girl?" The baron's booming voice echoed down the hall from his study.

She couldn't help but wince at his appalling manners, but she absolutely refused to acknowledge Whit's questioning expression. Denial was one of the last tactics available to her, and she'd every intention of putting it to good use.

"It's Lord Thurston, Uncle!"

"You bring a fart catcher, Thurston?"

Whit's only reaction was a raised eyebrow. "I beg your pardon?"

"He means a valet," she muttered and felt the heat of embarrassment flood her cheeks. It might be mortifying, she reminded herself, but it wasn't catastrophic. Yet.

"Yes, I know what he means." Whit turned toward Eppersly's voice. "As it happens, I come unattended!"

"Good! No room!"

"I'm sure whatever arrangements can be made will be more than adequate."

"Good!" There was a brief flash of thinning brown hair in the doorway. "Show him up, girl! What's the matter with you?"

"Is he always so charming?" Whit inquired when her uncle's head had once again disappeared into the study.

"You can hardly blame him, sneaking your way in as you have." It needled, tremendously, to speak in defense of her uncle, but it was easier than apologizing for him.

"He could have said no," Whit pointed out. "I sent an acceptance last night, and the estates aren't more than five minutes' ride from each other."

She didn't have a single believable rebuttal to that statement, so she ignored it instead and headed up the stairs. "You can carry your own luggage or you can wait for it. The staff is busy with other things at the moment."

He hefted his bag and caught up with her in the middle of the staircase. "Is the house short of staff, then?"

"Ask my uncle," she suggested, knowing full well he couldn't do so without insulting the baron.

She led him to a room at the very back of the hall. It was separated from the other guests by a storage room and two linen closets, but it was the best the house had to offer, its amenities disdained by the other guests only because they found the extra walk disagreeable. She opened the door and stepped inside, pleased to find the worst of the mildew smell had aired out.

"The doors there lead to a private balcony." One that she was relatively certain wouldn't collapse under his weight. "There's a bureau there for your things." She'd made certain all the drawers opened first. "We're having some difficulties with the bell pulls, I'm afraid. If you need something"—Get it yourself, she thought—"you'll have to hunt up a maid or footman."

"Mirabelle—" He reached for her, but she sidestepped his grasp and opened the door.

"Dinner is served at half past eight," she informed him, and left with the fondest wish that he'd remain in his room for the remainder of the party. Or at least until dinner.

# Eighteen

Mirabelle spent the remainder of the day alternating between putting fires out in the kitchen—mostly figuratively speaking, but with one small literal exception—and answering an endless line of summons from her uncle.

"Fetch me the case of port from the cellar. I don't want those thieving excuses for footmen going anywhere near it alone."

"Mr. Hartsinger likes fresh linen in his room. See it's done before he arrives."

"Change your gown. You're a disgrace."

"Why aren't you welcoming my guests, girl? Think I brought you home to sit on your fat arse all day?"

The fact that the baron felt qualified to be the judge of anyone else's physical appearance had never failed to astonish her. He was the single most corpulent individual of her acquaintance. The man was, in a word, *round*—not oblong, not a bit thicker 'round the middle and tapered at the ends. No, when his arms were at his sides, he made a nearly perfect circle, with only the slight protrusions that were his head and feet to throw off the illusion.

The head itself—and that was how she thought of it, as "the head"—was large and rapidly becoming hairless, and his nose was smashed flat against his face so that he looked like a ball with beady blue eyes and very fat lips. His feet were short and so small that she always had the impression—and the hope—they might give out under his weight and send him toppling over at any moment.

Sadly, that much desired event had yet to occur, and Mirabelle could only console herself with the knowledge that her obnoxious and inconveniently well-coordinated uncle kept her busy enough to leave little time for worrying over the additional guest in the house.

Mostly.

It helped that all the guests appeared to be occupied in their rooms at present—unpacking, she supposed, or writing missives to wives and sweethearts, informing them of their safe arrival. Mirabelle suspected there'd be a wife or two disappointed with the news.

But there would be no separating Whit from the others at dinner—not that she couldn't try. She sent a maid with an offer to have his meal brought to his room and when that failed, she sent maids with the offer to bring meals to every other member of the house. Only Mr. Cunningham agreed to the arrangement.

So in a matter of hours, Mirabelle found herself sitting at the dinner table with some of the most disgusting human beings in England . . . and Whit.

Dinners at Baron Eppersly's house were casual affairs. Very, very casual affairs.

So casual, in fact, that one might even go so far as to call them slovenly. Mirabelle personally felt they resembled nothing quite so much as a voracious pack of slobbering hyenas scrambling over dead prey. She'd never actually seen a hyena, mind you, but she'd read of them in books, and she rather thought the group fit the description.

Beyond the revolting sight of grown men eating without the slightest regard to etiquette—for heaven's sake, why did her uncle insist on the good silver if he was determined to use his fingers as fork, spoon, and knife?—Mirabelle also dreaded the start of dinner because it appeared to be a silent signal for the men to begin drinking in earnest.

The wine flowed in, and manners flowed out with equal measure. Guests who hadn't paid her the slightest bit of attention earlier suddenly found her to be a fascinating topic of conversation. Or so it had always been in the past.

They left her alone for the first hour that night. The addition of Lord Thurston to their ranks seemed to be enough to keep them occupied. Initially, they plied him with questions full of suspicion.

"What brings you to our humble gathering?" Mr. Hartsinger asked.

"Surprised you found the time—between your mama's fine house parties and your seat in the House of Lords," Mr. Waterson commented.

"Didn't I hear you once mention to Lady Killory that indulgence in spirits is the sign of a weak mind?" Mr. Harris inquired.

But Whit answered them all with wit and humor. "I'm here for the very reasons you mentioned, Mr. Waterson. I required an excuse to get away from the simpering women at staid house parties, not to mention the simpering women in the House of Lords. And you'd have made the comment too, Mr. Harris, if it'd been you the lady was breathing sherry on. Best way to get rid of her."

And soon enough, the conversation had gone from an interrogation, to a rollicking round of reminiscing about the late Lord Thurston and how his son might live up to the old man yet.

Mirabelle tried to make herself smaller in her chair. If she could only get through the meal without being noticed, without being called on to speak, she'd still have to suffer the shame of having Whit see her uncle and his friends in their limited dining glory, but she wouldn't have to actually—

"Quit slouching girl!" her uncle snapped.

*Blast.*

"Ugly enough as it is," he added. "No need to bring bad posture into the bargain."

*Damn.*

"Leave off the girl, Eppersly," someone said, she wasn't about to look up to discover who. "Not so bad looking I wouldn't have a go at her!"

*Oh. Bloody. Hell.*

She couldn't look at Whit. She couldn't have faced him now if her life depended on it. Was he laughing? She couldn't hear him laughing, but she could hardly make anything out over the cacophony of snorting her uncle called a laugh. Was Whit angry? Offended? Shocked? She wished she had the nerve to find out.

"What say you, Thurston?" one of the guests called. "You ever had a piece of—"

She threw herself into a vicious fit of coughing. The force of it scratched her throat and made her eyes water, but she didn't care. If the man finished that question, she wouldn't die of humiliation on the spot, but she'd want to.

The baron grunted and snapped greasy fingers at a footman. "You. You there."

"Simmons, sir."

"Did I ask for your name?" he demanded, before jabbing a finger at Mirabelle. "Idiot. Just pound the chit's back for Christ's sake."

"Pound the . . . ?"

"Go on, man!"

Mirabelle took a gulping breath and held the footman off with a hand and a wan smile. "That won't be necessary, Simmons, thank you."

Simmons looked to the baron for confirmation. The baron gave one disinterested shrug and went back to his meal.

"Excuse me," she mumbled, and fled. It was possible

she'd be berated for the early departure tomorrow, but it was equally possible her uncle had already imbibed enough to not care, or forget entirely. And she was certain she couldn't spend another second in that room. She raced to her own room, slammed the door shut, and locked it.

She had no idea how long she simply stood where she was, shaking and panting raggedly. Was that it, then? Would she be ruined because of one careless comment? When she felt her knees begin to buckle, she snapped herself back, forcing aside panic for reason. The guest had indicated that, given the chance, he *would* have a go at her, not that he ever *had*. It was a small but significant difference. One comment was cruel and mortifying, the other could irrevocably ruin her name. As it was, her reputation was merely scratched a bit. As was her pride. And her heart—Whit might not have laughed at the jest, but he hadn't defended her either.

"Well bugger him," she snapped to no one and refused to feel the least guilty for using such a vulgar invective. She'd heard her uncle use it a hundred times. "Bugger all of them."

As soon as was humanly possible, she'd begin searching for the proof of her uncle's innocence as a counterfeiter. As soon as she had it, Whit could leave. If she was still welcome at Haldon after that, she'd simply tuck this party away as a tremendously embarrassing memory. If not . . . well . . .

"Bugger it," was the best she could come up with.

It was another two hours before she gained the courage to again leave her bedroom. The others wouldn't be in bed yet, but there was always the question of whether they had managed to move themselves into her uncle's study or if they had drunk so much so quickly that they found it inconvenient to leave the dining room. She hoped for the latter. Her uncle sometimes fell asleep in whichever chair he was currently occupying and if the chair happened to be in the study, it would mean putting off the snooping she had planned in that room for a later night. As she was immensely anxious about snooping in her uncle's sanctuary, she found the idea of delaying it distinctly unappealing. Better to get it over and done with than to worry about it for another day.

She followed the sound of braying laughter to the dining room door. That was it then, she decided. Her uncle would either sleep there or have a pair of unfortunate footmen haul him to his room. But he wouldn't be back in his study this night.

She turned to leave, then stopped and turned back again, curiosity getting the better of her.

Was Whit still in there?

She peaked through the crack of the door, and discovered that yes, he was—the blighter.

For a man who wasn't there to enjoy himself, he was doing a suspiciously realistic impression of a dedicated reveler. He was drunk, she noted with disgust, and while that may have been unavoidable if he wanted to gain the group's trust and approval, she was certain he needn't look so bloody happy about it.

He was slouched, grinning rather stupidly, in an ancient highback chair with his cravat gone and his coat unbuttoned. He held both a wine bottle and the rapt attention of several men as he slurred out the tale of the man-eating boar he'd hunted in France. Nearly lost his life to the beast, she heard him say, and she wondered idly if she'd lose her dinner. If there was an ounce of truth in that story, she'd eat her blue chemise.

It was better that he have a fine time of it, she reminded herself. She could have found him sitting apart, watching the baron with disgust and contempt . . . and wondering how he might go about removing the Cole family from everything, and everyone, associated with Baron Eppersly.

Swallowing an irritated grunt, she turned back to her room. It wouldn't be more than another hour before they began to pass out, but she'd wait two just to be safe.

She waited three hours with the idea that, in this house, it was better to be very safe than very wrong.

She left her room with a plan of sorts in mind. She'd try the door to the study first, and if it proved locked, she'd make a trip around the side of the house to see if she couldn't shimmy up to the window. If she couldn't—and having no shimmying experience to speak off, there was a very good chance that would be the case—or the window was locked as well, she'd simply have to find a way into the study during the day. The very idea of such an attempt had her stomach twisting into knots. It'd be so much easier to be caught during the day, and if her uncle found out she'd been snooping about his study, he'd . . .

*Don't think about it. Don't think about it right now.*

She crept down the steps, taking care to skip the boards that creaked. In all probability, she could stomp down the narrow passage with no more stealth than a herd of elephants and no one would be the wiser. The guests had fallen asleep too drunk, and the servants too exhausted to notice, let alone care that someone was moving about in the house. Still, it never paid to take chances in her uncle's home.

To her immense relief, she found the door to the study unlocked. Whether he'd been too drunk to remember to lock it himself, or was simply in the habit of assuming no one would dare enter without invitation, she didn't know. Having made a point over the years of avoiding her uncle's favorite haunt, she'd never before had reason to test the door handle.

Twisting it now, she pushed open the door just enough to allow her to slip inside. She closed the door behind her, then leaned back against it with an enormous sigh.

She'd done it. She was in her uncle's study. She'd actually found the courage.

Remembering that her uncle's study was not a place she generally cared to be, she pushed off from the wall and set her mind to the task at hand.

Like most studies, the room was decorated and furnished for the comfort of a man seeing to his business: dark masculine colors, large oak desk, plush leather chairs. But since her uncle rarely bothered himself with anything as mundane as seeing to business, where there would have been bookcases in other studies, there were hunting trophies in this one.

Bucks, does, foxes, and birds of every variety were stuffed and mounted along the walls like a macabre parade of disembodied heads. Mirabelle tried to ignore them as she lit a pair of candles on the desk, but there were so many. She felt a lick of nerves and had the irrational image of accusing glass eyes glaring at her back.

She flipped through a pile of papers and tried to not let the fact that Whit had been right—she hadn't the least idea of what she was looking for—discourage her. She was so caught up in not paying attention to her nagging doubts, and not paying attention to the gruesome room around her, that she failed to notice the footsteps in the hall until they were nearly at the door.

She whirled, stunned as the footsteps came to a stop.

Dear Lord, she hadn't a key to lock the door.

Near to panicking, she grabbed a hideous brown vase off the mantel and positioned herself behind the door just in time. It opened slowly and quietly.

She lifted the vase. She'd knock whoever it was over the head and hope it rendered them unconscious, or at least stunned enough for her to make her escape without being seen.

A foot appeared. With a prayer that she had the timing right, she stepped forward to bring the vase down.

She caught a brief glimpse of light brown hair and blue eyes before Whit's hand lashed out to grasp the vase a moment before it connected with his head.

"I don't think that will be necessary."

"Whit." She spoke in what she thought might have been a whisper, but it was a bit difficult to say, really, with her blood rushing in her ears.

Smiling grimly, he released the vase and turned to close the door. "Scared you a bit, did I?"

"I knew it was you," she sniffed, setting down her impromptu weapon.

"Then why the vase?"

"As I said," she drawled, "I knew it was you."

"Arrogant little thing for one snooping about in the middle of the night."

"No more than you. I thought you were drunk."

He walked to the desk chair and settled himself comfortably, as if, she thought with annoyance, he was in the habit of breaking into other men's studies and making himself at home.

"You thought wrong," he informed her.

She fisted her hands on her hips. "Well if you must be here, make an attempt at being useful, for once, and search the desk drawers."

"Already done."

"I . . . you *are* drunk."

"Not in the least. I'm just a good deal faster than you. I searched the room as soon as the others took themselves off to bed. That was well over an hour ago." He leaned back in the chair and gave her a patronizing smile, one that made her fingers itch to pick the vase back up. "You'll need to be a bit quicker, imp, if you want to participate in this little game."

"This isn't a game." Suspicious, she narrowed her eyes at him. "What are you doing here, if you've already gone over the study?"

"Looking for you. I went to your room. You weren't there."

"How do I know you aren't trying to trick me into leaving? Maybe this is no more than a ruse to—"

"Bottom drawer on the right holds a half bottle of port, two tattered handkerchiefs, a loaded dueling pistol, and a stack of dusty stationery."

She scowled, hesitated, then stalked over to pull open the drawer. The contents were exactly as he described them.

"Now then," he said, making a point to study his nails. "I believe you owe me an apology."

The vase, she thought, might be out of reach, but the bottle of port was temptingly handy.

"That won't be necessary, either," he said and reached over to slide the drawer closed.

She scowled at him and rose. "I don't suppose you're going to tell me whether you found anything in your search."

"You have my word I'll inform you of anything of note that I find, but as it happens, there was nothing in here."

"Of course there wasn't. There isn't going to be anything anywhere. Why don't you give up on this—"

"I didn't search you out to discuss, yet again, the probability of your uncle's guilt."

She opened her mouth to deliver a scathing retort, but thought better of it. His voice had been clipped, and though his posture remained casual, she could see the tension in his muscles. And there was that telltale clenching of his jaw.

"You're angry with me," she said and resisted the urge to fiddle with the waist of her dress. "I wasn't really aware that it was you when I swung the vase, Whit. And I wouldn't have hit you with the bottle. I'm not a murderess, I'm just . . . occasionally tempted."

"This has nothing to do with the vase or the bottle. But since you asked, yes, I am angry with you. I have, in fact, never been angrier with you in my life."

She considered that, and him, for a moment before coming to a decision. "I don't care."

She headed for the door, but he was out of the chair and grasping her elbow before she could escape.

"You'll answer one question—" he began.

She pulled at her arm. "I'm not one of your servants to be ordered about, nor a member of your family inclined to humor your arrogance. Let me go."

"Not until we've settled this." He leaned down in an obvious attempt to intimidate. "Sit down. Now."

He'd taken that tact in the past, more than once, and Mirabelle could only assume it was an instinctual sort of behavior, because she couldn't remember a single time it had worked for him. She couldn't remember a single time it hadn't backfired spectacularly, actually. And since she'd always had affection for tradition, she gave in to the urge to respond in the way she always had—with claws.

She smiled at him, a sweet, slow spread of her lips.

"I find you, and that order, utterly . . ." She leaned forward until their bodies pressed together, and studiously ignored the hum of need the contact ignited. ". . . completely . . ." she smiled a slow, secret smile. "Resistible."

As a final insult, she lifted a hand to pat at his cheek for the second time in as many days. He quite literally growled— which she found immensely satisfying—and grabbed her before she could step away—which she would have found unnerving if she'd been given the time to think on it. But the next thing she knew, she was spun about, backed up, and crushed against the wall. His hands pinned her wrists against the wood, his breath panted on her cheek as he lowered his head.

She closed her eyes, waiting, wanting.

And, eventually, severely disappointed when it was a hand rather than his lips that clasped over her mouth.

Her eyes flew open. "Mfflg."

"Shh."

She heard it then, the steady fall of footsteps coming down the hall. No, not steady, she realized, uneven.

She slapped his hand away. "It's only Christian," she hissed. "Let me go."

"Christian," Whit's brow furrowed for a moment. "The stable boy?"

"The stable hand," she corrected. "He's a man grown."

He shot her a curious look. "Friends, are you?"

"Yes."

"How friendly?"

She felt the slap of that insult as if it had been his hand. Was that how he saw her now, after the humiliation at dinner? She gave him a mighty shove, which didn't dislodge him much, but tipped his balance just enough for her to slip out of his arms and away. "You're determined to be a complete ass tonight, aren't you?"

He blinked and took a step towards her. "No, Mirabelle, I hadn't meant—"

"I don't bloody care what you meant," she lied. She did care, and his shocked and regretful expression soothed the hurt and temper, but not quite enough to tempt her to continue the conversation.

"Good night, Whit."

She had enough sense to glance into the hall first before darting out and up to her room.

# ❋ Nineteen ❋

Occasionally, the guests at her uncle's parties grew a bit too rambunctious, and Mirabelle had found it expedient during those times to remove herself from the house. She'd had the same room at the back of the building since the first day she'd arrived, and every man who frequented the parties knew where to find it. Most never cared to, but once in a great while, one of them would get randy and drunk enough to imagine himself capable of shouldering down her bolted door, or—worse, as the locks she'd paid a great deal of money to have secretly installed were incredibly sturdy—attempt to talk his way through.

Rather than bother with the fuss of them, she sometimes slipped out her window, down a rain pipe and into the stable. With the help of Christian, she'd made a nice little nest for herself in the hayloft where she could sleep in peace, complete with blankets and pillows. She doubted anyone had ever noticed her absence during the night, and if they had . . . well, they likely wouldn't remember it by the morning.

Perhaps it was cowardly of her to hide from Whit, but she wasn't ready yet to face his questions or his reactions to her answers. Avoidance was no nobler a tactic than denial, but her options, she knew, were limited and dwindling.

Christian was filling water buckets in the stalls when she entered, a task she thought must be difficult for him given his limp, weak arm, and the fact that he went without help. She wanted to offer assistance, but knew it would scratch at his pride.

He set the last bucket down and walked to her slowly. A

stooped man with clothes gone to rags, he would have been a sight to frighten if it wasn't for his quick smile and bright green eyes. The layer of dirt that seemed a permanent feature on his face and bared arms made it impossible to determine his age, but she'd guessed it to be somewhere near five-and-forty.

He'd come to work for her uncle only a few years ago. She'd avoided him at first—as she did all the men of the house, servant or not—until one day he'd found her in the hayloft, hiding, while her uncle ranted and raved over a broken vase in the house. He'd brought her a blanket, sat down next to her, and told her stories of growing up in Ireland. She'd felt safe with him since.

"Wild tonight, are they?" Christian asked as she came in.

"Why do you ask?" she inquired as he came to a stop in front of her. "You were just in the house."

"Aye. And you were in the study. Are you wanting to discuss both, or should we let them be?"

"Let them be," she decided. "I'm too tired for anything else."

"Had a round with Lord Thurston?"

"I'd rather not speak of it . . . He can be such a tremendous ass."

"You've a whole house of arses just now," he pointed out.

"Yes, but I *expected* it of them."

"Ah, he's disappointed you, then," he guessed.

"Yes. No." She threw up her arms. "I don't know."

"Might want to figure that one through, lass."

She sighed and walked toward a rope ladder hanging from the loft. "I'd rather just ignore it for tonight."

"Fair enough."

He held the ladder while she climbed. When she reached the top, she pulled it up after her.

"Have what you need then, lass?"

"Yes, thank you," she called down. "And you?"

"Aye."

She pulled her bedding out from a small box hidden in the hay. She shook out the worst of the dust before spreading out the blanket, tossing down the pillow, and crawling atop her makeshift bed.

In the past, the soft snorts and neighs of the guests' horses combined with the reassuring shuffling of Christian's feet as he moved about the stable had never failed to lull her to sleep. But tonight she lay awake, her eyes open and staring at the wood ceiling above.

What was she going to do? It had only been one day. One day and already her uncle and his friends had humiliated her in front of Whit. And to make matters worse, Whit was clearly angry.

That wasn't anything new, she reminded herself. Whit had been angry with her more often than not in the past. But things had changed—wonderfully, to her way of thinking—at Lady Thurston's house party. They'd become friends, perhaps more, and now . . . and now she was sleeping in a hayloft while Whit was likely standing in his room cursing her name.

She shifted onto her side in an effort to get comfortable.

She could leave, of course. She could let Whit take care of the ridiculous counterfeiting charges. She could tell her uncle to go straight to hell and walk out the door and down the road to Haldon. She was welcome there . . . as a guest. At least until Whit returned and kicked her back out again.

Dear God, where would she go?

If only this business had happened two years from now. She'd have her five thousand pounds and the little cottage at the edge of town it would afford her. She wanted to invite Kate and Evie and Lady Thurston to visit her, to be guests in her home. She wanted her pride for more than just the next two years. She wanted it for a lifetime.

She wanted, she thought ruefully, a great many things.

"We've company coming, lass." Christian's voice cut through her musings like a knife.

"What?" She shot to her knees and scrambled to the edge of the loft in time to see Whit stride through the door. Slowly, carefully, she crouched back down again.

"Christian, isn't it?" Whit inquired.

"Aye."

"I'm looking for Miss Browning."

"Best to be looking in the house this time of night," was Christian's reply.

"And so I have."

"The lady doesn't care to be found, I guess. You'd be Lord Thurston, would you?"

"I would."

"You've a reputation as a gentleman."

"Earned, I hope."

"Might a lowly stable hand ask what you're about, searching out a lady while the house sleeps?"

Whit inclined his head. "I mean her no harm. You have my word."

"She speaks well of you and your family. Speaks of naught else while she's here." He nodded once and jerked a thumb toward Mirabelle. "She's to be found in the loft."

Mirabelle gasped and sat up. "You *traitor.*"

Christian merely shrugged and ambled toward the stable doors. "If you're not wanting him to pester you, keep your ladder where he can't be reaching it."

Whit walked down the aisle until he stood nearly under her.

"Are you going to come down, imp? Or shall I come to you?"

She held up the end of the ladder for him to see. "Unless humanity has been much mistaken, and pigs really can fly, you're out of luck."

"I come to you, then."

He eyed the floor of the loft, several feet above his grasp. Then he took several steps back.

"What are you doing?" she asked warily.

He ignored her. He crouched, got a running start, and leapt up to grab the loft floor at her knees.

She was too stunned to do more than gape as he hauled himself up by his hands until he could throw one elbow over, and then the other. By the time it occurred to her that it would be an easy enough thing to lift up his arms and send him falling to the ground—which happened to be about the time she stopped staring at the play of muscles under his shirt—he was hauling his legs up and the chance was lost.

"I can't believe you did that," she whispered in astonished voice.

"You just saw me, didn't you?"

"Yes, but . . ." She leaned forward to look over the edge. It seemed an awful long ways down. "It must be twelve feet—"

"Ten at the most," he assured her as he settled himself in the hay beside her. "I'm naturally spry. Why are you sleeping in the stable?"

"You're like an enormous spring," she breathed, looking at him again.

"The stable, Mirabelle. Why are you sleeping here?"

She opened her mouth to make another comment on his agility before deciding he'd just ignore it anyway. Settling back against a square bale, she frowned at him.

"If I'd been interested in answering your questions, I would have done so in the study. Besides, you seem to have your own ideas of what I might be doing in the stable . . . with Christian."

"I didn't inquire after your friendship with Christian with the intent to insult you," he said. "I asked with the hope that you would tell me he was someone you trusted. I should like to know you've had someone here you could rely on. It was nothing more than that, I promise."

"Oh. Well." She shifted her seat in the hay, unaccountably annoyed with his explanation. She wasn't in the mood just now to argue with him, but she was certainly in the mood to be angry with him. And being angry with him *now,* allowed for the possibility of an argument later.

"I won't ask for you to accept my apology as of yet," Whit continued, "as I suspect I'll just be asking for it again when we're finished here. There are things I need to know, Mirabelle."

"Whit—"

He reached out to grip her hand and give it a gentle squeeze. "Please. Haven't we come far enough in the last week for you to talk to me?"

Her hand fisted under his, not in anger, but in a kind of fearful agitation. She knew what he wanted to ask. She'd rather let it alone, to pretend they were sitting in the hayloft of a stable somewhere else, for some other reason. She didn't think the desire foolish, she thought it completely understandable . . . and unrealistic.

As much as she might wish otherwise—and she did, badly—avoidance and denial would no longer work. Better to answer his question—or questions as she rather thought would prove to be the case—than to have him draw his own conclusions. And better to have the chance to skew those answers when necessary.

She let go of his hand, pulled her knees up to her chest and wrapped her arms around them. "Ask your question, then."

He paused a moment before speaking. "I want to know why you never saw fit to mention the fact that your uncle is unkind to you."

"My uncle is unkind to near everyone," she evaded.

"He's friendly enough with his guests."

"They're men," she responded with what she hoped would pass for indifference. "Men who live for nothing more than their next kill and the next bottle of spirits. No one else can stand them, so they pack together, do as they please, and agree to keep it amongst themselves."

"A sort of honor among thieves?"

"Among rats," she decided. "And I lack a tail."

That surprised a brief laugh out of him. "Are you always the only woman in attendance?"

"No. Some of the guests have been known to bring . . . other guests."

"I see. And where is your chaperone?"

"This is my uncle's home. A chaperone isn't necessary to preserve my reputation."

"Your reputation is the least of my concerns at the moment."

"At *every* moment if the current situation is any indication."

He ignored that statement. "Are they always as . . . difficult, as they were tonight?"

"No." Sometimes it was much worse. "You're asking a great many questions, Whit."

"I want a great many answers," he replied. "But right now, what I want most is for you to return to Haldon."

The words were like a soothing balm on a burn, and she closed her eyes as a rush of relief and longing swept through her.

She couldn't return yet, not if she wanted her inheritance, but that Whit should offer after today . . . It was her greatest fear put to rest.

Almost.

He'd witnessed her uncle behaving as the obnoxious sot that he was, but Whit hadn't yet seen the absolute swine her uncle could be. And what would happen when he did? She'd be right back where she'd started—terrified, ashamed, wondering.

"Mirabelle?"

She opened her eyes to find him watching her with quiet concern.

It wasn't fair, she thought, to have kept her uncle's behavior a secret from those who could suffer from it—those who had shown her so much kindness.

Better that he should know. Better that she get the whole of it over, once and for all.

She searched for the right words and realized there were none that would suit as well as the blunt truth.

"My uncle is horrible," she admitted. When he failed to respond, she took a deep breath and pressed on. "I'm not speaking in hyperbole, Whit. At his worst, which you've not yet seen, he's truly awful. Five minutes in any respectable drawing room in London and he'd ruin the family name forever."

"I imagine he would."

"The family name," she reiterated. Honestly, how could he not catch on? "*My* name."

"Are you concerned he might take a sudden interest in traveling to London?"

"What? No." She rubbed the palms of her hands against her legs. "I'm trying to point out that he's a liability, which makes me one as well. I should have told you sooner, I know, but—"

"A moment." He held his hand up, his brow furrowed. "You consider yourself a liability."

"Of a sort, yes. You've worked so hard to secure your family's place in society and an association with me could conceivably damage the progress you've made. I know I should have said something before this, but I was . . . afraid . . ."

"Afraid you would no longer be welcome at Haldon," he finished for her.

She nodded.

"I see. I must have told you—" He grimaced and swore. "Hell, dozens of times that I didn't care for your presence at Haldon. Why would this be any different?"

"You said I was unwelcome, not that I wasn't allowed. You poked fun, but never said I wasn't to come."

"And you would have respected my decision in that regard?"

"I'd have adhered to it," she equivocated. "It's your house, your family. I know I should have said something sooner, but—"

"Yes, you should have."

Her stomach, already in knots, fell to her toes. "I know. I'm very sorry. It wasn't right to keep it from you. It's only that I love your family and Haldon, and—"

She broke off when took her chin in his fingers. "You should have, Mirabelle, because I could have long ago put your fears to rest on the matter. Look at me." He gently tugged her chin up until she met his eyes. "You're not responsible for his sins."

Hope bloomed cautiously. "Others would disagree."

And wasn't that the point? What others thought?

"Others would be wrong." He let his fingers spread to cup her cheek. "I value, and cultivate, my family's good standing in the *ton*. But not to the detriment of those I care for. Haldon will never be closed to you because of your uncle. I give you my word."

She closed her eyes again—this time to hold back the tears she felt gathering.

Whit never broke his word.

The weight of the fear she'd been carrying for so long dropped away and she suddenly felt light, almost weightless. And exceedingly tired.

She opened her eyes when his hand withdrew from her cheek.

"Thank you," she whispered.

She noticed his jaw tense at her words, but was in too much of a happy stupor to think on his odd reaction. "I suppose you should be getting back to the house," she whispered.

"In a while. Why don't you lie down for a bit?"

"I'm not tired just yet," she lied. She was more than

ready to fall asleep sitting up, but she wasn't at all comfortable with the idea of sleeping while he just sat there. Heavens, who would be? She was even less comfortable with the idea of him leaving. The stable loft seemed so much more pleasant, warmer, safer for having him in it.

"You needn't sleep," Whit said. "Just lie down."

"While you sit there and stare at me?"

"Would it help if I were to lie down beside you and stare?"

"Is the staring really necessary?"

"I'm afraid so. You're irresistibly sweet to look at when you're sleepy."

"I'm not sleepy," she objected but maneuvered herself to lie down on the blankets. It felt wonderful, absolutely sublime to lay her head down, but she wasn't ready yet to fall asleep.

"Whit?"

"Hmm?"

"I can't go back to Haldon right now. It would compromise your mission if your family were to play a role in defying my uncle's wishes. The baron wants me here—or needs me here, anyway."

"Your parents' will," Whit murmured. "Did they know the sort of man he was when they had it drawn up?"

"I've no idea. I've very little memory of them. They preferred adult company."

"I see."

"I recall my nanny very well, though," she said with a fond smile and a yawn. "Miss McClelland. She was very kind to me. She had the most beautiful bright red hair, and I could never understand why she was always about hiding it under a cap." She snuggled deeper into the hay. "I used to make excuses—transparent ones if memory serves—to go to her room in the evenings so I could watch her brush it out. She'd tell me stories while I sat on her bed."

"I'm glad you have that memory." He brushed a hand down her own hair. "Do you know what happened to her?"

"I searched her out once I was old enough to do so. She took a position with a nice family in Scotland, then retired when the children grew into adults. I considered attempting to begin a correspondence with her but . . ."

"But what?" he prompted.

"Well, it was near to twenty years ago and who knows how many children she had reared before me. She wouldn't remember who I am, like as not."

"I doubt that. A woman isn't likely to forget a child she cared enough about to tell bedtime stories."

"Perhaps." She closed her eyes for moment. Just for a moment, she told herself. "I wonder if she ever—"

"Mirabelle?"

"Yes."

"Go to sleep."

She pried open blurry eyes. "Aren't you going back inside?"

"Later." He brushed a hand down her hair in gentle strokes as her eyes fluttered close again. "Later."

While Mirabelle slept and Whit sat watching Mirabelle sleep, a very drunken gentleman staggered down the hallway to knock on a door. After several moments without receiving an answer, he knocked again, and again, and then turned the handle to peek inside. Discovering he'd gained admission to a broom closet, he snickered and stumbled back to the center of the hall.

It took him two more tries to correctly count the doors between his room and his destination, but eventually he managed to knock on the right door.

He didn't bother, or perhaps simply failed to remember, to wait for an answer this time. He fumbled his way into the room.

"What the bloody hell are you doing here?" a second

drunken voice snapped—slurred really, but he wasn't in a position to notice.

It took his eyes a moment to find the form lying on the bed, and a moment more for his uncooperative feet to find their way to that same bed.

"Come to a decision. Here." He dug through his pockets, which seemed exceedingly deep just then, before finally discovering and producing a folded piece of paper that he held up with a triumphant, "Ha!"

The second man craned his neck and squinted at it. "That it?"

"It is." He tried bobbing his head, but it did terrible things to his vision. He caught at the bedpost to keep from falling over and thrust the paper closer to the prone man. "Just need your signature on the line."

"You're certain? Won't take it back just because you offered while in your cups?"

"Insulting," he huffed. "Made up my mind. I want her."

"Well then, fetch me a pen." The second man snatched up the paper. "You can have her."

It was much later before Whit slipped away from Mirabelle and clambered down the ladder. He tossed the rope back up to the loft before seeking Christian in an empty stall at the end of the stable.

"You'll see to it she's back inside before the others wake?"

"Always have," Christian replied as he tugged on his boots. "Near to dawn now, but they'll not be up till well past noon. You needn't worry."

Needn't worry, Whit thought, and nearly laughed. "You've been a good friend to her."

Christian sent him a hard look. "Aye, well, she needed one, didn't she?"

# ❋ Twenty ❋

The single redeeming factor of having a house full of men who spend eight hours of the day eating and drinking to excess, is that they have the tendency to spend the remaining sixteen hours in bed.

The house was quiet when Mirabelle went back inside a bit before noon, and quiet still after she had washed and dressed and slipped down the stairs to find herself a bit of breakfast in the kitchen.

She found bread that hadn't gone completely stale yet and a small hunk of cheese with only a few bad spots. Her mouth watered at the thought of eggs and kippers, but those were for the guests. Wishing there were hot chocolate to be had, she made a pot of weak tea and settled down at a scarred table to eat her meager meal.

Whit found her there not ten minutes later. A wide beam of sunlight cut through the small row of windows, leaving the table, and her, in a soft glow. He'd wager, the way the light fell across her soft brown hair, that it would be warm to the touch. All of her would be warm to the touch—her hair, her skin, her mouth. He ached to reach out and take that warmth for his own. She'd feel like heated silk beneath his hands, warm cream against his tongue.

He closed his eyes and swallowed a groan. It had been hell last night, and heaven, to have her lying next to him. And he unable to do more than stroke her hair. He'd gone back to his room to toss and turn in bed.

He wanted her, more than any woman he'd ever known or desired, he wanted Mirabelle. But as appealing as a roll between the sheets was to him right now—and it was tremendously appealing—he needed to concentrate on her safety first and foremost. He took a moment to compose himself, then pasted on what he hoped was a friendly, but otherwise unremarkable, smile and stepped into the room. "Good morning, Mirabelle."

She turned her head to smile back at him. "Good morning. I'd thought perhaps you'd sleep longer."

Hard to do on a mattress that felt like a slab of rock beneath his back, while visions of her naked and moaning on a pile of hay danced through his head. "Had all the sleep I needed. Not much of a breakfast you have there," he commented to change the subject.

She looked down at her plate and shrugged. "It was available. Would you care for some?"

"I'd prefer eggs. Where is your cook?"

"Asleep, I imagine, though I couldn't say for certain."

"No matter, I'll make them."

"You? You can cook?" She said it with such stunned disbelief, he couldn't help laughing.

"I was a soldier, you'll recall."

"You were an officer," she returned. "I've never heard of an officer cooking his own meals."

"I didn't, but I learned how. I enjoyed spending time with my men, and that included those who cooked. I can't prepare a six-course meal, mind you, but I can manage a few eggs." He frowned at the stove. "This would be easier over a camp fire."

"Easier than a stove?"

He shrugged and began loading wood. "It's how I learned. I suppose the eggs are still with the hens?"

"Yes, I was going to collect them after I ate, but if you like—"

"I'll get them," he interrupted, and grabbing a nearby pail, went in search of his breakfast. He didn't have to go far, as the hen house was located only a few feet from the manor. He ducked his head under the door and gently pushed the annoyed birds aside until he'd collected enough eggs for a meal. If it wasn't enough for the other guests, they could bloody well get their own. Mirabelle didn't need to be working as a damn kitchen maid.

He found her still at the table when he returned, absently picking at her food.

"I return victorious," he declared, holding up the full pail.

The silliness of it made her smile, as he intended. "Did they put up much of a fight?"

"Nearly lost an eye," he told her as he lit the stove.

"That would have been embarrassing for you—to have survived a wild boar attack, only to be felled by a chicken."

"Heard that, did you?"

"Some of it, anyway. I hadn't realized you'd such a talent for fabrication."

"Hmm?" He poked at the fire and answered absently. "Ah, no. The boar was real enough. I don't care for hunting overmuch, but it had to be removed after it attacked one of the local villagers. Do you suppose this fire is hot enough?"

She was glad to have his back to her just then, because she was certain she looked a fool gaping at him. He'd really fought a wild boar?

"Mirabelle?"

She snapped her mouth closed when he turned to look at her. "Er . . . it seems adequate to me."

"Excellent."

She returned her attention to her food, determined not to dwell on the image of Whit stalking the deep woods in search of a man-eating beast. He'd have looked a bit rugged, she imagined—disheveled, and determined. And in uniform.

Good Lord, she wasn't certain if she were more frightened or intrigued by the idea. She strove for something else to think of. "Um . . . Speaking of hunting, the others will do so today."

He paused in the act of breaking open an egg to stare at her. "They actually do that?"

"Oh, they put quite a lot of effort into pretending."

"How does the baron go about it?"

"He takes the carriage."

"He takes the carriage," Whit repeated. "I cannot form a picture."

"You'll have very little trouble with that by the end of the day. Though you can't let him know you've seen it. It's a ridiculous system he has, but it's something of a tradition at this point. He sends the others out before him, with one excuse or another, then he has the carriage brought round with all his hunting supplies and two footmen. He takes the carriage to a secluded spot down the road, and hunts from the comfort of the cushioned bench."

He stared at her for a moment, his expression caught somewhere between bewildered and amused. "I can't believe there's some truth to that rumor. He can't ever have gotten something that way."

"He shot a rabbit once. Poor thing wandered past at the wrong time." She made a face at the memory. "The footmen are sent out with guns of their own, and anything they kill he takes as his own."

He shook his head and returned his focus to preparing a meal. "Do the others know?"

"If they do, they're wise enough not to mention it." She thought about that. "Which is the very same thing as saying no, I suppose."

"And are *they* ever successful in their hunt?"

"Not regularly, although Mr. Cunningham brings something back from time to time."

"The ill guest?" he asked, retrieving a fork to whip the eggs.

"Yes. Pity he's not feeling well. I suspect you'd rather like him." When he snorted derisively, she continued. "I'm in earnest, actually. He's tremendously obnoxious, but he's not an unkind man, and there's a bit of wit about him—it's crude, but it's there."

"You get on with him, then?"

"I do," she responded, sounding a little surprised by the admission. "Well—mostly."

Whit nodded and watched the eggs congeal nicely in the heating pan. "Perhaps I'll have the chance to take his measure at dinner."

"Before then, if he decides to go out with the other gentlemen."

He shook his head. "I'll not be accompanying the others."

"You have to. It's a hunting party, Whit. It would look strange for you not to go. Even Mr. Hartsinger will be going, and he always has a look about him as if he's not sure which end of the gun to hold."

Apparently unwilling to search the kitchen over in hopes of finding a clean plate, he picked the pan off the stove and brought it to the table. "It won't look strange if I plead a sore head after last night."

"Perhaps not," she conceded with a smile. "But you will look puny."

He shrugged, but not before she saw the wince. "Can't be helped. I need to search your uncle's room. Eat."

"Oh, thank you." She picked up her fork and speared a bite of egg. "If Mr. Cunningham is still ill, you might as well go with the others, because his room is only one over from my uncle's. I think it might have been the baroness's room at one point, complete with a connecting door."

"Damn it."

She scooped up another bite. "These are really quite good, Whit."

He merely grunted thoughtfully and stabbed at the food.

"There's the attic," she told him. "If he were printing counterfeit bills, he'd need a bit of space to do it, wouldn't he?"

He looked up at her. "You're right."

"Of course, I doubt my uncle has managed the steps to the attic in over a decade," she added.

He shrugged and took a greater interest in his breakfast. "It could be he has the servants carry things to and from for him and simply has the equipment stored there when others are in residence. It can't hurt for me to look."

"For us to look," she corrected. "And stop scowling at me. You've never seen the attic. Believe me, you'll need the extra set of hands."

The attic was only accessible by climbing a narrow set of steps off the servants' wing—and by the layer of dust covering those steps, Mirabelle estimated that no one had hauled anything in or out of the room in a very good while. But after discovering that Mr. Cunningham was still abed with the ague, Whit insisted they wait until the others had left, then forge ahead.

They climbed the dirty stairs and pushed open the door.

Trunks, crates, boxes, cloth bags, furniture, and every other item one might imagine finding in an attic was, in fact, to be found in that attic. They were stacked and piled and tossed about haphazardly so that the room looked something of a maze—a dusty, cobweb-ridden maze.

"Won't this be fun," Mirabelle said with a wry twist of her lips.

"It will certainly be time-consuming."

"We can't look through it all. The others will be back in only a few hours. They're really not that dedicated to the sport."

"Concentrate on the crates and trunks near the front of the room," he instructed as he moved off to the side. "Keep an eye out for anything locked."

She shrugged and picked a trunk at random. The lid opened with a load groan and a cloud of dust. She erupted into a fit of sneezing. When she finally recovered, Whit was standing over her holding out his handkerchief.

"Here you are," he said. "Better?"

"Than what?" she laughed, and took the cloth to wipe her watering eyes. "Thank you."

He shook his head when she tried to hand it back. "Keep it, hold it up to your nose and mouth the next time you open one of the trunks."

"What of you?"

"I'll manage," he said and walked back to his crate before she could argue.

They worked in silence for the next two hours, moving from trunk to trunk and crate to crate. As she dug through another pile of moldering men's clothing, Mirabelle came across a large lidded jar rolled up in a pair of breeches.

"How odd," she murmured to herself. Odder yet, there was a folded piece of paper inside.

She took the lid off and tried to pull the paper free, but it was stuck to the bottom and the jar was so deep she couldn't do more than grasp at the paper with her fingertips. She twisted her wrist and pushed until her hand popped through with a small sucking sound.

*Yes!*

She grasped the edge of the paper with her fingers and slowly peeled it back from the bottom. Miraculously, it came off in one piece.

*Yes! Yes! Yes!*

She pulled her hand back . . . and the bottle came back with it. Annoyed, she gripped the glass with her free hand and pulled. Nothing.

*No.*

She pulled harder, twisted her hand and wiggled her fingers. She tried yanking, tugging, gripping the jar by the rim and pushing. Nothing.

*No! No! No!*

She gaped at her hand, utterly appalled. It *had* to come out. It had gone through, hadn't it? Why the devil couldn't she get it back out again? She tried again, twisting her wrist this way and that, until finally admitting defeat. There was no possible way to get herself out of this ridiculous situation without help. She took a deep breath and concentrated on not sounding anxious.

"Er . . . Whit?" There, that sounded nonchalant, didn't it? She'd hesitated a bit, but she didn't think he'd noticed.

"Yes, what is it?" With his head still in a trunk, his voice sounded muffled and distracted.

"I was wondering . . ." Oh dear, how to put it? She licked lips gone dry. "I was wondering . . ."

Alerted by her hesitation, he emerged from the box and glanced over.

"Did you find something?"

"Not exactly," she hedged.

Rising, he brushed his dusty hands on his dusty coat. "What do you mean by 'not exactly'? What are you hiding, imp?"

"I'm not hiding anything," she said automatically. "Not exactly . . . Well, I *am,* to be honest, but it hasn't anything to do with my uncle or a counterfeiting operation, or—"

"I don't much care what it's about. I just want to know what it is."

*Damn and blast.*

"Oh, all right." She blew out a hard breath, only a little bit because she felt she needed to, but mostly just to stall. "I was trying . . . that is, I was attempting to reach something, you see, something stuck and . . . well, I hadn't realized . . ."

"Out with it, imp."

Resigned, miserable, she pulled her hand out from behind her back and held it up in front of her. She wanted, very badly at that moment, to hang her head in an aggravating mix of shame and apology, but pride kept her from dropping her chin. It might have shifted—along with her eyes—a little to the side in an effort to avoid eye contact, but that couldn't be helped.

He didn't react at first except to blink, clasp his hands behind his back, and run his tongue slowly over his teeth.

"I see," he finally said.

"It won't budge," she grumbled, still unable to meet his eyes.

"Yes, I assumed that was why it was there."

"And I can't very well go back out there like this."

"You certainly can't."

Annoyed by his continuing lack of reaction she dropped her hand and huffed. "Aren't you going to laugh at me?"

"I certainly will."

"Well, do you think you might trouble yourself to get on with it, so we can move on to the matter of—?" She wagged her bottle-hand at him.

"In good time. I want to be able to properly appreciate the moment. And this room—and our being in it together—place certain constrictions on the volume and length of that appreciation."

"Would you please just fetch some soap and water, Whit?"

"Of course," he replied, his lips twitching. "Wait here."

"Where else would I go like this?" she muttered, as he left.

It seemed to take forever for him to return again—long enough, in fact, for her to give serious consideration to wrapping her hand in an old shirt and seeking him out. If she could have come up with a single reasonable explanation for having her hand wrapped in a shirt, should one of the servants notice and inquire after it, she would have done it.

"Do you have any idea how difficult it is to find soap in this house?" Whit demanded when he finally returned carrying a bar of soap and a small basin of water.

"Some," she answered. "As I've been waiting here like this while you searched."

"I assumed there'd be some in one of the closets on the servants' floor, but I couldn't find a single one that wasn't filled to the ceiling with other things . . . tools and books and old clothes and nearly everything but what really ought to be in those closets."

"Like soap."

"Like soap," he agreed, as he knelt to set his burden at her feet. "And brooms and the usual cleaning supplies. Where do they keep all that?"

"They don't, mostly, though some of it can be found in the kitchen." She motioned with her free hand. "Where did you find that?"

"I had to go to my room. Sit on the trunk and let me see your hand."

She considered telling him she could do it herself, but then realized with only one free hand, she probably couldn't. Not as quickly as he could, and speed was of the essence when one's hand was stuck in a bottle.

She sat on the trunk. "Did anyone see you or ask what you were doing poking into closets?"

"Nary a soul. I heard snoring coming from several of the servants' quarters, however. Why does your uncle keep them on?"

She shrugged and watched him lather the soap. "No one else will work for him."

"Ah." He reached for her elbow and held her arm out as he ran the soap around her wrist.

"Whit?"

"Hmm?"

"I was wondering . . ."

"Wondering what?"

"I wanted to ask you before, but, between this, that, and the other—"

He looked up from his task. "What is it you want to know?"

"What is it you do, exactly, for William Fletcher? And how did you come to be doing . . . whatever it is you do?"

He went back to soaping her wrist. "You shouldn't know anything about it."

"A little late for that," she reminded him. "I answered your questions last night. And it wasn't something I cared to do."

He was quiet for a long moment, until Mirabelle began to think he wasn't going to respond at all, but then he set the soap down and began to use his fingers to rub the soap into her skin.

"I work, on occasion," he told her softly, "as an agent for the War Department, of which William is the head."

"Oh. Is he really?" She frowned in thought. "All this time, I thought he was simply a friend of the family."

"He is a friend of the family. He just also happens to command a small army of spies."

"Is that what you are? A spy?"

"Not exactly," he responded, and with enough coolness that she knew he wasn't going to elaborate any further on that topic. So she tried another.

"Is it often dangerous?"

"Not often, no. Certainly not more so than fighting a war."

"Why do you do it? You've so much responsibility already."

"I wish to give my family something they can be proud of."

"They are proud of you," she pointed out. "They're immensely proud of you. You're very nearly the perfect son, brother, and lord of the manner. Bit annoying, actually."

"Why thank you," he replied easily. "This is different. It's . . . bigger. It's something I can pass down to my sons—

should I be blessed with them. It's a legacy that can overcome several centuries of shame."

"You're ashamed of your heritage?" she asked with some surprise.

"I believe you met my father on several occasions," he said dryly. "Though he was rarely home."

She frowned at him. "He seemed a jovial enough man. I know he wasn't the most responsible of men, but—"

"The rumors you've heard scarcely touched on his sins. He was a useless combination of dandy and rakehell with no care for anyone but himself. He wasn't killed in a fall from his horse as is commonly believed. He died in a duel over an opera singer."

"Oh." Good Lord, she'd no idea. "I'm sorry."

"Ah, well. He's gone now and few people know the truth. Fewer still whose stories would be given more weight than my own accounting of events. Your uncle knows."

"He does?"

"Yes, as do some of his guests. They ran in some of the same circles, you see, but as I said, no one cares to gainsay the Earl of Thurston these days. Not loud enough to cause concern, at any rate."

But there were rumors of the truth, she knew. She remembered the whispers in the ballrooms and parlors right after the earl's death, but like everyone else, she'd brushed them aside as petty gossip. Whit hadn't had that luxury, she realized now. He never would.

"I am sorry, Whit."

"As I said," he replied taking hold of her elbow and the glass. "It's over and done."

He pulled her arm gently and her hand slid free of the jar.

"Oh." She flexed her fingers experimentally.

"Does it hurt?" he asked, rubbing her wrist with the pad of his thumb.

"No." It felt the very opposite. His touch sent her nerves to humming. "It feels . . . fine."

"Just fine?" he asked and bent his head to press his lips against the tender skin on the inside of her arm just below her elbow.

"Er . . . nice. It feels very nice."

"Only nice?"

"Well, it is just my arm."

"I see."

He rose to his knees, slid his hand around to the nape of her neck, and brought his lips to hers.

There was the softness again, the gentleness, and the need. She scooted to the edge of the trunk and after a moment's hesitation, let her hands slide up to his shoulders. It was all still so new to her. The kissing, the touching, the way both made her feel wanton and unsure at the same time. She wasn't at all certain what she should do, or shouldn't do. But she was sure she wanted to continue doing it as long as humanly possible.

"You've the sweetest mouth," he murmured against her lips, and she felt her heart skip an extra beat in her chest. "I told myself once it would taste bitter."

She pulled back. *"Bitter?"*

He smiled at her. "It shouldn't come as a shock that I was angry with you at the time."

"Angry with . . . you'd thought of kissing me before? Before all this?"

"Once, when I was a younger man." His grin broadened as he remembered. "We were yelling at each other over something or other, and I had the sudden notion of shutting you up with a kiss. I kept from doing so by convincing myself that you'd taste bitter."

"You'd thought of kissing me," she repeated with a slightly dreamy smile.

"I wasn't yet twenty. I thought of kissing near to everyone in a skirt who wasn't a blood relation . . . . Thought about it quite a lot, if memory serves."

She brought her foot forward to press down on his own until he winced around the smile. He tugged gently on her hair.

"Jealous, are you, darling?"

She rolled her eyes at him, which wasn't a particularly convincing denial, but worked well enough to have him standing up with a laugh and opening the paper she'd gone through so much trouble to retrieve from the jar.

"What is it, then?" she asked, prepared to be told she'd made a fool of herself over an old gambling chit or invitation to dinner. But when his face tightened, she stood and edged forward, impatient and nervous. Had she actually found something?

"What is it, Whit?"

Her heart drumming in her throat, she accepted the paper when he held it out to her. She skimmed its contents—twice. She wasn't sure what she'd been expecting, but she'd rather thought it would be something a bit more incriminating than a simple delivery receipt for common household items.

Baffled, she held the paper up. "What is this?"

"A delivery receipt for—" Whit leaned forward to read. "—one case beeswax, small; one case port, large; two cases—"

She pulled the paper back. "I can read, Whit, I just can't fathom why you think it's important."

"Look closer, imp."

She did, but nothing grabbed her as being out of place. She shook her head. "I'm sorry, but I fail to see the relevance—"

He reached over and pointed at an item. "Two cases Gold Crown Ink."

"And . . . ?" she prompted. "I've never heard of it, but—"

"Gold Crown is remarkably similar in appearance to the actual ink used in the printing of some bank notes."

She frowned thoughtfully. "If it's readily available to

anyone who wants it, then it's not conclusive evidence against him, is it? Perhaps he simply likes the color."

"It's not readily available," he informed her. "It has to be ordered."

"People order inks all the time, Whit, and for a variety of reasons."

"Two cases of it?"

"That is odd," she agreed and looked over the list yet again. There were subtotals and totals at the bottom, invoice numbers, signatures, and the date and means of delivery. She glanced at the date again and laughed.

"This receipt's almost a decade old," she informed him.

"I noticed."

She handed the paper back to him with an amused shake of her head. "If my uncle has been making poorly constructed bank notes for ten years, I should think someone would have noticed before now."

"I'd thought of that," he told her, taking the paper and stowing it away in his pocket. "There are several possible explanations. First, he could have been working on the process, attempting to improve—"

"My uncle works at nothing," she scoffed. "Let alone at *improving* something."

"Second," he continued, "he may have had to wait for the remainder of the supplies, or wait until he believed the trail linking him to the supplies disappeared."

"He hasn't that sort of discipline, Whit."

"Third, and my personal choice—he's been passing them off to someone else who circulates them out of the country."

"Oh." That she could actually imagine, particularly since it involved an accomplice. In her opinion, her uncle simply wasn't capable of committing a complicated crime without someone guiding him along the way. "I suppose that's a possibility. But you can hardly prove it with one old receipt."

"No, I cannot. But I've most of the week left yet."

"You're certain he's guilty now."

He considered that before shaking his head. "I don't know. To be honest, I don't care for your uncle."

"Few do," she pointed out.

"True, but only the two of us are responsible for obtaining evidence of his guilt in a serious crime."

The two of us, she thought, and tried not to grin at his casual reference of them as a team. It pleased her well enough that she would forgo pointing out that she was looking for the proof of her uncle's innocence, not his guilt. "You're afraid you're making mountains out of molehills—seeing things that aren't there because you've already made up your mind about my uncle."

"Not afraid exactly," he argued with just enough affronted dignity to have her grinning after all. "It's something to be aware of, that's all. Why are you grinning?"

"No reason," she lied. "I enjoy seeing you use that great sense of yours."

"I wasn't being sensible when I envisioned beating him black and blue over dinner last night."

"You weren't being original, either. I have that fantasy at least twice a day during my stays here."

"You've cause enough. I want to send you back to Haldon."

"We've been over and over—"

"I said I wanted, not that I could."

She nodded in understanding. If it were possible, she'd have them both back at Haldon. "I need to see to dinner before the others return."

Whit shook his head. "You won't be coming down to dinner again."

"It can't be avoided, Whit. My uncle expects me to play hostess, or his version of it."

He took her arm and led her towards the door. "I'll handle Eppersly. Stay in your room and lock the door."

She was perfectly willing to obey that order.

"You'll come for me? You won't search on your own?"

There was a long, telling hesitation before he answered. "I'll come."

Whit waited until the baron had a chance to settle himself into his study after the hunt before seeking him out.

"How's that head of yours, boy?" the baron asked as Whit made his way into the room.

He bit back the instinctive need to retaliate for being called "boy" and took a seat in front of the desk, letting his back slouch and his legs stretch out before him. He hoped it made him look appropriately slothful.

"Still attached to my shoulders, I'm afraid. How was the hunt?"

The baron heaved out a grunt. "Damn poachers. Man can't find game on his own land anymore."

"Damn shame," Whit agreed and congratulated himself for not smiling.

"Don't suspect you came in here to discuss hunting, Thurston."

"I didn't, in fact. I came to discuss your niece."

"Mirabelle?" The baron scowled. "What the devil for? Seems you'd have enough of her at Haldon."

"I do, which is why I'm discussing her now." He made himself fidget with his cravat. "I realize she's family, Eppersly, but can't the chit stay in her room for a day or two?"

"Heard you two don't get on."

"She's a bloody nuisance. And she . . ." He cast a nervous look at the open door before leaning over to whisper across the desk. "She talks to my mother. A man can't very well enjoy himself around a woman who gossips regularly with his mother, can he?"

The baron twisted his lips. "Can't, now you mention it. I'll see she stays in her room."

Whit didn't have to feign his relief, though the gratitude

was for show. "It's appreciated. My father always said you were a sensible man."

The baron nodded as if he had reason to believe that comment was anything other than the lie it was. "Pity he's not still here. No need to worry yourself over his censure."

"No need at all."

"He went well in the end, though. Had a wager with some of the others, how each of us would go. Won a hundred pounds on your father. The others figured he'd die of the pox."

"Cuckolding you, was he?"

The baron blinked once, then threw his head back to roar and snort with laughter.

"Your father's son!" he managed when the greatest part of his mirth had passed. "Had a tongue as sharp as yours."

"Yes, I recall," Whit muttered, and managed, just barely, to keep the sanguine expression of a slightly amused, but mostly bored young man on his face.

"We'll make a proper man of you yet."

"I look forward to the instruction." As he might, he thought ruefully, a cannonball to the head.

# ❋ *Twenty-one* ❋

*F*or Whit, dinner was no more pleasant that night than it had been the night before, but it was markedly less tense for him with Mirabelle safely tucked away in her room.

The men drank themselves half stupid in the space of an hour and wholly stupid a quarter hour after that. So it was with great relief that he saw the last of them drag themselves off to bed before the clock struck eleven.

He swayed and tottered himself as he made his way out of the dining room, but that was for the benefit of the staff.

"Where'z the baron?" he demanded of one of the footmen as he lurched into the hallway. "Good man, the baron. Good man. Where'd he go?"

"To bed . . . my lord," the footman replied, sidestepping Whit's tottering form. "All the guests have gone to bed."

"To bed! Already? Night's young." He gave a forced hiccup. "And they mocked me. Ah, well. Old men. What's to do? That is . . . what's a man . . . Never mind."

"Very good, my lord."

"Where'z my room, then?"

The footman let out a hefty sigh, gripped Whit's arm and hauled him up the stairs and down the hall. Because he was only willing to take the ruse so far, Whit fished out the key from his pocket himself.

"Got it. Got it. Not a bleeding infant," he muttered.

"If you're set then, I'm for my own bed."

Whit forced the key into the lock after a few bumbling tries, and waved a hand at the footman. "Off you go."

He didn't need to turn his head to know the man rolled his eyes before leaving. Couldn't blame him, really, though a decent footman would have made certain a guest had made it to his bed without first tripping over his own feet and cracking his head open on a piece of furniture.

He listened. The sound of the footman's steps dimmed and then disappeared up the third-floor stairwell. By the haggard look on the man's face, Whit suspected he'd told the truth—he was for bed.

It must be an exhausting job, he thought, as he stepped into his room for a candle and stepped back out again, to put up with the likes of the baron and his guests. Then again, the staff didn't do much besides, as far as he could tell. Plenty of time to rest between the drunken mayhem.

He made the brief trip to Mirabelle's room and stopped.

For a few long minutes, he simply stood outside her door considering, weighing, arguing, and otherwise working himself into a fine temper.

She had every right to participate. He had every right to keep her safe.

He should keep his word and knock.

He should keep her as far removed from all this as he possibly could.

He should bind and gag her, toss her into a carriage, and send the stubborn woman back to Haldon, *that's* what he should do.

This was a mission, he fumed, not a Mayfair dinner party. And this wasn't the same as digging through trunks in the middle of the day. Had they been caught, he could have readily fabricated a believable explanation for why the two of them were in the attic.

He was helping her find a portrait of her mother, or she was helping him find an extra blanket for his room. There'd been dozens of perfectly good excuses available.

But there was no good excuse for two people to be snooping through a room in the dead of night.

Thoughts of what could happen to Mirabelle if they were found out made his hands ball into tight fists.

He wasn't having it. He wasn't going to be worrying over her instead of worrying over the mission. He sure as hell wasn't going to spend the remaining nights of the party, standing in the hallway, arguing with himself.

She'd see reason, damn it, or he'd make use of that bind and gag.

Temper firmly established, he knocked sharply on the door.

At the quick rap on her door Mirabelle rose from her seat by the window and, out of habit, grabbed the heavy candlestick she'd pilfered from the library ages ago. The bolts on her door were sturdy, but still . . .

"Open the door, imp."

Relieved to hear Whit's voice, she set down the candlestick and opened the door.

"Are they all asleep, then?" she asked as she slipped out of her room.

He took her arm and promptly escorted her back inside.

"You're staying here."

Taken aback by the brusque command, she did little more than stare at him while he closed and rebolted the door.

"Three locks," she heard him mutter. "Chit has three locks on her door, but can't see the sense in staying behind them."

The insult broke her stupor. She'd had the sense to have them installed, hadn't she? And it had been no easy feat to time that around her uncle's comings and goings.

She crossed her arms across her chest and glared at his back. "What the devil has gotten into you?"

"You," he snapped, whirling around and jabbing an accussing finger at her. "*You've* gotten into me."

Later, she would think that a very lovely sentiment. At present, however, she just found it baffling. "What on earth are you talking about?"

He raised his finger up an inch, much in the manner of someone about to deliver a vehement lecture. Willing to indulge him—a little—if it meant getting some answers, she waited. And waited . . .

"Whit?"

He dropped his finger. "I was going to yell at you."

"Yes, I could tell. Care to tell me why?"

He hesitate before answering, his brow furrowed in thought. "I can't stand the idea of something happening to you," he finally admitted softly.

She didn't need time to appreciate that particular sentiment. She could have used a bit of it to come up with an appropriate response, however, because all she could think to say was, "Oh."

"The very thought of it, of you coming to harm, had me standing outside your door for the last ten minutes, arguing with myself like some sort of lunatic—"

"You've been fuming outside my door for the last ten minutes?" She found herself grinning, rather pleased with the image. "Really?"

His lips twitched and the lines across his brow disappeared. "Yes, really. And I—"

"Were you pacing?"

"I beg your pardon?"

"Were you pacing?" she repeated. "Or were you standing still, clenching your jaw at the door?"

He ran his tongue across his teeth. "I can't imagine why it would matter."

"It doesn't, particularly," she replied with a shrug. "Except that I'd like to have a clear picture of it in my mind, to use later when you're laughing over my hand in the jar."

He laughed softly now, as she had hoped he would. "I wasn't pacing. I was standing quite still, thinking I should storm in here and shout at you."

"But you didn't," she pointed out. "Didn't shout, anyway."

"No," he agreed and crossed the room to stand in front of her. "How could I? I'm angry with your uncle, not you. And you were just standing there, looking so quiet and patient, and—"

"Confused," she added for him.

"Lovely," he corrected and reached up to cup her face. "How is it I never before noticed how lovely you are?"

She opened her mouth . . . closed it again. "You say these things at random intervals just to unnerve me, don't you?"

"It is fun to watch you flounder," he admitted. "But I say them at random simply because they occur to me that way."

He caught a lock of her hair and rubbed it between his fingers. "Soft. I thought of it on our walk around the lake, the way the darker strands blend into the softer browns."

She licked her lips nervously. "Like a chestnut."

"The color's the same." He reached up to gently trace the arch of one eyebrow with his thumb. "I thought of your eyes, dark and rich—"

"Chocolate."

"Chocolate," he agreed. "—while I was undressing in my room, the night we agreed to a truce."

Her brain snagged on one comment. "While you were undressing?"

"Yes. I think of you at the damndest times . . . your skin, your lips, and the beauty mark just above them." His hand moved to cup the back of her neck. "This tender spot just below your ear."

"You do?"

"Mm-hm." He pulled her closer, and closer still, until he spoke against her lips and she felt the heat of it down to her toes. "And I think of this, nearly every waking moment of the day."

He kissed her then. Not with the softness he'd shown in the past and not with the wildness she'd experienced the night of the ball, but with a fierce determination that frightened and excited her.

His mouth moved strongly over hers, demanding she give, and yield, and take. Until she could do nothing but obey. His hands moved to stroke possessively—down her arms, up her back and down again. She felt the warmth in the wake of every touch.

He caught her around under the knees and hauled her into his arms. The sudden move made her gasp, as did the the feel of his arousal pressing against her hip when he settled on the edge of the bed with her in his lap. He nipped at her ear and snuck a hand under her skirt to stroke her calf.

"Whit, I—"

"Shh." He pressed his lips to the side of her neck just below her ear. He'd been right, she thought with a ragged breath, it was tender there.

He moved down toward her shoulder, pressing kisses along the way. Aroused, and uncertain what to do with that feeling, she struggled against him. "Whit—"

"Shh. Let me, Mirabelle," he whispered, and she felt a shudder tear through her at the sensation of his hot breath against her skin. "Just for a moment. I'll stop when you ask. I promise."

Stop? Why the devil would she want him to stop? She'd only wanted to say something nice, something sweet and poetic as he had. She only wanted to get closer, damn it.

Frustrated, she reached up to tangle her hands in his hair and brought his roving mouth back to hers. She kissed him with all the determination and possessiveness he'd shown that night, all the desperation they'd felt in the carriage, and all the restless desire she felt now.

She kissed him with all her heart and the deepest wish that he could see inside it.

A growl worked in his throat. And the next thing she knew, she was lying down, his weight pressing her firmly into the mattress.

"I'll stop," he whispered again, even as his hands worked under her to undo the buttons of her gown. "I'll stop if you want me to."

She tugged his coat down his shoulders in response.

They pulled and yanked, tearing at clothes in a frenzied rush to find the skin underneath. He caught her hand as she reached for his buttons of his breeches.

"Not yet, Mirabelle. Not yet."

She gaped at her hand in his. Had she really just tried to do that? Was she supposed to do that? She swallowed hard and met his eyes. "I don't know what to do."

"I do," he whispered gently. "Let me show you."

She dipped her head in a nod, then closed her eyes on a

sigh as he bent his head to press kisses along her collarbone, careful to be gentle where the skin was still tender from her fall. "No thinking, Mirabelle. Just feel."

"Yes." She sighed again. "Oh, yes."

That sound, that incredible sound of a woman yielding, nearly drove Whit over the edge. He struggled in his need to be gentle, and in his need to ravish. He'd never wanted like this. Not even when he'd been a green boy, panting after everything in skirts, had he ached so painfully for a woman. If she'd touched him, if he'd let her fingers continue on their quest to free him, he wouldn't have lasted.

He lifted his head to watch her for a moment while his hand brushed down to mold a breast. He'd managed to pull her dress off—all the while thinking that when they were married, he was going to order her an entire wardrobe of gowns with oversized button holes—and now he reveled in the soft skin her thin chemise left exposed.

He brushed a thumb across a nipple and watched as it peaked through the material. Her answering moan shot a shiver of lust through his system. His fingers glided along the neck of the chemise, gently pulling it back to expose her.

"It's . . . it's not the blue chemise," she whispered with a hint of apology.

"It's perfect," he heard himself tell her in a voice gone hoarse. "You're perfect."

If she responded, he didn't hear her. With his own blood roaring in his head, he gathered the material at the hem and bunched it up to pull it over her head before laying her back down again.

"Beautiful."

He took his time with her, torturing them both by tasting, sampling, teasing. He explored every inch of her form and delighted in its curves and dips, the subtle flare of her hips, the flat expanse of her stomach.

She moaned and twisted beneath him, and when she gave

a soft cry and raked her nails down his back as he brushed at the heat between her legs, he gave in to the desire to take.

To distract her, and please himself, he kissed her hard and deep as he stripped off his breeches and tossed them aside.

"Put your legs around me, imp."

She complied blindly, and this time it was he who gasped as he slipped into her wet entrance that first inch. He stayed there, caught between bliss and agony. His arms shook as he fought back the painful urge to just finish the job in one glorious push.

He could be gentle. He *would* be gentle.

He kissed her softly as he eased inside, seducing her body into accepting his. He waited for her to cry out, to tell him to stop.

But she only wrapped herself more tightly around him and kissed him back.

Until he came to the barrier that marked her as an innocent. He almost offered to stop. Almost. He was only a man, for pity's sake.

"I'm sorry, sweetheart," he whispered instead. And with a strong surge of his hips, pushed through to bury himself completely inside.

She unwrapped herself in a thrice. "Oh, ouch!"

He dropped his forehead to hers. "I'm sorry, imp. Give it a minute. Just a minute."

A minute turned into two, and then three as he courted her again with long kisses and soft caresses. He whispered in her ear, sweet nonsense that made her smile and sigh, wicked nonsense that made her blush and squirm.

When her body relaxed under his again, he shifted his hips cautiously, gauging her reaction as he began to move inside her.

Her reaction was everything he could have hoped for and more. She moved with him, her arms banding around his shoulders as her legs once again banded around his waist.

In the soft light of two flickering candles, they rose together. She striving for something she couldn't name. He striving to keep himself from grabbing that something before she had the chance.

He listened to her breath quicken, her soft cries grow faster and higher in pitch, and he willed her to reach out and take.

When she did, when she shuddered and bucked in his arms, he let himself go.

A full moon on a cloudless night can create a play of light and shadow that renders even the dreariest view an interesting landscape of black and grey. From his position in the woods at the edge of the side lawn—which was inarguably a very dreary view under most conditions—McAlistair sat and frowned at the scene before him. Pretty it might be, but convenient it was not. Better it be black as pitch so he could move across the ground without being seen.

Ah well, he had hidden in the bright sun of midday before this. Gone unseen and unheard in well-lit ballrooms and crowded bazaars.

He stood, stretched, picked his path, and moved forward to glide among the shadows. He crossed the lawn in long silent strides. His gaze tracked a brief flickering of light on the second floor before returning to the stable.

A man was waiting for him inside. Well, perhaps waiting was a poor choice of words, as it implied a kind of welcome. This man was crouched behind a stall door and taking aim with a gun.

Wasn't the first time, McAlistair reminded himself. He said nothing, only waited as the crouching man looked him over, then grunted and straightened, tall and sure, before lowering the pistol.

"Come then, have you?"

McAlistair nodded in response.

"Wondered if he might be after sending you. Seems he's after sending near to everyone."

He thought of the note left for him at his camp. "Orders," was all he said. Orders to watch and protect.

"True enough. Though it might have been wise to have sent me some sort of warning. It's lucky you are I didn't blow a hole through you."

He shrugged.

The other man rolled his shoulders. "It's coming to an end, I suppose. About bleeding time." He jerked his head at a stall at the end of the aisle. "Not much more to do now than wait. I've some pilfered brandy hidden, if you're wanting it."

McAlistair considered it. "Wouldn't mind."

# Twenty-two

Mirabelle lay in a daze beneath Whit. So *that* was what her uncle and his friends spoke of so often and so crudely. She'd known, from their uncensored comments, what happened between a man and a woman behind closed doors, and she'd known, from the way they'd spoken of it, that a man found great pleasure in the act. But she hadn't known, hadn't even suspected . . .

Unable to find the words, she sighed happily.

Whit stirred and levered himself up onto his elbows. "I'm crushing you."

"No. Well, yes," she amended and smiled at him. "But I rather like it."

It wasn't exactly poetry, but it was the best she could do under the circumstances. He smiled in return, and wrapping his arms around her, rolled them both to their sides. They stayed that way for a long moment, watching each other in contented silence. She could, she thought as drowsiness set in, look into his blue eyes for the rest of her life.

A hard howl of wind and the answering creak of wood was a swift reminder that it would be best to start the rest of her life when she wasn't lying next to a naked man in her uncle's home. Even if it was in her own room.

She shot up to a sitting position and made a grab for her chemise. "We should dress. What if someone heard us? What if someone comes looking? What if . . ."

She trailed off when she realized he'd neither moved nor responded. She looked over to find him lying still, his gaze settled somewhere below her collarbone.

She narrowed her eyes at him. "What are you doing?"

"Making a mental note for the future to startle you while you're naked as often as humanly possible."

She grabbed his shirt and tossed it at him. "Dress."

Laughing, he caught the shirt. "None of the guests could have possibly heard us, imp. The closest room is several doors down. And none of the servants would care enough to come looking if they had—which I highly doubt." He gave her a wicked smile. "You're quiet in your lovemaking."

She blushed and struggled into her chemise. "Nonetheless, I'd feel better if we were just . . . elsewhere. We could go to the stable."

Whit made himself comfortable again on the bed. "Thank you, but no. I don't fancy the idea of Christian trying to run me through."

"Why on earth would he do that? He couldn't possibly know."

He cocked his head at her and smiled. "Have a look in your mirror, darling."

"My mirror?"

She scrambled to her knees and found her reflection in her vanity. Good Lord, was the woman staring back really her? Her chemise was rumpled beyond recognition, her hair tousled and snarled beyond repair. Her lips were swollen, her lids were heavy, and her skin practically glowed. No wonder Whit didn't want Christian to see her. She looked wanton and ravished.

And decidedly pleased with both.

*Almost* as pleased as Whit, she thought, catching sight of his reflection. He'd leaned back against the pillows, his hands behind his head, the counterpane comfortably around his waist, and a very satisfied smile on his face. He hadn't put his shirt back on, and her eyes traced the smooth muscles of his chest and arms. She'd touched there, she remembered, a little awed. She'd run her hands and fingers there, gripped and . . . her eyes narrowed on a spot on his shoulder.

Were those scratches? She spun around for a closer look. They *were* scratches—a whole row of them across his shoulder.

Whit flicked his gaze over, then back to grin at her.

"You're quiet," he reiterated. "But you're lively."

"I did that?" She took in his satisfied expression. "And you don't mind?"

"Not in the least," he assured her, and with enough conviction that she took him at his word. He shifted and held a hand out to her. "Come back to bed, imp. If someone was interested in knocking on the door, they would have done so by now."

"I—" That was true, she admitted, a little embarrassed now that she'd overreacted at the thought of being discovered. Her only excuse was that she'd been a bit . . . well, disoriented was the only word that came to mind.

"But what of the search?"

"Your uncle's in his room, and I suspect we'd be wasting our time going through the attic again." He turned his palm up. "Come back to bed."

*She* suspected he was avoiding a search of the house with

her at night, but she took his hand anyway and let him pull her down. Whatever was waiting to be discovered, could wait until tomorrow. She was, sadly, not going anywhere.

She snuggled next to him, with her head in the crook of his arm, and the reassuring beat of his heart under her hand.

And for the first time since being orphaned, Mirabelle fell asleep under her uncle's roof with a smile on her face.


She woke alone in the morning, feeling stiff, sore, nervous, and irrepressibly happy. She and Whit had . . . Well, she and Whit *had*. And that said quite enough.

She washed in the cold water left in the basin from the day before and changed into one of the light brown dresses she'd brought from Haldon. She wished she had thought to bring the lavender dress. She wanted so much to feel pretty today, and it was exceedingly difficult to feel pretty in brown. A woman should feel pretty after spending the night in the arms of the man she loved, shouldn't she?

She stopped in the act of straining to reach the back buttons of her gown.

In the arms of the man she loved? Had she just thought that? She let her own arms fall to her sides.

She *had* thought that. And she still did.

She loved Whit.

Of course she loved Whit. She wouldn't have even considered doing . . . allowing . . . enjoying . . . Well, she just wouldn't have considered it, that's all. Except that she loved him.

Shouldn't she have realized before now? Shouldn't there have been thunder and lightning and a great deal of music in her head at the very moment she fell in love? Kate's books always seemed to indicate that was how it happened.

She scowled at nothing in particular and tried to remember if she'd recently overlooked an internal storm and symphony. None came to mind.

She didn't feel any different toward him now than she had the day before, which was exactly how she had felt the week before, which was exactly how . . . how she had always felt.

Because she had always loved him.

That realization didn't arrive with music either, but it did feel as if it came weighted. She rubbed absently at the sudden tightness in her chest. All this time she'd loved him. While they'd fought and snarled and otherwise made themselves generally unpleasant to one another, she'd loved him.

Had he known? She wondered in a sudden panic. Should she tell him? Did he love her in return?

No, no, and—she wasn't certain, but all signs indicated— maybe.

He couldn't possibly have known, as she hadn't even been aware of it herself. She couldn't possibly tell him, as she had no idea how he felt. And she couldn't possibly know how he felt, as he'd never told her more than that he found her beautiful.

Remembering, she blushed, and decided that much would have to do for now. She'd keep her newfound love to herself. Perhaps, in time, he'd give her some hint, some reason to hope for more. But for today, she'd accept their mutual care and desire and be grateful for it.

Resolute, she finished dressing and left her room with the intention of going to the kitchen.

She'd prepare breakfast this morning. It wasn't an effort to charm Whit, she assured herself as she reached the bottom landing of the stairs. He'd cooked for her yesterday and it was only fair that she take a turn at the stove. Even if she was a little unclear on how it worked. How difficult could it be, really? A little wood, a small fire, close the door—

"Good morning, my dear."

Mirabelle jolted at the greeting and at the hard grip that closed around her forearm. She had to repress a shudder as Mr. Hartsinger turned her to face him. He'd always made her uncomfortable. In part, she was certain, because he was the only one of her uncle's friends she wasn't entirely certain she could outrun.

He was tall and rail thin with greasy black hair that fell past his ears in messy clumps so that he reminded her of a very old mop. He was an odd addition to her uncle's gathering, and a relatively recent one, this being only the third time he'd come. He didn't claim to be a great sportsman like the others, and while he partook of the wine and spirits with as much enthusiasm as the rest of the group, he often remained quiet and slightly apart during the festivities.

She might have liked him a bit more for it, but there was something about him that made her extremely uneasy. His bony fingers gripped too hard and his small dark eyes seemed to be always laughing with a dark and bitter humor.

"Mr. Hartsinger." She gave a mental sigh of relief when his hand released from her arm. "You're up rather early."

"I've a few things to see to before I leave this evening. I must cut my stay short, I'm afraid. My responsibilities at St. Brigit's beckon."

"Oh, well . . ." Thank heavens. "I'm sorry to hear that."

"Not to worry, my dear. We'll see each other again."

"Yes, of course, my uncle is loyal in his invitations. We'll meet again in the fall, I'm sure." She wasn't entirely sure it was possible for someone to actually be loyal in invitations, but the diplomatic, if possibly nonsensical, reply came easier than another lie.

He certainly didn't seem to mind it. He laughed, a high-pitched kind of whinny that made her skin crawl. "Perhaps not then, my dear, as work keeps me occupied, but soon enough, soon enough."

"Er . . . yes." She couldn't think of a single way to respond to that, as any future meeting with him would be more than soon enough for her.

"You've a lovely way about you," he murmured and to her absolute disgust, reached out to trail a bony finger down her cheek.

She jerked back. "Mr. Hartsinger, you forget yourself."

"I do indeed, my dear," he replied with that same eerie giggle and dropped his hand. "I do, indeed. I'd hate for us to start off badly. You'll accept my apologies, won't you?"

*No.* "I'm certain you're eager to be going," she muttered and retreated back toward the staircase.

She didn't run up the stairs, but it was a very near thing. Like she had with the animal trophies in her uncle's study, she could feel his dark eyes chasing her up every step. Whit could cook his own breakfast after all, she decided as she reached the landing and hurried toward her room.

Unable to stop herself, she glanced back over her shoulder to be certain he wasn't following her.

And ran head first into a solid wall of shirt and muscle.

She yelped and threw her arms out, even as she was steadied by two strong hands.

"Mirabelle," Whit said over her head. "Easy. What is it?"

She pressed a hand to her heart, willing it to return to a natural rhythm. "Nothing. It's nothing. It's ridiculous."

Whit's grip tightened on her arms. "Tell me."

She shook her head and laughed nervously. She'd overreacted terribly. The man hadn't done anything worse than take a small and essentially harmless liberty. "I'm being foolish. Mr. Hartsinger frightened me, that's all. There's something so sinister about the man's appearance. I met him in the foyer—"

He used his grip to push her behind him. "Go to your room. Lock the door."

"But—"

"Now."

She grabbed him before he could leave. "He didn't hurt me, Whit. He didn't even try. Honestly," she insisted and pulled him around to face her. "He frightens me just by *being*. And you can't very well demand satisfaction for that."

He gave her a hard searching look before nodding. "Stay in your room, anyway. I'll have breakfast brought up."

She waited until she saw the violence fade from his eyes before releasing him and stepping up to give him a soft kiss. "Thank you."

"For what?"

"For coming to my defense."

A line formed across his brow as he lifted a hand to trail his finger down her cheek, much as Mr. Hartsinger had. But her skin didn't crawl as it had in the foyer, it lit up as it had in her room.

She pressed closer to him. "Perhaps you could bring me breakfast."

The line of worry cleared as he smiled. "Perhaps I could."

Whit brought her breakfast, as promised, but he didn't stay as she had hoped. His participation was required for the second day of the hunt. He couldn't avoid joining the others for two days running. It made her exceedingly nervous, the idea of him being in close proximity to a pack of armed idiots, but when she mentioned as much, he merely grinned, gave her an annoyingly chaste peck on the cheek and promised to return to her in one piece.

He was just smug enough, and therefore irritating enough, that she was a little bit happy to see the back of him as he walked down the hall.

She spent the early hours of the afternoon, after the others had left, once again ensconced in the attic. She dug and sifted through decades worth of odds and ends, and it occurred to her that her uncle must not have been the first master of that house with an aversion to tossing anything out.

Heavens, why would anyone want to keep a fifty-year-old wig and accompanying box of wig powder? She pulled the overly elaborate coif out of a trunk and marveled at the sheer size and weight of it. It must have been tremendously uncomfortable to wear.

"I remember my mother owning something similar to that."

Though she immediately recognized the voice behind her as Whit's, she couldn't stop herself from starting and dropping the wig.

"For pity's sake, Whit," she admonished with a hand against her thrumming heart. "What the devil are you doing back here?"

"Delighted to see you too, darling," he returned and leaned down to press a quick kiss to her lips. "Even though you're not in your room."

Her blood warmed at the contact. "I never promised to stay in my room for the whole day, and you're supposed to be hunting with the others."

"As far as they know, I still am. I wandered off."

"You wandered off," she echoed.

"I informed the group that, like the good baron, I prefer to hunt alone."

"Oh," she smiled at him. "That was rather clever of you."

"Wasn't it just?" His eyes scanned the mess she'd made unpacking the trunks. "Have you found anything?"

She brushed off her gown and rose. "No."

"Let's try your uncle's room, then."

"But Mr. Cunningham—" she began.

"Is fast asleep, snoring like a tremendous lion. I knocked on his door just to see if it would disturb him. It didn't." He took her hand, leading her out of the room. "I want this done and you safely back at Haldon."

"What if he should wake?" she asked as they made their way downstairs.

"Then we hide, or we run. It's not more than a twenty-foot drop out the window."

She narrowed her eyes at him. "Are you trying to frighten me into not going?"

"Yes."

"Well, it won't work." Probably. What if her uncle should take it in his head to return early? Or what if they couldn't hear Mr. Cunningham's snores through the walls of the room and he woke without them realizing it? Or what if—?

She stopped and frowned outside Mr. Cunningham's door. Whit was right, the snoring coming from the other side was prodigious. Worse than the noise her uncle made, something she had, until this moment, believed impossible.

"That doesn't sound healthy," she whispered as Whit opened the baron's door.

"It doesn't even sound natural."

He ushered her inside and closed the door behind them. "At least we'll have warning if he wakes. Start at that end." He motioned to the bureau. "I'll take the desk and armoire."

While Mr. Cunningham gurgled and rasped on the other side of the wall, Mirabelle picked through her uncle's personal effects. And came to the conclusion that she had been much too hasty in insisting that she participate in this part of the search. She hadn't realized it would entail going through her uncle's undergarments.

Grimacing, she used the handkerchief Whit had given her that first day in the attic to gingerly push aside the contents of the drawers. It took her only moments to find the large wooden box hidden under a pile of stockings. She hesitated briefly before reluctantly lifting the lid—the possibilities of what a man like the baron might hide under his stockings were varied, and distinctly unpleasant.

The box opened easily, and inside she found several large stacks of ten-pound bank notes.

Well . . . bloody, bloody, hell.

Perhaps they were real. Perhaps her uncle was simply a miser. Perhaps—

"Mirabelle."

She turned to find Whit standing next to her, holding a small brown package, and with his face set in grim lines.

"What is it?" she whispered.

"Proof," was his answer.

Or more proof, she thought miserably, and pointed at the drawer.

He looked in, frowned, and took a stack of notes to put in his pocket. Then he had her by the arm and was leading her out and down the hall. He didn't speak again until they reached her room.

"You found something else? What is it?" she asked again as he shut and locked the door behind them.

He handed her the package by way of answer.

She pulled out the contents, and swallowed hard. She didn't have to ask what it was that she held. Its purpose was obvious enough. It was a metal plate, one side etched with ridges like a stamp. And those ridges formed the shape of a familiar looking ten-pound bank note.

So it was true. Her uncle was a counterfeiter. She wouldn't have believed it for a moment if she hadn't been holding the proof right there in her hands. She continued to stare at it, astonished, until Whit spoke.

"Mirabelle?"

She blinked, the spell broken, and handed the plate back to him. "What will you do with it?"

"I'll deliver it to William, along with the notes and the receipt of delivery you found in the attic. What happens after that is up to him. I'm sorry, imp."

She nodded. She had no respect for her uncle to lose, no trust that could be betrayed, and no pride that could turn to shame. But she was now in the exceedingly uncomfortable position of being related to not only a pathetic drunkard, but a criminal as well.

She'd never be anything more at Haldon now than a guest taken in out of charity, she realized, and had to fight back the sob she felt building in her throat.

Whit was too honorable to break his word, but giving shelter to the desolate niece of a felon was a far cry from . . . from what, exactly?

Taking her as a wife?

Her heart raced with longing, even as it broke.

The Earl of Thurston would not make an outcast his countess.

"Mirabelle?"

She swallowed back the tears and disappointment. He'd never given her any indication that he'd planned to offer for her, she reminded herself sternly. He'd made no promises. He'd said nothing of love. If she'd ever harbored a secret desire to become mistress of Haldon, that was her mistake.

Determined to salvage some pride, she put on a brave face and gestured at the plate. "Will this become public knowledge, do you think?"

"I very much doubt it." Whit answered, carefully enough that she recognized his intent was to reassure. "William wouldn't care to see you hurt by this, no one does. He might threaten exposure as a means to acquiring the names of any possible accomplices, but a messy trial wouldn't be to anyone's benefit."

"There has to be someone else," she insisted tiredly. "There has to be. He simply isn't capable of doing this sort of thing on his own."

"After a few days in his presence, I'm inclined to agree. William might have some ideas on that."

"Will you wait to tell him, Whit? Just until tonight? I'd like . . . I'd like to think through . . . I'd like to make some plans."

She'd like to be alone before the well of tears she'd pushed back broke free.

He hesitated before answering. "As long as the men are still out. But you're to stay in your room. And while you're thinking, pack a bag. I want you back at Haldon before dinner."

# ❋ *Twenty-three* ❋

$S$he spent the first hour alone in her room sobbing hopelessly into her pillow. When the tears ran dry, she dragged herself up, washed her face and, as Whit had suggested, began to pack.

She wouldn't be coming back. She would never come back. She would likely live the remainder of her life at Haldon as a guest.

Her uncle had destroyed whatever chance she may have had with Whit, and that was a painful wound she couldn't imagine ever healing. But like pouring salt on the cut, her uncle's behavior would also rob her of an inheritance.

To permanently leave her uncle's house without his written consent—and he would never consent to give up his three hundred pounds a year—before she turned seven-and-twenty, meant forfeiting her inheritance. And every last pound would go to . . . she couldn't quite remember. To "The Ladies' Society for The Cultivation of Virtue," or some such nonsense.

Staying, of course, was no longer an option, not with the very real possibility of scandal looming over her head.

Exhausted and frustrated, she crammed a bonnet into her valise. Which was rather stupid, she chided herself—destroying her own things in a fit of temper. She took a solid kick at her desk instead.

It was all so unfair.

Oh, but the five thousand pounds her parents had intended for her, gone—and her chance at independence with it. She'd never be a member of the Cole family now, but her inheritance at least could have insured she not be a charity.

Nothing she could do or say would convince her uncle to willingly forfeit his yearly allowance. Likely, not even a charge of counterfeiting would keep him from pursuing his money.

Blast and damn. If only she had six hundred pounds available to simply pay him off. She latched her valise, picked it up . . . set it down again.

She *could* pay him off. Why ever hadn't she thought of it before? She ran to her desk, pulled out pen and paper, and drafted a very simple contract.

She'd need to hurry. She'd heard her uncle's carriage return not minutes ago. Whit was likely having their own transportation back to Haldon readied at that very moment.

Not ten minutes later, she made the brief and always unpleasant walk to the study to find the door open and the baron, returned from the hunt, behind his desk nursing a glass of port.

She cleared her throat as she entered the room. "Excuse me, uncle."

"You scare the boy off?"

"Beg your pardon?"

"Thurston, you twit. He's hitching his team up even now. He and Hartsinger both. Thought I told you to stay in your room."

"I have. You did. I didn't frighten him off." If he was angry with her already, she didn't stand a chance.

He shrugged. "Boy needs aging. Why are you here?"

She straightened her shoulders and stepped deeper into the room. "I've come with a proposition of a financial nature."

"Proposition of a financial nature," he mimicked badly and guffawed into his glass. "Gel ain't got so much as a pound to her name and she wants to make a proposition of financial nature. Stupid cow."

She waited until he was occupied with slurping at his drink before continuing in measured tones. "According to the terms of my parents' will, the three hundred pounds you receive for my care, such as it is, will cease in less than two years. At that time, the monies set aside for my dowry will become mine to spend as I please. If you should see fit to release me early from your house, I will agree, in writing, to recompense you for your cooperation as soon as I receive my inheritance. Nine hundred pounds, I believe, would be fair."

"Nine hundred pounds?" he repeated, suddenly looking a bit more interested.

"Interest on your investment, as it were. It's a tidy profit to be made in so short a time."

He downed the drink in his glass and poured another with shaking hands. "You'll give me nine hundred pounds to let you go?"

"In essence, yes."

His thick tongue came up to wet his lips as he studied her in silence. He was considering it, she thought, she ought to be thrilled. So why did the way he was looking cause her stomach to tighten in dread?

"And you'll agree to it in writing," he repeated slowly. Slowly and suspiciously enough to have her hesitating before answering.

"I . . . I will."

"How do I know you'll make good on it?"

"I just said I'd put it in writing," she reminded him, confused. "I don't know what else—"

"Not good enough." His thick fingers began a steady thrumming on the desk. "Not nearly good enough. I wouldn't have the means to take it to court if you changed your mind."

"I'm not going to—"

"I want collateral."

"Wha . . . ?" She spluttered at the sheer absurdity of the demand. "Collateral?"

"Something wrong with your ears, girl? That's what I said."

"But you know very well I haven't anything—"

"You've friends," he hinted slyly. "Wealthy ones."

The dread turned to anger. The man, she thought, was an abomination. "If I were comfortable asking the Coles for a loan," she informed him coldly. "I wouldn't be having this exchange with you."

"Your comfort is immaterial."

"It's becoming clear that this entire conversation is immaterial," she returned. "If you'll excuse me."

"I'll not. Sit down, girl." When she hesitated he slammed his drink to the table, splashing the liquid. "I said sit!"

She sat down, a lifetime of fear easily brushing aside pride.

"I need a minute to think this through," he muttered. "Can't be rash."

To her great surprise and dismay, he levered himself out of his chair and began a lumbering pace behind the desk. She watched, disgusted, and just a little bit awed, as he heaved his mass slowly from one side of the room to the other in a display of physical exertion she hadn't thought him capable of in years. The floor creaked and moaned beneath him, rivulets of sweat tracked down his face to pool in his cravat, and in between his heavy puffs of breath, he muttered to himself in fits and starts.

"Didn't see it before . . . Legal contract . . . Specific dates . . .Independent of the will." He paused momentarily to pour himself another drink before resuming his walk. "Chit'll be trouble . . . This way's better . . . He'll handle her."

As he continued his one-sided rant, Mirabelle began to wonder if he'd forgotten she was there, or just didn't care.

He hadn't forgotten. He ended his pacing with another

finger jab in her direction. "I'll take your offer, but you'll have Thurston's coffers to back your word."

"He won't agree to it." And she'd be damned if she would ask him.

"You'll see that he does. And I want four thousand."

"Four thousand what?" she asked, baffled. Perhaps the man had lost his mind at some point, and she simply hadn't noticed.

"Pounds, you stupid chit. What else?"

"Pounds! You want four thousand pounds?" She gaped at him. "You can't possibly be serious."

"Does it look to you as if I'm playing, girl?"

It looked, she thought with a small bubble of hysterical laughter caught in her throat, as if he were on the verge of exploding. But knowing she could never be so lucky, she forced herself to speak in calm and reasonable tones. "Four thousand pounds is too large a sum. If—"

"You'll pay it all the same."

She shook her head. She'd rather all five thousand go to the ridiculous charity. "It would make more sense for me to wait out the will."

"Then you can wait it out in St. Brigit's."

"I beg your pardon?" She couldn't possibly have heard him threaten to send her to the asylum.

"I see I have your attention now," he jeered.

"You can't do that," she forced out in a horrified whisper. "You won't do that."

"Can and will. Have that contract to me in a fortnight or you'll spend the remainder of your years in a cage."

"You would've put me there before this if you'd thought it worth your while. The expense alone—"

"Will take a pretty penny of the funds the will allows me, it's true, but I'll part with it you may be sure. Don't believe me? Here." He rooted through the desk. "Here. Deal's all but done. I'll not be gainsaid, girl."

He held out a letter she didn't recognize from the night

she and Whit had been in the study. The letterhead read *St. Brigit's Asylum for the Infirm*. And the contents—what little she could make out around her blurring vision—detailed the acceptance of one Miss Mirabelle Browning as a future occupant.

"But . . . I only just came to you. I . . ."

"Doesn't follow I couldn't have thought of it first, does it?"

She shook her head slowly. "No . . . No, this is wrong."

Her mind whirled with a disorienting mixture of fear and anger and panic, but beneath it all was the notion that it was all somehow wrong. It didn't make sense. Why was he so determined to have Whit's cooperation? Why spend the money for sending her away when it cost him nothing to risk taking her word? Why would he already have the paper from St. Brigit's?

Because he'd been planning to send her there long before today, she realized, and remembered what Mr. Hartsinger had said.

*We'll see each other again.*

But why? An asylum cost a good deal of money. Why would he want to part with that money now when the terms of the will were . . . ?

The terms of the will. He'd broken the terms of the will. Fear and panic were instantly drowned in a wave of blinding fury.

"There is no money, is there?" she breathed. Slowly, seeing red, she rose from the chair. "The dowry is gone. You've already spent it."

"I haven't the slightest idea of what you mean."

"You thought to send me away before I could alert the authorities."

"You're ranting, girl."

"But I offered you a better way, didn't I? Have me sign a contract and then ship me off. That's why you needed Whit's agreement, isn't it? You knew I wouldn't be able to fulfill my end of the bargain and thought to cheat him out of a fortune."

"Careful what accusations you throw at me."

"You stole my dowry." Her future. And the one hope she'd had in all the years she'd been forced to live under his roof. Gone. Gone for who knew how long. "You stole my inheritance. You're nothing but a thief."

"Watch your tongue." He shook the paper at her. "I hold your future here."

"You stole my future! You revolting, overblown, useless waste of——!"

The tumbler caught her on the cheekbone. A whopping crack seemed to echo in her head and she had the sudden and pointless thought that he could move a great deal faster than she had given him credit for. She hadn't even noticed he'd pulled his arm back.

What came after that, however, would always remain something of a blur to her. There was pain, she knew, where the glass had struck her hard enough to break the skin, but above and beyond that, there was fury. Great heaving waves of fury that crashed over her head and swept her away.

Without thought, without even realizing her intent, she bent to pick up the fallen glass. Then rose, looked at it for a moment . . . and hurled it back at him.

She ignored his howl of pain as the glass bounced off the side of his head.

"You bloody bastard!" She reached for a brass paperweight on the desk and winged that as well.

"You coward!" An inkwell came next, then a ledger, a candlestick, a box of snuff. "You're repulsive! Repugnant! Abhorrent!"

He grunted and yelped as each object found its mark, and he shuffled around the desk in an attempt to escape. She stalked him, tossing objects and insults and keeping the safety of the wood between them until they'd traded positions.

"Blighter! Rotter! Despicable counterfeiting . . ."

Her hand once more reached for the desk . . . and came back empty. She had only a moment to look down at the desktop; only a moment to notice it was empty; and only a moment to grab one of the drawers and yank it open, before he was on her. Even as she registered that he was coming around the desk, she shoved her hand into the drawer and groped blindly. She felt his fingers twist painfully into her hair even while her own fingers brushed something cool and smooth. She fumbled with it once, when he yanked her back hard enough to catch her head against the side of the desk, but then she latched on. And when she pulled her hand up again, she was holding a gun.

# ❀ Twenty-four ❀

Ten minutes more—that was all she was getting.

Whit stood in the front drive and watched his men from Haldon haul his trunk from his room. It took some doing, as Mr. Hartsinger's carriage was currently blocking the front steps.

The sun had set, and the last of its light was fading rapidly. He'd give Mirabelle those ten minutes, he decided, and not a second more. It would be hours yet before dinner, but her uncle had returned early, and every moment she remained in the house made him anxious.

He'd wanted to pack her off the moment they'd discovered the printing plate. Hell, he hadn't wanted her to come in the first place, but he'd lost that argument. Now that they had proof her uncle was involved in counterfeiting—and with the very good chance he had an accomplice—Whit was determined to get her out and away from the whole messy business.

He'd been hard-pressed not to take her arm in the baron's bedroom, lead her downstairs, out the front door, and straight into a carriage he could send to Haldon. And he'd continued to fight that urge every minute since he'd agreed to give her time to pack and think. She had a right to both, he reminded himself. She was leaving what might be loosely termed her home, and walking away from her only surviving relation.

If, upon his arrival, the baron had gone directly his room, she'd have had to do her thinking elsewhere. But Eppersly had waddled into the study instead, where he would no doubt remain until dinner. There was no chance of him discovering the missing plate and bank notes until Mirabelle was gone from the house.

"All ready here, my lord."

Whit nodded at the driver. "It'll be only a minute more."

He noticed the fading light again. No reason he couldn't try hurrying Mirabelle along, just a bit. He spun on his heel toward the house . . . and then saw it—the slightest movement in the shadows near the stables. He stopped, peered through the dim light and watched as a dark shape slipped inside.

He turned to the driver and spoke quietly. "Hand me your crop."

"My lord?" the man asked, even as he handed over the whip.

Whit took the handle, found a grip he liked. "If Miss Browning comes out, see that she stays in the carriage."

Trusting his man to follow the command, Whit worked his way around to the back of the stable. It occurred to him that whoever he was following might have a perfectly good, or perfectly legal at any rate, reason for skulking about. It could be someone meeting a lover, or a servant avoiding work.

Or it could be a thief or the baron's coconspirator.

It certainly wasn't Christian. The dark figure moved with an agility the stable hand lacked.

Whit entered the stables silently, his muscles tense, the blood rushing in his ears.

A light flickered and the sound of movement came from a stall two doors up.

He let his feet roll beneath him, heel to toe, to lessen the noise of footsteps on hay. He stepped behind the closest post, craned his neck around the wood to peer into the stall.

And looked directly into the eyes of his quarry.

"McAlistair." Whit didn't jump—though it was a near thing—but he did let out an agitated breath at the sudden surprise. "Why not pull out a gun and shoot at me?"

"Might have. Once."

Whit responded with an annoyed grunt, and lowered the crop. "What are you doing here?"

"Orders."

In an instant, Whit's blood turned to ice and the cold of it made his heart seize painfully in his chest. He had the man by the front of his collar before he'd even realized his intent. "Mirabelle's in that house," he snarled. "You'll not do a bloody thing while Mirabelle's in the house."

McAlistair shook his head. "Retired. Remember?"

Whit loosened his hold, took a deep breath, and let his hands drop. "Of course. Of course, forgive me."

McAlistair made a slight movement of his shoulders that may, or may not, have been a shrug.

"Why did William have you come?

"Protection."

The insult stung. "I can bloody well protect myself."

"For the girl."

That insult stung more. "I can bloody well protect her as well."

"Orders," he repeated and pulled a letter from his coat pocket.

Whit reached for it, skimmed over the impersonal note from William informing McAlistair of his new mission, and handed it back. "How long have you been lurking about the grounds?"

"Two days."

Since the start of the party, Whit thought, and nodded. William liked to play to his agent's strengths. Whit was best at charming his way in. McAlistair was best at sneaking.

"The mission's over," Whit informed him. "I need only get Mirabelle to—"

"Someone's coming."

Mirabelle's mind whirled with the same dizzying speed as the day she'd tumbled down the hill. The room was out of focus, and her movements felt stiff and somehow disconnected from the rest of her.

She had a pistol in her hand. That was clear enough. And her uncle was backing away into the corner of the room. She could see that, as well. It was a fine sight, she decided, as she rose from her knees and moved around to the front of the desk. A very fine sight, indeed.

Shouldn't he pay for every insult, every humiliation, every moment of fear? Shouldn't he pay for hurting her, for stealing her future? She could see that he did. She could make certain he paid, and paid dearly.

She gripped the gun with shaking hands, and leveled it at his chest. "I ought to," she heard herself say as if from a great distance. "I ought to."

A loud click sounded behind her ear. "But you won't, my dear. Not today."

Dread, cold and hard, filled her as Mr. Hartsinger stepped around her, his own pistol aimed at her heart.

"It's not so much that I'd mind you shooting him," he said with his nasty giggle. "But murder invites attention, and I can't have that. Be a good girl now and lower your weapon."

With no other choice, she slowly dropped her arm.

The baron shuffled forward, a stream of blood issuing from his nose from where she'd caught him with the snuff-box. "Should beat you senseless," he snarled, snatching the gun out of her hand.

"Then we wouldn't be able to find out what she knows, would we?" Hartsinger pointed out with contempt. "Now then, my dear, you and I are going to take a walk, calm as you please, to my waiting carriage. If you give any indication of duress, I'll shoot you in the back. I'd just as soon not, but—"

"And I'll shoot your friend. What's his name—Christian," the baron interrupted. He sneered when she looked at him with surprise. "Didn't think I knew about that, did you?"

"You didn't know about that," Mr. Hartsinger muttered. "Until I pointed it out."

"Well, I know about it now," the baron snapped before waving the gun at Mirabelle. "And if you give us any trouble, girl, I'll aim between his eyes."

And likely shoot off his own foot, Mirabelle thought. Only, by the way her uncle's face was once again turning red, it was clear she hadn't just thought it. In her muddled state of mind, she'd said it out loud.

She wasn't given much of a chance to regret the error, just the time it took for her uncle to turn the gun around and bring the butt of it down on her head.

Hartsinger lowered his arm and stared at Mirabelle's crumpled form.

"You idiot," he snapped at Eppersly, snatching the baron's gun away and tossing it safely out of reach. "How do you propose we get her out of the house now?"

Whit and McAlistair watched from around the stall walls as a heavyset man with a thick crop of dark hair entered through the front and called out. "Christian? Christian, my good man, have you seen our girl today?"

It must be the perpetually absent Mr. Cunningham, Whit decided. Mirabelle had said he was an amiable sort, and Whit couldn't imagine any of the other guests would refer to Mirabelle as "our girl," or know to ask Christian about her whereabouts.

Odd though, that man didn't appear to be suffering the aftereffects of a long illness. He walked down the center aisle with a clipped step and continued to call out in a booming voice. "Christian? Are you in here?"

Whit leaned forward and squinted his eyes. He knew that voice. He knew the man. The hair color was different, and there was something off about the nose, but he knew him . . . and not as Mr. Cunningham.

He straightened and stepped forward from the stall. "Any particular reason for you to be looking for her, Mr. Lindberg?"

Lindberg started, then winced. "Thurston. Blast. Ah, well. It was only a matter of time, I suppose."

"Before what?" Whit asked.

"Before this business ended," Lindberg responded cryptically and moved forward to close the remaining distance between them. "Hello, McAlistair."

McAlistair sniffed once. "You reek."

"God, man, what is that?" Whit took two steps back. "Bad fruit?"

"Old cabbage and a healthy splash of vinegar, actually. Pungent, isn't it?"

"It's noxious. Why the hell are you attending the baron's party, disguised, and smelling of old cabbage and vinegar?"

"Didn't want the girl getting too close," he explained. "What if she recognized me in London?"

"She couldn't bloody well recognize you as you've spent the whole of the party in your room."

"Yes, well, *this* time. But I learned you were to come, you see, and—"

"Explain 'this time,'" Whit instructed.

"I've played the role of Mr. Cunningham for more than ten years."

Ten years? "Why?"

"To watch over the girl, of course." He shrugged his broad shoulders. "Just following orders."

"There's a lot of that going round," McAlistair murmured.

Lindberg blinked and smiled. "I believe McAlistair just made a joke."

A new voice sounded from the doors. "Are we all here, then?"

Whit whirled around to see Christian striding forward with long, uneven steps. Whit shot a glance at McAlistair.

"Didn't you hear him coming?" McAlistair always knew when someone was approaching. Before McAlistair could respond, however, Whit's eyes widened in realization of something and he turned back to Christian. "You're not stooping," he accused. "Why aren't you stooping?"

Christian came to a stop in front of them, his limp and weak arm still apparent, but his back was straight and his shoulders squared. "It was only for the girl's benefit. I fancied I was less of threat to her that way. Evening, McAlistair. Lindberg, your smell is bothering the horses."

"Can't be avoided," Lindberg responded. "It appears things are drawing to a close. Or a head. I'm not quite sure which."

Whit looked at each of the three men and the hand holding the crop tightened. "I want answers—"

"William sent us," Christian informed him.

Though he hadn't meant to have the answers now, he couldn't help responding. "Do you mean to tell me you've had this same mission, for years?"

"Only four," Christian replied and shrugged. "I've had worse."

"Holy hell." He held up his free hand when Lindberg looked as if he might add something to that. "Not now. I need to get Mirabelle out. You," he snapped at Lindberg,

"Go keep Eppersly occupied. The rest of you meet me at Haldon in an hour."

He didn't wait to hear if there were any objections, but simply turned and strode from the stable. He'd deal with William and the others after he'd gotten Mirabelle safely to Haldon. A man could only worry over so many things at once. He had to have priorities.

And Mirabelle was his first.

Crossing the now darkened yard at a trot, he noted with some relief that Mr. Hartsinger's carriage was gone. There'd be no need to sneak her out now. With the baron in his study, and the house filled with disinterested staff, he could simply walk her down the front steps.

But just to be certain, he stopped at the study doors once he was inside. Reassured by the sound of huffing breath and creaking floorboards on the other side, he headed upstairs to Mirabelle's room, peeking in the library and billiards room for returned guests along the way.

He found her door unlocked, which irritated him some. But he found the room empty, and that flatly infuriated him.

Hadn't he expressly told her not to leave her room?

He turned a circle in the small space, taking in the gown laid across the bed, the mess of papers at the desk, and the packed valise on the floor.

She'd gone looking for something, he assured himself, even as a chill of unease settled over the anger. Like as not, the stubborn chit was in one of the countless storage rooms, digging out some memento or other.

The shuffle of heavy feet in the hall had him striding out of the room again.

"Something's wrong," Lindberg said, panting a bit from his quick climb up the steps. "Study's a wreck. Eppersly's sporting a bloody nose and wouldn't let me past the door. Where's our girl?" he added on a shout as Whit sprinted past him.

"Missing! Fetch the others!"

Whit barreled into the study, throwing the doors open with a crash. He took in the contents of the room in one sweep of his gaze. Furniture turned over, papers and items from the desk scattered, the baron holding a bloody handkerchief to his nose, and—most terrifying of all—a pistol lying in the corner.

Eppersly hastily shoved the handkerchief in his pocket. "Thurston, my boy—"

"Where is she?" Whit demanded, crossing the room in a few long strides. He fought the urge to wrap his hands around Eppersly's neck and squeeze the information out. Unfortunately, the man couldn't answer if he couldn't breathe.

Eppersly made a sad attempt to straighten his cravat. "Where is who?"

"Mirabelle," Whit ground out, curling his hands into fists. "Where is she?"

"Mirabelle? I don't know what you're talking about." Eppersly blinked rapidly, the very picture of a dim-witted man attempting to play stupid.

Which was twice the idiocy Whit had the patience for. His fist shot out, connected, and Eppersly went down like a felled oak.

It may not have been as satisfying as strangling the bastard, but then, Whit wasn't entirely confident his hands could have found a neck under all those rolls of fat. And it was *immensely* satisfying to plant his boot on the man's chest and hold him down.

"Where is she, you miserable—"

"You don't understand!" Cowed, Eppersly shook on the floor. "She's mad! She went mad! Attacked me!"

Whit was almost glad for the excuse to lean in until the baron garbled and choked.

*"Where?"*

"Hartsinger," Eppersly gasped when Whit let up again. "Hartsinger took her."

The confession hit Whit like a shot to the chest, robbing him of breath and leaving him reeling.

*She's mad.*

*Hartsinger took her.*

"You sent her to St. Brigit's?" he hissed.

"Smuggled her out in a trunk," Lindberg's voice informed him from the doorway. Whit glanced over to see him enter the room with McAlistair and Christian. "The staff here will do anything for a coin. And admit to it for a little more."

Shoving aside panic, Whit stepped off the baron and turned to Christian. "Can you fight?"

"I've a brace of loaded pistols in the stable," Christian answered with a nod.

"Good. Saddle the horses. Lindberg," Whit continued as Christian left, "take the carriage to Haldon, tell William what's happened."

"Of course."

"McAlistair, there's a pistol in the corner—"

"Now see here!" Eppersly interrupted, struggling to a sitting position. "You've no right interfering! No right! You don't even like the chit!"

Whit didn't bother responding. He simply pulled the printing plate and bank notes from his pocket and handed them to McAlistair. "Find out what he knows. If he gives you any trouble," he said clearly, "kill him . . . Have you ever killed a baron?"

McAlistair considered it briefly before shaking his head. "Duke once. Two counts. A Russian prince."

"Well then, a baron wouldn't be much of a feather in your cap, would it?"

He left the room to the sound of Eppersly's whimpering.

# ❀ Twenty-five ❀

$\mathcal{M}$irabelle woke in stages, fighting her way through a fog of pain and confusion. She was vaguely aware of being curled on her side in a small space, and of a bumping and rocking sensation. But nausea and exhaustion dragged her back to oblivion before she could work through what that might mean.

When next she woke, her world was still, stale, and absolutely black. She blinked her eyes experimentally to be sure they were open. When the darkness around her didn't alter, she reached out and discovered a hard surface mere inches from her face. Not blind then, she reasoned, shoving at the barrier, but trapped. With panic creeping steadily through her blood, she searched the meager space around her with her hands and feet, and found only that she was boxed in on all sides. A trunk? She shifted and squirmed, trying to find or force a way out.

And there *was* a way out. There had to be.

It was like being buried alive.

The possibility of such a horror sent the panic racing. She cried out, kicked, and clawed at her confinement.

An answer came in the form of a loud creak, a rush of fresh air, and a great burst of light in her eyes.

"Now, now. There's no need for all that," a familiar voice admonished.

"Let me out," she demanded even as she scrambled up. "Let me—"

"I hardly intended to keep you strapped to the top of the carriage for the whole trip."

A set of bony fingers gripped her arm and helped her climb out of the trunk. Shaking them off, she stumbled across a few feet of dirt road toward a carriage, then simply bent at the waist and let the cool night air fill her lungs.

"That's it, my dear. Take a few more deep breaths," the voice advised. "A strike to the head can be a bit off-putting to the system. The man's a brute. You're well rid of him."

A strike to the head, she thought dully. A road and carriage. A high-pitched voice and bony fingers. Memories came trickling back.

Oh, Lord. She'd been kidnapped—struck over the head, stuffed in a trunk, and taken away. It was beyond comprehension, surreal enough that she had trouble wrapping her mind around it. Young ladies being hauled off against their will was the sort of thing Kate's novels were rife with—a clear indicator of how far removed the scenario was from reality.

She straightened slowly and held her hand up against the blinding light. "Where are we?"

"On the road home, my dear," Mr. Hartsinger said, lowering the lantern.

"Home?" What was the man talking about? What sort of abductor brought his captive home? "You're taking me to Haldon?"

Hartsinger giggled. "Of course not, silly girl. I'm taking you to your new home, St. Brigit's."

St. Brigit's.

Suddenly, her circumstances didn't seem surreal at all. Kate's stories of damsels in distress might have been fiction, but the tales Evie told of sane but inconvenient women being sent to asylums were terrifyingly real.

Her eyes jumped from one side of the darkened road to the other. She couldn't outrun a carriage, particularly feeling as dizzy and sick as she did, but if she could dart off the side into the trees, perhaps she could hide . . . .

"Ah, ah, ah. None of that," Hartsinger sang, lifting the

pistol she'd forgotten he had. "And I shouldn't bother looking to my driver for help, if I were you." He jerked his chin toward the shadowy figure pushing the trunk off the side of the road. "I pay him handsomely. Now, into the carriage with you."

She considered disobeying. If it was a choice of being shot on the side of the road or spending the rest of her life locked in an asylum with the likes of Mr. Hartsinger, she'd take the bullet.

Fortunately, that choice wasn't required of her. She need only bide her time until she had the opportunity to escape. Or until Whit came for her.

Feeling determined about the first, and absolutely certain of the second, she climbed into the carriage.

Whit had known fear before. He'd felt it the day Mirabelle had fallen down the hill. And the night she'd insisted on participating in the mission.

As a soldier, he'd experienced that sick dread that proceeds every battle, and the weighted horror that comes as men die in the blood and gore of combat.

But nothing, absolutely nothing, compared to the marrow-deep terror he felt now.

He spurred his horse on, knowing it was dangerous to ride hell-for-leather with only the shadowed moonlight to show the way. He had no choice.

How much of an advantage did Hartsinger have? Five minutes? A quarter hour? Even more? How long had they been in the stable, standing about, while Mirabelle was being dragged away?

In a trunk.

Was she still in there? Trapped and frightened?

He almost preferred that idea over the alternative—that Hartsinger had taken her out and was now alone with her in the carriage.

A man could do a great deal of harm to a woman when he had a carriage and a quarter-hour's time at his disposal.

He signaled to Christian to take the next turn left. It was another risk, using the narrow trail, but it was their best chance to pull ahead of Hartsinger and ambush him where the trail met the road. With any luck, they could take out the driver from the cover of the trees, avoiding an out-and-out chase that would further endanger Mirabelle.

"There now, isn't this cozy?" Hartsinger sighed as he settled on the bench opposite Mirabelle. Keeping the gun trained on her, he lifted a hand to knock on the roof, starting the carriage off. "Would you care for a blanket? There is a bit of chill tonight."

If she could have risked opening her mouth without losing her supper, she would have gaped at him.

Was the man being solicitous?

"Oh my, you do look surprised," he tittered. "And I suppose you have reason. Pity, though, this isn't at all how I would have chosen things to begin. I'd envisioned a slightly less dramatic homecoming for you. But, well, needs must."

"St. Brigit's is not my home," she bit out between clenched teeth.

"Certainly it is. The contract your uncle signed is legal in every way. You'll be very happy there," he assured her, growing excited. "I intend to give you your own room, you know, complete with window and fireplace. And a soft bed, as well . . . although, I'll admit," he added with another giggle, "when it comes to that, I'm thinking of my own comfort as much as yours."

Seeped in pain, her head pounding mercilessly, the meaning of that statement didn't immediately register with Mirabelle. But eventually understanding dawned, and with it came revulsion—thick greasy waves of it. Her stomach spasmed painfully, until she feared that just keeping her mouth closed wouldn't be enough. She pressed herself into the corner, taking shallow breaths until the worst of it passed.

"But business before pleasure, I'm afraid," Hartsinger continued, as if nothing were amiss. "Tell me what you know of this counterfeiting business."

Though the movement cost her, she shook her head.

"You don't mean to pretend ignorance, do you, because it will never work. I was eavesdropping on you and your uncle, you see." He grinned broadly. "I cannot tell you how much I enjoyed watching you pelt the baron with his own effects. And I would have left you to it, if you hadn't referred to him as . . ." He glanced at the ceiling, remembering. "A . . . despicable counterfeiting . . . and then you broke off, I believe. So tell me, my dear, whyever would you call him such a thing?"

She had no intention of cooperating with the man. But she was in no condition to fight him either. She tried for distraction. "You're an accomplice," she accused.

He frowned thoughtfully. "I don't think I care for that word. It has a sort of secondary ring to it. Let's just call me the architect. Our little operation was my doing. Which still leaves the question of how you discovered it."

"Does it matter?"

"Indulge me," he suggested.

"No."

"Tell me," he repeated, raising the gun. "Or you go back in the trunk."

"I was snooping in the baron's room," she snapped. "I found the bills and plate."

His face went blank. Then cold and hard.

"What plate?"

Mirabelle wasn't given the chance to answer. Seemingly out of nowhere, the sharp report of a pistol cut through the night air.

The carriage lurched, taking on a sudden burst of speed, and the force of it threw Hartsinger into her. She shoved at him instinctively, using her hands and feet to knock him back . . . and knock the pistol from his hand. It bounced off the bench to land on the floor.

There was a mad scramble as they both dove for the weapon. By virtue of being closest, she got there first, but the benefits of that were limited, as it gave him the opportunity to land on top of her.

Even hurt and frightened as she was, the notion occurred to her that she had never experienced anything so repulsive as Mr. Hartsinger's full weight squirming against her back. She threw an elbow out and caught him in the ribs, but that earned her little more than a grunt, and provided him room to sneak a hand under her to claw at the gun.

Certain she wouldn't be able to throw him off and knowing she hadn't the space to aim the gun without hurting herself, she did the only other thing she could think of—she curled around the weapon, squeezed her eyes shut, and closed her mind against the feel of his grasping hands.

The carriage was slowing. Wasn't it slowing? Wasn't the rattle of the wheels easing? Her heart leapt at the sound of hoofbeats at the side of the carriage, and the distant sound of Whit calling her name. If she could just hold on long enough . . .

Hartsinger's hand gripped the gun, slid off when she jerked, and then gripped again.

Her heart sank as quickly as it had leapt. She wouldn't be able to hold on. She wasn't strong enough. Hartsinger would have the gun in a matter of seconds. And he wouldn't use it to shoot his only bargaining chip. He'd aim for Whit.

Without further thought, she twisted the gun, instinctively aiming to the side, away from her face, and with her last ounce of strength pushed herself back as far as Hartsinger's weight allowed.

Then she pulled the trigger.

The sound was deafening, a painful blast that left her ears ringing. And the heat that seared along her rib cage had her crying out.

But even over the noise and pain she could hear Mr. Hartsinger screeching. Had she shot him? Her purpose in discharging the gun had been to render it useless, but if she'd managed to wound him in the process, all the better.

"Mirabelle!"

She heard Whit call for her again and the unmistakable bang of a carriage door being flung open. Then came the blessed relief of Mr. Hartsinger being flung away. But she didn't open her eyes until Whit's strong, familiar hands lifted her up to a sitting position.

"Where are you shot? Mirabelle, where—" His eyes found the rip in her clothing and the burn mark on her rib cage and he swore, low and viciously.

"I'm not shot." She glanced down and squinted. "Well, maybe a little. "

He ran shaking hands along the wound. "It's not bleeding. You're not bleeding."

"No. I aimed away."

"You—?" He swore again and, though it was a bit hard to tell, she thought he shook his head. "Where else are you hurt? Mirabelle. Sweetheart, look at me."

She'd like to, she thought, if only he would be still a moment. But he kept moving, running unsteady hands over her—her arms, her back, her face. And he kept shifting his head to kiss her—her eyes, her mouth, her hair. Because trying to pin him down made her dizzier, she simply wrapped her arms around him and burrowed in.

He followed suit, gripping her so tight she might have protested if it hadn't felt so right.

"You're all right," he breathed. He lifted her up and out

of the carriage, and pressed his face to her neck. "I heard the shot. Tell me you're all right."

She nodded against his chest. "I'm all right."

She felt a tremble go through him before he pulled back and framed her face with his hands. "Did he hurt you?"

"No."

He brushed his thumb gently beneath the broken skin of her cheek. "I was late."

"No, my uncle did that," she explained, feeling a little steadier. "You were just in time—"

"I was late," he repeated, and she realized he wasn't referring to just that night.

"You're here now," she whispered. And because he was, and because he seemed to need it as much as her, she wrapped her arms around him a second time.

"I want to go home, Whit," she said into his coat. "My head hurts. Will you take me home?"

"I will, sweetheart." His fingers feathered gently through her hair. She felt him tense when he found the knot where the butt of the gun had struck her.

"I am all right," she assured him. "I just want to go home."

"And I'll take you, darling, I promise." He set her gently on the carriage step. "But I need just a moment. Can you wait just a moment?"

She nodded, expecting him to do something with the horses and carriage. Instead, with rage in his eyes, and his features set in hard lines, he reached inside and grabbed Hartsinger's weapon. "Stay here."

She didn't stay. How could she, when Whit was marching off with a pistol in his hand? She followed him around the side of the carriage, annoyed that she needed to use it for support. In the dim moonlight she could make out someone standing over two men on the road. The first, whom she assumed was the driver, was holding a bleeding arm.

And the second, whining loudly and dabbing at a nasty gash along his shoulder, was Mr. Hartsinger.

"She shot me. The chit shot me," he trailed off nervously as Whit strode past and retrieved fresh shot from the back of his saddle. "Miss Browning has been legally signed into my care. This isn't your concern, Thurston."

Whit loaded the gun and stepped forward to stand over Hartsinger. "Do I appear unconcerned?"

Though Mirabelle found the sight of Hartsinger cowering on the ground gratifying, the uncharacteristically frigid tone of Whit's voice sent chills up her spine. He didn't really mean to kill the man, did he?

Hartsinger certainly seemed to think so. "Consider what you're doing, man! It would be murder! You'll hang—"

"I'm an earl," Whit reminded him.

That gave Hartsinger pause. Peers of the realm weren't sent to the gallows. "You'll be banished!" he tried instead. "The authorities will—"

"Difficult for a man to report murder," Whit interrupted, priming the pistol and aiming it squarely at Hartsinger, "with his head stuck on a pike."

Mirabelle started forward. "Whit, no!"

He flicked a glance in her direction. "Don't you want his head stuck on a pike?"

*Oh, rather.* "But he's the accomplice."

"Is he?" Whit asked, but didn't lower the weapon. "Well then, it's not really murder at all, is it?"

Hartsinger's mouth began to work rapidly, though it was a moment before sound came out. "A lie. The girl lies—" he shrieked and ducked when Whit raised his weapon an inch. "A misunderstanding! The lady misunderstood! I implore you—!"

"Whit, please," Mirabelle cut in, and wondered if she could walk the distance to where he stood without falling. "I just want to go home. You promised you'd take me home."

For the first time since leaving her beside the carriage, Whit turned and really looked at her.

And lowered the gun. "So I did. Tie them up, Christian. See McAlistair gets them."

Unsteady, Mirabelle reached behind her to grip the carriage. "McAlistair?" She took a second look at the tall man standing beside Whit. *"Christian?"*

"I'll explain—" Whit broke off at the sound of approaching horses. "That would be Alex," he commented and striding to her, lifted her off her feet into his arms. "With any luck, he brought a second carriage."

Alex had, as it turned out, and in short order Mirabelle was tucked warmly next to Whit and on her way to Haldon.

The carriage rocked gently beneath her, lulling her into a lethargy that fear had earlier kept at bay. She stared unseeing out the dark window, longing desperately for sleep. But her mind refused to settle. Everything had changed. Her plans, her future, her hopes—all had been dashed in the course of a single day.

"Mirabelle?" She felt Whit's hand move from her shoulder to brush at her hair.

"He took my dowry," she said softly. "My uncle, he stole it." She looked to him. "I don't know what to do. I had it all planned. Now I don't know what to do."

When the tears came, he simply gathered her in and held on.

# ❧ Twenty-six ❧

𝓗aldon was a riot of noise and activity when they arrived.

Nearly every servant had descended on the front hall looking for a way to help. Kate, Evie, and Sophie surrounded Mirabelle and bustled her off to her room. William Fletcher appeared from the library looking harassed, followed by Lady Thurston who looked to be doing the harassing.

Mr. Lindberg returned from a second trip to the baron's, carrying the contract that assigned Mirabelle to St. Brigit's. And with the news that the baron had babbled an extended confession within minutes of being left alone with McAlistair. Lord Eppersly claimed to have been blackmailed by Mr. Hartsinger into using the bank notes after attempting, in desperation, to pass several off in payment to the asylum for Mirabelle's future care. He denied all knowledge of a printing plate, and when asked how he'd come about the counterfeit notes, would only answer that it was meant to be a grand joke.

Assuming that no other information would be available on that score until McAlistair's return, Whit made his way upstairs and for the second time in a fortnight, found himself standing outside Mirabelle's room, anxiously waiting for news. He refused offers of food and drink, and demands for explanations alike. The thought of eating made his stomach churn, and he couldn't provide answers he didn't have.

The physician, paid handsomely to be available to the Cole family at a moment's notice, arrived within a half hour. He spent what seemed to Whit to be an exceedingly large amount of time in Mirabelle's room before finally emerging to announce that Miss Browning's wounds were not life-threatening, though she would likely have a very unpleasant headache and a very unattractive black eye by morning. The physician then provided a list of instructions for dealing with a blow to the head that Whit passed on to Mrs. Hanson with the express order that every member of the household was to memorize its contents.

Then he went in search of William. He found him once again in the library, and once again, apparently, being harassed by Lady Thurston.

They stood in front of the fire, and barely spared him a glance when he entered.

"You said she was safe," Lady Thurston accused William in a voice sharp enough to cut glass. "Nothing of this sort was supposed to happen."

Whit came to a stop in front of a small reading table and glared at the pair. "What are you talking about?" he demanded, and was roundly ignored.

"I never would have suggested the ruse if I thought for even a moment her safety would be compromised," William replied defensively.

"What ruse?" Whit demanded, for all the good it did him. Neither his mother nor William even flicked their eyes in his direction.

"Mr. Lindberg and Christian should have informed us of the potential danger—" Lady Thurston began.

"Neither have ever reported the baron becoming violent in their presence," William cut in. "And none of us suspected Hartsinger's involvement."

"How did you know of Mr. Lindberg—" Whit tried.

"Have they had blinders on for all these years?" Lady Thurston snapped.

"Lindberg and Christian are outstanding members of my—"

"Enough!" Whit slammed his fist on the table. "That is bloody well enough!"

His mother drew herself up. "Whittaker Vincent, I will not tolerate that sort of language in my house."

"Lady Thurston, it is *my* house, and at the moment, I don't give two damns for your tolerance. *Sit down.*"

"Well," she huffed. She straightened her shoulders, indignant, but looked about her, found a chair to her liking, and sat on the edge primly. "Well."

William followed suit, taking a seat next to her, though his posture was of a man resigned, not offended.

Whit stifled the urge to pace. "I want answers. William, you start."

"Yes, yes of course." William reached up to tug at his cravat, but finding it already undone, yanked it off instead. "Your mother and I felt . . . No, no, I should start from the beginning, shouldn't I?" He heaved a great sigh. "Seventeen years ago, I made a deathbed vow to the late Duke of Rockeforte. I was tricked into it, to be honest, but nevertheless—"

"What vow?" Whit cut in.

William shifted in his seat and the slightest trace of a blush rose to his cheeks. "I promised . . . I promised to see that his children . . . found love."

Whit scowled at him. "You can't be serious."

"I am," William responded with a scowl of his own. "As he was—though I suspect he's laughing over it even now— the blighter."

"His children . . ." Whit repeated, and remembered the strange mission he and Alex had been assigned nearly two years ago. Alex had been given the task of wooing Sophie in the hopes of catching her and her cousin in the act of spying for the French. They'd been only marginally successful in that regard, and it'd been a damn odd way to go about the business.

"Were you responsible for Sophie and Alex meeting?" he asked.

"Yes, and I should like to point out that although this particular mission hasn't gone quite as planned, at least you haven't found it necessary to fight off a pack of would-be assassins." William perked up a bit. "I believe I might be improving."

Whit ignored his mother's derisive snort. "Improving in what, exactly? What has any of this to do with Mirabelle, or me? Neither of us are related to Rockeforte by blood."

"No," William agreed. "But you were his children all the same."

"He loved you," Lady Thurston said quietly. "Though you were too small to remember well, he loved each of you as if you were his own. In some ways, he was more of a father to you than your own."

Because he did remember, Whit only nodded and turned to William. "You thought to bring Mirabelle and me together."

"That was my idea," Lady Thurston admitted. "I had hoped . . . no, I knew, from the very start, that the two of you were meant to be. It was fate."

Whit allowed that statement to sink in before answering. "Mother, I love you, but that is the single most preposterous thing I have ever heard."

"Not at all," William argued. "I saw it as well, clear as day. Well, once she pointed it out to me. I'd never seen a girl more suited to you."

Whit happened to share the opinion, but he couldn't stop from asking William, "Why?"

"Because, my boy, she *bothered* you."

"She bothered . . . *that's* your qualification?"

William smiled in fond memory. "Should have seen your face the first time she came to Haldon. I've never seen a boy of thirteen look so utterly confounded, nor so angry about it."

"Mirabelle is the only person you have ever lost your head over, Whit," his mother said gently.

"Yes, and look what it's cost her." Angry with himself, with them, with the whole ugly affair, he gave in to the need to move. He strode to the fireplace to glower at the flames.

Lady Thurston watched him, a line of concern forming across her brow. "Mirabelle's injuries are not of your doing. The fault lies with her uncle and Mr. Hartsinger, first. William and me, second."

"That's neither here nor there," Whit murmured with a shake of his head before looking to his mother. "You knew of the counterfeiting operation?"

She winced. "I did, though I hadn't thought it particularly dangerous for Mirabelle. She was protected, and she'd been attending her uncle's parties for years. I thought it an excellent opportunity for you to see that the time she spent there was unpleasant."

"You *knew?*"

"Only that she was unhappy there," she was quick to explain. "But that alone was hardly argument enough to convince you to attend one of the parties. Particularly in light of the past the two of you share. I did not realize that she was in physical jeopardy." Her voice faltered. "Do you think I would have allowed her to go otherwise?"

William leaned over to pat soothingly at her hand. "After the duke died, I had Lindberg charm his way into an invitation through one of the other guests. He's kept an eye on her during the parties. His reports indicated a notable . . . lack of manners, shall we say, among the other guests. But he felt confident in his ability to protect her."

"He was wrong."

"He managed the job for considerable amount of time," William argued.

"Neither here nor there," Whit said, shaking his head. "What of Christian?"

"Ah. I sent him a little under four years ago. He'd been party to a particularly sensitive mission and needed to remain out of sight for a bit. I sent him to the baron's, preferring to err on the side of caution where both he and Mirabelle were concerned . . . though it would appear I failed in that."

"We'll argue who's at fault later," Whit replied, though he had no intention of doing anything of the sort. He knew exactly whose responsibility it had been to protect Mirabelle—his. "Explain the counterfeiting. The baron claims to know nothing of the plate."

"I had Alex plant the plate."

Whit blinked. "You . . . what? What the devil for?"

"So you could find it," William answered without a hint of shame at planting evidence.

"What if he'd been innocent?" he demanded.

"Then I wouldn't have planted it."

Whit ground his teeth at that bit of circular logic. "You were certain of his guilt."

"Yes, but I wasn't certain how careful the baron might be in hiding the proof of that guilt, and with Mirabelle in the house, time was of the essence. I hadn't thought her in any real danger, but erred on the side—"

"William."

"Right. You were to spend a day, perhaps two, searching before finding the evidence. Long enough to see what sort of man the baron is and, if necessary, to insist Mirabelle return permanently to Haldon."

"She wouldn't accept the invitation from anyone but you," his mother added. "I should know, as I tried."

Whit stared at her. "Did it never occur to you, to just *tell* me what sort of man the baron was?"

"You knew as much as we did, Whit," she replied softly. "The baron's propensity for drunkenness has never been a secret."

Bloody, bloody hell.

She was right. There had always been whispers of Epperly's fondness for drink. But overindulgent fops were more common in the *ton* than handkerchiefs. He'd thought, when he'd bothered himself at all over the matter, that Mirabelle's uncle was just another useless and essentially harmless wastrel. Like his father.

He dragged a hand through his hair. "Why now? Mirabelle and I have been at odds for years."

Lady Thurston sighed. "I had very much hoped that the two of you would find your way to each other naturally, but you were taking too long about it, and time was running out."

"Running out for what?"

"There is less than two years left before Mirabelle receives her inheritance," she elaborated. "She plans to purchase a house of her own with the funds. She'll no longer live at Haldon, where the two of you would be so often in each other's way."

"She could have visited," Whit pointed out, though the point was moot, now that Eppersly had stolen the money.

"After so much time spent being a guest, I suspect she would have preferred we come to her more often than not." She tossed him a doubtful look. "And I don't believe for a moment that you would have joined us. Knowing as much, I tried first to see if a forced truce would work."

"It *was* working."

"Yes, and the mission to the baron's was to finalize matters."

He laughed without humor and turned to William. "My mission to uncover a printing plate you'd made and planted yourself."

"I didn't make it," William argued.

"Your father did," Lady Thurston informed him. "More than ten years ago."

Whit held up a hand for silence, and wondered that it wasn't in a fist, or full of the hair off his head. This conversation was going to drive him mad. "You," he snapped at William, "told me, not two minutes ago, that you planted that plate. And now you," he said turning to Lady Thurston, "tell me my own father is responsible for forging it?"

"It was meant to be a prank," his mother elaborated.

"A prank," he repeated.

She nodded. "Yes. Your father and Eppersly thought it up—over a bottle of port, no doubt—and imagined it would be a fine joke to play on their friends. They hired an engraver of little talent who'd look the other way for a few extra coins, and they ordered the ink from the same sort of man."

"They bought the paper in a London shop," he guessed.

"Actually, if I remember correctly, they took the paper from my writing secretaire, and used it to print a number of notes."

He thought of the bank note William had shown him that first day in his study, and the stack of identical notes from the baron's bureau. "That's why the note was such a poor counterfeit. They didn't see the need to bother with—"

"It's an excessive amount of bother for a simple joke, in my opinion," Lady Thurston cut in with a huff. "But yes, as they'd never meant for anyone other than their friends to see the notes, they didn't trouble themselves to make them perfect."

"What happened?"

"I found them out and put a stop to it. Your father put away the plate, and the baron agreed to put away his share of the notes they had already printed. That was the end of it, for a time."

"Until one of the notes surfaced this past month," William added. "Your mother had told me of the intended joke long ago. I'd seen the printing plate and a sample of the counterfeit bills. I knew where it came from. I suspect Eppersly is telling the truth. He attempted to pass off a few of the bills to Hartsinger, who caught on to the trick and blackmailed the baron into giving him more of the bills to circulate. I imagine he's passed them on to friends out of the country. Might have been able to continue the ruse a bit longer if Eppersly hadn't tried using one in Benton."

"But rather than put a quick end to it with a quiet raid, you planned this mission."

"Two birds with one stone," William replied.

"When William suggested the possibility," Lady Thurston added. "I went to the attic and hunted up the plate."

"The attic," Whit grumbled. "Of course."

"I beg your pardon?"

"Nothing."

"Were you caught searching?" Lady Thurston asked. "Is that how Mirabelle came to be injured?"

"No." Realizing it was his turn to answer a few questions, Whit stepped away from the fire and took a seat across from them. He told them what he learned from Lindberg's report.

"For heaven's sake," Lady Thurston breathed when he had finished retelling the events of the evening. "What was she doing in his study? Do you suppose she knew of the contract?"

Whit shook his head. "I don't know what she was doing there, though I doubt she knew of her uncle's intent to send her off to an asylum. We'll have to ask her."

A soft rap at the door by a footman kept Lady Thurston or William from responding. "I'm sorry to interrupt, but Miss Browning is asking for you, my lady."

"Go ahead," Whit encouraged. "I'd like a few moments with William at any rate."

Whit waited until she'd left before speaking. "You sent McAlistair. Why?"

William shook his head. "I hadn't expected him to be of any real use. Figured he would just skulk about the grounds a bit."

"Then why give him the orders to go?"

"As I said earlier, I preferred to err on the side of caution. With the two of you searching the house, the possibility of danger to Mirabelle increased. I wanted to be certain she was protected. Have a few champions, as it were."

"How many champions did she need?" He held up a hand before William could answer.

He knew how many she'd needed. One. Him. And he hadn't been there.

He'd failed.

"Damn it." He dragged a tired hand down his face. "You were right, and it was best that he was there." He smiled ruefully. "He wasn't at all happy about it."

William merely snorted. "Past time the man came out of hiding, and it was as good a way as any to ease him back into the world of the living."

"Difficult world for a man who deals in death. Does my mother know what he was?"

"Not unless you told her."

Whit shook his head. "No. When he came to stay on the grounds, I told her only that he was a soldier."

"Ah." William brushed at his pant legs and stood. "Well, if there's nothing else, I'm in dire need of a drink, and then I believe it's time for me to be going. I'll just—"

"You've a bit left to do yet," Whit cut in with a hard glance. "We'll be going over this again."

William slowly resumed his seat. "Again?"

"Again. And a third and fourth time if I feel it's necessary. Then you're going to go upstairs and explain it all to Mirabelle as many times as it takes to satisfy her."

"Bloody hell," William muttered and sat back down. "I'm the bloody head of the bloody War Department. That bloody well ought to count for something."

"I wouldn't give a damn if you were the bloody king," Whit retorted. "Mirabelle is upstairs, hurt, frightened, and—"

"Ha! It worked," William said suddenly. His scowl bloomed into a satisfied smile. "The mission was a success, wasn't it? You're in love with her."

Whit shifted in his seat before he could stop himself. "I'll not lend credence to this ridiculous farce—"

"No need, I can see it on your face. And you're squirming in your chair. You're bothered again."

"I'm nothing of the sort," Whit argued, and resisted the urge to shift again when William leaned forward to pat him once on the knee.

"Try not to worry yourself over it. Love can be a cruel mistress, it's true. But like all fancy women, if you treat her well, she'll reward you with the most delightful surprises."

After William was finally permitted to leave the room, Whit considered getting foxed with the idea that if he was going to be just as useless as his father, he might as well be just as drunk to boot. But he didn't pour the drink. He just stood at the sideboard in his study, staring at the bottle, wavering between talking himself into it and talking himself out.

"Go on and have one, Whit." Alex's voice came from behind him. "I'd say the occasion more than warrants it."

"You knew of this." He spun around and started forward, more than ready to tear his oldest friend limb from limb.

Alex held a hand up. "I knew of, and I participated in, William's matchmaking scheme. Nothing more."

Whit punched him anyway.

"Bloody hell!" Alex's head snapped back with the blow, but he didn't fall. "What the devil was that for?"

Whit pointed at him. "For attempting to manage my life, and Mirabelle's as well."

Alex wriggled his jaw experimentally and threw him an ugly look. "I didn't hit you when William played Sophie and I for fools, did I?"

"No, but I didn't get to knowingly participate in that," Whit returned sharply. "Don't tell me you haven't been enjoying yourself immensely these last two weeks."

Whit refused to feel guilty. If a man couldn't take a facer now and then in the name of friendship, what good was he?

Alex appeared to be of the same mind. He gave his jaw one last rub with the back of his hand before extending it to Whit.

"Fair enough," he grumbled "I should point out, however, that the person most deserving of a broken jaw is William, not I."

"To hear it told, your father holds the greater share of blame."

"I can't argue with that." Alex moved around him to pour two snifters of brandy. "How is Mirabelle?"

Whit shook his head at the proffered drink. "The physician reported that—"

"Yes, I've heard the physician's report." He looked at Whit pointedly. "But how is she?"

"I don't know." Unable to sit, he walked to the window and looked out into the darkness. "I'll speak to her after my mother and William have had their say."

"It'll be a wait."

And because it would be, and because he recognized Whit's mood, Alex made himself comfortable in his chair. He couldn't stop his friend from brooding in silence, but he could damn well make certain he didn't brood alone.

# ❋ *Twenty-seven* ❋

*H*is heart was pounding.

Whit walked down the hall toward Mirabelle's room with the realization that his hour-long brooding session had accomplished nothing more than to make him nervous. It was ridiculous. He hadn't been nervous the last time he'd seen her—being ushered away by the women. But then, he'd been too worried and angry to be anything else.

Now the anger and the worry had drained, leaving only the nerves. There were questions still to be asked, and he was fairly certain the answers would be painful.

Lizzy answered his knock and by unspoken agreement, left him and Mirabelle alone.

Mirabelle watched him with wary eyes as he moved to stand at the end of the bed.

"Have you come to lecture me?" she asked in a tired voice. "Because if you have, I'd just as soon you wait until tomorrow. I've already received an earful from your mother."

"I haven't come to lecture you, but I would like you to tell me what happened if you're feeling up to it."

She sighed but nodded. "Fair enough."

She waited until Whit took a seat next to the bed, then elaborated on what had occurred—on her idea to pay Eppersly to release her early from his house, the subsequent fight, and her forced carriage ride.

"The contract is real, Whit. It—"

"I know," he cut in. "McAlistair and Lindberg found it in the study."

"It wasn't there when we searched."

"No, it was dated the day after."

She paled even further and her eyes grew round. "Someone else from St. Brigit's won't come for me, will they? They can't use the contract to—"

"No, sweetheart." He stepped around the bed to grip her trembling hand. "I promise, no. It's done now."

Her throat move in a swallow. "How can you be sure?"

"Because I personally saw to it that the contract went to ash in a fireplace, and because by this time tomorrow, Hartsinger and your uncle will be on their way . . . elsewhere. William will see to it. I promise."

"Oh." She let out a long breath and closed her eyes for a moment. "All right. That's all right then."

"Better?" he asked, giving her hand a quick squeeze.

She opened her eyes and offered a small smile. "Yes, frightened me, that's all . . . He came by earlier—William, I mean—but he didn't mention what would happen to them."

"Did he explain the rest?"

"He did. I . . . I don't know what to say." The small smile widened. "They went through a great deal of trouble."

"They caused a great deal more."

"So did I."

He didn't immediately argue, though it was his first instinct. "That would depend, I think, on whether or not you suspected your uncle capable of something like this."

He gestured at her bruised cheek which, as the physician had indicated, was rapidly progressing to a black eye. He forced himself to ask the question he had been dreading most.

"Had he hit you before, Mirabelle?"

She hesitated before answering, which was answer enough.

"Not in a very long time," she finally whispered without meeting his eyes.

"But he had hit you."

Her nod was barely perceptible. "A few times, when I was a child and hadn't yet figured out how to evade his temper."

"Was this before your first visit to Haldon?"

She shook her head, and winced at the resulting pain. "Not all."

"Yet you said nothing," he responded and let go of her hand.

She rubbed the heel of it against the counterpane. "It stopped, Whit. Or, at least, I learned how to avoid it. I was already frightened you'd discover my uncle's shameful behavior. There didn't seem, to me, to be a good reason to tell anyone."

"We could have helped you."

"I know. I regret that." She closed her eyes on a sigh. "I'm so very sorry, Whit. I wish I had done this all so differently."

And he wished she wouldn't apologize. It only served to

make him feel worse. "An apology isn't necessary. You're not responsible for this."

"Of course I am," she argued tiredly "I chose to keep secrets out of pride, and—"

"This was my failure, and I take full responsibility for it."

"*Your* failure?" Mirabelle gaped at him, completely bewildered. "What are you talking about? You haven't failed at anything. You—"

Swearing suddenly, he strode back to the foot of her bed, where he began to pace.

"Whit?"

He stopped abruptly and gestured at her face. "You have marks on you."

"From my uncle," she said, confusion warring with exasperation. "Not from you."

"Yes, your uncle and Mr. Hartsinger. Men from whom I should have protected you. I should have . . ." He trailed off, dragging a hand through his hair and resuming his agitated walk.

She watched him for a minute before trying to speak. "Whit—"

"How many times?" he suddenly demanded, whirling on her again. "How many times did I tell you I wanted you gone from Haldon, that you weren't welcome here?"

"You didn't know. You couldn't have—"

"It was my business to know. It was my responsibility as head of this house to see to your welfare."

"And so you did."

He barked out a humorless laugh. "By taunting you? Insulting you?"

"No," she said softly but firmly. "By letting me taunt and insult you back."

He opened his mouth, closed it again. "What the devil are you talking about?"

"You seem to have a distorted memory of our disagreements, Whit," she sniffed. "I wasn't a helpless puppy you kicked about and left cowering in the corner."

"Of course you weren't." His voice gentled as he came to her. "I didn't mean to imply . . . Sweetheart, you're the bravest woman I know. The most courageous—"

"For pity's sake, don't," she snapped, swatting at the hand he'd lifted to brush at her hair. "I was a brat, Whit, and well you know it."

He dropped his arm and eyed her sternly. "You were nothing of the sort."

"I was everything of the sort. I poked and prodded, teased and insulted. I instigated more than half our fights and participated fully in all of them."

"That doesn't change what—"

"*And*—I thoroughly enjoyed every moment of it." When he only looked at her, disbelief evident on every feature, she continued. "Have you not stopped to consider why I was so *quick* to battle with you? Why I never tried to gain the favor of a wealthy and powerful peer?"

"Likely because I wouldn't let you," he muttered.

"No. I may have said that myself not so long ago and believed it, but it wouldn't have been true. I fought with you because I adored it. I fought with you because I could . . . because you let me."

"Let you?" he scoffed. "Bloody hell, I hardly gave you a choice."

"Of course I had a choice," she huffed. "It would have been easy enough to stop baiting you, easy enough to ignore the barbs you offered. And you would have ceased delivering them after a time—sooner, if I'd thrown in a few tears. But I'd never been the least inclined to cry or—"

"I made you cry not a week ago," he reminded her with a sharp look. "In the room next to the study."

"Because I was ashamed of my uncle, of myself, of . . ." She tossed her hands up. "You're missing the point."

"The point is that I should—"

"Allow me to make *my* point," she finished for him with an annoyed glare. She waited until he'd held up his hand before continuing. "I've lived most of my life under the thumb of a man I was too afraid of to look in the eye. I can't explain what it meant to me, to be able to say and do as I pleased without fear. To know that no matter how angry I made you, you'd never raise your hand to me, never hurt me. I very nearly reveled in that."

"A man can wound with more than just his fists," Whit informed her quietly.

"But no more or less than a woman," she countered. "I took great pleasure in, and great advantage of, that equality. You didn't fail me, Whit. You—" She took in his skeptical expression and changed tactics. "Perhaps . . . perhaps we could come to some sort of agreement."

He sent her a look that was part exasperation and part amusement. "Another agreement?"

"We have had some success with them," she reminded him with a small smile.

He considered her, and the idea. "I suppose we have," he admitted after a time. "What did you have in mind?"

She pursed her lips thoughtfully. "How's this? I will accept your apology for not protecting me in the manner you feel you should have. If you will accept mine for not informing you that I was in need of said protection."

A corner of his mouth twitched. "I've some reservations regarding the wording, *but,*" he was quick to add when her face turned mutinous, "I will agree to the general sentiment."

"Then you'll cease slouching about as if the burden of guilt was too much for you to bear?"

"I haven't been slouching," he retorted, and wondered if he could straighten his shoulders without being too obvious about it.

"And you'll not treat me as if I were a cracked piece of porcelain or a sadly wilting flower?"

He gave her a pointed look. "I assure you, neither idea has ever occurred to me."

"And you'll—"

She broke off when he simply leaned down and pressed his finger to her lips. "I've agreed to your terms, Mirabelle. Now you'll accept the fact it may take me a bit of time to become fully comfortable with them."

She tried talking around his finger. "But—"

He used his thumb and index finger to press her lips together. "You'll accept it."

She pointed at the hand that kept her from responding, in acceptance or otherwise.

For the first time since entering her room, he smiled. "Blink once for yes."

She narrowed her eyes first, but eventually complied.

"Good." He freed her lips and bent to gently kiss her forehead. "Then we'll consider the matter settled for now."

"I should toss you from the room for that," she groused.

"Probably, but then you'd be left with nothing to do." He took a seat in the chair next to the bed. "And the physician indicated that sleep was not the best course of treatment at this time."

She shrugged and plucked at the counterpane. "I couldn't sleep, at any rate. My mind won't settle."

"It's been a difficult day for you," he said softly.

"Difficult doesn't quite cover it," she replied with a rueful twitch of her lips. "But that's not what's troubling me now, not entirely. It's the future."

"The loss of your inheritance?" he asked gently.

She nodded. "I'd had so many plans, and now I'm uncertain of what to do. I was thinking . . ." Suddenly nervous, Mirabelle adjusted the covers on her lap. "I was thinking that a reference from you would go a long way in helping me secure a position—"

"You want to leave," he interrupted stiffly.

"Yes. No." She blew out a breath. She wasn't at all sure what she was going to do yet. She simply wanted to know which options were available to her. "Not this very minute."

"But when you're well again," he guessed.

Confused, and a little annoyed by the accusation in his voice, she sat up straighter against the pillows. "I'm not particularly unwell now."

He jabbed a finger at her. "Attempt to get out of that bed and I'll bloody well tie you to it."

"I'm not getting up." She'd tried it earlier, and had nearly fallen on her face for the effort. "And I don't understand why you're upset."

"Don't understand why I'm upset?" He dropped his finger to glare at her. "You tell me you want to leave, and you don't understand why I'm upset? What's wrong with your staying at Haldon?"

"Nothing!" She threw up her hands, frustrated. "And everything. Surely you didn't expect me to always remain at Haldon, a hanger-on?"

There was a pause before he spoke. "I did once," he finally admitted softly. "And rather liked the idea of it."

"Really?"

He leaned back into the chair, remembering. "I imagined the two of us, old and gray, still sparring with each other as if no time had passed."

"Oh, well. That wouldn't have been so terrible, I suppose."

"Perhaps." He caught her gaze and held it. "But I want something else now."

"For me to remain at Haldon until we're old and gray, less the sparring?" she guessed.

"Yes, but not as a guest."

She found something else in the counterpane to pick at. "However kindly you may rephrase it, I am not family."

He leaned forward and took her hand. "You would be, if you consented to becoming my wife."

Her mouth dropped nearly to her chin. "Your . . . your wife? You mean marry you?"

"That is the usual way of becoming a wife, I'm told," he answered with a twitch of his lips.

"I don't know what to say." She really didn't. It was beyond her scope. She'd thought that chance lost. How could he marry the niece of a criminal? "I . . . You're asking me to marry you."

"Not as I had planned to, but yes—"

"You'd planned to ask me?"

He shrugged and smiled. "Well, it really ought not to be something a man does on a whim."

"No . . . no, it shouldn't." She continued to gape, feeling a little lightheaded and more than a little stupid. "I really don't know what to say to you, Whit, I—"

"Yes would be a fine start." His smile fell. "You're not going to say yes, are you?"

"I don't know," she answered honestly. "I . . . How can you ask this? I'm the niece of a criminal."

He frowned at her. "I told you once before—you're not responsible for his sins."

"Yes, but just taking me in is quite a bit different from . . . from . . ."

"Just taking you?"

"From making me the Countess of Thurston," she corrected, slanting him an annoyed look. "There's no guarantee my uncle's actions won't become public knowledge at some point. People will talk—"

"Damn the talk," he snapped.

"How can you say that? You worked so hard securing your family's popularity—"

She cut off at his laugh. "Mirabelle, *popularity* has never been a problem for the Cole family. The *ton* was exceedingly fond of my father."

"But . . . I don't understand."

"He was witty and charming. He threw lavish parties, agreed to every wager tossed to him, drank with the young bucks, flirted with the old ladies—"

"You said he was a dandy and a rake," she accused.

"And so he was. The *ton* loved him for it." He shook his head when she began to argue. "But they didn't respect him. He couldn't be trusted—with money, with the ladies, with keeping his word. He was a favorite diversion, nothing more."

"Oh." Her brow furrowed in thought. "If it's not society's good favor you've been courting, then what have you been doing?"

"Behaving as a gentleman, I hope," he said simply. "I'd have the Cole family known for their honor."

She licked her lips. "And if marriage to me should throw that honor into question?"

He made a noise that was half sigh and half groan. "To begin with, I'll see to it your uncle's behavior will never become public knowledge. I'm an earl, aren't I? And an agent of the War Department, besides. There are things I can do. Beyond that, there is nothing dishonorable in offering for an honorable woman. And you are an honorable woman— a beautiful, intelligent, and courageous woman. Anyone incapable of seeing that is an idiot. Why should I care for the good opinion of an idiot?" He drew her hand to his lips, pressing a kiss to her palm. "Marry me, Mirabelle."

Marry him. He truly wanted to marry her, despite everything. Her heart, so terribly heavy only an hour before, stuttered and then raced until she felt marvelously lightheaded.

"This is so . . . I hadn't expected . . . I . . . Can I ask you a question?"

Whit winced and set down her hand. "When a person

has to ask to ask, it's a fairly good indicator that what is going to be asked, will be unpleasant."

She gave herself a moment to decipher that statement. "I'm still too muzzy to even attempt responding to that. I only wanted to know . . . did you realize you'd have to offer for me before you . . . before we . . . ?"

"Made love?" he finished for her.

"Yes."

His brow furrowed in thought. "Realize is an odd choice of word, in this case. The wrong one, I think. I have always been aware of what is expected of a gentleman in such circumstances, but if you're asking if I was thinking of it at the time, I'd have to answer no." He reached out to brush the back of his fingers gently across her uninjured cheek. "I thought only of how much I wanted you."

"Oh."

"Does that upset you?" he asked, cocking his head at her.

"No." How could it, she thought? She'd been lost in him. It would have cut at her heart to know he hadn't felt the same. "But now you're thinking of it, and offering, because it's expected of you?"

"No," he replied sternly.

"Then . . . why are you offering?"

He stood up from the chair and gently nudging her over a bit, took a seat on the edge of the bed.

"Because I want to marry you," he said simply. "For me. I want to know you'll always be here at Haldon where you belong—where I can see your chocolate eyes, touch your chestnut hair, taste your creamy skin—"

"I'm quite the confection."

"You are that," he replied and took a quick taste of her lips. "I want to know you'll always be about to make me laugh, to encourage my sister in her music, to support my cousin in her attempts to free the women of England—"

"You know about that?"

"Of course I do. I want to know you're safe and happy. And I want you here because *I* need that to be happy. I want to have a life with you, children with you." Careful of her injury, he took her face in her hands, his blue gaze staring into hers. "I want to marry you Mirabelle, because I love you."

"*Oh.*" A smile, slow and delighted, crept up her face. "Oh, that's very nice."

A corner of his mouth hooked up. "Not exactly the response I was hoping for, but—"

"I love you too."

The other half of his mouth moved until he was grinning. He pressed a gentle kiss to her mouth. "You're right. It's very nice."

She laughed, threw her arms around his neck, and kissed him back. She wasn't gentle, as he had been, but threw herself into the kiss. She kissed him for everything she was worth, determined to show him the contents of her heart, the depth of her love. She let the pain and fear of the last few days flow away. And let Whit fill the space they left behind.

He set her away with a groan. "No more of that until you're well," he managed around a pant. "And we're married."

"I'll make you happy, Whit." Unable to resist, she pressed her lips to his for another quick but hard kiss. "When I'm not driving you mad."

"Are you saying yes, Mirabelle?" he demanded. "Will you marry me?"

She framed his face in her hands. "Yes. Absolutely, yes. There's nothing I want more."

"I'll make you happy, as well," he promised.

"And drive me mad a bit?" she asked.

"To distraction," he assured her and leaned forward to rest his forehead against hers. "I've loved you the whole of my life, imp . . . even when I didn't like you."

"Of course you did," she said with a sly smile. "It was fated."

# ❋ Epilogue ❋

*A*lthough he would have preferred the speed and simplicity—particularly the speed—of a small wedding by special license, Whit agreed to wait until the banns had been read before taking Mirabelle as his wife.

It allowed his bride time to fully heal—and what woman wished for the accessory of a black eye on her wedding day? And it gave time for Madame Duvalle to create her wedding dress, a simple elegant gown in the ivory silk she had somehow known was meant for Mirabelle.

Unbeknownst to Whit, it also fit perfectly over blue satin.

Whit's mother was given the chance to indulge in an extravagant to-do—something she'd been denied with Alex and Sophie's wedding.

To her delight, Whit's annoyance, and Mirabelle's amusement, Lady Thurston spared no expense, even going so far as to demand two extra trips to London to find and purchase all the necessary accoutrements.

But in good, if lengthy, order, he and Mirabelle stood at the altar and exchanged their vows. He smirked when she faltered at the promising to obey bit, and she teased him on the drive home by feigning an interest in the tradition of occupying a suite of her own.

And they celebrated on the back lawn of Haldon surrounded by their friends and family . . . and nearly every member of the *ton*.

"I can't believe your mother was right," Mirabelle commented as they stood together a little ways from the crowd, taking a moment for themselves.

"About us?"

"About the weather. She was adamant it wouldn't rain—that it couldn't rain, I believe were her exact words. And here it is, warm and cloudless. How could anyone possibly know that?"

He threaded his fingers through hers. "She has a firm belief in fate. Although she did decorate the ballroom, just in case."

"She decorated everything."

"This is true."

She smiled as she watched Whit's mother accept a drink from William. "She's so happy," she said before turning to Whit. "You're not still angry with William, are you?"

He brought her hand to his lips for a kiss, and one discreet nibble on her knuckles—it was their wedding day, after all.

"I'm not still angry," he replied as she blushed. "How could I be, when he brought us—albeit in a rather foolish way—together."

She pulled her hand away and darted a nervous glance at the guests. "I'll thank you to stop embarrassing me."

"Every single guest over the age of eighteen knows exactly what you and I are going to do the very moment they leave—"

"And every one of them would thank you not to begin until they do." She slapped at his hand when he laughed and reached for her again. "I'm attempting to have a serious conversation, Whit."

"Well, don't," he advised. "It's our wedding day."

"And therefore I shouldn't be serious?"

"You should be celebrating."

"I am," she replied and dodged another grasp. "But I want to know if William means to continue his missions."

She nodded toward Evie, who stood a distance away in a small group of guests. It was clear she wasn't listening to whatever was being said. Her gaze and thoughts were focused on the hills beyond the lawn.

Whit paused in his attempts to snatch up his wife. "William intends to fulfill his promise to the late duke, though I tried to talk him out of it." He aimed a dark scowl at the man in question. "He won't tell me what he has planned either, the blighter. Says I won't be able to stop myself from interfering."

"You won't," she agreed, and looked from Evie to William. "Perhaps I can pry something out of him."

"Unlikely," Whit scoffed. "The man's lips are sealed tighter than a drum."

She continued to eye William speculatively. "Hmm. I believe a brief talk with the man is in order."

"He's an agent for the War Department, Mirabelle. A brief talk isn't going to . . ." He trailed off as she moved away from him towards William. "You'll tell me what he says!"

She cast a wink over her shoulder. "I'll think on it."

# Emily Bryan

## *Vexing the Viscount*

As children they'd sparred with play swords. She'd scarred his
chin, and he broke her heart. Now, more than a decade later,
the true battle was only beginning...

Daisy Drake needed Lucian Beaumont, Viscount Rutland.
Tired of being labeled "on the shelf," she craved adventure.
And Lucian held all the clues to a long-buried Roman treasure. Surely her desire to join his search had nothing to do
with his dark curls and seductive Italian accent. Too bad Lucian wanted no help from her—until she donned the dis-
guise of an infamous French courtesan and promised to teach
him all she knew about the pleasures of the bedchamber. Of
course, she only knew what had been written in naughty
books. But Daisy had always been a quick learner. And night
by naked night, they'd discover treasure neither expected to
find.

ISBN 13: 978-0-8439-6134-8

✂

# ☐ **YES!**

Sign me up for the Historical Romance Book Club and send my FREE BOOKS! If I choose to stay in the club, I will pay only $8.50* each month, a savings of $6.48!

NAME: _____

ADDRESS: _____

TELEPHONE: _____

EMAIL: _____

☐ I want to pay by credit card.

☐ **VISA**          ☐ **MasterCard**          ☐ **DISCOVER**

ACCOUNT #: _____

EXPIRATION DATE: _____

SIGNATURE: _____

Mail this page along with $2.00 shipping and handling to:
**Historical Romance Book Club**
**PO Box 6640**
**Wayne, PA 19087**
Or fax (must include credit card information) to:
**610-995-9274**
You can also sign up online at **www.dorchesterpub.com**.
*Plus $2.00 for shipping. Offer open to residents of the U.S. and Canada only.
Canadian residents please call 1-800-481-9191 for pricing information.
If under 18, a parent or guardian must sign. Terms, prices and conditions subject to change. Subscription subject to acceptance. Dorchester Publishing reserves the right to reject any order or cancel any subscription.